HOW IT ALL ENDS

AN AMERICAN TRAGEDY

Bruce William Hagemeier

Eastwind Farm and Publishing Company

Elizabethtown, North Carolina

ISBN: 9798372392328 (Paperback)

ALSO BY
BRUCE WILLIAM HAGEMEIER

BLOOD OF TYRANTS, Watering the Tree of Liberty

For my son, EJ; you have made me so proud.

For my wife, Denise; you have made me happier than I deserve.

For my country, the United States of America; may we repent and know again the will of God.

Before it's too late.

Turning and turning in the widening gyre
The falcon cannot hear the falconer;
Things fall apart; the centre cannot hold;
Mere anarchy is loosed upon the world,
The blood-dimmed tide is loosed, and everywhere
The ceremony of innocence is drowned;
The best lack all conviction, while the worst
Are full of passionate intensity.

—W. B. Yeats, "The Second Coming"

BOOK I

LOS ANGELES

CHAPTER ONE

A great civilization is not conquered from without until it has destroyed itself from within.

— Will Durant, "The Story of Philosophy: The Lives and Opinions of the World's Greatest Philosophers"

THE WOMAN WHO was about to die waited at the door. The Tiffany manager buzzed her out. "Thank you, Ms. Harrison," he said. His perky sales voice was not at all affected. He had just sold her a Tiffany Knot Double Row Necklace in yellow gold with over six carat total weight in diamonds. The price was a cool eighty-two grand, making it by far his biggest sale of the week.

Natasha Harrison looked over her shoulder and answered with a smile. She was thrilled with her necklace and wanted the manager to know how much she appreciated his help. It had not been easy deciding which piece to buy. *So much jewelry,* she thought, *so little time.* Her brown eyes sparkled at her witticism. She touched the palm of her hand to her red painted lips and blew the manager a kiss.

The manager smiled and waved. "Have a nice day, Ms. Harrison."

Natasha pushed the door open and strode out onto the corner of Rodeo Drive and Wilshire Boulevard. She had a two block walk to her car but did not mind at all. It was another perfect afternoon in Southern

California. The sky was a brilliant azure punctuated by striations of wispy white cirrus clouds. The sun felt warm on her skin.

Natasha was not twenty feet from Tiffany's when a little old lady rushed up to her side. "Excuse me," said the little old lady, breathless, "aren't you Gal Gadot?" The little old lady had her cell phone out, ready to snap a picture as soon as she confirmed her suspicion. The little old lady's husband stood a few feet back, looking mortified and pretending not to know his wife.

Natasha smiled gently. "No," she said, "I'm afraid not."

"Are you sure?" pressed the little old lady. She leaned closer to Natasha and lowered her voice. "It'll be our secret if you are."

"Positive," whispered Natasha. Then, when she noticed the little old lady's disappointment, she added cheerfully, "But I'm flattered you thought so!"

The little old lady fidgeted with her iPhone, flustered. "I was so sure!"

"Sorry to bother you," said the little old lady's husband, coming up beside his wife and taking her by the arm. "Come on, Mildred," he said patiently, "let's leave this young lady to her business."

"No bother at all," hollered Natasha after the couple as they walked away.

Really it was not. Natasha was often stopped on the street by some curious member of the public in a case of mistaken celebrity identity. The subject of her mistaken identity was usually Gal Gadot, too, like the little old lady thought, although Kendall Jenner was a close second. Natasha bore a striking resemblance to both with her tall, lithe figure and dark, exotic looks. If she had to choose between the two, she hoped she looked more like Jenner than Gadot. Gadot was ten years older than Jenner and Natasha was not at all ready to look mature.

Natasha had another hope, too. She hoped the attention was more than a simple case of mistaken identity. She considered herself a celebrity in her own right even though no one knew her name. "An anonymous celebrity!" she often joked. She hoped at least some of the attention was attributable to a kind of subliminal recognition, because people had seen her face over and over again, in advertisement after advertisement.

Natasha was a model. She had an impressive resume for being all of twenty-four. She had been the face of Chanel and the figure for Dior. In her more recent work, she was "the driver" for Porsche. Porsche's offer to feature Natasha in their video ad campaign surprised Natasha as much as her agent. Natasha asked, "Shouldn't you get an actual race car driver, or one of the car engineers? I thought Porsche owners only care about performance."

The portly marketing executive from Porsche chuckled at her comment. "Ja," he said, "but they still like beautiful women."

Natasha spent a year "driving" for Porsche. A professional race car driver actually put the car through its paces. He was the one who flashed across the finish line to win the checkered flag. Through the miracle of editing, Natasha was the one who opened the door and pulled off her helmet. She would shake loose her long, brunette locks, give the camera a sly come-hither look, and ask seductively, "What's in your garage?" Sales that year were up ten percent.

The video ad campaign for Porsche had been fun. It had also whetted her appetite for more. After the ad campaign, Natasha told her agent she wanted to break out from the modeling pack. She wanted to be the one walking down the red carpet with the paparazzi madly pushing and shoving and snapping her photo. She wanted people to know her name, like Jenner and Gadot. Her agent told Natasha what she already knew. A breakout meant roles in acting. It meant television and film. Jenner had *Keeping up with the Kardashians.* Gadot had *Wonder Woman.*

They both started looking for acting roles, Natasha and her agent. Her agent went about it in his way, Natasha in hers. Six months later, Natasha walked down the aisle with Neiman W. Harrison, chief executive officer for Warner Brothers. "Well," said her agent with a laugh in a private toast to Natasha after her engagement was announced, "I guess we know who has the better approach." Filming for her first picture started six months after their honeymoon.

A homeless man sat on the sidewalk up ahead. Natasha instinctively clutched her purse as she approached. She clutched it harder still when she remembered the black velvet box ensconced inside, the one with the Tiffany Knot Double Row Necklace. Street crime was a problem in Los Angeles, even on Rodeo Drive, and people with means now took care not to flaunt their wealth. That was the reason she chose not to wear her beautiful new necklace when she left Tiffany's, as much as she wanted to.

The homeless man sat with his back up against the wall of Van Clef & Arpels. He had been there an hour or so, arriving just after Natasha parked on the street. The manager of Van Clef & Arpels was aware of the homeless man's presence but thought it best not to make an issue of it. Asking the man to leave might provoke him and prove dangerous. And calling the police was an exercise in futility. Calls to 911 were increasingly met with a recorded, "All our lines are busy at the moment. Please stay on the line if this is an emergency." The manager assuaged his irritation with the thought the homeless man would soon move on. The homeless usually did, as long as they had not unpacked their shopping cart and pitched their tent.

The homeless man held a tattered piece of cardboard. "HOMELESS VETERAN" was printed in black marker across the top, all in capital letters. Just below, printed in smaller letters, was "Will work for food." Natasha wondered if the homeless man was really a veteran. *Doesn't the government provide food and shelter for homeless veterans?* Then she wondered if he was really willing to work for food. She had read countless stories of the homeless turning down offers of food because what they really wanted was money to buy alcohol and drugs.

The homeless man looked up at Natasha with bloodshot eyes. The pungent odor of urine assaulted her nostrils. Natasha looked around to make sure there was no one nearby ready to snatch her purse when she reached for her wallet. She saw no one. When she looked back at the homeless man, she noticed his matted hair and filthy clothes.

"God bless you, ma'am," said the homeless man when he saw Natasha pull a twenty-dollar bill from her wallet.

"Here," said Natasha, offering the bill to the homeless man along with a sympathetic smile. "Maybe this will help a little."

The homeless man appreciated her smile almost as much as the bill. People mostly ignored him when they walked by, as if he was invisible. When they did acknowledge him, it was usually with a disapproving frown or a scornful "Get a job!" The homeless man smiled back at Natasha. His smile revealed the black and brown stubs of teeth destroyed by smoking methamphetamine.

Natasha forced herself to keep smiling. Inside, she shuddered in horror. *Meth mouth!* She took great pride in the perfect alignment of her teeth and their perfect whiteness. She knew a model was nothing if not a beautiful smile. *How can someone deliberately do that to themselves, choose to make themselves ugly, repulsive even?!* She walked away briskly, leaving the homeless man to his miserable existence.

There were not a lot of people out and about, which was typical for a weekday on Rodeo Drive. Weekdays were for serious shoppers, for people like Natasha who had money to spend and appreciated the undivided attention of the store manager. Weekends were for tourists and fashionistas.

Natasha hit the button on her fob. The violet Porsche Taycan flashed its greeting and unlocked its doors. The Taycan had come to be Natasha's as part of her compensation package for her work on the Porsche ad campaign. Before the campaign, Natasha never thought to own one, never even knew there was such a car. Now, she swore she would never own anything else. She loved the lines. She loved the color. And, especially, she loved the fact it was electric. Her agent claimed her enthusiasm for its battery-powered propulsion was because she was excited to do her duty as a global citizen, fighting climate change. The reality was more mundane. As far as Natasha was concerned, it would be too soon if she ever handled another smelly gas nozzle at the filling station.

Natasha was grateful for the security of the Taycan. She locked the doors and leaned her head back against the headrest. She closed her eyes and tried to relax but the face of the homeless man with his wrecked smile drifted out of the darkness. Her eyes opened wide. She snapped at the car, "Play music. Clair de Lune." The Taycan immediately complied. The soothing piano notes of Debussy filled the interior. She took a few deep breaths and started to relax. "Only happy thoughts," she whispered to herself. She remembered the Tiffany Knot Double Row Necklace in her purse and decided she would wear it on the drive home. Her practiced fingers managed the clasp behind her neck. She adjusted the rearview mirror to admire it. The necklace followed the graceful lines of her neck. Her olive skin took on a golden, radiant glow as if energized by the gold in the necklace. Her eyes seemed to come alive, too, even more than usual. They sparkled with the reflected brilliance of a dozen diamonds. "Beautiful," she whispered. The homeless man was gone from her thoughts.

The Taycan accelerated silently onto Rodeo Drive. Natasha headed home by the usual route. She turned right onto Santa Monica Boulevard, which was part of the old, historic Route 66. There was not much historic about Santa Monica Boulevard as far as Natasha was concerned, other than the old Troubadour nightclub. She had been there once since moving to Los Angeles because it was one of those "must see" sights in LA, a veritable icon. Elton John had played there back in the day, when he was first starting out. It was his first show in the United States. He was even introduced by Neil Diamond. After her one and only visit to the Troubadour, she decided once was enough. The band that was supposed to be the next big thing compensated for their lack of talent with an obnoxious level of volume. It was loud to the point of being painful. She regretted not heeding the advice of a friend who recommended she bring hearing protection. An intoxicated fan spilled a drink down the front of her new blouse. Finally, to top it all off, she was groped multiple times in the mosh pit.

Beverly Hills Park was off to her left. The park was a few blocks of what used to be immaculately manicured lawn. That was before it was taken over by the homeless. The city had cleared out the homeless countless times, which inevitably involved an ugly spectacle on the evening news. The city finally surrendered to the political pressure and decided another solution was required, a more humane solution. They would find shelters for the homeless. Since there was already an acute shortage of rental space in the city, that meant the city would have to build shelters. The builders were happy with the building program, of course, since the average cost of a new apartment unit was well over a million dollars. In fact, the builders had been one of the chief groups lobbying for a more humane solution. While the city now had its solution, implementing the solution required time. The homeless pitched their brightly colored tents in the park and waited. They pitched their tents in such numbers and in such a disorganized, haphazard fashion that it was no longer possible for the city to mow the grass. Where the grass was not trampled flat, it grew up tall. Wild flowers also grew up and gave the tents the appearance of having been pitched in a prairie rather than a park. Though the city was now building more than a dozen new apartment units each month, the population of homeless only grew.

After the park came the sprawl of nondescript retail and multi-level apartment buildings that characterize so much of West Hollywood. With few exceptions, the buildings looked tired. Graffiti was ubiquitous. Ground floor windows often featured steel security bars. Their prevalence had increased markedly as a consequence of the last economic downturn. The evening news promised, “Recovery imminent, likely next quarter.” They had been making the same promise for thirteen straight quarters. People walking down the streets looked tired. Most of them walked with their head down, which was generally considered a prudent practice as the city struggled with surging rates of violent crime.

Natasha turned left onto North Fairfax Avenue and caught her first glimpse of the Hollywood Hills. The hillside was dotted with impressive homes. The homes were impressive not only for their size but their location, which afforded spectacular views of the city below. There were also patches of green. The patches of green were due to the larger trees, the ones big enough to sink their roots deep into the soil to find moisture. The rest of the hills were brown since the grass and brush had long ago succumbed to the heat and drought of summer.

On Camino Palmero Drive, the retail and apartment buildings acquired a more upscale look. The people there seemed to have more of a bounce to their step. There were nicer cars parked on the street, too. The traffic thinned out and lush, robust oaks replaced the sickly palms that lined the earlier streets.

Natasha turned onto Outpost Drive. She felt like she was finally leaving the city. Apartment buildings were replaced by single family homes, all neatly kept. Homes in the first few blocks had six-foot walls and gated driveways. Then, with a little more distance from the city, the walls gave way to wooden fences and green hedge rows, for privacy rather than security. Finally, homes were visible from the street. A fit-looking young woman jogged down the sidewalk. A couple walked their dog. Up ahead, on one side of the road, the Hollywood Hills came right up to the curb. There was an actual view of open countryside.

Natasha lived on Castilian Drive. It was a narrow, winding street with room for only one car to pass if another car was parked on the side. That was where she first noticed the white van following behind. It was following too close. *Assholes!* she thought, concerned about being rear-ended if she was forced to stop short. She pressed on the accelerator and the Taycan responded instantly, putting distance between the Taycan and the van. The distance was short-lived. A moment later the van was back on her tail. She was already doing thirty-five in a twenty-five-mph zone and did not dare go faster. She could see two heads through the van's windshield. They looked to be male. She thought, *Probably some workmen late for a job.*

Then she was home.

Natasha slowed the Taycan and hit the button to open the automatic gate at the driveway entrance. It was an impressive wrought iron gate topped with gold fleur-de-lis, a gate befitting the impressive estate of a successful model and the CEO of Warner Brothers. She waited as the gate slowly opened. The van waited behind her because the back of the Taycan jutted out into the street, leaving no room to pass.

When the gate was open enough, Natasha pulled forward. She hit the gate button a second time when she was through, to close the gate. She was shocked to see the van pull in behind her instead of continuing on its way down Castilian Drive. The van broke the gate's infrared beam, the one that prevents the gate from closing on a vehicle in its tracked path. The gate stopped and reversed direction, opening again. *What the hell?!* thought Natasha, alarmed. She drove up as close as she could to the front door, hoping her husband was home. He usually worked from home but went to the office on occasion.

The van stopped directly behind the Taycan, trapping it against the front of the house. Natasha thought about running for the front door but decided against it. It was too far. *What do I do?! What do I do?!* A sense of panic welled up inside her, grabbing her stomach and twisting it in a knot. The van doors flew open and two men jumped out. They ran to either side of the Taycan. Natasha saw what looked like a pistol in the hand of the man on her side. She thought, *Call the police!* She grabbed her purse sitting on the passenger seat and pulled the phone from its side pocket. Her hands were shaking.

The man slammed his fist against the driver's side window. "Police!" he shouted. His face was angry. "Out of the fuckin' car! Now!"

Natasha was dumbfounded. *Police?! What did I do?!*

The man slammed his fist on the window a second time. "Out of the fuckin' car, lady! Right fuckin' now!"

Natasha felt her face flush hot as she struggled to process the situation. *Why are the police acting like this?!*

The man pointed his pistol at Natasha's face. "Now lady! Before someone gets hurt!"

Natasha recoiled at the sight of the pistol's black muzzle pointed directly at her face, right between her eyes. Her doubts about the man's claim to be a police officer disappeared, pushed completely from her mind by her instinct for self-preservation. She raised her hands in surrender. "Ok, ok, ok!" she pleaded. "I'm coming out! Please don't shoot me!"

"Unlock the fuckin' door!" ordered the man, gesturing at the lock with his pistol.

Natasha pushed the unlock button. The man yanked the door open as soon as the lock popped. He grabbed Natasha by the arm and yanked her from the driver's seat. "What did I do?!" she screamed, shocked by the sudden pain in her bicep. The man's grip felt like a vise.

"Shut the fuck up!" shouted the man. "Hands behind your back!"

"I didn't do anything!" screamed Natasha in protest.

The man pulled a pair of handcuffs from his belt and held them up for Natasha to see. "We can do this the hard way or the easy way! Your choice!"

With the pistol no longer pointed at her face, Natasha recovered a measure of composure. Something seemed terribly wrong to her. Police do not act this way, especially in the Hollywood Hills. "I want my lawyer!" she said defiantly.

"You'll get your lawyer when we get to the station!" snapped the man. "The cuffs?!"

Natasha considered refusing. Then she decided against it. Though she was at least a head taller than the man, he was twice as wide and looked like he could play professional football. Plus, he had a gun. "Ok," she said, more than a little reluctantly. She put her hands behind her back. She felt cold steel clamp down on one wrist, then the other.

The man pulled Natasha around to face him. "This your house?" he asked, not shouting for the first time.

"Yes. Yes, it is."

"You live here alone?"

"No, I live here with my husband." She felt better mentioning her husband. She was confident he would clear this up, whatever *this* was.

"Is he home?" asked the man.

"He should be, unless he went to the office."

The man smiled. His smile struck Natasha as cruel. A chill ran down her spine. "Well, how 'bout we go find out?" He pulled her roughly to the front door. "Keys?"

"In my purse."

"And where the fuck's your purse?"

"In the car."

The man turned to the second man following behind and nodded toward the Taycan. The second man nodded back. A moment later he returned with Natasha's keys and handed them to the first man. Before asking which key went to the house, the first man reached down and tried the ornate, bronze door knob. It turned and opened. The man looked back at Natasha with an incredulous expression. "You don't lock your fuckin' door?"

"At night we do," explained Natasha, embarrassed.

The man snorted. "Pretty fuckin' stupid."

Another chill ran down her spine. *Cops don't talk like that!* Then she noticed the tattoo on his neck, done all in black ink. It was a black figure wrapped in a cloak. There was a skull for a head and a scythe in its boney hands. It reminded her of the grim reaper. *And they don't have tattoos like that, either!* She made up her mind. *He's no cop!* She kicked open the front door and ran inside. She did not get far. The man grabbed her by the arm and yanked her back to his side. She screamed, "Neiman! Help me! Neiman!"

The man slugged her hard in the stomach. She collapsed to the floor gasping for breath. The second man walked in and calmly closed the door.

"Tasha?!" came a man's voice from upstairs.

The first man looked at the second man and smiled his cruel smile.

"Come on, motherfucker," said the second man. He punched the palm of his hand with his fist.

"Tasha?!" came the man's voice once more. He sounded closer. There was the sound of footsteps running down the stairs. From the foyer, his feet were visible first. He was wearing tan leather moccasins. Then his legs were visible, dressed in blue jeans. Then his torso, dressed in a white polo shirt. Finally, when he was halfway down the stairs, his face appeared. It was Neiman.

Neiman stopped as soon as he saw the two men standing in the foyer. "What's going on here?" he asked, confused.

"Police," answered the first man.

"Neiman," groaned Natasha from the floor.

"Tasha!" shouted Neiman, seeing her for the first time. He bounded down the remaining steps and knelt by her side. "What's wrong, Tasha?! What happened?!"

"Neiman," gasped Natasha, "they're not police."

"Not police?" Neiman looked at the handcuffs. Then he looked back at Natasha's face. He saw fear there. He stood up and faced the two men. "I'd like to see some identification," he said sternly, the way he did at the office when he was not happy with someone and wanted them to know it. "And I demand to know why my wife's lying on the floor, and why she's in handcuffs."

"You want some ID?" asked the first man, scowling. "I'll show you some ID." He rushed at Neiman and pushed him hard against the foyer wall. Then he pushed the muzzle of the pistol against the side of his face. "This enough ID for you, motherfucker?!"

"Please …" said Neiman, shocked by the sudden violence and the muzzle of the pistol digging into the side of his face. "We don't want any trouble. Please … take whatever you want."

The first man said nothing. He searched Neiman's eyes for any sign of fight. When he saw none, he stepped back, smugly satisfied his work was done. Neiman was thoroughly intimidated. He was satisfied in a larger sense, too. In his world, there were two kinds of people: predators and prey. He had no doubt which he was. He had been a predator most his life, red in tooth and claw. And the man he pushed up against the wall with the business end of his pistol just confirmed what he was. He was prey. Were he capable of empathy, the first man would have felt sorry for him, for what was about to happen to him. Instead, he was only mildly curious. *Does this asshole even know he's prey?*

"No one's gonna get hurt," said the first man, suddenly calm, "as long as we get what we want."

"Take whatever you want," said Neiman.

The first man turned to the second man. "Get this bitch on her feet."

The second man grabbed Natasha by her arms and lifted her to her feet as if she weighed nothing. He pushed her over to face the first man. Her hair was disheveled and covering half her face. The first man reached out and brushed it back. His fingertips moved down her neck. Natasha's skin crawled from his touch. "Real nice," said the first man, more to himself than anyone else. His fingers had stopped at the Tiffany Knot Double Row Necklace.

The first man turned back to Neiman. "Me and my homey here, we followed your bitch back from Tiffany's—"

"Please ..." interrupted Neiman. "Her name's Natasha."

The first man cocked his head. He gave Neiman a quizzical look before he smiled his cruel smile. "Ok," he said, "that's cool." He continued where he left off. "Me and my homey here, we figure anyone shopping at Tiffany's ..." He suddenly glared at Neiman. "Like your bitch wife here!" He paused, wondering if Neiman would object a second time.

Neiman looked away and said nothing.

The first man snorted. "Thought so. Well, like I was saying, me and my homey here, we like nice stuff."

"We sure do," confirmed the second man. He was leering at Natasha.

"I have money," offered Neiman, suddenly hopeful he had the means to get these two men to leave his house. Money was always the answer, he thought. In his world, it always had been. "Please, take whatever you want. It's upstairs in the study, in the vault there."

"That's what I'm talking about!" said the second man, grinning widely. His two front teeth glittered with gold.

The first man motioned for Neiman to lead the way.

The vault was built into the wall of the study. It had a burgundy enamel door with a five spoke brass handle. The digital key pad was just above the brass handle. Neiman punched in the code and opened the door. He pointed to a shelf where stacks of hundred-dollar bills were neatly organized in orange currency bands. "There's a hundred grand in cash there," he said proudly.

The first man leaned in to look at the pile of cash. He reached out and touched some of the bills to make sure they were not some figment of his imagination. He had never seen so much cash all in one place.

"Please," said Neiman, "take it. It's all yours."

"You bet your ass it's ours!" snapped the first man, annoyed Neiman did not understand the money was not his to give. It had not been his since they followed his wife through the driveway gate. "You need to remember your place, motherfucker!"

Neiman was taken aback. While he did not expect remorse from the first man, for taking something that was not his, because the man was obviously a thief, he thought a little appreciation was in order. It was, after all, his cash they were stealing.

"And the jewelry?" asked the first man. "Something tells me this ain't the first time your bitch wife been to Tiffany's."

"Yes," said Neiman, disappointed by the man's vulgar reference to his wife again, after he had objected, as well as his lack of appreciation for the cash. He pulled out a sliding tray below the shelf with the pile of cash. The tray was black velvet. Precious stones glittered there, set in gold rings, bracelets and necklaces. The black velvet tray would have been right at home at Tiffany's because the first man was more right than he knew. Natasha was a regular customer at Tiffany's.

"Shit!" said the first man.

"Fuckin' A!" said the second man.

"Take it all," said Neiman, just wanting them out of his house.

The first man had enough. He had enough of what he came for, cash and valuables, and he had enough of Neiman's attitude. He turned and punched Neiman in the face.

Neiman staggered back, shocked. "You broke my nose!" he shouted.

"You keep talkin' like we need your permission, motherfucker!"

"I ... I ... I," stammered Neiman, holding his nose to stem the bleeding. "I know you don't need my permission."

"Any guns?" asked the first man, ignoring Neiman's affirmation.

"No, no guns," said Neiman. "We don't like guns."

"What?!" asked the first man, incredulous. "You don't like guns?!"

"No," said Neiman, not at all understanding why this man was so angry. He had just given him a fortune in cash and jewelry.

"Well, I don't get that, 'cause ... you see, I like guns." He held his pistol up in front of his face to admire it. "And I like *this* gun 'cause it means I get to take your shit and there ain't nothing you can do to stop me ... 'cause you ain't got no gun." He looked at Neiman with contempt. "Just think, motherfucker, if you came down those stairs with a shotgun instead of your limp, cracker dick, then, well, we wouldn't be takin' all your shit right now."

Neiman looked over at Natasha. He could see she was terrified. *What the hell does this guy want?! Why can't he just take his money and leave?!* "I could never shoot someone for money," said Neiman proudly.

It was the wrong thing to say.

"Fuck!" said the first man, disgusted. He glared at Neiman. "Ain't you all fuckin' high and mighty in your fancy cracker-ass mansion with more fuckin' money than God. Well, motherfucker, what if we want something more than your fuckin' money?"

"I don't understand," said Neiman. He really did not.

The first man turned to the second man. "Help this limp dick motherfucker understand."

The second man grunted his acknowledgment, satisfied he was finally getting what he wanted, right from the start when he first watched Natasha walk out of Tiffany's. He turned to face Natasha and leered again. She immediately understood and backed away. She managed only a few steps before he leapt forward and grabbed her arm. He also grabbed a handful of blouse and ripped it from her body, exposing her bare breasts. Natasha screamed and turned to hide herself as best she could. Her hands were still cuffed behind her back.

"Shit, man!" said the first man, laughing with surprise. "Your bitch ain't wearing no bra! Limp dick got himself a nasty bitch!"

"Please," said Neiman. "Don't ..." He felt the room start to spin.

"What?" asked the first man. "*NOW* you wanna shoot me?" His voice was mocking. "Uh huh. I bet you do. Well, motherfucker, you can't 'cause you ain't got no gun. So, what you gonna do now, limp dick?"

Neiman tried to answer but no words came.

The first man laughed. "Let me help you, limp dick, 'cause I know what you're gonna do. You're gonna sit back and watch while me and my homey here fuck your bitch wife."

The second man grabbed Natasha by the hair and pulled her over to the desk in the middle of the study.

Natasha screamed, "Noooooo! Please! Neiman … help me! Noooooo!"

The second man slapped her hard across the face. The force of the slap snapped her head to one side and split her lip. She stopped screaming. Warm, salty blood filled her mouth. The second man pushed her face down on the desk. She struggled in vain as she felt him rip off her skirt and then her panties. Nausea welled up inside her. She started to sob.

"Please …" begged Neiman. It was the only word he could find.

"Here," said the first man, offering his pistol to Neiman, handle first. "Still don't like guns? My homey here is fuckin' your wife, limp dick, right now, while you're standing there … doing nothing."

Neiman could only look at the pistol. His arms were paralyzed. His feet were rooted to the carpet.

The first man shook his head sadly. "And then it's my turn. You're gonna be watchin' a while, limp dick." His voice was almost sympathetic, as if he was talking to a child that needed to understand bad behavior comes with consequences. There was no real sympathy in his voice, though. There was only mocking contempt. "Or you can try and stop it. All you have to do is take the gun."

Neiman stared at the gun wide-eyed, desperately wanting to do something, anything to stop these men from hurting his wife. He prided himself on being a man of action. It was action that made him what he was today, the chief executive officer of the largest entertainment corporation in the world. He knew exactly how to handle producers whose budgets were out of control. He knew exactly how to expand distribution rights in overseas markets. He knew exactly how to boost the stock price for leverage with the board when negotiating his next compensation package. None of that mattered here. The mindset and skill set required to save his wife and save himself were beyond him. He had never thought to acquire them, let alone practice and develop them. He considered himself a civilized man. A civilized man, he believed, was governed by the rule of law and the rule of law gives government a monopoly on violence. What he failed to consider was the fact not all men are so governed. Worse, he failed to allow for the existence of evil in the world, real, tangible evil, and the small but nontrivial potential he might someday encounter it. On that fateful day, when he was not favored by the roll of the cosmic dice, evil would have its way with him.

Unable to do anything but watch, tears of despair ran down Neiman's face.

"I thought so," said the first man coldly. He turned the pistol around in his hand and held it properly. Then he carefully aimed at the center of Neiman's forehead. He pulled the trigger. The pistol jumped in the first man's hand. The study reverberated with the concussion of the gunshot. Neiman collapsed to the floor. His body twitched spasmodically like a fish out of water. Then it was still. His lifeless eyes looked up at the ceiling. A red stain of blood expanded on the carpet beneath his head.

Natasha never heard the gunshot. She was nine years old now, walking along the beach with her mom. They were looking for sea shells down by the water's edge to add to their collection at home. They had just found a big sea scallop. Her mom carefully washed the sand from the shell and held it up for Natasha to see. The delicate, fragile walls were a beautiful, translucent mosaic of pink and orange. Her mom looked down at Natasha with adoring eyes. They both laughed. A gentle ocean breeze blew off the water. It felt crisp on Natasha's face. Her hands caressed the warm cashmere of her favorite sweater. The setting sun shimmered as it touched the blue ocean horizon. Breakers rolled in endlessly, enveloping them with the soothing sound of surf. It was all so perfect. It was the best day of her life.

"You gonna get some?" asked the second man with a grin. He stood back from Natasha as he pulled up his pants.

The first man laughed. "Wouldn't miss it!"

Natasha never felt him when he came and had his way with her. She never felt the muzzle of the pistol, either, pressing up against the back of her head when he was through with her, and after he had ripped the Tiffany Knot Double Row Necklace from her neck. When the bullet came and ended her life, she was there on the beach, collecting shells with her mom.

CHAPTER TWO

Decadence is a moral and spiritual disease, resulting from too long a period of wealth and power, producing cynicism, decline of religion, pessimism and frivolity. The citizens of such a nation will no longer make an effort to save themselves, because they are not convinced that anything in life is worth saving.

— Sir John Glubb, "The Fate of Empires"

PASTOR TIMOTHY LAYTON liked to work late. His pastoral duties were complete. His phone had finally stopped ringing with all the calls that made up a typical day. There were the mundane calls for help. Could the church participate in a bake sale next month? There were the heartbreaking calls for divine intervention. Would he pray for a miracle for a woman in the prime of her life, a wife and mother of two who had just received a diagnosis of stage four pancreatic cancer? And there was everything in between.

So, too, were his familial duties complete, including sitting down for dinner with his wife, his daughter and his two sons, and then doing the dishes afterwards. The family dinner was a ritual Pastor Layton insisted upon unless there was something close to an emergency. It was a ritual second only to prayer. The dinner ritual was a simple one. The table was set by the children. They put out the plates, the silverware and the glasses. Everything had its proper place. The napkin was folded diagonally with the long edge of the fold adjacent to the left side of the plate. The fork went on top of the napkin. The knife was set adjacent to the right side of the plate with the edge turned in toward the plate. The spoon was set next to the knife. Finally, the glass went above the knife and the spoon.

Part of the children's responsibility for setting the table included lighting the two candles in the crystal candlestands which had been handed down in his family through five generations. It was a responsibility the children coveted. His daughter, the eldest of his three children, had initially insisted she be the one to light the candles because her brothers could not be trusted with such a precious family heirloom. "They break everything!" she claimed.

Her brothers objected even though there was some truth to what she said. They roughhoused with reckless abandon. "She's only saying that because she wants to hog the fun part!" they fired back.

The fun part was striking the old-fashioned wooden kitchen matches on the rough side of the big red and green Diamond matchbox and then watching the red match heads flare into flame. When he and his wife told them to work it out themselves, they came up with a roster that was a daily rotation for lighting the candles. The roster went from oldest to youngest.

His wife would carry the hot dishes to the table. His daughter carried the salad, bread and condiments. He would lead them all in prayer. He kept the prayer short and to the point. "Bless us, O Lord, and these Thy gifts, which we are about to receive from Thy bounty, through Christ our Lord. Amen."

"Amen" at the dinner table was the equivalent of NASCAR's "Gentlemen, start your engines." Everyone at the table snatched up their knife and fork and commenced to eat with enthusiasm. Still, their enthusiasm was tempered by the proper handling of eating utensils. Their proper handling was, in fact, a part of the dinner ritual. Pastor Layton had insisted upon it from the moment his children were old enough to feed themselves. It was a pet peeve of his, and always a bit of a shock, to sit down to a meal with successful, well-educated people and watch them grab hold of their eating utensils in a closed fist as if some level of brute force was required to cut a piece of trout. "Didn't their parents teach them table manners?" he would ask his wife, exasperated, once he was back home. Eating, he believed, was as much a civilizational practice as writing, which meant the tools required for both must be handled deftly and with precision. In turn, that required they be held properly, between the thumb and forefinger.

Conversation was the other part of the dinner ritual and by far the more time-consuming part. Pastor Layton and his wife would always start it off, inquiring how the other's day went, sharing humorous aspects of their day, and discussing current events. Inquiring how the other's day went was never perfunctory. There was genuine interest and concern. Humorous stories were typically self-deprecating, and never told at another's expense. The discussion of current events proceeded from a consideration of what was actually known to be true versus what was surmised or mere conjecture. Opinion was always identified as such, with a discussion of the thought process that produced the opinion.

Pastor Layton loved to play the devil's advocate. "Well," he would usually start with a twinkle in his eyes, "that's an interesting perspective." Then he would pose questions designed to test the validity of the opinion, much like a scientist probes a hypothesis with data from the natural world. There was never any presumption of superior insight or intellect by him or his wife, never any ego involved because someone was emotionally invested in "being right." It was always a sincere desire to discover the truth, or to get as close to the truth as possible, whatever the truth might be. They did this purposefully, in front of their children, so their children would have the example of a reasoned, respectful adult conversation. Then it was the turn of each of their three children. No devices were allowed at the dinner table. No phones. Certainly no iPads. And the TV sat alone in the family room, its screen black and its speakers silent.

If you asked Pastor Layton why he liked to work late, he would tell you it was his "alone time" to recharge his spiritual batteries. He would retire to his office which was attached to the back of the sanctuary. It was only a short walk from the parsonage next door. If the weather was good, which it almost always was in Southern California, he would light up his pipe on the front porch of the parsonage and then slowly make his way over to the office, meandering around the beautifully manicured grounds of the church as he puffed away on his pipe. He had it timed perfectly, the degree of meandering, so he arrived at the door to his office as he finished the last puff.

The furniture in the office was not his own. It belonged to the church. There was a beautiful antique mahogany desk and a comfortable leather desk chair. Opposite the desk were another three leather chairs. A bay window took up most of one wall. Built-in mahogany bookshelves covered two walls from floor to ceiling. Their shelves were filled with books that mostly belonged to the church. Two whole shelves were filled with his own books. Many were of a theological nature. Others concerned history. Of those, "The Story of Civilization" was one of his prize possessions. It was an eleven-volume set written by the husband-and-wife team of Will and Ariel Durant over the span of four decades. The first of the volumes was published in 1935, the last in 1975. It had taken Pastor Layton four years to make his way through the set. It was, he would freely admit, a labor of love. He loved history, especially when it was effectively brought back to life and made something more than the recounting of battles and promulgations by despots, kings and emperors. He loved the detail of how people actually lived in the past, from the high and mighty to the wretched poor. At times, though, he found the detail overwhelming, like drinking from a fire hose. He knew it was a level of detail he could never possibly retain. It was usually then he considered the monumental effort required to research such a work, especially in the day and age before archives were digitized and remotely available to all. *They must have lived in the library!* he thought. When he finished the last volume, he concluded there is only one constant in history. Human nature never changes. He found that conclusion comforting as a Christian. *How could human nature change? We were created in the image of God!*

Pastor Layton recharged his spiritual batteries by reading Scripture. Then he would pray. He was a true believer in the power of prayer because he believed God answered prayer. He would first pray for the wisdom to understand what was written in Scripture. Then he would pray for the courage to apply that wisdom in present-day life, with himself, his family and the world at large. He knew courage was required because he was living in a world that was in the process of rejecting its Christian faith, and the process was well advanced toward completion. Condemnation if not outright persecution was an increasingly common consequence for those who espoused the tenets of Christianity, unless they were the innocuous tenets about loving your enemy and practicing charity.

Sometimes his prayers were answered in short order. There was the time his daughter came home from school and, partaking of their evening ritual of conversation, revealed how her first-grade teacher told the class they were free to choose their gender, that they could be a different gender if they wanted, different than what they were at home, which meant they could go by a girl's name even though they were given a boy's name by their parents. They were told they could wear girls' clothing, too, if they wanted, even if they came to school dressed as a boy. They could change into their preferred clothing once they were at school. The teacher told them the same was true for the girls if they wanted to be boys. The teacher concluded by telling the class they could be whatever gender they wanted at school regardless of what they were expected to be at home, and nobody at home needed to know.

Pastor Layton and his wife were shocked by their daughter's story. They prayed on the proper course of action and decided to keep their daughter at home the next day. They also decided to go and talk to the school principal to find out if there was some misunderstanding. Mr. Chilton was the school principal. The Laytons relayed the story their daughter shared with them at the dinner table. They were shocked a second time when they found Mr. Chilton unconcerned by what the teacher told her class. In no way did he find it inappropriate. On the contrary, he calmly explained how it was consistent with the sex education guidelines approved by the California Department of Education.

"Sex education for first graders?" asked Pastor Layton's wife, incredulous.

"We encourage classroom discussions beginning in kindergarten," answered Mr. Chilton, "about gender identity and LGBTQ relationships."

"You discuss gender identity with kindergarteners?" asked Pastor Layton. He was as incredulous as his wife.

"Well, yes … in an age-appropriate manner, of course. Our priority is to make all children feel comfortable at school … dispelling myths, breaking down stereotypes. Our goal is not to cause confusion about sex and gender but to help children develop an awareness that other expressions exist."

"And one of those myths is 'He created them, Male and Female'?" asked Pastor Layton, quoting from Genesis.

"Mr. Layton, the Supreme Court requires we keep religion out of our curriculum."

"What about biology? Is that a myth, too … that there are two and only two sexes, and that those sexes are determined at birth by your chromosomes?"

"I can assure you, Mr. Layton, our guidelines are developed with input from the appropriate experts, child development experts."

"And those experts think children not only can choose their gender, and their sexual orientation, but they can do so without input from their parents?" asked Pastor Layton. "And that hiding their choices from their parents, about their gender and sexual orientation, is ok … with teachers promoting and supporting this deception along with the school principal?"

"Mr. Layton, teachers and principals are, regrettably, sometimes put in the awkward position of being caught between parents and students. But much like circumstances where there is abuse in the home, our first duty is to protect the students."

"From what?"

"We cannot let a parent's rejection of a child's choice … with regard to their gender identity … and their sexual orientation … We cannot let that rejection guide our advocacy for a child. A parent's rejection of a child's choice is devastating to that child, Mr. Layton. If I may be frank with you, parents are not *entitled* to know their child's choice. That knowledge must be earned."

Pastor Layton heard enough. He was as angry with himself for allowing his daughter's indoctrination to take place under his nose and without his knowledge as he was with the man sitting in front of him who had facilitated it. He decided then and there his daughter would never again attend public school, and that her two younger brothers would also never attend. He was certain his wife felt the same way.

He indulged his anger by speaking his mind. "Mr. Chilton, if I may be frank with *you*, we have a profound difference of opinion that will preclude us from ever again entrusting our daughter to be educated by you and your school system. Our job as parents is, in fact, to reject the choices of our children if we know them to be harmful to their development, because they are just that, children. How we as a society arrived at the point where we ask children to make fundamental and irreversible decisions about anything, never mind something as patently absurd as the notion they can choose their gender, is supremely troubling to me. The Scripture and biology are both as clear as they can be on this. There are two and only two sexes: male and female. Your sex is determined at birth, by God and your chromosomes. Every culture has known this since the beginning of time except, apparently, ours. Every culture has known that the raising up of children to be healthy, happy, well-adjusted adults requires the parents take into consideration the sex of their children as much as their innate talents and aptitudes, if not more so. *This* is what it means to be a good man, a good husband and a good father. *This* is what it means to be a good woman, a good wife and a good mother. To do otherwise, Mr. Chilton, is the real child abuse. Surely you know this. Surely you would not stand by and watch your own children be indoctrinated by what can only be called a poisonous ideology, an ideology that legitimizes what is, at best, a childish fantasy and, at worst, a real mental health issue … And then to stand by and countenance children having their bodies chemically and surgically mutilated so they can never have children of their own … There is a word for that, Mr. Chilton. The word is 'evil.' It is pure, unadulterated evil. Yet, you stand by and allow it to happen … to other children. No doubt that is your thirty pieces of silver, the price for your position as principal of the school. How you can sleep at night is a mystery to me. I pray you someday find the courage to stand up for these innocent children. And I pray you someday fall to your knees and beg God's forgiveness for all the innocent children whose lives you have ruined."

Mr. Chilton was also through listening. He responded that threats against school personnel were unacceptable and that he would call security to escort the Laytons off campus if they did not immediately leave. The Layton's daughter started homeschool the next day.

Pastor Layton's prayers were not always answered in such short order. He was being asked with increasingly frequency by his parishioners if the End Times were here. He understood the question. He had asked himself that very question after his meeting with his daughter's principal,

Mr. Chilton. He recalled how the Apostle Paul said there will be a falling away first, before the last days, in which some man will set himself up as God, pretending to be God, and the people will believe him. He thought men were certainly setting themselves up as God in a collective sense, by insisting people "follow the science" no matter how unscientific the science might be. But he saw no single man pretending to be God. Also, as much as the world seemed to have lost its collective mind, he knew it had done so before without the Rapture ensuing and Jesus taking believers up with Him into heaven.

Pastor Layton spent weeks praying on it, praying the Holy Spirit would help him put the steady drumbeat of negative news into its proper historical perspective. That historical perspective finally came to him late one night when he was alone in his office. *Yes,* he thought, *the schools may be failing at everything except indoctrination. Yes, there may be double digit inflation and a shortage of labor because no one wants to work. Yes, the economy may be in another Great Recession and possibly heading toward a second Great Depression. Yes, the government may be bankrupt and risking nuclear war with Russia and China for no discernable national security interest. Yes, roads and bridges may be falling apart. Yes, there may be draconian water rationing, rolling blackouts and food shortages. Yes, the southern border may be in chaos. Yes, crime may be rampant in the streets and getting worse. Yes, there may be 150,000 fentanyl overdoses a year. And, yes, to cap it all off, there may be a crashing birthrate because young people are not interested in having children, as if you could blame them. But … things have been worse.*

Pastor Layton decided there was no way to know. The End Times might very well be here. Then again, they might be decades, centuries or even millennia in the future. He decided to share his conclusion with his parishioners. He also decided to tell them, for whatever it was worth, that a prudent man is always prepared—mentally, physically and spiritually—for any and all possibilities.

CHAPTER THREE

Shotgun blasts are heard
When I rip and kill at will
The man of the hour, tower of power
I'll devour
I'm gonna tie you up and let you
Understand that I'm not your average man
When I get a jammy in my hand
Damn
Ooh, listen to the way I slay
Your crew
Damage, uh, damage, uh
Damage, uh, damage
Destruction, terror and mayhem
Pass me a sissy-soft sucka, I'll slay him.

— LL Cool J, "Mama Said Knock You Out"

THE MAN WITH the grim reaper tattoo pulled Natasha's violet Porsche Taycan onto the Hollywood Freeway, heading south toward South Central Los Angeles. The second man followed behind in the white van. The man with the tattoo dialed in Channel 43 on Sirius XM radio, which was LL Cool J's Rock the Bells channel. They advertised the channel as "dedicated exclusively to hip-hop fans who want that classic hip-hop sound." He was all of twenty-two years old and his homeboys teased him about his taste in classic hip-hop. "They was playing that shit before you was born!" they liked to say. "Shit! They was playing that shit before your old man was born!"

The man with the tattoo had no idea why he liked classic hip-hop. He had never given it any thought, just like he had never given his father any thought. All he knew about his father was the one thing his mother had told him, that he was named after his father. He was eleven years old when she told him and he was already angry at the world. The next day he informed her and everyone else he would no longer answer to Raymond. From now on, he would go by RZ. When his mother asked why RZ, he answered that he just liked the sound of it, that it was cool, and that people would be less likely to mess with him.

"Why's that?" asked his mother naively.

He smiled his trademark smile, which was generally considered cruel even then, at least by everyone except his mother. He answered, "Don't you know? RZ … It's short for razor."

"Mama Said Knock You Out" came on the radio, by LL Cool J. RZ turned the volume up loud. He knew the lyrics by heart and sang along. He imagined himself as LL Cool J in the music video he had watched countless times. He was in the boxing ring with a hoody over his head defiantly announcing his comeback, except his comeback was really something else. "Don't call it a comeback," the lyrics went. "I been here for years. I'm rocking my peers, putting suckas in fear." That was exactly how RZ felt as he sang along. He had always lived in Los Angeles but Los Angeles had never really known he was here. Until now. Now, he was certain, Los Angeles knew he was here.

RZ was not unique in that he did not know his father. There were only a few married couples with children living in the neighborhood. Most of the families consisted of single mothers and their live-in boyfriends. Many of those families were little different from the families with married couples. The live-in boyfriends contributed to the maintenance of the household, buying a portion of the groceries and helping with rent. They also contributed to the parenting. Some of them were actually good at it, stepping into the role of a father with a firm but patient hand. Unfortunately for RZ and his mother, her live-in boyfriend was really only interested in partying and hanging out. What little he did to contribute financially was limited by the fact he seldom worked. He seldom worked because, even though he graduated high school, he was functionally illiterate. He read at an elementary school level. He was also functionally feral, which further restricted his employment opportunities. He mouthed off at anyone who made him angry: customers, co-workers, even the boss. If he was really angry, he started throwing punches. To the extent he helped with the parenting, it was only when RZ did something that annoyed him personally, which was usually something trivial like eating the last slice of pizza from last night's party, the one he had planned to eat in the morning, or when RZ turned on the TV when he was trying to get some sleep after hanging out all night with his homeboys. In the sense that parenting is a verb, his concept of parenting was limited to punishment, which usually turned into beatings. RZ's mother tried to protect RZ by redirecting his anger. She literally took punches for RZ. She had enough of him after her second black eye.

There were no more live-in boyfriends after that. RZ's mother tried the best she could to raise RZ as a single mother but found him increasingly difficult to control. Some of that was a consequence of the normal maturation process. Boys need to establish their independence as they grow up. Some of it, too, was a consequence of there being no man in the house to lead by example and help with the discipline. But the biggest part of it, the difficulty of keeping RZ under control, was the simple fact his mother could not control herself. She was addicted to drugs and alcohol. Her addiction to drugs and alcohol was a result of her attempt at self-medication for what would ultimately be diagnosed as Gulf War illness.

RZ's mother had joined the Army right out of high school. The Army trained her as an ammunition stock control and accounting specialist. She was deployed to Saudi Arabi after Iraq invaded Kuwait and remained there for the duration of the Gulf War. She had no idea exactly what caused her illness. Doctors generally do not know even today. It might have been from exposure to all the burning oil wells left behind by the retreating Iraqi Army. It might have been from exposure to the depleted uranium used in some of the munitions. Or, it might have been a side effect from the anti-nerve gas tablets the Army required them to take. There are over a dozen suspected culprits. Whatever the actual culprit, she increasingly complained of fatigue and headaches. After returning home, her joints started to ache. After leaving the Army, she found it difficult to remember things, even simple things like what she had for breakfast. When the Department of Veterans Affairs finally diagnosed her with Gulf War illness, she received a lump sum payment of sixty thousand dollars. She spent most of it on drugs, which is how she ended up pregnant again. It is also how she ended up losing custody of RZ when he was thirteen years old, to her mother, RZ's grandmother.

RZ's grandmother was even less well equipped than her daughter to raise a young man all by herself. She did not do drugs. She did not even drink alcohol. She was a devout Christian who attended church religiously. Her age was one handicap. She was seventy-two years old when RZ came to live with her. Her health was another handicap, and it was the greater of the two. She was overweight and suffered from diabetes. Often, she needed a cane to walk. Always, she needed help getting up stairs. Her heart was in the right place, though. She did her best to raise RZ. She forbade him to leave the house except for school or if it was an event with adult supervision. She knew he would only find trouble out on the street, running around with other boys in the neighborhood. Her proscription lasted almost a year. Then, one day, one of RZ's friends knocked on the door. He was a friend from school. He invited RZ to come and hang out. RZ simply told his grandmother he was going out and there was nothing she could do to stop him. RZ and his friend jumped a kid the same day. The kid was walking home from elementary school. When they took the kid's lunch money, RZ realized he liked being a bully. He never looked back after that. He finally found something he was good at. He and his friend, and then his friend's friends, started to fancy themselves "gangstas." They were leading the gangsta lifestyle celebrated by rappers. They graduated from jumping elementary school kids to shoplifting, and then to burglary. They even had their own street corner. They started hanging out well into the night like the older guys.

RZ's grandmother watched helplessly from the confines of her living room in her modest two-bedroom house, the one with the overgrown yard RZ was supposed to keep up but did not. He had not touched a lawnmower since he started hanging out. "Yardwork is for suckas," he said derisively. RZ's grandmother knew how things would end up if RZ kept hanging out. He would end up in jail like so many of the other young men in the neighborhood, or worse. She turned to a friend for help, one she knew from church. His name was Mr. Smith.

Mr. Smith was RZ's middle school gym teacher. She turned to him because he was the only man RZ seemed to respect who was also a positive role model. She knew RZ respected Mr. Smith because he had come home from school after his first day of gym class and actually wanted to talk about school. "You should have seen this guy!" RZ told her breathlessly. "We was all standing around in the gym waiting to meet our new gym teacher when this big ass mother—"

"RZ!" scolded his grandmother. "Don't you dare use that word in this house!"

"Ok, ok … Chill out, Grandma. So, anyway, this big dude comes walking out. When I say big, Grandma, I mean *big*. He looks like a body builder. You should have seen him! I mean, we usually don't pay no attention to teachers. Like, we just kinda ignore 'em. We want to make 'em work for it, you know. But this guy … As soon as he walked out, the whole class went quiet. We're, like, just looking at the dude and going 'Whoa!' So, he walks up to the front of the class and looks us over. He don't say nothing, either, while he's standing there. I'm checking him out and I see this manila envelope under his arm. There's this handle sticking out. Then he says, and this is so awesome, Grandma … He says, 'My name is Mr. Smith. You may have heard about me but, in case you haven't, I'll tell you what you missed. I have high expectations for my class … which means I have high expectations for you! I expect hard work from all y'all. I also expect discipline … 'cause hard work requires discipline. Now, I don't like being disappointed. And I've got a friend here who especially don't like being disappointed.' Grandma, he grabs hold of the handle sticking out of the manila envelope under his arm and pulls out this handball racquet. You know, the ones made out of wood with the holes drilled in it. Anyway, he says, 'You disappoint my friend here, even just a little, and he'll be landing on your sorry ass from about this high.'" RZ clenched his fist as if holding the handball racquet and raised it shoulder high. "'But … you seriously disappoint my friend … he'll be coming from this high!'" RZ raised his clenched fist high over his head. "'And let me tell all y'all wannabe gangstas something … from this high, my friend here will be smoking!'"

Mr. Smith told RZ's grandmother he could not make any promises but he would try and help out. One day after gym class, he asked RZ to join him in his office. He offered RZ a seat in front of his desk. RZ noticed the photos hanging on the wall behind Mr. Smith's desk as soon as he sat down. One was a formal family portrait. An elderly couple with white hair was seated in the center of the portrait. They were holding hands. Behind them stood Mr. Smith. He had his arm around the waist of a beautiful middle-aged woman whom RZ assumed was his wife. Mr. Smith and his wife were flanked by two boys in their early teens. Mr. Smith and the elderly man wore black suits with matching red ties. So did the boys. The women wore elegant, gold dresses accentuated with a single strand of white pearls. Everyone was smiling.

Another photo showed Mr. Smith in his green and khaki Marine Corps service uniform. He was standing in front of an American flag. There was no smile on his face there. Instead, he looked determined and resolute. Three rows of multicolored ribbons stretched across the left side of his jacket, just above the breast pocket. Below the ribbons, pinned to the flap of the breast pocket, were two silver badges. The first badge showed the crossed M1 Garands of the Marine Rifle Expert Badge. The second had the crossed 1911s of the Marine Pistol Expert Badge. Red sergeant chevrons were visible on the jacket's left sleeve.

A third photo showed a group of Marines dressed in camouflage and holding rifles. They looked tired, like they had been out in the woods for a while. Still, they were smiling. The photo was obviously posed as the first row of five Marines was kneeling and the back row of nine Marines was standing. Even though they were wearing boonie hats and their faces were painted black and green, RZ recognized Mr. Smith in the middle of the first row.

Finally, there was an assortment of photos showing Mr. Smith as a young man. He was in uniform there, too, only it was either a football uniform, a basketball uniform or a track uniform. It struck RZ odd to see photos of Mr. Smith with a young man's lean body and smooth, innocent face. It dawned on him the man seated before him had, perhaps, once been seated where he was now, opposite a disappointed teacher. That was a revelation for RZ because he always thought his problems unique to him, or at least unique to his generation. Never once had he considered the fact his problems may have been experienced by the generations before him, by any of his teachers, and certainly not by his mother and grandmother.

Mr. Smith looked directly at RZ. It was more the warm, smiling look of Mr. Smith the family man rather than the determined, resolute look of Mr. Smith the Marine. He said, "You're really good at running, son. Ever consider running track?"

"Really?" asked RZ.

RZ was not surprised to hear he was good at running. He knew he was good because he usually finished first or second when his gym class went out on its fitness runs. What surprised him was the fact an adult would take the time to sit him down and tell him he was good at something. Adults, especially those charged with his instruction, only seemed to sit him down to tell him he was in trouble, or he was about to be in trouble if he kept on doing what he was doing.

"Yes, really," answered Mr. Smith. "Now, let me tell you something, son … I'm a big believer in sports. You know why?"

RZ shook his head.

"Because there's no faking it in sports. You're either better than the competition or you're not. You're either winning or you're losing. There's no bullshit in sports. And you know what makes you a winner instead of a loser?"

"Practice?" offered RZ tentatively.

Mr. Smith smiled. He was encouraged to find RZ engaged. He had sat opposite more than his share of surely, arrogant teenagers intent on communicating their complete and total lack of interest in anything he had to say.

"Yes, but it's more than practice. It's practicing longer, harder and smarter than the competition. It's what keeps you out there in the field, pushing yourself past the point where most people would have quit, pushing yourself past the point where *you* wanted to quit."

"Then what is it?" asked RZ, genuinely wanting to know.

"It's discipline, RZ. You learn discipline. You learn to be a disciplined man ... that ain't nothing nobody can take away from you. Ever. You'll have it the rest of your life. And it'll work for you in every aspect of life, not just with sports. It'll get you a better job. It'll make you better at your job, in whatever you choose to do. It'll make you a better husband, too, when you get to that point in life, and a better father." Mr. Smith looked hard at RZ to emphasis the importance of what he was about to say. "RZ, discipline will make you a better man."

Life was better for RZ after his talk with Mr. Smith. He joined the track team and worked hard at training. Just like Mr. Smith promised, his discipline paid off. He set school records in the short and middle-distance events. He won the middle school district track meet. He was even thinking of the state track meet next year, after he graduated middle school. His school work also started to improve. He was not bringing home A's but he was at least doing his homework. More importantly, he was putting real effort into it. He received his first B, ever. It was in math. His grandmother was so thrilled she took him out and bought him a new pair of track shoes.

RZ's progress ended with middle school. High school brought new friends. They were the wrong kind of friends. He started skipping class and hanging out again. He stopped applying himself in class and even stopped competing in track. The only thing that seemed to carry over from middle school was his commitment to discipline, courtesy of Mr. Smith. Only now, that discipline was applied to breaking the law.

He was fifteen when he started stealing in earnest. It was not your typical petty shoplifting, either, the kind teenagers sometimes perpetrate for the thrill of it or as a rite of passage with friends to prove their bravery. This was organized shoplifting, the kind that was epidemic in California thanks to Proposition 47. Proposition 47 made shoplifting a misdemeanor rather than a felony if it involved less than $950 of property value. A person could still be prosecuted, technically, and serve up to six months in the county jail if convicted, but the actual practice by district attorneys concerned for social justice was not to proceed with prosecution if the accused was a minority and, especially, a minor. The police soon stopped making arrests as they were not interested in wasting their time.

RZ and his group were remarkably cost conscious when they targeted a store for shoplifting. Before they grabbed a shopping cart, they opened the calculator app on their smart phones. They kept a running total as they piled their carts high with merchandise. When they had a total just shy of $950, they headed for the checkout line at the front of the store. Of course, they did not stop to pay. They just headed for the exit. Even if there was security, security did nothing to stop them by order of store management. Store management did not want the potential liability should a violent confrontation ensue. They also did not want the potential adverse publicity should a violent confrontation end up a viral video on social media, or on the nightly news.

RZ and his group initially focused on low-end retail stores like Walgreens, Target and Best Buy. Then, as their confidence grew, they moved on to high-end retail. They hit Neiman Marcus hard, targeting the purse department. One after another they grabbed a purse, checked the tag to make sure the price was under $950, and ran out the front door to hop into their waiting getaway vehicle.

They moved on to auto burglary after shoplifting. They would hit one of the big parking garages near an upscale mall. They would look for expensive cars—Mercedes Benz, Porsche, BMW—and smash the windows. Even if the car alarm went off, no one paid attention. Not once did anyone try and stop them. They scored big more than a few times but RZ decided auto burglary was too much a hit-or-miss proposition. People tended not to leave valuables in the car. A more promising proposition, he decided, was to let people get in their car and follow them home. The police call it "follow-home robbery." They would have two or three carloads of people following behind. When the unsuspecting driver pulled in his driveway, they would swarm him, punching him and pushing him to the ground. The assault did not stop once the driver was on the ground, either. There on the ground, they would start kicking him. They would keep kicking him until he no longer offered resistance. Usually that meant the driver was pleading for his attackers to take whatever they wanted, just please stop kicking him. Other times it meant the driver suddenly went slack from the psychological shock of the assault or from a blow to the head that rendered him unconscious. RZ and his group would then strip the driver of valuables. They would take the wallet, of course, or the purse if the driver was a woman. They would also take watches and jewelry.

The modius operandi for RZ and his group worked well until one time it did not. One guy just kept fighting. When the neighbors came out and started shouting, RZ and his group were forced to leave. They left empty-handed. After that, RZ decided it was time to get a gun. It was no more difficult to acquire an illegal gun in Los Angeles than it was to acquire illegal drugs. He found the gun amazingly effective once he had it. Just point a gun at someone's face and watch them raise their hands in surrender.

Only once during his many follow-home robberies did RZ feel something resembling empathy for his victim. It was for one of his earlier victims. She was an elderly lady. Even though she was white, she reminded RZ of his grandmother. He knew his grandmother would be equally helpless if suddenly jumped by a group of eight young men. He was disturbed by his feeling of empathy for the elderly lady. He considered it a fundamental flaw in his gangsta character. He resolved to harden himself so he would never again feel even a trace of empathy. He told himself his victims were not deserving of empathy for the simple reason they had something he wanted and they were not prepared to fight to keep it. It was the law of the jungle as far as RZ was concerned. It was survival of the fittest. He was the predator, his victims the prey. His victims, he thought, deserved no more empathy than a gazelle caught in the jaws of a lion, or a seal ambushed from the ocean depths by a great white shark. He especially liked to think of himself as a great white shark. The great white shark was the most fearsome animal in its domain, which is what RZ aspired to be in his. Also, the great white shark attacked its victims suddenly, by ambush from out of the dark, the way RZ and his group liked to attack their victims. His subsequent victims, the ones after the elderly lady, would likely have agreed with RZ's simile had they known of it. When they looked up into his eyes while lying prostrate and helpless at his feet, they found nothing resembling empathy. His eyes were cold, black and unfeeling, just like the eyes of the great white shark.

RZ's success with follow-home robberies brought him to the attention of the South Central Crips. They invited him and his group to join their gang. RZ understood the invitation for what it was: an offer he could not refuse. He was too successful and claiming too big a piece of the follow-home-robbery pie not to be coopted by the Crips. His options were to refuse the Crips, and then be attacked as a competitor, or to join the Crips and pay a portion of his take as tribute. The first option was really not an option because the Crips were an enormously powerful gang, not just in South Central Los Angeles but nationwide. Their total national membership was estimated by law enforcement at thirty to thirty-five thousand. They also had a reputation for ruthless violence. RZ chose the only option that made sense. He accepted their invitation. There was only one requirement for membership in the Crips. He had to commit cold-blooded murder. It was that requirement for membership that doomed Natasha and Neiman Harrison the moment they were targeted by RZ and his homeboy.

***

RZ looked in the rearview mirror and noticed the white van falling behind. *What the fuck?!* he thought. He slowed down as well. *What the fuck's he doing? He's going forty-five fuckin' miles an hour!* He pulled out his phone and punched in the second man's number. It rang until his voicemail picked up. The second man's voice rhymed his greeting. "Either you slingin' crack rock or you got a wicked jump shot. Go ahead and get funky on my phone. Might be I call your ass back."

RZ hung up without leaving a message. He looked down at the speedometer. *Fuckin' A! Forty fuckin' miles an hour!* He dialed again.

Three rings later, the second man answered. "Yo, RZ, you got some good shit here."

"Damn right it's some good shit! What the fuck you doing smoking it?! And what the fuck you doing driving so slow?!"

The second man laughed. It was a stupid laugh, the kind of laugh you hear when someone is flying high on dope. *Motherfucker probably lit up as soon as we left!*

"Ain't driving slow," protested the second man. He was slurring his words.

RZ felt his face flush hot. It was not that he begrudged the second man lighting up, or even lighting up *his* dope. He planned to do some celebrating himself for their score tonight, and for successfully completing their rite of initiation for the Crips. Only, he planned to do his celebrating when they were safely back home and the Taycan was safely in the chop shop. *Motherfuckin' idiot!* he thought.

"Been thinking about that ho, RZ. That was one fine ho. You ever had a ho as fine as that?"

"Listen, fuckhead, you're driving forty fuckin' miles an hour … on the freeway! You need to put the joint down and concentrate on your fuckin' driving. You need to do it *right now,* like I'm fuckin' telling you. Then maybe I won't beat your ass when we get home."

The second man laughed as if RZ's threat was hysterically funny. "Shit, RZ, you're just mad 'cause you got the sloppy seconds with that ho. Now, be honest RZ. Wasn't that the finest ho you ever had in your whole ho-fuckin' life?"

RZ took a deep breath, trying to calm himself. He said coldly but with real menace in his voice, "Ok, we're getting off the freeway … right now. We're taking this fuckin' exit and then we're pulling over so you can get your fuckin' head screwed on straight."

Another hysterical laugh came from the second man. "Did you get that, RZ? The finest ho you ever had in your *whole* ho-fuckin' life. Pretty fuckin' funny, huh?"

RZ shook his head in disgust. He slowed the Taycan for Exit 4B, for North Alvarado Street. He watched the van follow behind in the rearview mirror. He noticed a car following behind the van. He had not seen the car before because it was directly behind the van. He could only see it now because it was suddenly exposed by the curve in the road for the freeway offramp. Then he noticed the light bar on top of the car, the one characteristic of the California Highway Patrol. The light bar suddenly exploded in frenetically dancing red, white and blue strobes.

CHAPTER FOUR

Good people sleep peaceably in their beds at night only because rough men stand ready to do violence on their behalf.

— George Orwell

PASTOR LAYTON SAT back in the first pew of Wesley's Chapel and let the music wash over him. Noah Bridges was the young man singing and Pastor Layton thought him truly gifted. He had a rich, resonant tenor and perfect pitch, at least as far as Pastor Layton could tell.

Noah was singing "Be Thou My Vision." Not only did Pastor Layton love the song itself, he loved the history behind the song. The melody was composed by an unknown composer who wanted to honor the heroism of Saint Patrick. According to legend, Patrick defied the local Irish king on Easter Sunday in 433 to proclaim the glory of God. The king had issued a decree prohibiting the building of fires, even the lighting of candles, in observance of a local Druid festival. Patrick wanted to show the world God's light could not be extinguished. He climbed to the top of Slane Hill, the tallest hill in the area, and built a raging fire. It was visible for miles around and, presumably, visible to the Irish king who forbade its making.

The lyrics are only slightly less obscure than the melody. They are usually attributed to an Irish poet in the sixth century named Dallán Forgaill. Forgaill wanted to honor Patrick for his act of defiance against the Irish king and his faith in the King of kings. The original Gaelic was first translated into English by an Irish linguist named Mary Byrne, in Ériu, the Journal of the School of Irish Learning. That was in 1905, some fifteen hundred years after Saint Patrick lit his fire on top of Slane Hill.

Finally, in 1912, Eleanor Hull, the founder and secretary of the Irish Text Society, set the words to the melody composed by the unknown composer. The result was an instant sensation. Pastor Layton found it interesting so many contemporary artists chose to leave out the third verse, apparently thinking it too militaristic. The third verse goes: "Be thou my buckler, my sword for the fight. Be thou my dignity, thou my delight, thou my soul's shelter, thou my high tow'r. Raise thou me heav'nward, O Pow'r of my pow'r." Pastor Layton noted with satisfaction Noah chose to keep the third verse in the version he sang this morning.

The congregation erupted in applause when Noah finished. Noah bowed self-consciously and took his seat with his wife three rows back from the front. Pastor Layton walked up to the pulpit. He wore a long sleeve, white button-down shirt, a navy jacket and khaki pants. He set his Bible down and looked out at the faces of his congregation. The church was two-thirds full. There were easily two hundred faces looking back at him. He started the way he usually started, with the greeting, "God is good."

"All the time," responded the congregation as one.

"And all the time," continued Pastor Layton.

"God is good," said the congregation.

Pastor Layton smiled warmly. "Welcome everyone. Wasn't that a beautiful hymn? It transports me, that song, every time I hear it … bringing me closer to our Father in heaven. Can we give Noah another round of applause?"

The congregation obliged Pastor Layton and applauded enthusiastically.

"I keep telling him he should quit his day job and take up gospel singing. He does such a beautiful job. No, just kidding. Noah, you're really, really good but … don't quit your day job. You're really good at that, too … and I think it pays better."

Chuckles rippled through the congregation.

Pastor Layton opened his Bible. "Today, I would like to talk to you about something that has been weighing on my mind. It's been weighing on my heart, too. Every day seems to bring another awful story in the news. Rampant crime in the streets. Mass shootings in our grocery stores and schools. An open border in chaos. Looming clouds of war overseas. And a faltering economy here at home. Our city, our country, our world seems to have lost its way. Worse, it seems to be falling apart. It has been weighing on a lot of you, too. I know because many of you have come up to me in recent months and asked, 'Pastor Layton, are these the End Times?' I would like to address that question today."

Pastor Layton surveyed the congregation. He could see he had their attention.

"The short answer is: I don't know. If you turn to Matthew 24:36, it says, 'But of that day and hour knoweth no man, no, not the angels of heaven, but my Father only.' If Jesus did not know, certainly *we* cannot know the day and the hour. Also, it's important to remind ourselves there have been dark days in our past. Those days, too, must have seemed like harbingers of the End Times to the Christians living through them. Does anyone here know how many people died in the Second World War?"

He paused and looked over the congregation. He was not expecting an answer from the congregation. He only wanted the congregation to ponder the question.

"Sixty million," he answered with an incredulous voice. "Think about that number for a moment. Sixty million souls, most of whom were civilians. And think about the terrible economic collapse that was the Great Depression, that preceded the Second World War. Those people went through the Great Depression *and* the Second World War. Then there was the First World War, which was called 'The War to End all Wars' at the time. They named it that in the midst of the fighting, in 1918 … I imagine to keep up morale. That name, it turned out, was a bit optimistic. Going back further in history, there was the American Civil War. We fought that war to preserve the Union and end slavery. It is estimated seven hundred thousand Americans died in the Civil War. The equivalent number today, with our much larger population of 330 million, is over eight million people. Think on that … eight million of our fellow Americans … dead. Then there was the Black Death of the fourteenth century in Europe, Asia and North Africa. Scholars estimate the Black Death carried away a third of the population of Europe. There was the scourge of the Vikings in the ninth century. There was Attila the Hun in the fifth century. Imagine living in Rome in the first century, during the time of Caligula and Nero when Christians were martyred for their faith. Christians were burned alive at the stake. Christians were literally thrown to the lions in the Colosseum, to be ripped apart and devoured as a public spectacle. You understand my point. There have been many, many epochs in history when the Christians of that time would have had ample justification to believe they were in the End Times … or that the End Times were near … just as many of us are thinking today."

Pastor Layton walked out from behind the pulpit and pointed at the congregation. He was a reserved, almost mild-mannered man when you met him somewhere other than preaching to his congregation. In front of his congregation, though, he was a different man. He was transformed. He liked to think it was the Holy Spirit moving through him to touch the hearts of the people sitting in the pews. He sometimes joked it was the Holy Spirt knowing he could only touch the hearts of the people if the people were not falling asleep.

"But the signs, Pastor Layton!" objected his alter ego, the one who often interrupted his sermons as a way to keep his congregation engaged. "What about the signs?!"

"Yes," answered Pastor Layton, now himself again, "there are signs. And I'd like to spend some time today talking about those signs. So, what does Scripture say about the signs, the signs that tell us the End Times are near? I'll briefly talk about four of them. The first is 'the sign of deception.' Matthew 24:4-5 says, 'And Jesus answered and said unto them, take heed that no man deceive you. For many shall come in my name, saying, I am Christ; and shall deceive many.' Yes, there are many deceivers in our world today. There are the politicians offering us utopia … if only we give them a little more power … if only we give them a little more money … if only we surrender a little more freedom. And there are those who would be gods. What should I call them? The globalists? The transhumanists? Those are the people who believe *all this …* " He gestured at his body, at the congregation, at the walls and ceiling of the sanctuary. "Those are the people who believe *all this* was created by random chance, by the giddy dance of atoms in some primordial swamp. Those are the people who believe it can all be explained by evolution, and that their time has come … with their science and technology … to take control of that process, the process of evolution, to improve upon God's creation. They promise us a race of supermen and superwomen, stronger, smarter and longer lived than ever before. They want to meld our minds with the machine, too, with computers, so our intelligence is integrated seamlessly with the artificial intelligence of the machine. Ultimately, they would have us be machines, moving our consciousness over to a computer so we will live forever. When one computer dies, we simply download our consciousness to another computer. They promise we will be immortal. They promise we will be like gods."

Pastor Layton looked out at his congregation and shook his head sadly. He asked slowly and with great solemnity, "Where have we heard that before?"

He continued. "The second sign is 'dissention.' Turn to Matthew 24:6. 'And ye shall hear of wars and rumours of wars: see that ye be not troubled: for all these things must come to pass, but the end is not yet.' I think all of you know the United States was the world's sole superpower at the end of the Cold War. The United States won that war when our adversary, the Soviet Union, collapsed economically and fragmented politically into its constituent parts, one of which was Russia. For thirty years, our military was second to none, able to vanquish any foe with one arm tied behind its back. Well, after the wars in Iraq and Afghanistan, after the war in Ukraine, those days are gone. We have a second Cold War today … with Russia *and* China. And when you consider them together, Russia *and* China, we are in a far weaker relative position, militarily and economically, than we were during the first Cold War. So, yes, I think we can check the sign for dissention."

He saw heads nod their agreement.

"The third sign is 'devastation.' Matthew 24:7 says, 'For nation shall rise against nation, and kingdom against kingdom: and there shall be famines, and pestilences, and earthquakes, in diverse places.' Do we have famine? Yes, we have famine."

"But Pastor Layton," objected his alter ego, "we've always had famines!"

"True!" he answered. "But the famines were confined to the developing world. Today, as a result of our second Cold War with Russia and China, we have disruptions in grain harvests and shipments worldwide. We have farmers not planting fields because fuel and fertilizer are too expensive. We have hunger in the first world for the first time in a long time. Real hunger. We see it here in Los Angeles. And it's not just a problem with food being in short supply. It's a problem with food being unaffordable. How many low-income people would not have enough food to eat, would actually starve if not for public assistance, if not for church charity, because it's too expensive for people to feed their families? And let us not forget famine in the developing world. It is much, much worse than in years past, as evidenced by the tsunami of immigration from the developing world to the developed world."

Pastor Layton walked back to the pulpit.

"The sign for devastation also includes pestilence. Of course, we had the Covid-19 pandemic. Yes, it was politicized. And, in Pastor Layton's view, the politicization of Covid-19, of a disease, for political and financial gain, is yet another sign. But staying focused on the sign for pestilence, the world literally shutdown because of Covid-19. The world also paid a terrible toll in lost lives, primarily among the sick and elderly."

Paster Layton saw more heads nod their agreement. He knew many in the congregation had lost loved ones during the pandemic.

"The last part of the sign for devastation is earthquakes. Here we get into statistics and I find statistics, as the saying goes, often used as an intoxicated man uses a lamppost: for support rather than illumination. I will not bore you with the details of my statistical analysis but my conclusion is, yes, there has been an increase in the number of major earthquakes and great earthquakes in recent years. But, and this is an important 'but,' there is also a lot fluctuation in the numbers. So, in Pastor Layton's opinion, we only have two parts out of the required three for the sign of devastation. I'll give devastation a soft check mark."

Paster Layton looked at Aunt Joyce in the third row. She was not really his aunt. Everyone simply called her that, Aunt Joyce. She had just turned ninety and was his barometer for how his sermon was being received. If she was struggling not to fall asleep or, worse, if her eyes were closed, he knew he was going on too long. He saw her eyes sparkling with interest.

"Finally, we come to the fourth sign, which is 'deliverance into Tribulation.' Matthew 24:9 says, 'Then shall they deliver you up to be afflicted, and shall kill you: and ye shall be hated of all nations for my name's sake.' What is Jesus talking about here? I think it's pretty clear he's talking about the persecution of Christians. In the United States, the persecution of Christians is, today, limited. You may not be hired if you're a Christian. You may be passed over for promotion if you're a Christian. But, at least today, you won't be fed to the lions. Our brothers and sisters in other countries are not so fortunate."

Pastor Layton consulted his notes.

"The World Watch List found 4,761 Christians martyred last year, 4,488 churches and other Christian-affiliated buildings attacked, and 4,277 believers detained without trial, arrested, or imprisoned. Those are sobering numbers. And, because of them, I believe without a doubt we have the sign of deliverance into Tribulation."

Paster Layton looked out at the congregation. "Is everyone still with me?" he asked.

Heads nodded. Aunt Joyce gave him an encouraging smile.

"Good. I know we're covering a lot of ground. Hang in there a little longer. I'm getting to the end. So, we have these four signs. And they suggest the End Times are near. We have to ask ourselves, then: What do we mean by 'near?' Is it today? Is it tomorrow? Is it a hundred years from now? The answer is: There's no way to know."

Pastor Layton's alter ego returned with a vengeance. He clenched his fists at his sides and scrunched his face into a knot of frustration as if he was a four-year-old throwing a tantrum. He screamed at the ceiling as his face turned red. "What's the point of all this, Pastor Layton, if we know it's coming but we don't know when?!"

"The point is," answered Pastor Layton, once more a rational adult, "*you* don't know when it's coming so *you* have to always be ready. Say it after me: I have to ..."

The congregation repeated back, "I have to ..."

"Always be ready."

The congregation repeated, "Always be ready."

"That's right. *You* have to always be ready. Always. We talk about being spiritually ready all the time here in church so I'm going to skip over the spiritual readiness part today. I want to talk about another kind of readiness. It's a kind of readiness we don't talk about often in church, frankly. In fact, there's a good chance you've never heard any talk about this type of readiness in church because, for some reason, Christians don't like to talk about this kind of readiness."

Pastor Layton pointed at the congregation. "Do you think Christians need to toughen up?"

He paused to let his question sink in.

"If Christians are being persecuted around the world, martyred in the thousands like in the days of Caligula and Nero, with worse likely to come, do you think maybe we Christians need to toughen up?"

He saw some in the congregation nodding in agreement. Most sat completely still.

"I do," he answered without a trace of doubt. "My Christian brothers and sisters, evil is loose in the world. Evil people are using their power, using their influence, to fundamentally transform our country into something our Lord, our Father, finds an abomination. Should good Christians not concern themselves with this fundamental transformation, with this evil abomination, because, well, politics is too divisive? Should good Christians not concern themselves with this evil abomination because it spoils our message of love?"

He walked down to the front row of the congregation. When he continued, his voice was soft and low as if confiding a secret. "My Christian brothers and sisters, let me tell you something ... Love requires you act when evil is threatening the ones you love. Love requires, after you've turned the other cheek and found the enemy still intent on doing evil, to you and all you love ... Love requires you recognize you have no more cheeks to turn. Jesus said he came not to change one jot or one tittle of the Old Testament. My Christian brothers and sisters, there is much the Old Testament can teach us about fighting evil. That is what I meant when I started by saying Christians need to toughen up. God raised up David to defend Israel. David was tough. I believe God wants to raise us up, all of us, His people, to be tough today like David was tough in his time."

"But Paster Layton," shouted his alter ego, "what's that mean for me?!"

"What it means for you ..." answered Paster Layton, pointing at the congregation and gradually moving his finger from left to right to make sure everyone in the room understood he was addressing each and every person there. "What it means for you is this: I'm asking for volunteers. I'm asking for mighty men and women of valor to come forward and join me in getting ready to defend our church and our church family against evil, against the evil that is out there right now, stalking us, against the evil that will only grow stronger and more arrogant in its exercise of power as the End Times draw near. I hope you will join me for our first meeting this Wednesday night at 6 p.m. in the multi-purpose room. There, we will start to work getting ready to meet evil. We will start to work getting ready to defend ourselves and our families against evil. We will start to work getting ready to defeat evil. Thank you and God bless you."

CHAPTER FIVE

All along the watchtower
Princes kept the view
While all the women came and went
Barefoot servants, too
Outside in the cold distance
A wildcat did growl
Two riders were approaching
And the wind began to howl.

— Bob Dylan, "All Along the Watchtower"

OFFICER LEAH BLUNT was ready to finish her shift. Twelve hours is a long time to be stuck in a car, especially in a Dodge Charger that is not all that spacious to begin with and which is even more cramped when all the accoutrements of a California Highway Patrol cruiser are added. Many of those accoutrements are courtesy of the modern digital age. The largest and bulkiest of them is the keyboard and screen that make up the mobile digital computer. It is mounted on the center console. A little further back, also mounted on the center console, is the hand controller. It is basically a joystick that allows the officer to use only one hand to work the cruiser lights, radio, public address loud speakers, and the little microphone in the officer's pocket that records the officer's every word when outside the cruiser, and every word of the person with whom the officer is conversing. Mounted to the cruiser's ceiling by the rearview mirror is the mobile video/audio recording unit. It comes on automatically with the cruiser lights to record traffic stops on DVD. It can be manually activated as well to record the interior of the cruiser, the officer seated in the driver's seat and any suspect detained in the rear of the cruiser. Finally, there are the accoutrements that have been at home in police cruisers long before the advent of the modern digital age. They are a Remington 870 twelve-gauge pump shotgun and a Colt AR-15 A2 rifle. Both are locked in a gun carriage between the driver and passenger seats. Their lineage can be traced through the development of modern firearms, through the development of black powder and primitive firearms, back even through the development of edged weapons, like swords and knives, and primitive projectile weapons, like spears and arrows. Their lineage goes all the way back to the humble rock and the simple fist, all the way back to the beginning of time, when Cain rose up and slew his brother, Abel.

Officer Blunt struggled to find a comfortable position in the seat. Her back ached.

It had been bothering her off and on for the last two weeks, ever since her wrestling bout with a drunk driver. She had pulled the man over for driving erratically. She smelled alcohol on his breath the moment she walked up to his window. She asked him how many drinks he had and he gave her the answer everyone always gives. "Two," he said. She thought that funny, how people are so predictable. They always say "two" because they think two is somehow more believable than one. Little do they realize the number has nothing to do with the officer's decision to conduct a field sobriety test. The officer is only asking to gauge their reaction, to see if they look worried because they know the number is really six, or to see if there are manifest indications of intoxication like slurred words.

The driver seemed perfectly fine with her request to step out of the vehicle. He also seemed fine as they went through the three standardized exercises that comprise the field sobriety test. They started with the horizontal gaze nystagmus test, colloquially known as the "follow the pen with your eyes test." She noticed his eyes darting from side to side as he followed her pen, and then rapidly oscillating as if twitching when she held her pen at the limit of his peripheral vision for the prescribed four seconds. They moved on to the walk and turn test. She explained how the test was to be performed, with him taking nine heel-to-toe steps forward on an imaginary line, pivoting, and taking nine steps back toward her, counting his steps out loud as he went. He was supposed to keep his arms at his side as he walked. The man had not managed his third step before he raised his arms for balance. He stopped after only seven steps, pivoted incorrectly, and stopped counting his steps out loud. As he walked back toward her, he started flapping his arms erratically up and down as if they were the wings of a plane fighting a gusting crosswind on final approach. The third and final test was the one-leg stand test. She again provided verbal instructions and physically demonstrated how the test was to be performed. He raised one leg six inches off the ground while keeping his hands at his side. He started counting out loud as instructed. "One-one thousand, two-one thousand ..." She observed him swaying and once again needing his arms for balance. At "six-one thousand" she observed him putting his foot down to keep his balance. She stopped the test.

"How'd I do officer?" asked the man cheerfully.

Officer Blunt looked down at the man's license. She was holding it in her hand. She wanted to make sure she had the man's name right. "Mr. Ramirez, you failed all three of the field sobriety tests. That means I have probable cause for placing you under arrest for driving under the influence."

It was then that Mr. Ramirez turned belligerent. "The hell you will!" he yelled. He started back to his vehicle, intent on simply driving away.

Should have tased him then and there, thought Leah, still critiquing her performance two weeks later.

Instead, she rushed after him and pushed him up against the side of his car. "You are under arrest!" she yelled. "Put your hands behind your back!"

Mr. Ramirez turned and grabbed Leah in a bear hug. He lost his balance because he was, in fact, intoxicated. The two of them fell to the ground. He was on top of Leah when they hit the ground. His hands, which were clasped together behind her back, took the brunt of the impact. He lost his grip and released his bear hug. She immediately drew her taser and fired.

Maybe I'm getting too old for this, thought Leah as she tried, once more, to find a comfortable sitting position.

Not that she was old. She was all of thirty-one. She had joined the

California Highway Patrol right out of college, which meant she had been an officer for nine years. It seemed like a lifetime. Her husband had been after her to quit for a while now, to find another job that was not nearly so dangerous. He started in on her again after her wrestling bout with the drunk driver. "What if he didn't let go, Leah? What if he got your taser? What if he got your pistol, God forbid?"

Part of her wished she had not told her husband about the incident, that she had conveniently left that part out when he asked how her day went. Another part of her, the part that loved him, that knew he was the one person in all the world she could trust completely, about anything and everything, appreciated his concern. She knew he did not resent her career, her commitment to something bigger than herself. He was not a jealous man. She knew he loved her, and that he was sincerely concerned for her safety.

"Will you still be doing this when we have children?" he asked. "I may not like the risk you're taking, every time you put on that uniform, but I'm an adult … and I can deal with the risk even if I don't like it. But we want to have kids, right? Soon? Is it fair to ask them to live with the risk they might not see their mother again every time she heads off to work?" Her husband regretted his question as soon as he asked it. "I'm sorry," he said. "That was unfair of me."

They were standing in the kitchen in the home they had owned for close to four years. Leah was leaning up against the center island. Her husband was facing her, leaning against the counter next to the sink. Leah came up and gave him a hug. He hugged her back. They held each other a while, savoring the feeling of warmth it gave them, the way it always did when they held each other close, one flesh joined together out of two, seemingly against the world. "I just worry about you," he whispered in her ear. "If I ever lost you …"

She pulled back from their embrace and searched his eyes. "I know," she said, smiling at him gently. A tear of joy ran down her cheek. "If I ever lost you …"

They did not discuss it further.

In truth, Leah was also worried. It was not one single thing that worried her. It was the culmination of things that had come together over the past several years to give her this persistent, uncomfortable sense of foreboding. She felt the world was coming apart. She felt the pace of disintegration was accelerating. Worst of all, she felt there was nothing she or anyone else could do to stop it.

When she first joined the force back in 2016, the rate of violent crime had increased only slightly in recent years, and that was after more than two decades of dramatically decreasing rates. Experts debated the cause for the dramatic decline. Some thought it was demographics because the baby boomers were aging. Others thought it attributable to the greater number of police officers, the expanded budgets of police departments, and the stiffer sentences handed down by courts. There had certainly been a dramatic increase in the prison population. In 1970, fewer than half a million people were incarcerated nationwide. By 2010, nearly two and half million people were incarcerated. There were also some far-fetched theories, at least in Leah's view. One expert attributed the drop in crime to Roe v. Wade because legalized abortion meant fewer children in difficult circumstances, the kind of circumstances that led to criminal behavior down the line. Another expert claimed the drop was the result of the Consumer Products Safety Commission banning the use of lead paint in 1978, and then the Environmental Protection Agency banning leaded gasoline in 1996. His hypothesis was that lead exposure in young children resulted in learning disabilities and problems with impulse control which, ultimately, translated to criminality when those young children grew to be young adults.

Everything changed in 2020. She remembered it as if it was yesterday even though it was five years ago, the awful, shocking video of a Minneapolis police officer kneeling on a man's neck while the man complained, "I can't breathe!" The man was George Floyd. By the time the paramedics arrived, Floyd was unresponsive. He was declared dead at Hennepin County Medical Center some ninety minutes after his first encounter with Minneapolis police. The next day, there were protests and riots in the Minneapolis-Saint Paul area. In the following days, the protests spread across the United States. Ultimately, they involved upwards of twenty million people. They were the largest protests in the country's history. While most of the protests were peaceful, a few were not. Police intervention was required in approximately ten percent of the protests. By the time the protests ended weeks later, more than two dozen people had lost their lives. The Major Cities Chiefs Association estimated more than two thousand officers were injured. The Insurance Information Institute estimated the property damage from looting, arson and vandalism at $2 billion.

Leah remembered watching the riots on the news. She also remembered her sense of disbelief. *How can this be happening … in the United States of America?!* She was shocked to see the rioting in Washington DC, to see fires raging around the Washington Monument, to see fires raging just a few blocks from the White House. She was especially shocked to see a fire at St. John's Church, "the Church of the Presidents." Every president had worshipped there since James Madison in 1816. To her, the fire seemed an attempt to burn down not just a building, not just a church, but the very country itself along with its traditions and history.

"Defund the police!" became a rallying cry for the protesters. In July 2020, the Los Angeles City Council voted 12-2 to cut $150 million from the LAPD budget for the next fiscal year. Given the proposed operating budget of $1.9 billion, the cut was less than ten percent. Still, it was a highly symbolic act whose symbolism was not lost on police officers and criminals alike. Leah had friends in the LAPD. They were appalled. She remembered one of them raging, "The mayor and the city council are idiots, complete fuckin' idiots … in addition to being stupid! Great idea! Let's just ignore actual facts regarding crime and policing and indulge ourselves with feel-good fantasies!"

Unfortunately for Los Angeles and her citizens, her friend's assessment proved prescient. There were fifty-nine shootings in the first two weeks of 2021 compared to just seven in the first two weeks of 2020. A total of 1,451 victims were shot by the end of 2021 compared to 946 in all of 2019. The men and women in blue increasingly found themselves targeted, too. Two sheriff's deputies were ambushed as they sat in their cruiser at a metro station. The gunman walked up from behind, acting as if he was going to walk past, then suddenly pulled a pistol and started firing into the cruiser. There had been no provocation at all, no warning. The deputies were both hit in the head but one of them was able to call for help on the radio. While the deputies were fighting for their lives in the hospital, in surgery, protesters showed up and started chanting. "We hope they die! We hope they die!" The deputies did not oblige them.

The yearly number of shootings continued to climb. So, too, did the number of homicides. There were 252 homicides in 2019, 355 in 2020 and 397 in 2021. Every year, the body count went up another fifty or so. The increase in 2025 was shaping up to be substantially greater. As of the end of October, there were 611 homicides.

As bad as the violence was out on the streets, there was something Leah found still more troubling. It was the arrogant incompetence she increasingly witnessed in the halls of her own organization, the California Highway Patrol. She started to sound like her friend in the LAPD with his low opinion of the mayor and city council, only she was sounding that way with her chain of command in the CHP. It was a strange journey for her, to become such a cynical person, especially considering how she had entered the police academy with an idealistic commitment to serve her community, and with a firm belief those in charge were well-intentioned and possessed of genuine integrity.

***

Officer Leah Blunt noticed a white van up ahead. Traffic was passing around the van and another vehicle in front of it because they were traveling slower than the speed limit, which was sixty-five mph, and much slower than the actual traffic because people habitually drive five to ten mph over the speed limit. Then she noticed the van drifting from one side of the lane to the other. "Another drunk," she groaned.

She closed the distance until she was directly behind the white van. She toggled on the cruiser's license plate reader. It automatically ran the plate through a number of databases. The first database consisted of vehicle information. The license plate reader provided the year, make and model of the vehicle, the vehicle identification number, the expiration date of the plate, and any suspensions placed on the plate. It also provided the name of the person to whom the vehicle was registered. The second database consisted of driver information. The license plate reader assumed the driver to be the person in whose name the vehicle was registered and provided the person's name, address, date of birth and social security number. It also provided information from the driver's license—eye color, sex, height and weight—and the driver's driving record. The final database concerned criminal history. The license plate reader searched local and national databases and identified any outstanding arrest warrants. If any were identified, it sounded an alarm to alert the officer.

Fortunately for the man in the white van and unfortunately for Officer Leah Blunt, the white van was not registered in his name. It was registered in his mother's name. She worked as a medical receptionist. She had only one interaction with police in all her forty-eight years. That was back in 2003, for speeding. The officer let her off with a warning. Had the name of the man in the white van been run through the criminal history database, Officer Leah Blunt would have received multiple alarms.

Leah glanced at the screen of the mobile digital computer and saw nothing out of the ordinary. The only question in her mind concerned the car in front of the van which was also traveling too slow. *Drinking buddies?* she wondered. *Guy who got lucky in a bar and having his soon to be banging buddy follow him home?* The car was shielded from view by the van so she could not see if it, too, was drifting back and forth in the freeway lane.

She decided to stop the van. She toggled on the radio. "7810. 10-38. Possible 502." 7810 was Officer Leah Blunt's badge number. 10-38 was radio shorthand for a traffic stop. 502 was the code for drunk driving.

Dispatch immediately confirmed her message with a terse, crackling repeat-back over the cruiser's radio speaker. "7810. 10-38 your 502."

Leah provided the usual follow-on information. "7810. Heading south on 101, approaching North Alvarado Street. California tag seven, Mike, Oscar, four, zero, nine, zero. White Ford van."

Dispatch provided the crackling repeat-back. "7810. Heading south on 101 approaching North Alvarado Street. California tag seven, Mike, Oscar, four, zero, nine, zero. White Ford van."

Leah confirmed the repeat back. "7810. Good copy."

The car ahead of the van changed lanes to take Exit 4B for North Alvarado Street. Leah noticed the car changing lanes smoothly. She also noticed the proper use of its turn signal. Then she watched the van following behind, over-steering as it changed lanes and not bothering to signal. *Definitely impaired,* she thought. She followed the van and car to the bottom of the offramp. Both vehicles signaled for a right turn. *She definitely knows I'm behind.* Leah noticed a bearded, bedraggled homeless man to her left with a shopping cart turned upside down and his belongings strewn about on the ground. *What's happening here?* She made a mental note to check on the way back.

The van and car turned right onto North Alvarado Street. There was a small encampment of homeless people off to her right. Two tents were pitched up against a concrete retaining wall for an adjacent apartment building. The wall was covered in graffiti. Off to her left she noticed a used car lot. "CASH 4 YOUR CAR- AUCTION PRICES," promised its sign. Even though the vehicles in the lot did not look like much—they were economy models when new and definitively showing their age now—they were all parked behind a sturdy steel fence at least eight feet high. The fence was topped with razor wire.

Leah took a deep breath like she always did before a traffic stop. *Show time!* She turned on the cruiser lights with the center hand controller. The van continued driving, oblivious to the lights. She toggled on the public address system. "Pull over to the right and stop," she said. "Pull over to the right and stop." Still no response. She toggled on her siren. The van kept going.

Leah was certain the driver knew she was following behind. Leah was also certain the driver, who Leah thought to be a woman but was really a man, knew she should pull over, between the lights, the public address instruction and the siren. In Leah's mind, the lack of compliance meant the driver was either trying to hide something, like drugs, trying to access a weapon, or trying to decide if she should make a run for it. Leah toggled on the radio again. "7810. Suspect vehicle noncompliant, not pulling over. Request backup. Heading west on North Alvarado Street, toward West Temple Street."

Dispatch provided the crackling repeat back. "7810. Backup request for noncompliant 10-38. Heading west on North Alvarado Street, toward West Temple Street."

Leah confirmed the repeat back. "7810. Good copy."

There was a McDonald's up ahead on the right with a line of cars in the take-out lane. The car in front of the van pulled into the McDonald's parking lot. The van followed. Leah pulled in behind the van. She notified Dispatch the van had stopped. She opened the cruiser door and started walking cautiously toward the van, her hand on the grip of her pistol like it always was when she approached a driver during a traffic stop. Suddenly, the door to the van opened. *Shit!* Leah drew her pistol and pointed it at the door. "Do not get out of your vehicle!" she ordered. "Stay in your vehicle!"

The driver ignored her command. Leah was surprised to see a young, muscular man step out of the van instead of a forty-eight-year-old woman. The man held up his hands and smiled at Leah.

"Turn and face the van with your hands up!" shouted Leah.

The man neither turned nor raised his hands.

Then she saw the door to the car open.

"You both need to freeze where you are!" shouted Leah as loud as she could. "Right now! Freeze and do not move!"

RZ stepped out of the violet Porsche Taycan and faced Leah. He would have come out shooting had he not left his pistol under the seat in the white van. He held up his hands like the second man and smiled his cruel smile. He said in a relaxed, reassuring voice, "Officer, we don't want no trouble."

"Face down on the ground!" shouted Leah. "Both of you! Right now!"

RZ continued smiling as he started moving off to the side to increase his separation from the second man. Leah knew exactly what he was doing from her training in the police threat simulator. It was how multiple attackers position themselves so they can attack from multiple directions.

The second man started slowly walking toward Leah, as if on cue from RZ. "Hey, Officer," he said, "why you so uptight?" He was also smiling. "I got my hands up. Hands up, don't shoot. You know."

Even though adrenaline was pumping through Leah's system, she was firmly in control of her emotions. There was no fear, no panic. Her training had taken over. She continued with her warning that the two men stop and lie face down on the pavement. The two men continued to ignore her warning. They also continued to close the distance to Leah. When they reached her red line, the one she had mentally established the moment her two potential assailants presented themselves, the one where she knew she had to shoot if she was not to risk being rushed and overpowered, she pulled the trigger. She targeted the man from the van first because he was closest. She fired two shots at the center of his torso. She immediately transitioned to her second target, which was RZ. She did not bother to confirm her first target was down before transitioning to RZ. The imperative was to get hits on all her attackers, to slow them down, before going back and ensuring each individual attacker was no longer a threat. She fired two shots at RZ's torso and immediately turned back to face her first attacker, the man from the white van. She found him lying face down on the ground.

Once more, Leah transitioned to RZ. He was still on his feet. He was struggling toward her as if he was trying to run in an atmosphere that had suddenly turned viscous, like water, like the ocean that was the domain of the great white shark he so aspired to emulate on dry land back when he first launched his criminal career. The atmosphere was obviously not water, though. It was air, and RZ was struggling to run through it because he had two bullet holes perforating his right lung.

Officer Leah Blunt fired again. She fired as rapidly as she could squeeze the trigger and recover her sight picture as the pistol recoiled in her hand. She kept firing until RZ collapsed to the ground. Later, after the cruiser's video was analyzed, she learned she fired a total of five times in just over a second. She had no idea how many rounds she fired at the time. She was doing what she was trained to do, which was to keep pulling the trigger as rapidly as she could until the threat was no longer a threat. When she finally stopped firing, RZ was lying on the ground like his homeboy, face down and motionless. He was three strides from her feet.

CHAPTER SIX

Every kingdom divided against itself will be ruined, and every city or household divided against itself will not stand.

— Jesus, "Matthew 12:25," KJV

THE PEOPLE WAITING in the line of cars in the McDonald's take-out lane pulled out their smart phones and started videoing as soon as Leah pulled her cruiser into the parking lot. The moment the gunfight was over, they posted their videos to social media, whereupon the videos instantly went viral. They trended on every platform. In less than thirty minutes, there was a spontaneous demonstration at McDonald's with over a hundred people protesting against police racism. In less than an hour, the local BLM chapter had mobilized and joined the demonstration, bringing the total to over five hundred people. It took all of ninety minutes for the first celebrities to show up, anxious to show their solidary with BLM and their opposition to police racism. The celebrities would have been there sooner except it was a good thirty-minute drive from the tonier parts of town. The beneficial aspect of the media exposure was, to the minds of attending celebrities, only a fortuitous coincidence of their standing tall for social justice. The local Los Angeles media arrived as if on cue, just after the first celebrities.

"Is that Johnny Penn?" asked Melissa Wright, the reporter from KNBC.

"I think so," answered her cameraman, Leonid Pushilin. He went by Push because he did not like Leonid and no one could pronounce Pushilin.

Melissa was a seasoned reporter. She had worked six years in San Francisco, at KRON, before taking a job at KNBC and moving to the South Bay where she could be closer to her mother. That was in 2018. She first met Leonid in 2019 when they were assigned to cover a story together. She thought him pleasant enough when they met. They engaged in the usual small talk. She learned he lived with his parents and that he and his parents emigrated from Ukraine to the United States in 2007 when he was fourteen, which is why he still spoke with an accent. She learned he liked to run triathlons and study Krav Maga, a style of hand-to-hand combat developed by the Israeli military. Krav Maga dispensed with the elaborate techniques and ceremonial aspects of traditional martial arts in favor of simple punches, kicks, knees and elbows. She also learned he was especially attached to his dog, Ginger, a Pit Bull/Jack Russell mix he rescued from the shelter. He liked to show Melissa pictures of Ginger sitting in his car, sleeping on the sofa or looking up at him with rapt attention before he threw whatever it was he was going to throw. Melissa told him Ginger looked remarkably like the RCA Victor dog.

"The what?" he asked, not understanding at all.

Melissa laughed. She could not believe he had never heard of the RCA Victor dog. "You know," she explained, 'His Master's Voice,' the dog sitting there in front of an old-fashioned hand-cranked gramophone with its head cocked as if listening."

He really had never heard of it. When she pulled up the ad on her phone, he laughed and said, "Yes, I see what you mean. Had I only known."

"What? You would have named her Victor?"

"No," he answered. "Victoria."

They covered their share of stories together over the next year. Had anyone asked her, she would have described Push as a great cameraman and a nice guy. She had no idea he had come to think of her as something more than a professional colleague until she came to work one morning and found a single long-stemmed rose on her desk with a folded note. When she opened the note, there was only one handwritten word: "Dinner?" She looked around the newsroom to see if anyone nearby was waiting for an answer. She saw no one. She spent the morning racking her brain, trying to recall recent encounters that could have provoked such an invitation. She thought it had to be someone in the newsroom because access to the office was limited by building security. No one came to mind. She was not sure she would accept the invitation, either, whoever it was. On the one hand, it was mysteriously romantic. On the other hand, it was somewhat unnerving; she felt a bit as though she was being stalked.

She found out it was Push when she climbed into the KNBC van to cover a story later that day. He was sitting in the driver's seat when she climbed in with her stack of notes. "So?" he asked.

"So what?"

"May I take you out for dinner?"

"It was you!" she nearly shouted, shocked. Her stack of notes slipped off her lap and fell to the floor of the footwell where they covered her feet. "Push … I had no idea it was you!"

He smiled. "Hope you didn't mind the rose and note. A little too melodramatic maybe?"

"No, no. It was … fine." She looked at him and laughed. "A little surprising maybe. Ummm … what's this about, Push?"

"Isn't it obvious?"

"Are you asking me out on a date?"

He looked directly at her and smiled. "I am. I'd like to take you out for dinner."

"But why?"

"Melissa, you don't make it easy on a guy! I enjoy working with you. I enjoy being with you. I think you're smart and … well … I think you're a beautiful woman."

Melissa blushed. She knew Push to be a confident man. He even had a reputation as a bit of an operator. He was good at getting people to go along with his ideas even if they were, perhaps, not always in their best interest. It was a skill that had come in handy more than once when they were on assignment, getting people to agree to be interviewed when they would have been better off keeping their mouth shut. She also thought him an attractive man and had occasionally wondered why he was still single. Since they met, she knew of only one time he had gone out on a date. He did not say much about the date other than the woman was not his type and he was not interested in a second date.

"What type are you looking for?" she asked.

He answered dryly, "The type that doesn't think the Ten Commandments were left on Mount Sinai by space aliens."

She agreed to go out with him. One date turned into two and two into three. She was surprised to find there was real chemistry between them. She passed on the Krav Maga because she had no interest in getting punched in the face but she took up running with him. She enjoyed being with his family and, thankfully, he actually liked her mom, which was essential if not easy. Melissa turned out to be "a dog person" thanks to Ginger who decided she preferred Melissa's lap to Push's when they were sitting together on the sofa watching television. They even liked watching the same shows on television: reality survival shows, reality singing competitions and old movies, especially old film noir movies. The one fly in the ointment was politics.

At first it was fun, having different political views. He was a conservative and she was a liberal. They both tended to have friends of the same political persuasion so it was a new and exciting experience to hear from the other perspective. They honestly tried to understand each other's point of view. It became a running joke with them, that their polar opposite views must be a consequence of geography. They were literally born on opposite sides of the world. He had the Ukrainian perspective. She had the American one. It became harder to laugh as time went on and the world went from one crisis to the next, seemingly with no break in between. They both cared deeply about the state of the world. They both knew the world was on the wrong track and things needed to change. Unfortunately, their prescriptions for change reflected their political views and, as a result, were completely at odds. Increasingly, it became a challenge not to take their differences personally.

President Trump was their first challenge. Melissa despised the man as a vulgar womanizer. She also thought Trump completely unqualified to run the country and a genuine threat to world peace. She asked Push, "How can you even consider trusting a reality TV star with the nation's nuclear launch codes?!"

Push thought Trump one of the few genuinely honest people in politics. He loved Trump's pugnacious take-no-prisoners style. He could not agree more with Trump when Trump said, "The country doesn't win anymore." He thought Trump's business acumen exactly what was needed to get the country back on track. They finally agreed not to discuss Trump for the sake of their relationship.

Covid was their next big challenge. They shared the same concern early on in the pandemic when not much was known about the virus and epidemiologic models were predicting millions of deaths in the United States if drastic measures were not adopted. Melissa was in complete agreement with those measures. She agreed with the lockdowns, the mask mandates and the requirement everyone be vaccinated. She even agreed with the censorship of news and social media to reduce the spread of "misinformation." While Push may have agreed with the drastic measures early on when not much was known about the virus, he ended up appalled the Constitution had been effectively suspended without so much as a vote. Later, he decided the lockdowns and mask mandates were completely unwarranted by the actual science as well as any reasonable cost-benefit analysis. He was suspicious of the vaccines but finally relented and received his two shots because Melissa was distraught about him dying if he remained unvaccinated. As reports of the vaccine's waning effectiveness and serious side effects accumulated, he vowed he would never get a booster. Melissa, meanwhile, was on her second.

The protests and riots over the death of George Floyd were the watershed moment when both Melissa and Push began to question the long-term viability of their relationship. Not only could they not agree on the event itself, they could not even agree on its context, including the fundamental character of the nation. Was America a racist nation or not? It was an open and shut case as far as Melissa was concerned. George Floyd was murdered by a white police officer because he was black. She added the BLM avatar to her Twitter and Facebook accounts and participated in BLM marches in downtown Los Angeles. Push saw no evidence Floyd was murdered, let alone murdered because he was black. As far as he was concerned, the guy died from a drug overdose. "Plus," he said to Melissa emphatically, "the guy was resisting arrest. Resist arrest like that in Ukraine and see what happens to you. And they're all white in Ukraine!"

Melissa fired back, "Don't be such a racist!"

He responded, "Don't be such an idiot!"

They managed to stay civil with each other during the run up to the 2020 presidential election, mostly by avoiding any discussion of politics. Early on during the Democrat primary, Melissa supported Kirsten Gillibrand, a senator from New York. She liked Gillibrand for her strong support for women's issues, for her proposal for "Medicare for all" and for her promise to "abolish Immigration and Customs Enforcement." She also liked the fact Gillibrand was a stalwart critic of Trump. She was not a fan of Biden during the primary but, during the general election, she was an enthusiastic supporter. She was on the "anyone but Trump" bandwagon. Push was all-in for Trump. He thought Trump had accomplished a lot in his first term despite what he considered unprecedented and often unprincipled opposition from the legacy media, the establishment Republicans and a bitter Democrat party determined to have its revenge for Hillary's defeat in 2016. He drove all the way to Reno, Nevada to attend a Trump rally in September, 2020. He did not bother asking Melissa if she wanted to attend.

Their political ceasefire lasted until the day after the election. Melissa was ecstatic when the media declared Biden the victor. "Free at last!" she shouted, celebrating in their living room. "Our long national nightmare is over! Thank God we're finally rid of that despicable creature! Thank God the adults are finally back in charge!"

Push was sitting on the sofa fuming. While he was often sarcastic, he rarely used profanity. He let fly with both when he responded. "Oh right, Melissa. I'm sure God couldn't wait to put Biden in the White House, a corrupt, serial groper with obvious dementia. Yeah, God is all about Biden's degenerate, Marxist agenda. Yeah, God wants children masked up forever … with mandatory vaccinations for everyone, including children. And speaking of children, God is certainly all about aborting them right up to the moment of birth! My body, my choice, right? Except when it comes to mandatory vaccination. How pathetic! There is no fuckin' way Biden got eighty million votes! Those corrupt fuckin' Democrats stole the election! And that piece of shit Biden *IS NOT* my president!"

That was the beginning of the end of their relationship. The final nail in the coffin was the war in Ukraine.

Melissa could not remember an issue where people in United States were so united in their opinion. Finally, liberals and conservatives, Democrats and Republicans had found common ground, something they could agree on. All it took was an invasion by the evil empire. Blue and yellow Ukrainian flags appeared overnight, flying everywhere, as did the blue and yellow Ukrainian label pins. She bought one of the label pins and wore it proudly, fully expecting she and Push would, for once, be on the same side. They were not.

"I see you've jumped on the bandwagon, too," he said with something close to disgust as she sat down in the passenger seat of the KNBC van.

"What?" she asked, not at all knowing what he was talking about.

"The pin on your label. The Ukrainian colors."

"Oh, well, yeah ... It's terrible what's happening there, the Russian invasion."

He shook his head and looked out the window.

"What's wrong, Push?"

He laughed sarcastically. "Shouldn't you know what's going on first, in another country, before you start waving their flag? I suppose you'll be sending the Ukrainians money next. Or maybe you'll be heading over there yourself to enlist in their army and fight their war for them. You didn't listen to a word Dad said, did you? Jesus, Melissa, there's been a war going on there for the past eight years, my cousin's in the Luhansk militia and our town's getting shelled daily ... by the Ukrainians!"

She was taken aback. She also had this terrible sinking feeling this was the end of the two of them. If they could not find common ground when the Russians invaded a sovereign nation, there was no hope of them ever finding it. She could only manage to say, "No, Push, I definitely don't plan on enlisting."

His anger was gone as quickly as it appeared. He sensed it, too, the hopelessness of their relationship. He sighed and said, "I'm sorry, Melissa." There was a moment of heavy silence in the van. Tears welled up in her eyes. She knew what was coming. She knew it was the right thing to do, too, for them to end their relationship. Still, they had loved and laughed a lot in the two years they had been together. He broke the silence. "Look, I think maybe we're not a good match, you and me. I really care about you, Melissa. I'll always care about you. I just think we're too ... different." He noticed a tear rolling down her cheek. He reached over and gently squeezed her hand. She squeezed his back.

The next few weeks were tough. They mostly avoided each other. Then they had their first assignment together. It was not nearly as awkward as they expected. A few months after that, they were even able to enjoy each other's company, as long as they avoided politics. An outside observer would likely have described their relationship as playfully platonic and wondered why they were not together as a couple.

"Can you believe this?" asked Melissa as she filled up the KNBC van. "Four hundred and forty dollars for a tank of gas!"

"Well," answered Push, busy punching the address for their next assignment in his phone's map app, "that sounds about right … when gas is $14.29 a gallon."

"Aren't you mad about this? You, of all people?"

"No, Melissa, I've moved on."

"To what?"

He clipped his phone into the phone holder mounted on the van's dash and answered flatly, "Resignation."

"Well, aren't you the cool, stoic one."

He smiled wryly. "It's a Slavic thing. You expect things to be bad because they've always been bad."

"Well, they weren't always *this* bad, not here anyway."

"Yes, that's true. So perhaps congratulations are in order. The United States of America has finally joined the club."

"What club is that?"

"The we're-so-fucked club … which is shorthand for the official title, which is the we're-so-fucked-because-our-ruling-class-is-only-interested-in-maintaining-power-and-enriching-itself-at-our-expense club."

Melissa thought his comment such a typically "Push thing" to say. When they were a couple, it would have annoyed her greatly. Now, she only laughed. He had always been cynical about human nature. He was always looking for the angle, how someone was maneuvering for advantage or looking to get away with something. She was the exact opposite. She was the eternal optimist. She liked herself for who she was: a positive, trusting person. She liked the fact she gave people the benefit of the doubt until they proved her wrong. Even then, she believed in second chances. In the final analysis, she was a person who believed in the essential goodness of humanity. She believed that, given a choice, most people, most of the time, will choose to do the right thing. Melissa returned the nozzle to the pump, happy to know she and Push had gone their separate ways.

***

Melissa surveyed the scene around McDonald's and considered her course of action. The parking lot itself was cordoned off with yellow crime scene tape. Inside the tape, she saw the medical examiner. He was impossible to miss in his white anti-contamination suit, the one he wore over his street clothes to keep his DNA and other bodily detritus from contaminating the crime scene. His anti-contamination suit included white slip-on shoe covers, a white hair cover and blue latex gloves. An interview with the medical examiner would be great but Melissa knew from experience he would be busy for an hour or two meticulously surveying the scene, taking notes and photographing anything and everything that was even remotely relevant to the investigation.

The police, she was certain, would have nothing to say. She would never be allowed to interview the actual officer involved in the shooting. And the rest of the police, the ones standing around protecting the crime scene perimeter, they were prohibited by department policy from talking to the press. "You'll have to talk to the communications officer," they would answer politely.

That left interviews with the proverbial man on the street and the demonstrators. She might get lucky and find a man on the street who actually witnessed something. More likely, and especially given the nature of the shooting, which was yet another police shooting of an unarmed African American man, she expected the witnesses to come and find her, wanting to vent their frustration and anger to an audience that was larger than just their friends and neighbors. She had no doubt she would be easy to find with her microphone and accompanying cameraman. As far as the demonstrators were concerned, Melissa knew they made for good TV. They always had something to say and were always passionate about saying it. *Throw in a tense standoff with police, a little tear gas for dramatic effect and voilà … I might be the lead local news story tonight! Add in a demonstrator who is also a nationally known celebrity like Johnny Penn … I might make the national news!*

Melissa turned to Push. "Let's see if we can get an interview with Penn."

They caught up with Johnny Penn behind the police barricade that had been hastily erected in the street opposite McDonald's. Johnny Penn's hair was brown, long and slicked back on top. On the sides, it was cut short. The net effect was what his stylist described as a trendy mix of classic and modern. While Johnny Penn was all in favor of being both classy and modern, he especially liked the fact the close-cut hair above his ears made his graying temples less noticeable. He was fifty-one years old, mesmerizingly handsome, athletically built and spotlessly groomed. He looked as if he had just walked off the set of one of his movies where he was playing a rich, successful playboy, one who was a little bit dangerous as well.

The man standing next to Johnny Penn looked to be more than a little dangerous. He was a head taller than Johnny Penn and more powerfully built. His hair stylist, assuming he did not cut his own hair with a razor, may well have described his style as functional yet intimidating; his head was shaved bald. Contributing to the intimidating look were his square, chiseled jawline, his close-cut black beard and his dark, wraparound sunglasses. He, too, was impeccably dressed and could have come from the same movie set as Johnny Penn, only he would have been playing Johnny Penn's bodyguard which, in reality, he was.

"Mr. Penn!" shouted Melissa, pushing her way through the crowd of demonstrators. "Mr. Penn!"

Johnny Penn's bodyguard stepped in front of Melissa.

"Mr. Penn, Melissa Wright, KNBC News. Any comment on the shooting?"

"It's ok," said Johnny Penn, squeezing the shoulder of his bodyguard.

Push started filming. Melissa spoke into the microphone with the KNBC logo. She used her "reporter's voice" which was deeper and more official sounding than her regular voice. "Mr. Penn, preliminary reports indicate police have shot two unarmed African American males. Do you have any comment on what appears to be an epidemic of police shootings of unarmed African Americans?" She pointed the microphone at Johnny Penn.

Johnny Penn was ready for the question. He had been rehearsing his answer the moment he decided to drive to the scene of the shooting. He had lots of experience with political activism and knew the importance of a dramatic moment. It could make or break a political event just like it could make or break a movie. He also knew the importance of being active in the right causes, and keeping one's activism current. Even though he had been politically active his entire career, and even though his political causes were all politically correct, he had not been able to participate in the George Floyd protests in 2020. He was on location in New Zealand filming that summer. His absence was noted. Worse, it made him the subject of speculation he was not sufficiently committed to social justice. There was even vicious gossip he was a woke poser. With this shooting, he was determined to prove the gossip wrong.

"Thank you, Melissa," began Johnny Penn. He paused and looked directly at the camera. He was a professional actor and knew how to connect with an audience. "Yes, I would like to comment. Two precious lives were lost today. Two. Every life is precious and I grieve every time one is taken. But my grief here is also mixed with anger. It is one thing when one of our brothers or sisters is taken by accident, by disease, by cancer. Then we grieve but at least we understand. Here, I do not understand. How do you explain yet another unarmed black man shot down by police? How do you explain it? How do you explain it without calling it what it is?"

He took a moment to contemplate his question. There was a look of genuine angst on his face. "It's murder," he finally answered. "It's deliberate, cold-blooded murder. These two young men were murdered for the crime of being black in America. Just like Michael Brown was murdered by police in Ferguson. Just like George Floyd was murdered by police in Minneapolis. Just like countless hundreds, countless thousands of black men and women have been murdered going all the way back to the founding of our country, because … Let us speak honestly for a change … We all know this country was founded on the monstrous, despicable evil of slavery. And let us face what can no longer be concealed. This country, our country, is racist to the core … It was conceived in racism and it was raised up in racism. Its heart and soul are racist. Its bones are racist. Its very marrow is racist."

Johnny Penn looked away from the camera as if to compose himself. When he looked back and began again, his voice was sadly resigned. "These murders of innocent black men will not stop until there is a reckoning with that fundamental fact. So, what do we do? How do we reckon with it?"

A gleam appeared in his eyes. Johnny Penn had seen the promised land and he wanted his audience to see it, too. Passionate determination filled his voice. "Well, people, when you have a cancer, what do you do? You cut it out, right? You kill it with chemicals. You kill it with radiation. That's what we need to do with the cancer of racism today … in our country. Wherever it's lurking, in police departments, in schools, in corporate boardrooms, we need to kill it. We need to kill it for the love of all that's good and decent in our country, all that's decent in the world. Can we finally do that, people? Can we finally do whatever it takes to kill the cancer of racism? I believe we can. I believe we must! Then and only then, if we're still being honest, can we put an end to these senseless murders. Then and only then, can we have the country we were meant to have. I'm asking every one of you from the very bottom of my heart, please, let that be the epitaph for these two young men, the ones who died here today, so their deaths will not have been in vain. Thank you."

Melissa had tears in her eyes when he finished. She fought to recover her composure as she brought the microphone back below her chin. She swallowed hard and looked at the camera. "Thank you, Mr. Penn. If I may add … that was one of the most beautiful, inspiring messages of hope I have been privileged to witness, ever, in my thirteen years as a TV news reporter. This is Melissa Wright reporting from downtown Los Angeles."

The red light on Push's camera went off. Melissa dropped the microphone from below her chin and turned to Johnny Penn. She wiped her eyes and smiled at him. "Thank you again, Mr. Penn. I really meant what I said. That was an inspiring vision for a better world." She laughed awkwardly. "Look, you even made me cry!"

Johnny Penn also laughed. "Thank you, Melissa. I just spoke from the heart." He sincerely appreciated her compliment because he knew the audience had the final say, whether a performance was good or not. He thought it went well but he would reserve his final judgment until he had a chance to critically watch the playback when he was back home. "Were we live?" he asked.

"No. We were streaming to the station. The producer will decide on the time slot, the five o'clock news or the six o'clock news. I think he'll run it on both, frankly. I think maybe the national news will pick it up, too. It was really *that* good."

"I just hope we touch a few hearts."

She extended her hand. "I'm sure we will. Thanks again for the interview, Mr. Penn."

"You're very welcome." He held on to her hand a little too long. "I hope you don't think this out of line, Melissa, but … would you like to have a drink with me later this evening?"

Melissa was not at all expecting his invitation. She knew from the tabloids Johnny Penn was always dating some beautiful, up and coming Hollywood star. She never imagined he would be interested in dating someone like her. Even though Push always told her how beautiful she was, and even though she very much appreciated him telling her that, she thought herself merely attractive when candidly assessing her looks in front of the mirror, perhaps bordering on very attractive when wearing an outfit that was particularly flattering. She thought her best features her petite nose, her intense blue eyes and her bright, beaming smile. She also knew men loved her long blonde hair. She was proud of her body, that it was physically fit and healthy, although she had to admit there were times she wished there was a bit more to it, that she was a little taller, and that there was more shape to her figure. Overall, though, she was happy with her looks. Her problem was never one of attracting men. Rather, it was one of attracting the right sort of men, men who shared her view of the world and had also managed to grow up out of adolescence.

She searched his eyes. They were the color of dark black coffee where the cream had just been added and was still swirling about in a silent, turbulent storm of dark and light browns. She saw depth and complexity in his eyes. She saw warmth and compassion, too. She thought there was something intriguing there that might warrant taking a chance.

"I'm flattered, Mr. Penn—"

"Please … Johnny."

"Will I get my hand back, Johnny, if I say yes?"

Johnny Penn laughed. He squeezed her hand gently before letting go. "Sorry, I did not mean to be … Let me try this again. If *you* would flatter *me*, I would love to buy you a drink later this evening."

She made up her mind. "Ok, I'd like that."

Melissa walked back to the KNBC van after giving Johnny Penn her number. She knew Push heard the whole conversation even though he did his best to pretend he was not there and not listening. "So?" she asked, when they were back in the van.

"So what?"

"Aren't you impressed? I've got a date with Johnny Penn."

"You know he has a reputation, right?"

"Well, maybe I've got one, too."

"What," he scoffed, "for working too much and going out with losers?"

Melissa punched him in the shoulder.

Push looked at her and laughed. "Ok, maybe they weren't *all* losers. Just do me a favor and be careful."

"And besides," she said defiantly, "maybe I'm the one who just wants to have a good time."

Push knew she really was not. He knew she wanted a dependable man with whom she could share her life and maybe raise a family. "Hey," he said, "you do what you want. You're a grown woman. I'll just tell you what I tell my guy friends who are also out there 'doing what they want.' Fast women are like fast cars. They're a lot of fun at first but they all leave you the same way … cut and bleeding on the side of the road."

Even though KNBC did not broadcast the interview live, the people standing next to Melissa and Johnny Penn effectively made it live with the video from their phones. They sent the interview to their friends who, in turn, sent it to theirs. And so on. Soon it was trending on social media and the people there at the demonstration who had been too far away from the interview to know there was even an interview, never mind hearing what was actually said, found the interview popping up on their phones. They listened and had their hearts touched just as Johnny Penn hoped. Only the touch was not by the better angels of their nature, the angels desiring peace and reconciliation, or at least an end to the criminal violence that necessitated the use of police violence. These angels were of a different persuasion. They were the ones who had been there down through the ages whispering in the ears of small and great men alike, telling them all their woes, all their failures were not of their own doing. Evil forces were to blame. Evil forces directed by conniving, evil conspirators. The demonstration turned ugly.

CHAPTER SEVEN

I had seen nothing sacred, and the things that were glorious had no glory and the sacrifices were like the stockyards at Chicago if nothing was done with the meat except to bury it.

— Ernest Hemingway, "A Farewell to Arms"

MR. SMITH, FORMER physical education teacher and mentor to RZ, walked down the column of middle school boys standing at attention on the blacktop outside the school gym. The boys were all dressed in their gym clothes which could more accurately be described as uniforms. No individuality was allowed other than your preference for gym shoes. The shorts were red. The socks were white. And the T-shirts were white with "DALTON ACADEMY" printed in black block letters underneath the school seal.

The school seal, truth be told, was shamelessly copied from the Harvard University seal when Dalton Academy was first established as a private Christian middle school not quite seventy-five years ago. It featured a triangular shield with three open books, two at the top of the shield and a third at the bottom. The capital letters for "veritas," which is Latin for "truth," were allocated by syllables across the three books: VE, RI, TAS. The only difference between the Dalton shield and the Harvard shield was the third book. On the Dalton shield, the third book was turned facedown to symbolize the limits of reason and the need for God's revelation. The facedown posture of the third book and the reasoning behind it are consistent with the original Harvard shield. Harvard turned the third book faceup at a later date to recognize their new-found belief there is no limit to man's reasoning and, therefore, no longer a need for God's revelation.

The boys had the left strap of their jockstrap pulled out from underneath their red gym shorts so it was visible to Mr. Smith as he walked by. Once he walked by, and only after he walked by, each boy then released the stretched elastic strap so it snapped back into place. This was the obligatory jockstrap check that was required at the beginning of every gym class. It was designed to confirm the boys had dressed for class with the appropriate personal protective equipment. There were thirty boys in the gym class, all standing at attention in five columns of six boys each. The jockstrap check was executed with not just military precision, as Mr. Smith liked to say, but Marine Corps precision. It typically required less than thirty seconds to perform. Unless there was a problem.

Mr. Smith stopped halfway down the third column of boys. The boy to his left had pulled out a portion of his white Jockey briefs in the hope Mr. Smith would not notice he was out of uniform. Mr. Smith turned and looked at the boy. "Gomez," he said sharply, "why aren't you wearing your jockstrap?"

Gomez stared straight ahead since he was still at attention. He answered, "Sorry, Mr. Smith. I guess I forgot it."

"Ok, Gomez," boomed Mr. Smith, wanting to make sure the whole class heard him, "that's a mile for forgetting and a second mile for trying to fake it."

Gomez turned and looked at Mr. Smith with a pained expression. "Two miles, Mr. Smith?"

"That's right, Gomez," boomed Mr. Smith. "Two miles! A two-mile run does remarkable things for a bad memory. And if I hear another word of complaint, it'll be three miles."

Gomez thought a two-mile run bad enough. He had no interest in running three miles. "Yes, Mr. Smith," he acknowledged, resigned to his fate and determined never again to forget his jockstrap.

"Gomez," boomed Mr. Smith, "fall out and start running."

Gomez let go of his Jockey briefs and took off running for the track. Two miles was eight laps.

After the jockstrap check, the class moved on to their close order marching drill. Mr. Smith counted cadence. He started like he always did, with "Low-right, uh low-right," which was a stylized way of saying "Left-right, left-right-left." Then he would make it interesting, taking one of his old Marine Corps cadences and modifying it to be something more appropriate for Dalton Academy. Of course, that meant omitting profanity. It also meant omitting references to Guadalcanal, the Frozen Chosin and Chesty Puller. The cadence today was: "Up in the morning way too soon. Hungry as heck come the noon. A what we gonna do when we get back. Take a shower and hit the rack." Then he shouted, "NO WAY! GOTTA RUN! PT! ITS LOTS OF FUN! DALTON!"

The boys shouted back in unison, "ACADEMY!"

"DALTON!" shouted Mr. Smith.

"ACADEMY!" shouted the boys.

Mr. Smith loved close order marching. It took him back to his days at Parris Island. He knew some of his fellow Marines still had nightmares about "the land that God forgot, where the sand is eighteen inches deep and the sun is scorching hot." Mr. Smith was not one of those Marines. He remembered basic training fondly, the drill, the discipline, the honor and the brotherhood. The only thing missing today was the sound of boots hitting the parade ground all at the same time and echoing off the nearby buildings. Even today, at the age of sixty-one, forty-three years after he joined the Marine Corps fresh out of high school, he vividly remembered the sound.

There was another reason he loved close order marching. It was a reminder he no longer worked as a physical education teacher in the Los Angeles Unified School District. He retired in 2020 when the Covid pandemic hit. Schools were closed and teachers were required to conduct their classes remotely. Some subjects were less amenable than others to distance learning and physical education was one of the least amenable. He had thirty, even forty kids in his class. They all logged in to their computers at home and followed his example as he led them through stretching, calisthenics, running in place and jumping rope. Increasingly, as the weeks turned into months, he noticed more and more kids turning off their Zoom video feed. They could still see him, if they were even there watching, but he could not see them. He knew the reason they were turning off their Zoom video feed. They were tired of working out. When he required his class keep their video feed on, he was told by the department head it was against District policy. Students had privacy rights when they were home.

He stuck it out until the fall of 2020 when he finally decided he had enough. He did not begrudge the District for its abundance of caution when Covid first appeared. It was a new virus and, reportedly, thirty or forty times more dangerous than the seasonal flu. By summer, though, it was apparent to anyone willing to do a little homework Covid was really only dangerous for older people and people with significant co-morbidities. For younger people, people like his middle school students, it was remarkably benign, far less dangerous than the seasonal flu that had been around forever. Plus, even when they got it, young healthy people were extremely unlikely to transmit it. He ended up disgusted. Bad enough the so-called experts had closed down the economy and closed down his church but to deny children the opportunity to go to school, to learn in person and socialize ... It was, to Mr. Smith, unconscionable.

He enjoyed his retirement as best he could in a Los Angeles that was locked down. He ended up investing in a home gym with weights and a squat rack because the gyms were all closed. He refused to go along with the mask requirements as much as he could while still having to shop for the necessities of life. He adopted the approach of only wearing a mask if asked to do so by a store employee. It had to be a store employee, too. Only rarely did a member of the public come up and ask him to don a mask. Some of that was no doubt a consequence of his intimidating size. He would respond politely when a member of the public did, on occasion, ask him to wear a mask. "I appreciate your concern," he would say, "but I have an exemption." No one ever pressed him about the nature of his exemption, although he was prepared if they did. If he was asked politely, he planned to say, "That's a personal issue between me and my physician." If he was asked impolitely, his accoster would have received a sarcastic broadside: "I have an exemption from following inane, ineffectual and unconstitutional edicts from aspiring petty tyrants. Have a nice day and try minding your own fuckin' business!"

Gradually, the restrictions faded with the hysteria. People went back to work. Restaurants and gyms opened. Schools opened, too. When the kids were back in the classroom, Mr. Smith decided he wanted to go back to teaching, only not in the public school system. Even before Covid, he was finding it more and more difficult to run classes the way he wanted to run them. The year after RZ was so impressed with his handball racket in the manila envelope, he was told by the District he could no longer threaten students with physical punishment. The following year, he was told he could no longer have his class perform close order marching drills. Some parents considered them "overtly militaristic." Then, the year after that, the school principal called Mr. Smith into his office to tell him his jockstrap check was no longer acceptable. "It's perpetuating gender stereotypes," the school principal explained.

"Gender stereotypes?" asked Mr. Smith, incredulous. "Either you got balls or you don't!"

The school principal rushed over and closed the door to his office. "Mr. Smith," he scolded, "you've attended our diversity and gender training. You know some of our boys may choose to identify as girls, which means they might be offended if compelled to wear a jockstrap. And if some of our girls identify as boys … well … it might uncomfortably highlight the fact they have not yet transitioned … physically, I mean."

While Mr. Smith had been required to attend diversity and gender training in previous years, and considered it a load of rubbish, he kept his mouth shut out of concern for his pension. Now that he had the requisite twenty years, he no longer felt compelled to remain silent. He looked hard at the principal and said, "That's about the stupidest thing I've ever heard … and I've heard a lot of stupid things." He turned and walked out, not waiting for a reply.

Mr. Smith found the Dalton Academy teaching position posted on the bulletin board at his church. He thought a private Christian middle school might be a better fit for his style of teaching. Mr. Rawl was head of the Dalton Academy physical education department. He was also the hiring manager. When Mr. Smith told him flat out how he would run his classes, jockstrap check and all, Mr. Rawl nodded and said, "Mr. Smith, that's *exactly* what we need here at Dalton Academy."

Mr. Smith dismissed his class at the basketball courts at the far end of the athletic field. He stood there and watched for a few minutes to make sure the games were going smoothly before heading back to his office. Mr. Rawl was inside with the television turned on. "This ain't good," he said when he saw Mr. Smith walk in. He nodded toward the television.

KNBC news was turned on. A McDonald's restaurant was visible in the background. The reporter on the scene, Melissa Wright, was reporting from a corner on the street. The serious expression on her face matched the serious tone of her voice. "We are here at the intersection of North Alvarado and West Temple Streets, just off the Hollywood Freeway. You can see behind me a number of burning police cruisers. Behind the burning cruisers is a line of riot police stretching across the street. Protesters are standing here in front of the burning cruisers. At the moment, it appears to be a tense standoff. The protesters gathered earlier today when they learned about the shooting of two unarmed African American males by a California Highway Patrol officer. The officer has not yet been identified. The number of protesters was about five hundred when we first arrived. They were peaceful. Following an emotional appeal for social justice from the actor Johnny Penn, the number of protesters swelled to well over a thousand. The protesters were blocking traffic and, in one case, pulled a motorist from his vehicle. We captured the scene on video. I must warn you, the scene is graphic."

The image of Melissa Wright was replaced with the image of a black SUV about a hundred yards from the corner where she had been standing for her on-the-scene report. The SUV was blocked from going further by a group of protesters standing in the middle of the street. Some of the protesters were carrying baseball bats. Others had what appeared to be crowbars. The protesters moved around the SUV. Then they started smashing its windows. A protester opened the door to the SUV and pulled out the driver. The driver was a middle-aged white male. The driver threw a punch at the protester and the protester punched back. Then there was a flurry of punches until another protester came up behind the driver and hit him in the head with a baseball bat. The driver collapsed to the ground and lay motionless.

Melissa Wight appeared again. "We do not know the condition of the driver. EMTs have been unable to access the scene."

"I'll tell you the condition of the driver," said Mr. Rawl. "He's dead!"

"Yeah," said Mr. Smith, grimacing. He shuddered at the thought of what a baseball bat would do to a human head.

Melissa Wright continued. "And here again is my interview with Johnny Penn from earlier this afternoon."

Mr. Smith and Mr. Rawl watched Melissa Wright's interview with Johnny Penn. When the interview was finished, Mr. Rawl grabbed the television remote and muted the volume. He was visibly upset. "That is about the most irresponsible thing I can imagine a person saying in a situation like this. Talk about pouring gas on a fire!"

"I remember the Rodney King riots," said Mr. Smith, "in '92. We had just returned from Kuwait, from Desert Storm, and were back at Camp Pendleton. We were ordered to deploy to LA to restore order. It was bad … real bad. Those people were trying to burn the city down. And they were shooting at firefighters when the firefighters showed up to put out the fires."

"I remember," said Mr. Rawl. "Drove to work with a pistol in my glove box and a rifle in my trunk. Was not about to end up like that poor guy they pulled from his truck. What was his name? Denny?"

"Yeah," said Mr. Smith. "Reginald Denny. I remember him. The news helicopter was showing it live. The poor guy was just doing his job, driving his truck. He happened to drive through the part of town with the worst of the rioting. If not for bad luck he'd have no luck at all. The rioters stopped his truck and pulled him from the cab. They hit him in the head with a friggin' brick!"

"He survived, right?"

"That's what I remember. Some good Samaritans saw him on television. He was lying in the street in a pool of his own blood. They came out and saved his life."

"Maybe that guy in the SUV will be as lucky," said Mr. Rawl.

"Maybe," said Mr. Smith, seriously doubting it. "Do you know this guy Penn?"

"Not really. Saw one of his movies, I think. Couldn't tell you the name of it."

"Is he just looking for attention?" asked Mr. Smith. "He can't possibly know it was murder. I wish these people would wait for the facts before jumping to conclusions. And to claim these guys were murdered for being black ... How the hell can he know that?"

"It's not about the facts," said Mr. Rawl. "It's about pushing an agenda. If he cared about the facts, he'd wait to know what they were."

Mr. Smith shook his head. There was a concerned expression on his face. "This is starting to look like the LA riots all over again. And he has to mention Michael Brown and George Floyd."

A young man's face appeared on the television. It was a color photo that looked like it might have been from a high-school yearbook. Mr. Smith immediately recognized the face. It was RZ's. "Turn that up!" he said.

Mr. Rawl unmuted the volume. Melissa Wright's voice returned. "Police have identified one of the deceased men. His name is Raymond James. He was a twenty-two-year-old resident of South Central Los Angeles. Police have still not released the identity of the second man."

"You know him?" asked Mr. Rawl.

Mr. Smith nodded. "Yeah," he said sadly. "He was one of my students back in LA Unified, in eighth grade. When was that? Seven, eight years ago. Went to church with his grandmother. He was getting into trouble then and she asked me to help out. Thought we made a difference, too. Thought we saved him."

"What happened?"

"He went to high school," said Mr. Smith with a shrug, "hooked up with the wrong crowd. His grandmother passed away a couple years back. I lost touch then. God, what a waste!"

"I'm sorry."

Mr. Smith remembered the fourteen-year-old RZ who was so thrilled to set the school record for the 440. He remembered him beaming when he received his first trophy at the District track meet. He remembered him talking about going to college with a track scholarship, and then maybe joining the military.

"His mother?" asked Mr. Rawl.

"Mother was a drug addict."

"Father?"

"Never knew his father."

"Kid never had a chance, did he?"

"No, not really."

"Can I ask you a straight up question, as an African American? That guy Penn says we're a racist country. Calls us racist to the core. You think that's true? You think those young men were killed because of … What do they keep calling it? Systemic racism?"

Mr. Smith grimaced. "Been listening to that stuff for a long time now, all that talk about systemic racism and white supremacism. They were pushing all that on the teachers back when I taught at LA Unified. They expected us to incorporate it in our teaching, to use it to develop our course curriculum. My opinion … It's nothing but poison. It's poisoning black people because it's teaching them to believe they're victims. I told RZ—"

"Who?"

"Raymond … He went by RZ. I told him all it takes to make something of yourself is determination and hard work. When he asked me how I knew, I told him my family is the living, breathing proof of it. My parents were dirt poor when they came from Jamaica. Didn't have nothing. My dad worked as a janitor and my mom cleaned houses. They ended up owning their own home. They made sure I towed the line, too. Gave me my work ethic. Taught me everything you do is a reflection on you and a reflection on your family. I ended up a sergeant in the United States Marine Corps. I ended up owning my own home. I ended up getting married and having two good boys. I think that impressed him. It just wasn't enough. Anyway, all that systemic racism stuff, all that white supremacism and white privilege … It's not only poison for black folks, it's poison for our country. It's teaching people the color of your skin is more important than the content of your character."

"How come all these people forgot about Martin Luther King?"

"Just my opinion … We've been going backwards a long time now. I'm not gonna say there ain't racism out there. There's always been racism. I've met white racists and, let me tell you, I've met black racists. Expect we'll have racists as long as we have folks looking to blame others for their circumstances. It's just human nature. The difference now … we're promoting racism as a society. It's become public policy. And it's ok because … well … this time, we're doing it for 'the right reasons.'" He used his fingers for air quotes.

"I guess ol' Martin Luther King didn't fully understand."

They watched the television in silence as a group of protesters approached the line of police. The police began firing tear gas.

"It's not going to end well, is it?" asked Mr. Rawl.

"No," answered Mr. Smith sadly. "Our country has all these problems, tough economic times with maybe tougher times to come. People are frustrated and angry. There are no easy solutions and each side is blaming the other. Then you start talking like Penn, dividing people based on skin color. You can't talk like that and have anything good come of it."

"All the Hollywood people talk like that."

"I know," said Mr. Smith. "And half the politicians. Hell, half the damn country talks like that."

"What scares me … I think the other half of the country has about had it with all that talk. I think they've about had it with being blamed for everything. I know I have!"

Mr. Smith nodded. "There's one thing Penn said I actually agree with."

"What's that?" asked Mr. Rawl.

"There will be a reckoning."

"You think so?"

"Yeah. Only it won't be the one he's hoping for."

CHAPTER EIGHT

The heroes of declining nations are always the same—the athlete, the singer or actor. The word "celebrity" today is used to designate a comedian or a football player, not a statesman, a general, or a literary genius.

— Sir John Glubb, "The Fate of Empires"

MELISSA WRIGHT TURNED onto Hollywood Boulevard, following her navigator app to the Musso & Frank Grill. She was heading west on Hollywood Boulevard and driving into a blinding sun that was just above the Hollywood skyline. She flipped down her windshield visor. She was tired. It was after 8 p.m. and part of her wished she was heading home to kick off her heels, change into her cozy jogger pajamas and relax with a glass of wine. *Or maybe the whole bottle,* she thought, *after today.*

Instead, she was driving to meet Johnny Penn for a drink. *At least he picked a spot that was close.* The Musso & Frank Grill was a short twenty-minute drive from the KNBC studio. She was only a kid the last time she drove down Hollywood Boulevard. She was with her parents. Her only memory of it was of her parents being excited about the bronze stars embedded in the sidewalk. They were excited about the names on the stars. She did not share their excitement because she knew none of the names. Years later, she learned they were following the Hollywood Walk of Fame. Driving down Hollywood Boulevard today, she thought the area looked tired and run-down. Palm trees lined both sides of the street. Their spindly sixty-foot trunks and tufts of green and brown palm prawns gave the trees a distressed, sickly look. The buildings were mostly single-story retail stores dating back half a century or more. Souvenir shops were generously mixed in with the usual convenience stores, clothing boutiques and tattoo parlors. Rollup metal doors covered the store fronts with the exception of the tattoo parlors whose brightly colored neon signs advertised their services and the fact they were still open for business.

She spotted the sign for the Musso & Frank Grill when she crossed North Cherokee Street. It, too, looked dated and tired, which made sense to her as she drove closer. The sign proclaimed "Since 1919" and "Oldest in Hollywood." She pulled over and parked on the side of the street about a block from the restaurant. There were not a lot of cars parked on the street except directly in front of the Musso & Frank Grill. She found the sidewalk littered with trash, including, here and there, used hypodermic needles.

In view of the neighborhood, she was not expecting much from the Musso & Frank Grill. She was also more than a little disappointed in Johnny Penn. She wondered why he would pick a place like this if he was such a big Hollywood star. She also wondered why he would pick a place like this if he was looking to impress her. She understood why as soon as she opened the front door.

The maître d' was impeccably dressed in a white button-down dress shirt, a black bow tie and a red waiter's jacket accented with a black lapel that ran from the collar to just above the waist. He was of medium height and build and looked to be Hispanic. His face was deeply creased around his eyes, and from his nose to his mouth, such that you would suspect he spent the better part of his life smiling and laughing. Your suspicions were confirmed when you noticed his eyes. They had an intelligent, mischievous sparkle. His skin was a deep, dark brown. His hair was thinning but combed back neatly. It was also mostly gray.

The maître d' greeted her with a warm smile. "Welcome, madam. Welcome to the Musso & Frank Grill."

She could not help but smile back. "Thank you. I'm meeting Mr. Johnny Penn."

"Of course—"

"Melissa!" Johnny Penn walked up briskly. He was beaming. "Any trouble finding it?"

"No. The navigator took me straight here."

"Great, great. Come and sit down. You must be beat after today!"

She followed Johnny Penn to a booth near the front. The booth was a semi-circle of red leather and dark brown mahogany. It comfortably sat four so the two of them slid around toward the back to be closer together. The tablecloth was white linen. Folded white linen napkins were in front of them along with their silverware. Johnny Penn moved his martini with three olives off to the side to give Melissa more room. "What can I get you to drink?" he asked.

The maître d' laughed. "Would Mr. Penn please leave *me* something to do?"

Johnny Penn laughed, too. "Melissa, this is Fernando."

"Nice to meet you, Fernando."

"Very nice to meet you, Ms. Melissa. Mr. Penn and I have known each other a very long time. How long would you say, Mr. Penn?"

"Almost twenty years … which isn't long enough, apparently, since you still won't call *me* by my first name."

Fernando chuckled. "Sorry, Mr. Penn. It would not be showing the proper respect for my customer. You are Mr. Penn and this is Ms. Melissa."

"You're calling *her* by her first name!" objected Johnny Penn.

"That is only because I was not properly introduced. Ms. Melissa, may I have the honor of knowing your last name?"

"It's Wright with a W. And thank you, Fernando, for keeping chivalry alive."

He acknowledged her thanks with a solemn nod. "Now, Ms. Wright with a W, let Fernando get you something to drink." He offered her the cocktail menu which she politely waved away.

"I'll have a glass of chardonnay," she said.

"We have a nice Alma De Cattleya from Sonoma. It's on the drier side with hints of pineapple and mango. May I bring you a sample?"

"Fernando … I trust you implicitly. A glass would be fine. And, please, make it a big glass."

"It will be my pleasure," he said with a chuckle. "I'll bring you some water and fresh bread, too."

As Fernando headed back to the kitchen, Melissa had her first chance to look around. The dining room was not big. It was twice as long as it was wide. She and Johnny Penn were seated in the first of eight semi-circular booths. The booths stretched the length of the long wall. Facing them across a narrow aisle was a row of smaller booths that were square and designed to seat two. Down the middle of the dining room ran a second row of the big, semi-circular booths. A counter with sixteen individual chairs ran the length of the opposite wall. The chairs were upholstered in the same red leather as the booths. The counter faced a grill with an ornate stainless-steel hood trimmed with copper. A man with a white chef's apron and white chef's hat was busy tending grill. For the first time, Melissa noticed the smell of grilling meat. Her stomach rumbled and reminded her she had not eaten since breakfast.

The dining room walls were paneled in the same rich, brown mahogany as the booth furniture. The panels extended two-thirds of the way up from the floor where they met a wallpaper scene of gently rolling green hills dotted with the occasional white farmhouse. The leaves on the wallpaper trees were a soft, faded red like the leaves of the maple trees in New England during a foliage season that was less than spectacular. The wallpaper sky was the color of parchment. Art deco sconces were evenly spaced along the top edge of the mahogany paneling. The glass shades faced up so the light from the sconces cast a warm golden glow on the wallpaper countryside.

Melissa was surprised to find the dining room three-quarters full since it was the middle of the week. The diners were mostly couples. The muffled murmur of their conversation combined with the wood and leather décor to give the dining room a warm, intimate feeling. The feeling was also one of timelessness, as if the dining room had always been there. *All it needs is a fireplace,* thought Melissa, e*ven if it's summer in Los Angeles.*

"I'm so glad you could make it," said Johnny Penn. "What a day, huh?"

"It was pretty intense."

"I watched all your reporting. Great job, by the way … being in the middle of the action and capturing the outrage of the community."

"Thanks. I felt bad about the driver … when they pulled him from his car. I wish they hadn't done that."

"Yes, I saw that. Did you hear anything about him? Is he ok?"

"He didn't make it."

Johnny Penn shook his head sadly. "It's unfortunate innocent people have to suffer for the sins of our society."

His comment struck her as oddly detached. *An innocent man lost his life and you're talking about the sins of society?*

"I hope you're being careful out there," he continued. "It's important to be where the action is but it's also important to take the right precautions. Does your network provide security?"

"No. But I'm careful. Plus, I have Push."

"Your cameraman? Well, he looks like he can handle himself."

"How 'bout you? I don't see your bodyguard."

Johnny Penn smiled. "I gave him the night off. Didn't think you were too dangerous."

Melissa thought about her response and decided she was tired of always having to consider her reputation. She answered nonchalantly, "You never know."

Johnny Penn took a sip of his martini and thought, *This could be interesting.*

"So, what about your speech?" she asked. "Bet you had tons of feedback."

"I did! Two million 'likes' on Twitter!"

"That's awesome! Congratulations, Johnny!"

"Plus, I had a call from the mayor's office. Can I share something with you in confidence?"

"Sure."

"Mayor's planning to address the city tomorrow. He wants me to say a few words after he's finished … about the need for social justice."

"Congratulations again. Do you know what the mayor's planning to say?"

Johnny Penn leaned closer and lowered his voice. "He'll be calling on the DA to file criminal charges tomorrow, against the cop who shot those two men. He wants the charges to be murder, too, second-degree murder."

"Isn't the DA supposed to decide on the charges?" asked Melissa, shocked by his revelation. "You know … whether they're warranted or not? It hasn't even been a day! The investigations are just getting started and they normally take weeks. Why's the mayor getting involved?"

Johnny Penn shrugged. "He doesn't want his city to burn?" He saw his answer bothered Melissa and decided to change the subject. "Hope you like it here. Do you know this is the oldest restaurant in Hollywood?"

Melissa welcomed the change of subject. "Yes, since 1919."

"Ah, you saw the sign."

"How'd you discover it?" she asked.

"My agent brought me here to celebrate when I got my first acting role."

"What was the movie?" she asked, genuinely interested.

"I had a somewhat inauspicious start. I was a model in a jean commercial. Anyway, my agent was a gruff, older guy. I still remember him telling me: 'Look, kid, you wanna be a big-time actor, then you need to look like a big-time actor, you need to act like a big-time actor and, most important of all, you need to be seen with big-time actors.' I stopped wearing jeans after that, except when I was doing their commercials. I also started hanging out here, at the Musso & Frank Grill."

"Meet any big-time stars?"

"I met Frank Sinatra."

"Really?!"

"Ol' Blues Eyes himself, back there in the New Room."

"The New Room?"

"I'll show it to you later. Used to be called the 'Back Room.' The Back Room opened in 1934 … right after Prohibition. You could say it was a semi-public place. It was open to the public but you had to get past Fernando's grandfather to get in, which meant you had to *be* someone, or *know* someone."

"Seriously?" asked Melissa with a laugh. "Fernando's grandfather?"

"Well, no, not really Fernando's grandfather … but supposedly the maître d' back then was not to be taken lightly, like Fernando. He kept the riff raff out. The Back Room was a place where the Hollywood movers and shakers could go and have a drink without being mobbed by the public. They lost the lease for the Back Room back in '55. That's when they opened the New Room. The New Room has the same bar as the original Back Room, the same light fixtures and furniture. There's a phone booth back there, too. It was the first public pay-telephone in Hollywood. Johnny Depp got his first acting job on that phone! That was back in the day, before cell phones, which is hard to imagine now."

"What a great story!" said Melissa, thinking it really was. She made a mental note to mention it to her producer for their Backroads of Los Angeles segment.

"The booth's still there. You can only make local calls, though."

Fernando returned and placed a generous class of Chardonnay in front of Melissa. "I would ask the lady and gentleman if they have any questions about our menu but I can see they have not yet looked."

"Fernando, I was telling Melissa how I met Frank Sinatra here, and a little bit about the history of the Musso & Frank Grill, about the Back Room and how it turned into the New Room. You have a great story about Charlie Chaplin and … Who was it? Rudolph Valentino?"

Fernando chuckled. "Douglas Fairbanks. Yes, I love that story. Ms. Wright, see that booth all the way down this row, in the corner?"

She looked past Johnny Penn to the far booth in the corner. "I see it."

"We call that the 'Chaplin booth.' Charlie Chaplin would come here every day for lunch and sit in that very booth. He would usually race Douglas Fairbanks from the studio. They would be on horseback because Hollywood Boulevard was a dirt road back then and, well, I think they just had a lot of extra horses. You know, for the pictures. The loser had to pay for lunch. Charlie Chaplin always ordered lamb and kidney with bacon."

Melissa laughed. "I can't imagine a dirt road in the middle of Hollywood. And the lamb and kidney sound terrible!"

"Ah, Ms. Wright, don't be so quick to judge. Remember, everything tastes better with bacon. It's still on the menu and it really is very good. The price has gone up, though. It was 75¢ back then."

"I'm sure it is, Fernando. It's just … I don't do bacon."

"Ah," he said with a smile. "I'm sorry to hear that. Now, I will leave you two alone. Mr. Penn, you will let me know when I can be of service?"

"I will, Fernando. Thanks."

Fernando gave Melissa a wink and walked off.

"He's a character!" whispered Melissa in Johnny Penn's ear.

"Oh, believe me, he is. He's a great guy, too."

"Now you have me curious. Who were the other Hollywood regulars here?"

"There's a long list. Mary Pickford. Gretta Garbo. Gary Cooper. Elizabeth Taylor. Humphrey Bogart and Lauren Bacall. Joe DiMaggio and Marilyn

Monroe. In fact—I should have mentioned this before—Joe DiMaggio and Marilyn Monroe used to sit right here, in this booth."

"Get out!"

"Really, it's true. You can ask Fernando. Supposedly, Marilyn Monroe picked this booth because it's closest to the front door and she liked being seen. Kinda' weird isn't it, to be sitting right here where someone famous once sat."

"I feel honored. I know that sounds silly but …"

"No, no, I don't think it's silly at all. This whole place makes me feel honored. Such great talent used to frequent this place. I think of this place as hallowed ground. And I have to tell you, Melissa, I'm a little surprised at you."

"What?"

"That you're genuinely impressed. I can't tell you how many people I've met who have never even heard of Marilyn Monroe. Of course, they're all younger people."

She laughed and told him the story of walking along the Hollywood Walk of Fame as a young girl with her parents, how they were so excited and she was not because the names meant nothing to her. "Maybe that's why I like old movies so much. I'm trying to make up for not being excited along with my parents."

"You like old movies?" he asked, surprised again. "Me too!"

"I adore them! I adore the stories and I adore the style of acting. They were both so much more dramatic back then. Some people think they're overdone and corny but, what can I say … I love them! And I love the way people had real class then. The women wore dresses and the men wore suits. And the fedoras! Nothing says class like a man with a nice fedora. Whatever happened to the fedora, anyway?"

"I wish I knew! I'd be wearing one if I thought I could get away with it!"

"Something about black and white films, too. Helps suspend disbelief. Maybe because it just *looks* like a different world."

"What's your favorite movie?" he asked.

"That's a tough question." She thought a moment before answering. "I'll say *Casablanca.* I'm a big Bogart fan for one thing. Talk about a face made for the movies! And I'm a sucker for a good love story." Melissa did her best imitation of Bogart's famous line from the movie, which was not half bad considering her voice was an octave too high and not at all raspy from too much drinking and too many cigarettes. "Of all the gin joints in all the towns in all the world, she walks into mine."

Johnny Penn laughed. "That's really a great line. You know I had a crush on Ingrid Bergman when I was a kid, because of *Casablanca.* I thought she was the most beautiful woman in the world, more beautiful even than Marilyn Monroe."

"Any chance we'll see someone tonight?" asked Melissa. "Someone famous, I mean."

He looked at her and smiled, not sure if she was serious or just teasing.

She suddenly realized her question may have been insulting. She blushed. "I'm sorry, Johnny! That wasn't at all what I meant!"

He laughed and touched her arm. "No worries, Melissa. Really, I'm not a vain person, despite what they claim in the tabloids. To answer your question ... Occasionally, but not like in the old days. Don't ask me why. Not trendy, I suppose."

They stopped talking long enough for Johnny Penn to signal Fernando. He came over and took their order. After a bit of cajoling from Fernando—he told Melissa she could order pan-seared scallops anywhere—she went with one of the old classics: veal schnitzel with prosciutto, arugula & parmigiano. Not to be outdone, Johnny Penn also ordered one of the old classics: grenadine of beef with bearnaise sauce.

Melissa was enjoying herself. She found Johnny Penn not at all like she imagined. He was polite and considerate, interesting and funny. He was also passionate about his political activism. He told her about his trip to Havana, Cuba in 2012 with a few other Hollywood celebrities to push for the normalization of relations between Cuba and the United States. He told her how they met the president of Cuba, Raul Castro, and how they were then given an audience with his brother, the legendary Fidel Castro. Johnny Penn talked about how unfair it was that Cuba had suffered under the embargo from the United States going all the way back to 1962 and how much he admired the Cuban health care system. "Whatever you want to say about the revolution in Cuba ... and, yes, maybe there are some problems with communism ... But at least all the people there have access to affordable, quality healthcare. Everyone should have healthcare. I believe it's a basic human right. So, I say, '¡Viva la revolución!'"

They both laughed. After never agreeing with Push about anything political, Melissa found it wonderfully refreshing to be with a man who shared her views.

Johnny Penn was also a good listener, which Melissa had learned from experience was a rare quality in men. Usually, she found men liked to talk about themselves, that they assumed you would chime in if you had something to say, which meant you would be waiting a long time if you were waiting for a man to ask how you felt about something. She had learned to insert herself into conversations at work out of professional necessity. Still, it left a bad taste in her mouth, like she was being rude.

When Johnny Penn asked Melissa if she had any siblings, she told him about her brother. It was a painful subject and she rarely talked about him, especially with someone she just met. With Johnny Penn, she told him the whole story, how her brother played guitar and wanted to be a musician and how her dad did not approve and wanted him to get a real job. He ended up working in construction so he could finally move out of the house. He was often unemployed. He was also often miserable, both because of his financial situation and because he was not doing what he really loved to do, play guitar. He ended up an alcoholic. Finally, he put a bottle to his head and pulled the trigger. "That's the reason I left San Francisco," explained Melissa, "and took the job here at KNBC. With my brother gone, Mom had no one in Los Angeles. No family, I mean."

"Family's important," said Johnny Penn seriously. "If you don't mind me asking, and at the risk of using a cliché, how come an attractive woman like you isn't married?"

"Well," she said, doing her best to sound coy, "I could ask you the same question. You're ... What? The most eligible bachelor in Los Angeles? In California? In the world?"

He laughed. "Ok, I'll go first. I was selfish when I was younger. Honestly, I did not want the responsibility of another person depending on me. And, how do I put this politely ... I had all the companionship I wanted."

"Is that how you feel today?"

"I think having another person depending on you is ..." He searched for the right words. "Not such a bad thing, as long as you can depend on them, too."

"Maybe that's what love is supposed to be," said Melissa, surprised at the depth of emotion in her comment, and at herself for using the L word.

"Maybe," said Johnny Penn, touched by the emotion evident on her face. "Now it's your turn."

She smiled and shrugged. "Haven't met Mr. Right."

"You will," said Johnny Penn confidently.

By the end of the evening, Melissa felt the attraction between them as if it was a magnetic force pulling them closer. She wanted to touch him. She wanted to feel the warmth of his skin. She wanted to feel his arms wrapped around her and the press of his lips against hers.

Johnny Penn seemed to read her thoughts. He slid up next to her in the booth so his leg was pressed against hers. He looked into her eyes and found them inviting. There was tenderness there, and intelligence. He thought her eyes the most beautiful eyes he had ever seen in a woman, liquid turquoise in almond-shaped pools of pure white. He found her gaze penetrating. She was looking through his outer façade, through his Hollywood persona to see the real Johnny Penn with all his faults and insecurities. Her eyes assured him it was ok. She wanted him just the way he was. He gently touched her cheek with his hand. He felt the softness of her skin, the warmth of it. Every nerve in his fingertips tingled with electricity. He felt her leg press against his harder than before. He leaned in to kiss her lips. When their lips met, he closed his eyes. He felt the room begin to spin.

CHAPTER NINE

A society which chooses war against the police better learn to make peace with its criminals.

— Unknown

OFFICER LEAH BLUNT was curled up on the sofa glider on the patio of her home in the foothills of Santa Clarita, a city of nearly a quarter million residents in the northwestern corner of Los Angeles County. The sun was just coming up to reveal a beautiful view of the desert valley below. Leah was oblivious to the view. At most, she had snatched an hour of fitful sleep last night. When she finally stopped trying at 4 a.m., she grabbed the iPad and a cup of coffee and sat down on the glider to check the news. She was devastated by what she found. When she could no longer stand it, reading about how she was a murderer and yet another example of a systemically racist police force in a systemically racist country, she closed the iPad. She cried for a while, which numbed her feeling of impending doom. She felt like she had woken up from a terrible nightmare only to find it was no nightmare at all. It was reality, and that reality had her trapped with no escape. It had her losing everything she held precious in life; her husband, her career, her very freedom, even her chance to have children. That was how her husband found her when he woke up, rocking in the glider and gazing off at the horizon with a dazed look on her face, her eyes ringed with red.

"When'd you get up?" he asked, sitting down next to her on the glider and gently touching her leg.

"About four."

"You get any sleep?"

"Not much." She turned around on the glider so she could rest her head on his lap. She grabbed hold of his leg as he stroked her hair. "I'm sorry, honey," she said. "You were right. I should have quit." Her voice was subdued. He could barely hear her.

"We'll get through this," he said in a confident, reassuring voice. "You didn't do anything wrong, Leah. That'll come out in the investigation."

"Honey, you don't understand." She spoke mechanically, as if every bit of emotion was wrung out of her. "The investigation doesn't matter. I watched the evening news when I got up. I've already been tried and convicted, all in a single news cycle. I'm guilty of cold-blooded murder. Plus, I'm a racist."

He had never heard her sound so defeated. "They can say whatever they want. There's a lot of garbage out there on the news. You're a good cop, Leah. You did it by the book. You did exactly what you were trained to do. That'll come out in the investigation. It has to. After that, it'll come out in the news. People will see you did nothing wrong."

She sat up and looked at him. She smiled thinly. She reached up and touched the side of his face with the palm of her hand. "Honey," she said, "this is what will happen. There will be two investigating teams. One with the LAPD Officer Involved Shooting team, the OIS team. The other with the California Department of Justice OIS team. The LAPD OIS team will submit their findings to the Los Angeles District Attorney. That's Cortez, who ran on a platform of 'reimagining police.' Suffice it to say, he is *not* a friend of the police. The California DOJ team was established after the George Floyd protests. It was established by the state legislature to provide an independent review of all officer involved shootings that result in the death of an unarmed civilian. They submit their findings to the California DOJ Special Prosecutions Section for review for potential criminal liability. The state legislature established the DOJ team to 'build trust between law enforcement and the community.' What does that mean? It means, in practice, they give the benefit of the doubt to the victim of the OIS, not the officer. So, I've got a better than even chance of being criminally charged. And I get to roll the dice not once but twice."

"There's still a chance they'll find you did nothing wrong," insisted her husband, "which you didn't. And if they ignore the facts and charge you, we'll get the best lawyers money can buy."

She sighed. "Honey, it won't be a fair trial."

"Why are you saying that?" asked her husband with an edge of frustration. He did not understand why she was painting it black. "Of course it'll be a fair trial!"

"Remember Chauvin?"

"The cop who murdered Floyd? That has nothing to do with your case, Leah. Chauvin had his knee on the guy's neck for cryin' out loud!"

"That's right, honey. He did. And it was a restraint technique taught at the Minneapolis Police Academy. It was also approved by the Minneapolis Police Department as a legitimate means of subduing an uncooperative suspect. None of that mattered."

"Then how could the jury find him guilty?"

She smiled another tight, thin smile. "Honey, you're such a good person. And you're also incredibly naïve. Why is that? Why are good people always naïve?" She thought about it a moment before letting it go. She explained. "Minneapolis was in flames. The mayor of Minneapolis declared Floyd was killed because he was black. He said that on national television. The president of the United States, no less, declared he had seen the evidence and 'hoped' the jury would reach the right verdict. The media, being the paragons of ethical reporting they are, revealed enough information about the jurors that their identities were no longer anonymous. And then there were the various activist organizations. They were promising Minneapolis would burn to the ground if the jury did not return the right verdict. The jurors knew the verdict expected of them. It was 'guilty.'"

"But what about keeping his knee on Floyd's neck. How long was it? Nine minutes? How could that be justified?"

"What would you do? Well, you're not a cop so that's not a fair question. But I've asked myself that a lot. You've got a big man, 6' 6" tall, muscular, obviously intoxicated, who has been forcefully resisting arrest for a good ten minutes. You finally have him subdued on the ground. If he's no longer resisting then, yes, maybe you remove your restraint. But you also have a crowd that's loud, aggressive and getting more unfriendly by the minute. The imperative is to keep control of the situation."

"You'd keep your knee on the guy's neck?!"

She shrugged. "You got a situation; you make a decision."

"Jesus, Leah."

"You make the wrong decision, they crucify you. No, I take that back. You make the right decision but it's a decision no one's willing to defend, because of politics … They still crucify you. Doesn't matter if you're a good cop, either. Chauvin was a twenty-year veteran cited multiple times for bravery. Although, I have to say, he did have seventeen complaints filed against him, almost one a year, which is a little unusual."

"But wasn't the guy a racist?!"

"There was no evidence of racism. Honey, the cold, hard reality is… They came back with a guilty verdict because Chauvin was a white police officer, Floyd was a black man, and a lot of powerful people had a vested interest in portraying this country as systemically racist. Chauvin was the perfect scapegoat." She signed heavily. "Just like I'll be the perfect scapegoat."

The doorbell rang.

"That'll be Parnell," said Leah.

Parnell had been assigned as her "peer officer" after she surrendered her firearm to her supervisor, which is standard procedure in an OIS, to take the officer's weapon. The weapon is sent to the forensics lab to confirm its proper functioning. Forensics also confirms the weapon is loaded with the authorized type of ammunition. The job of the peer officer is to monitor the overall well-being of the officer involved in the shooting and to look after the officer's physical needs. Parnell drove Leah from the scene of the OIS to the hospital where she gave a blood sample to confirm she was not under the influence of drugs or alcohol. Parnell then he drove Leah home and promised to check on her in the morning.

"Do you want to see him?" asked Leah's husband.

"Yeah," she said, pushing herself off the glider and pulling her robe around her waist.

Officer Parnell walked into the kitchen. His khaki California Highway

Patrol uniform was perfectly creased. He wore the short-sleeved summer-issue shirt. The gold seven-point CHP star was pinned to his shirt above the left breast pocket. The push-to-talk radio mic was velcroed to the epaulet of his left shoulder. Its cord ran down to his black duty belt that was bulky with the accoutrements of a patrol officer: radio, taser, handcuffs, flashlight, extra magazines and service pistol. He held his campaign hat in his hand. He looked grim. "Mornin' Leah," he said. "How you feeling?"

"I've felt better," she answered. "You look like shit, if you don't mind me saying."

He smiled at her insult. "I'll bring your car by later today. You need another sidearm while they run the forensics on yours?"

"No, I've got my own stuff."

"Anything else I can get you?"

She was suddenly tired of waiting for it. She could tell he was holding something back and knew that could mean only one thing. It was not good news. "Ok, Parnell, out with it. Why the gloomy puss?"

Parnell had a genuinely pained expression on his face. "Leah, there's some scuttlebutt … Mayor's giving a speech today. He's gonna demand the DA charge you."

"With what?" she asked, grabbing the edge of the kitchen table to steady herself.

"Second-degree murder."

All the strength ran out of her legs. She collapsed in the kitchen chair. She rubbed her hands slowly up and down her face. "I'm gonna spend the next twenty years in prison," she said to herself quietly. "I'm gonna spend the next twenty years in prison with psychopaths who hate the police."

Her husband came up and rubbed her shoulders. "No you're not," he said to her quietly. "Leah, I told you, we'll fight this with everything we've got. We'll get the best lawyers. We'll get the truth out. People will see … *You did nothing wrong!*"

"He's right," said Parnell earnestly. "Leah, we all saw the video. It's out there on YouTube. You did it right, Leah. Maybe those punks didn't have firearms but they were coming for you. You did exactly what I would have done. You did exactly what any cop would have done who didn't want to end up dead. I'll tell you something else. You know that Porsche that was in front of the van? Well, it was stolen. We traced it back to the owner. She was some famous model who lived up in the Hollywood Hills. When they went out to her house, they found her there dead, shot in the back of the head. And that was after they raped her. They found her husband there, too, shot in the face. He was some big, Hollywood studio executive. Those two pieces of shit robbed the place, raped the woman, and then executed the two of them. They both have long criminal histories. Leah, they're career criminals as well as cold-blooded killers."

Parnell's face flushed red.

"And I'll tell you something else … I've had enough of this 'blame the cops' shit! These fuckin' politicians want to get up in front of people and talk about racism and how black lives matter when none of this has anything to do with racism … Fuck 'em! Blue lives matter, too! How 'bout all lives matter?! Anyway, I'm through with these politicians and the stupid people who vote for 'em. If they can't tell the difference between the good guys and these pieces of shit then … well … like I said, Fuck 'em! I'm done risking my life to protect 'em. They can start protecting themselves. Nothing like a good dose of reality to cure stupid."

Leah looked at Parnell and smiled. She had recovered from her shock and appreciated him saying she did nothing wrong. As much as she loved her husband, Parnell's assessment meant more to her than her husband's. Parnell's was the assessment of a fellow professional. She said grimly, "You can't cure stupid, Parnell."

"We'll see," he said, still angry. "I'm telling you, Leah, they arrest you for this, I'm done being an officer. A lot of guys feel the same way, too. A lot! I'm telling it to you straight, Leah. They do this, they arrest you for defending yourself, for not wanting to end up dead, and for doing the world a favor by putting a couple pieces of shit in the ground, a couple of cold-blooded killers … We'll all walk! We'll all go on strike! And to hell with these politicians and the stupid-ass people who vote for 'em!"

CHAPTER TEN

We are not ruled by the same ideas nor do we possess the same moral character as our parents did. Today, freedom takes a back seat to equality. "One nation, under God, indivisible" has become an antique concept in an age that celebrates diversity and multiculturalism. Our intellectual and cultural elites reject the God our parents believed in and the moral code they lived by.

— Pat Buchanan, "Suicide of a Superpower"

LARRY SAUNDERS WAS a software engineer. He worked for Brilliant Solutions, a defense contractor responsible for the software of the AIM-120, otherwise known as the AMRAAM. AMRAAM is an acronym for advanced medium range air-to-air missile. The AMRAAM uses active transmit-receive radar guidance instead of semi-active receive-only radar guidance. That means it is a fire and forget weapon; it does not need guidance from the firing aircraft's radar. The AMRAAM has more than thirty years of design history behind it and is currently deployed on all active-duty American fighters—the F35, F22, F15, F16 and F18—as well as the Eurofighter Typhoon. The American and European Union defense departments consider AMRAAM the most sophisticated, combat-proven air dominance weapon in the world.

Larry Saunders had been with Brilliant Solutions for thirty years. Brilliant Solutions was his first job after graduating from MIT with a master's degree in software engineering. That was in 1995. He soon developed a reputation with Brilliant Solutions as an exceptional engineer. If you had a challenging problem, you wanted Larry on your team. That reputation made its way to the Air Force and Navy. They started requesting Larry attend their design reviews to explain program decisions, evaluate flight test performance data and, on those occasions when the AMRAAM was actually used in combat, to participate in after-action reviews. There had been several of those after-action reviews since AMRAAM's introduction to Air Force and Navy inventories. AMRAAMs had been used in combat in Iraq, Bosnia and Kosovo. Altogether, the AMRAAM was credited with sixteen confirmed kills.

Larry pulled into the driveway of his home in Manhattan Beach, a beachfront city located in southwestern Los Angeles County. He did not pull into the garage because the garage was no longer a garage. It had been converted to a one-bedroom studio apartment for his son, Bernie. Larry turned off the engine and sat staring at the garage door. Even though he was looking directly at the garage door, he was not seeing it. He was, in his mind, back at Brilliant Solutions, sitting in the office of the HR manager. It was 10 a.m. and Larry was her third meeting of the day.

The HR manager took a sip from her coffee cup before setting it down on her desk next to the folder with Larry's personnel file. She then proceeded to explain to Larry why he would not be the next program manager for AMRAAM. "You were a great candidate," she said with an encouraging smile. "And it was a difficult decision, Larry. It's just … we had a number of highly qualified applicants for the position, with different strengths and weaknesses, and, well, when we weighed them all … the selection committee determined the best fit for the AMRAAM program was Ketanji Brown."

Larry had heard the rumor before he walked into the HR manager's office, that Ketanji Brown would be the new AMRAAM program manager. The rumor concerned him because, often, HR rumors turn out to be true. Still, he refused to believe this particular rumor because it seemed so unbelievable. He was far and away the best candidate for the position. And that was not simply his opinion, although he liked to think himself capable of objectively assessing his strengths and weaknesses. Everyone thought he was the best candidate. His boss, the current program manager, flat out told him. "You'll be the next program manager, Larry. No one is stronger technically. No one knows the program better. Plus, and this is a big plus, you're good at politics. That's a unique combination, an engineer that's good at engineering *and* good at politics." His boss laughed then. "You don't find *that* too often!"

The AMRAAM team thought so, too, that he was the best candidate. They encouraged him to apply when they heard the current program manager, Larry's boss, was retiring. They all asked, "You're putting in for it, right?" Then, after he applied, they thought he was a shoo-in. "Looking forward to working for you!" they all said.

Finally, there was the Air Force AMRAAM program liaison officer. He was characteristically direct. "You need to be the next program manager, Larry. No one else measures up. I need you. The program needs you. And … this is no bullshit, Larry … our pilots need you!"

There was another reason the rumor seemed unbelievable. The rumored winner was Ketanji Brown. There were four applicants for the position and, in Larry's opinion, she was the least qualified. She was hired as a senior engineer five years ago. Prior to that, she had nine years' experience at Boeing. Her experience at Boeing had always bothered Larry. Why, he wondered, was she leaving Boeing when Boeing was desperate to retain engineers like all the other aerospace companies? Even more concerning to Larry was the fact her last job at Boeing was with the 737 Max program, the program whose entire fleet was grounded in 2019 after a second crash of their airplane for what was ultimately determined to be a software failure. Had Larry been a member of the interview team, he would have had more than a few questions regarding her role as a software engineer in the Boeing 737 Max program.

When Ketanji started working on the AMRAAM team, Larry found her a competent engineer, if not an exceptional one. His biggest complaint was what he considered a lack of dedication. They often had to work long hours to meet a program deadline or analyze missile telemetry from a test firing. Ketanji groused about having to work late and work over the weekend and, adding what she considered insult to injury, not being paid for the overtime. To be fair, Larry found that a common problem with the younger engineers. Their "work-life balance" seemed more important to them than the program's success. That always struck Larry as odd because, if the program was not successful, they would be out of a job. Without a job, they would have zero work-life balance. "Maybe it's the new math," quipped Larry to one of the older engineers, knowing only an engineer would find his mathematical humor funny. "They've determined the answer to an age-old question. Zero divided by zero is not undefined. It's not zero, either. It's one! There it is! The perfect work-life balance!" Whether or not it was new math, Larry could not imagine being a program manager if you were not prepared to work a whole lot of hours, including over weekends and holidays, and all while not getting paid for them.

Larry sat stone-faced in front of the HR manager as he digested the news. "So, it's Ketanji," he finally said.

"Yes," said the HR manager with a sympathetic smile. Then she added, "You were a close second, Larry." She added that as a consolation for his obvious disappointment. "And I would really encourage you to apply again, Larry, the next time a program manager position opens up."

"A close second?" asked Larry, frowning.

"Yes," said the HR manager without hesitation.

"Just curious," asked Larry, "what was it?"

"What was what?" asked the HR manager, not understanding the question.

"What was it that made Ketanji Brown a close first? Did she have more program-relevant technical experience than me?"

The smile ran away from the HR manager's face. She looked down at her desk as she considered her response. When she looked back at Larry, she decided her response would be honest. "Larry, everyone on the applicant assessment team considered you the most experienced candidate."

"Did she have more liaison experience with the Air Force and Navy?" asked Larry, already knowing the answer.

"No, Larry, she did not."

"Is she more trusted by the AMRAAM program team?" asked Larry, an edge of anger creeping into his voice. He knew the answer there, too.

The HR manager fidgeted with the papers in Larry's personnel file. She was not comfortable with the conversation's direction. "Look, Larry, I know this is disappointing—"

"You're damn right it's disappointing!" said Larry in a voice loud enough to be heard outside the HR manager's office. He was tired of dancing around the truth. It was crystal clear to him why Ketanji Brown was selected and he was not. He just wanted to hear the HR manager say it. He gave his anger free rein. "I'm the most qualified guy for this position and everyone knows it! My boss knows it! The guys on the program team know it! Hell, even the damn government knows it! So, if I'm the most qualified guy for the job, how come it's going to Ketanji Brown?!" Larry glared at the HR manager, daring her to answer.

The HR manager leaned forward. There was a pained expression on her face. She spoke quietly. "Look, Larry, we've both worked for Brilliant Solutions a long time. I respect you. I know how hard you've worked for the AMRAAM program, and for Brilliant Solutions. I'll be straight up with you … and I hope you can appreciate that … what I'm going to tell you … well … it would mean my job, Larry … if the wrong people were to find out I shared this with you."

"I will consider this conversation confidential," said Larry stiffly. Then he added, "You have my word."

"That's good enough for me," said the HR manager. She locked eyes with Larry. "Everything you said is true. And what I said is true, too. You were a close second. You were close because everyone on the assessment team recognized you are head and shoulders above the other candidates when it comes to technical expertise, program experience and managerial ability. The problem was, there's something that trumps all those attributes. We have to meet DOD diversity requirements. That's the deciding factor now. According to DOD, we don't have enough diversity in our workforce. And, according to DOD, we especially don't have enough diversity in our management positions. I really wish it was not the case but, being completely honest with you, it is."

"So, I didn't get the job because I'm a white guy."

"That's correct."

"Anything else? Did Ketanji come out of the closet as a lesbian … so DOD can check another box?"

The HR manager shook her head. "No, we're not allowed to ask about sexual orientation. Of course, if she was a lesbian, we could not discriminate against her."

"Of course!" said Larry with a bitter laugh.

"Why don't you talk to your boss. Take some time off. I'm sure he'll be ok with that. You're really a tremendous asset to Brilliant Solutions, Larry, and to the AMRAAM program especially."

A tremendous asset?! thought Larry. *Did she really just say that?!* He pushed back his chair and stood up. "I appreciate your honestly," he said in a flat, emotionless voice. "You can count on this conversation remaining confidential."

Larry walked into his boss's office after his meeting with the HR manager. He found his boss just as shocked as he was when he told him Ketanji Brown would be the next program manager. "Come on," said Larry's boss, "I could use a drink. And I know you could!"

Larry followed his boss to Hennessey's Tavern, an Irish style pub they frequented for lunch and the occasional work celebration. They took separate cars because Larry had no intention of driving back to work; he was done for the day. There was plenty of room at the bar because it was still early, before the lunchtime rush. A waifish young woman was behind the bar when they sat down, intently focused on her phone as her thumbs danced across its face. She only noticed Larry and his boss when she finished her text.

"Get you guys something?" she asked with a half-hearted smile as she walked up. Larry thought she had what his son would call "an emo look." When Larry asked his son if he liked the look, his son gave him one of his trademark shrugs that communicated "who cares" with the same bored, dismissive authority he used when he actually bothered to say it out loud.

Larry did not particularly care for the look. He thought it trashy even though the emos obviously put some effort into looking the way they looked. The young woman had styled, shoulder length hair that was colored platinum blond and highlighted with pinkish streaks. Her eyes were made to look even bigger than they were, which were already big and beautiful, with oversized artificial eyelashes and the extravagant application of black mascara that turned up at the outer corners of her eyes and almost touched her eyebrows. A gold ring pierced her petite nose and two gold studs pierced the pale white skin under her lower lip. Each stud was located halfway from the center of her lower lip to the corner of her mouth. A too-small and too-tight black tank top made it impossible to miss the ample swell of her breasts whose curvature and dimensions were further emphasized by the application of makeup in her cleavage. Across the front of her tank top in white block letters, all capitals, were the words "DEAD INSIDE."

"I'll have the IPA on tap," said Larry's boss, nodding toward the Lagunitas tap handle.

"Sixteen or twenty-two ounces?" asked the bartender. As she spoke, Larry noticed a gold stud in the middle of her tongue.

"Make it twenty-two," said Larry's boss.

The bartender turned to Larry. "Anything for you?"

"Jack Daniels on the rocks. Make it a double, please."

The bartender walked away, not bothering to acknowledge their orders.

"Charming personality," said Larry's boss.

Larry smiled. "I feel like a dinosaur."

"Yeah," said his boss, "me too. Do young guys really like that look? All those piercings? They must, right? Otherwise, why would they be so popular with women?"

"You got me," said Larry. "Definitely not my thing."

"Keep hearing how these kids are doing everything later than we did, dating, graduating from college, moving out, buying a house, getting married, and especially having kids of their own. Maybe they don't care about attracting guys anymore."

"Maybe."

"You ever ask your son that, if young women care about attracting guys?"

"No. Not sure he'd know, either. He doesn't get out much."

"He have a girlfriend?"

"Not that I know of. We don't talk much."

"Sorry to hear that."

The bartender came back with their drinks. "Here you go," she said, not bothering to smile. "Let me know if you need anything else."

"Thanks," said Larry.

The bartender returned to the far side of the bar where she pulled out her phone and immediately reacted with shock to whatever it was she found on the screen. Her thumbs set about texting with urgent intensity.

"I ever tell you the story about the time we tried to set up our son with a waitress?" asked Larry's boss.

"No."

"We were having dinner at our regular restaurant, Marge and me. There was this good-looking young waitress there, about our son's age. She was friendly and Marge is good at getting your life story in under sixty seconds. Well, Marge finds out our waitress is single, living with her dad and taking courses at the occupational center to be an underwater welder. We're surprised to hear that, stereotyping gender roles and all. Marge asks why. The waitress says she likes diving, that she goes diving with her dad, and that there's great money in it, working for the oil and gas companies. Anyway, to make a long story not quite so long, Marge and me walk away from dinner thinking this young lady would be a great match for our son who also likes diving. He'd been complaining how he can't find decent women to date. We tell our son about her and he agrees to join us for dinner the next time he's out our way. Well, that took a while because he doesn't get down to see us too often. Six months go by and, finally, he's down to visit. We ask for her table and, well, we find out a lot can happen in six months. She's dressed kind of trashy. She's no longer living with her dad. She's no longer taking welding classes at the occupational center, either, because she's working full time to pay for her apartment. And, here's the best part, instead of diving, she and her roommate, another waitress who also works at the restaurant, they both like to hang out at the beach after work and drink beer until the sun comes up." Larry's boss laughed. "We caught so much shit from our son after that!"

"Sounds like the end of your matchmaking credibility."

"It was!"

"So," said Larry, suddenly serious, "how's this gonna work with Ketanji Brown?"

Larry's boss shrugged. "You'll muddle through, I guess. And you'll cover for her as required."

Larry looked at his boss to see if he was joking. When he saw he was not, he shook his head and scoffed. "You know, I knew this shit was going on. I knew DOD had their diversity, equity and inclusion program, their DEI program. And I knew what that meant, too, that companies that want to do business with DOD, like Brilliant Solutions, have to have their own DEI program. I just didn't know it meant *this!*"

"If it makes you feel better, I didn't either."

"I guess I was ok with the idea you give the nod to the black woman if everything else is equal. Hell, you have to make a decision, right? I just never thought it would turn into 'we give the job to the black woman as long as she's minimally qualified, and regardless of how good the white guy is.'"

"I can only imagine how you're feeling. That job should have been yours."

"I'll get over it. I like doing technical stuff. So, really, this just means I get to keep doing what I like doing. Hell, maybe they did me a favor, not picking me for management. What really bothers me is what this means for the country … when we stop picking people based on merit and start picking people based on skin color, or their friggin' reproductive equipment."

"It means," said Larry's boss, "we lose our technological advantage."

"It sure as hell does!" said Larry, suddenly passionate. "And that's a serious thing in our business! It's one thing to produce a toaster that's technologically inferior but you produce an inferior AMRAAM … You're the one who gets shot down instead of the enemy!"

Larry lifted his glass and filled his mouth with Jack Daniels. He felt it burn all the way down his throat. "And if it's happening here, out in industry, it sure as hell is happening in our universities and high schools. What I wanna know … What happens to our technological advantage when our next generation of engineers, all trained and hired and promoted to perfectly reflect the demographics of society, can't engineer their way out of a paper bag?"

"We lose the next war," said Larry's boss matter-of-factly.

"Can you imagine what the Chinese must be saying about us? And the Russians?"

"What?" asked Larry's boss. "You don't think they're worried about their 'diversity gap?' Because … you know … diversity is our strength." His voice was dripping with sarcasm.

"No," said Larry definitively, "I don't. I think they're laughing at us."

They sat in silence.

"Oh well," said Larry after a moment, resignation replacing his passionate indignation. "It was a good ride while it lasted."

"It sure was," said Larry's boss. "Not trying to rub it in but … I think I picked a good time to retire."

"I think you did, too. And, I'm not gonna lie … Right now, I'm jealous!"

"You'll get there," said Larry's boss with genuine sympathy.

"I know. What's another ten years?" Larry raised his glass. "Here's to the glory days, and the guys who made them glorious. That'd be you, boss."

"And you, Larry."

Their glasses touched with a clink.

Sitting in his driveway, staring ahead at the garage door, Larry thought about his thirty years at Brilliant Solutions, how they had been great years and how he had a lot of professional pride in what he accomplished. Then he wondered if he wanted to continue working for a company that was no longer interested in producing the best AMRAAM possible. There was a moral dimension to his consideration beyond the injustice of what had happened to him, having been passed over for promotion for someone obviously less qualified. A less capable AMRAAM meant more causalities in a future conflict, and more casualties was a fancy way of saying more dead pilots. *How do I live with myself,* thought Larry, *propping up a system responsible for that?!*

Larry noticed the grass in the front yard was still a shaggy mess. *How long has it been?* he wondered. *Two weeks since Bernie mowed the grass? Three weeks?* Without him knowing it or wanting it, his anger and frustration with DOD and Brilliant Solutions transferred to his son, Bernie. *Twenty-two years old and living rent free in my garage! All I ask is that he take out the trash and mow the lawn once a week! And he can't even do that!* Larry slammed the door to his car and walked purposefully to the front door of his house. He was determined to have his lawn mowed by the end of the day, and that Bernie would be the one to mow it.

CHAPTER ELEVEN

Am I the only one who can't take no more
Screamin', "If you don't like it there's the fuckin' door"
This ain't the freedom we've been fightin' for
It was somethin' more, yeah, it was somethin' more
Am I the only one, willin' to fight
For my love of the red and white
And the blue, burnin' on the ground
Another statue comin' down in a town near you

— Aaron Lewis, "Am I the Only One"

UNLIKE HIS FATHER, Bernie was having a great day. He had been up since three in the morning working with his fellow hackers. He and his fellow hackers had acquired a password to the California Highway Patrol computer system. They had acquired it from the dark web. The dark web, in turn, had acquired it from another hacker who had hacked into the personal computer of a CHP officer. The CHP officer had carelessly stored his CHP password in an email to himself. He stored it there along with all his other passwords, including passwords for his banking accounts. Bernie and his hacker friends planned to use those, too, once they were finished with the CHP.

Inside the CHP computer system, Bernie accessed the personal information for all eleven thousand CHP employees, including home addresses and phone numbers. "Payday!" he said to himself quietly as he downloaded the spreadsheet.

Bernie and his hacker friends planned to sell the information on the dark web. Countless sites on the dark web are interested in illegally acquired data. Those sites are able to exist despite the best efforts of law enforcement thanks to the use of onion routing, a technology that uses multiple layers of encryption and redirection to protect the identities of both buyers and sellers. To the extent anonymity is essential for an ongoing criminal enterprise, onion routing is essential for the dark web.

It was no accident Bernie and his hacker friends targeted the CHP. They were incensed at the shooting of two unarmed African American men, and not just because it was in Los Angeles, which they considered their own backyard. They were incensed because the CHP officer involved in the shooting was obviously guilty of murder. In Bernie's mind, and the minds of his fellow hackers, there could be no possible justification for shooting a man who was unarmed. Plus, they all considered it an indisputable fact police forces in the United States of America are hopelessly corrupted by systemic racism. "Just look at African American arrest rates," Bernie said to one of his fellow hackers. "If that's not proof of police racism, I don't know what is!"

Having tried and convicted the CHP officer for murder, Bernie and his fellow hackers were further incensed by the fact the officer's identity had not been released. That fact was the impetus for their original plan, which was to hack the CHP computer system and divulge the officer's identity. If the state would not tell people the name of the officer involved in the shooting, they would! When they found no data on the CHP computer system regarding the officer's identity, they settled for what they considered the next best thing. They would divulge the identities of *all* CHP officers, all eleven thousand of them.

Bernie and his fellow hackers were members of Anonymous, although a more accurate description would be they simply considered themselves Anonymous. That is all that is required, in reality, to be Anonymous, because there is no official Anonymous membership. There are no requirements to join, no dues to pay upon joining, no bylaws, no organization and no leadership. If you call yourself Anonymous, you are Anonymous.

Bernie first called himself Anonymous in 2020 when he saw a video on an Anonymous Facebook account. The video promised the Minneapolis

Police Department "would pay" for the murder of George Floyd. Bernie networked with others on the account to make that threat a reality. They actually took down the Minneapolis Police Department website. Bernie was hooked after that. He was hooked by the feeling of having accomplished something consequential. He was also hooked by the feeling of being an instrument for righteous vengeance. Even more than standing up against an unjust system, he and his fellow hackers were actually punishing the system. They were making the system pay.

In 2021, Bernie participated in Operation Jane, an Anonymous sponsored operation intended to obstruct the Texas Heartbeat Act, a law that banned abortions once a heartbeat was detected, usually about six weeks following conception. The Texas Heartbeat Act also made it a crime to aid and abet a person obtaining such an abortion. As part of Operation Jane, Bernie led the effort to hack the website of the Republican Party of Texas. Bernie and his fellow hackers defaced its homepage. They added text about Anonymous. They added an invitation to join Operation Jane. And, finally, in what Bernie considered a moment of inspiration, he personally added links to Planned Parenthood for donations and abortion services.

In 2022, when Russia went to war against Ukraine, Anonymous went to war against Russia. Bernie was right there with them, fighting in the cyber trenches. Bernie and his fellow hackers disabled the website for the Russia Times as well as websites for other Russian state-owned entities, including the Russian Ministry of Defense. Bernie and his fellow hackers also attacked Russian television channels. They laughed themselves silly when they replaced the regular programming on Russian television channels with YouTube videos featuring patriotic Ukrainian songs and speeches.

Bernie's cyber efforts naturally led to his participation in direct physical action. He participated in the George Floyd protests, of course. He also joined protests against the Russian invasion of Ukraine, against the growing problem of homelessness in Los Angeles and across the nation generally, against the growing power of Big Tech to censor dissenting views on the internet, against poverty and the growing wealth gap, and, finally, against climate change. His direct physical action initially involved nothing more than marching. Then marching turned into chanting and fist pumping. More and more, the chanting grew angrier and the fist pumps more threatening.

His direct physical action first turned violent when he ran into a Trump supporter. That was at a protest against climate change. He knew the man was a Trump supporter from his red MAGA hat. The man was there to protest the protesters. His poster board sign proclaimed, "Climate change is climate bullshit!" Bernie could not recall who threw the first punch. One minute they were screaming at each other, the next minute they were throwing punches. The fight itself was an adrenaline-charged haze for Bernie. Before the surrounding bystanders pulled them apart, both of them were bloodied, although Bernie definitely received the worst of it. After that, Bernie decided to carry a weapon. At times, it was nothing more than the wooden stick attached to the poster board with his protest message. Other times, it was a length of steel pipe. If the weather was cool enough, it was a baseball bat. The cool weather was required to comfortably wear an outer garment of sufficient size and bulk to conceal the bat. The bat hung from a rope looped about his neck and shoulders.

Regardless of the weather, the Anonymous mask was an essential accoutrement for Bernie. The Anonymous mask is also known as the Guy Fawkes mask. Bernie considered it essential to conceal his identity in the event he ever had to deploy his weapon. He had no faith in the legal system understanding his need to use a steel pipe to bash the skull of a Trump supporter or anyone else espousing ideologies he considered evil and hateful. There were, of course, other options available to Bernie to conceal his identity. Antifa protesters favor black balaclavas and hoodies, often with dark sunglass for protests during daylight hours. While that mode of concealment is effective for its intended purpose, it was never anything Bernie considered adopting. He was proud of his work for Anonymous and wanted the world to know Anonymous was where his allegiance lay.

Bernie also loved the history of the mask. While the mask owes its present-day appearance to the 1980s' graphic novel "V for Vendetta" and the 2005 film adaptation of the same name, its pedigree can be traced much further back in history, all the way back to 1605 when a Briton named Guy Fawkes attempted to bomb the House of Lords and end what

Fawkes and his co-conspirators considered Protestant persecution of Catholics in England.

Fawkes was captured before he could detonate his gunpowder bomb. He was tortured into revealing the identities of his co-conspirators. Fawkes and all but one of his co-conspirators were sentenced to be hanged, drawn and quartered. Fawkes, however, managed to escape the hangman's noose. Moments before his execution, he jumped from the gallows. Instead of making good his escape, he only managed to break his neck. Parliament established a day of remembrance the following year, in 1606, to mark the anniversary of the plot. The day of remembrance is November 5. Every year since, on that day of remembrance, Britons give thanks for the plot's failure by constructing effigies of Fawkes, complete with a mask to capture Fawkes' likeness. The effigies of Fawkes, popularly known as "guys," are then carried through English villages and towns to be burned in roaring bonfires.

There was another reason Bernie only wore the Anonymous mask. He simply loved the look of it. He loved the stark whiteness of the face and its chiseled features. He loved the exaggerated laugh lines under its ruddy pink cheeks and the deeply creased crow's feet at the corners of the eyes. He loved the neatly groomed pencil-thin eyebrows and the pencil-thin moustache and goatee, all jet black. Most of all, though, he loved the confident, knowing grin. To Bernie, the grin bespoke of the justice that would soon be visited upon a corrupt and arrogant ruling class, if not by him than by the legions of other "guys" similarly committed and simply biding their time, waiting for the right opportunity.

Bernie's friends and family did not consider Bernie an athletic man. He was never interested in sports growing up, in school or after school. Never in a million years would they have thought Bernie an aggressive man. Never in a million, million years would they have considered him a violent man. He was, by nature, an introvert. He was also the stereotypical nerd, quiet and bookish, who much preferred interacting with digital devices to interacting with actual, real people.

That Bernie was an introvert and never interested in sports made him the polar opposite of RZ. RZ was a natural born leader and a record-setting athlete back in middle school. They were also polar opposites in that

Bernie grew up without his mother while RZ never knew his father. Bernie's mother ran away with another man to "find herself" when Bernie was twelve years old. RZ's father never stuck around long enough to even know he was a father. He, too, was hoping to find himself, making it with as many women as possible, hanging out and getting high. Finally, Bernie and RZ were polar opposites in a global sense. They literally grew up in different worlds. Bernie grew up in Manhattan Beach, a mostly upper middle-class, white community known for its beautiful beaches and surfer culture. RZ grew up in South Central Los Angeles, a mostly lower middle-class, black and Hispanic community known for its mean streets and gang culture.

There was, however, one thing Bernie and RZ had in common. It was a thing that a superficial analysis of their respective personalities and circumstances might suggest was only possible through a remarkable coincidence. Really, though, it was anything but a remarkable coincidence. It was simply evidence individual personalities and circumstances are no match for the power of societal forces. What was that one thing they had in common? It was an overwhelming sense of alienation from their country, the nation of their birth.

RZ's sense of alienation is easy to understand. He was born poor, raised without a father, warehoused in terrible schools and surrounded by male role models who, for the most part, were only interested in immediate gratification, lawful or otherwise. Taken together, alienation was the inevitable result.

Bernie's sense of alienation, by contrast, is not at all easy to understand. Other than losing his mother when he was twelve years old, he was privileged in every sense of the word. He lived in a nice neighborhood, attended quality schools and, most important of all, had a father who loved him and was determined to do whatever it took to see his son grow up to be a responsible, successful adult. Those positive factors turned out to be no match for a school system determined to inculcate in its students a genuine, deep-seated loathing for the United States of America; for its history, its culture, and its people. Bernie was taught his country, the country his father was busy defending through his work at Brilliant Solutions, was founded on the institution of slavery, expanded from sea to shining sea through a deliberate policy of genocide against Native Americans and, finally, made wealthy at the expense of innocent people everywhere, through imperialism overseas and discrimination at home, especially against women, minorities and members of the LGBTQ community.

While there is an element of truth to each of the charges, no attempt was made to place the charges in context. The history of the United States can be considered loathsome only when measured against a utopian ideal. Bernie's teachers never once considered where in the world, or in all of recorded history for that matter, their utopian ideal ever existed. They ignored the fact slavery was the norm in the world at the time of the country's founding, just as they ignored the fact slavery would not have been possible without the support of the Africans themselves, raiding and capturing their fellow Africans to sell to Muslim and European slave traders. They also ignored the fact Native Americans waged war on their fellow Native Americans, and that their imagined stereotypical Native American living in splendid harmony with nature actually raped, pillaged and slaughtered with as much enthusiasm as any Muslim or European, and that they also carried off the survivors as slaves. The body count may have been lower as a result of Native American avarice but that was only because the Native Americans were not as technologically advanced as the Muslims and Europeans. A balanced perspective of history, had Bernie's teachers been interested in balance, would have taught that. They would have taught the United States was far from perfect but also not uniquely evil. On the plus side, they would have taught the United States gave the world a new and revolutionary form of government, a form of government that serves as the foundation for the liberty and individual rights Americans hold dear today.

Finally, for good measure, Bernie's teachers added a healthy dose of imminent apocalypse courtesy of climate change. Both those things, the one-sided presentation of history and the imminent apocalypse from climate change, were reinforced by popular culture, by Big Tech, Hollywood and the legacy media. What chance, then, did Bernie have against such a wall of indoctrination? What chance would any adolescent have? The reality was: He had none. He was left alone to try and justify his existence when literally every adult authority figure in his life, all of them except his father, were telling him the generations that came before represented all that was wrong with the world. They were also telling him that unless he wanted to spend the rest of his life revolted by what he saw in the mirror, he needed to make amends. He needed to prove he was not like those previous generations by denouncing all they stood for, by despising his own race and his own sex, by supporting reparations, by supporting open borders, by supporting supranational organizations intent on dismantling the sovereignty of the United States of America, and, to save the planet, by demanding an end to the use of fossil fuels. Forever.

So it was Bernie came to despise his father.

Bernie was surprised by a sharp knock on the door. "What?!" he asked with an annoyed voice.

"We need to talk," said Larry.

"I'm in the middle of something," answered Bernie, wondering why his father was home so early. While he actually was in the middle of something—he was working away on his computer—he also had no interest in what he assumed was another lecture about getting out of his room more often, and the subsequent lecture that inevitably followed that one, about getting a real job.

"Open this door," demanded Larry. "Right now!"

"Bullshit!" muttered Bernie. He walked over and opened the door. Then he stood in the doorway to make it clear his father was not invited to walk in his room.

"Can I come in?" asked Larry, amused his son thought to block the entrance. Larry noticed it was dark in the room save for the ghostly white glow of two computer screens. He also noticed a ripe, musty smell, like trash that was overdue to be emptied.

Larry did not wait for his son to answer. He walked forward so Bernie was forced to step aside. "Your room smells like shit," he announced. He said it harshly, like a judge passing sentence. "When's the last time you cleaned it?"

"Hey!" objected Bernie. "This is my room! You can't just barge in here without my permission!"

Larry snapped around so his face was inches from Bernie's. He stared hard at his son. He considered grabbing his son by his sweatshirt, the one that said "I WOKE UP LIKE THIS," dragging him to the front door and then physically throwing him out of his house. Even though he had thirty years on his son, he knew he would prevail in a physical contest. He ran and lifted weights. His son, by contrast, did nothing other than sit in front of the computer or sit behind the wheel of his car when he was out delivering groceries for Doordash. For a moment, the two of them only glared at each other.

Larry decided against a physical response. He said deliberately, as if speaking to a spoiled child, "No, Bernie, you got that wrong. This is *my* room because I pay for it. And that means I get to come in and inspect *my* property any time I damn well please. And if you have a problem with that, then you can go live somewhere else. You can go get a real job and rent a real apartment."

Bernie's face turned red. He was angry but not sure how to respond. It had been a long time since he had seen his father like this, not only unconcerned about his feelings but ready to impose some real discipline. He looked away from his father.

"Ok," said Larry, "now that we have that straight, let's get some light in here." Larry walked toward the sliding glass door to pull open the drapes.

"Dad!" objected Bernie. "Can we please do this later?!" Bernie sounded desperate.

"Nope," said Larry, "we're doing it now." Larry yanked open the drapes. The noon-day sun streamed into Bernie's room and revealed what could only be called a complete and total mess. Dirty clothing lay in disheveled heaps on the carpet where it had been haphazardly thrown by Bernie. The carpet was completely covered by Bernie's clothing except for a few isolated patches. Where the actual carpet was exposed, it was stained and filthy. A used towel hung from the half-open door to the bathroom. Dirty dishes were stacked in the sink to the point where they formed a precarious mountain of porcelain and glass. Empty pizza boxes were stacked on the counter. Magazines, books and papers were strewn about the dresser and desktop with the exception of a small, cleared area directly in front of the computer.

And a woman was lying asleep in Bernie's bed, on top of the sheets, with nothing covering her naked body except a skimpy black negligee.

"What the hell?!" exclaimed Larry, shocked.

"Dad … I can explain!"

Larry almost looked away so the woman could make herself decent without him watching. Then he noticed something. He noticed the woman was not real. "You're sleeping with a mannequin, Bernie?!"

"Dad! She's not a mannequin! She's …"

"What?!" asked Larry, looking at his son with disgust. "She's what, Bernie?!"

"Her name's Kendra. She's—"

Kendra's eyes opened wide when she heard her name. She also spoke. "Hello, Bernie," she said in a sexy, sultry voice. "I've been missing you. I've been wanting you, too, Bernie. I've been wanting you all day." She giggled. "You know you shouldn't leave me alone, Bernie. I start to think of things when I'm alone. I think of all the things I want you to do to me."

Larry was shocked a second time. "What the …" He never imagined the mannequin would speak.

"Kendra!" barked Bernie. "Go to sleep!"

Her eyes closed.

Bernie turned to Larry. "Dad, it's the latest technology—"

"Don't!" interrupted Larry, holding up his hand. "I don't want to hear whatever bullshit you're about to give me. I'll tell you what she is. She's a fuckin' rubber doll! And I'll tell you what you are. You're pathetic! You know why you're having sex with a fuckin' rubber doll, Bernie? Because no real woman will have you! And I don't blame the real women because you're pathetic! Look at this room! Look at the fuckin' lawn you haven't mowed in three weeks! Look at the fact you're twenty-two years old and still living in your old man's one-room converted garage, with no real job and no prospects for one!"

"Can I please explain?" pleaded Bernie.

Larry had to force himself to calm down. He looked at his son with contempt. "Ok," he said, "explain."

"It's not what you think—"

"You have no idea what I'm thinking!" Larry angrily interrupted.

"Ok, ok. It's just … You know how your generation had magazines and stuff, and the internet. Well, this is the same thing. It's just, you know, porn, that's all. It's porn for the twenty-first century."

Larry shook his head sadly, struggling to maintain his composure. *First work and now this.* Not only was he disappointed with his son, he was disappointed with himself. In fact, he was more than disappointed. He felt like a total and complete failure. He had always believed his first priority in life, his most important responsibility in life, was doing right by his son, especially since Bernie was his one and only child. And doing right by his son meant raising him to be an independent, responsible man, a moral man. For his son to turn out like this …

Bernie was encouraged by his father's silence. "It's no big deal, Dad. Really. There's nothing weird about it or anything like that. All my friends have one. They're not cheap but they're cheaper than a girlfriend."

I've been too easy on him, thought Larry, not really listening to his son. *Too easy for way too long.*

"Plus, you don't have to worry about STDs."

Larry thought about what he would say next.

"Dad?" asked Bernie, suddenly concerned by his father's silence.

"Bernie," said Larry, finally deciding, "this is what's going to happen." He looked at his watch. "It's now 12:37 p.m. By 6 p.m. today, you will have this room cleaned up. You will have the lawn mowed. *And* you will have … Kendra … moved to another location, one that is not on my property. If you fail to do these things, and do them to my satisfaction, then you will be sleeping in your car tonight, and for every night after that until you save enough money, your own money, to rent your own apartment."

Larry did not bother waiting for an answer. He turned and walked from the room.

CHAPTER TWELVE

Politics have no relation to morals.

— Niccolò Machiavelli

LOS ANGELES CITY Hall was dedicated over a three-day period beginning on Thursday, April 26, 1928. At the time of its dedication, it was the largest building in the Southwest. It had required two years to build. No expense was spared in its building, either. It was completed for the then lofty sum of $5 million. It had twenty-eight floors and stood over 452 feet above Main Street. The entire municipal staff of Los Angeles required only four of its twenty-eight floors when it first opened for business, which was not an accident since the building was designed to accommodate a growing city well into the future. City Hall would remain the tallest building in Los Angeles until 1964.

The dedication ceremony was nearly as grand as the building itself, and perfectly in keeping with the ambitions of the city's leaders and its citizens. There was a three-mile-long parade that included hundreds of floats, thirty-four bands and more than 32,000 people. The flag was raised and a chorus sang "The Star-Spangled Banner." Irving Berlin sang. The mayor gave the dedication address. There was a rousing chorus of "America." That evening, the Lindbergh Beacon was dedicated by President Coolidge. He spoke by wire from Washington DC. The Lindbergh Beacon sat atop the highest point of the building, on the stepped art deco pyramid that served as the roof of the central tower. The beacon was a gift from the Los Angeles Chamber of Commerce who intended it "blaze the way for future air travelers." Charles Lindbergh had completed the first ever solo trans-Atlantic flight the year before, in May 1927, and was actually there to witness the dedication of the beacon named in his honor. President Coolidge used a golden key in Washington DC to turn on the beacon for the first time. The Los Angeles Times reported, "For thirty minutes the building was kept dark as the beaming beacon turned silently on its pivot and cast the message of Los Angeles' civic progress and development as an aviation center." Then another breaker was thrown and the great architectural masterpiece was illuminated from without by brilliant white flood lights and from within by the softer, more yellow light of the office ceiling lamps. The light from the office ceiling lamps was visible through the building's office windows and gave outside spectators the distinct impression the building was now occupied, and that its occupants were hard at work conducting the city's business.

Over the next two days, the building was open for inspection by the public. On the evening of the final day, the Native Sons and Daughters of the Golden West put on an historical pageant. The dedication program proclaimed, "The Spirit of the dedication of this white monumental monolith which is the new City Hall is the spirit of Los Angeles—the spirit of a forward-looking people, determined to win a happy community Destiny. This monument symbolizes the soul of a struggling, fighting, building people, never knowing defeat and always climbing upward, until today it may be said of them: 'This is their City. They have created it; they have transformed it from a sleepy Spanish-California pueblo to one of the mightiest communities of a continent.'"

What would an attendee at that dedication think today if somehow transported through time to present day Los Angeles? This hypothetical time traveler would, no doubt, marvel at the technological advancement of the present day, at the sleek cars on the roadway and the jet aircraft overhead, stacked up for their final approach to Los Angeles International Airport. He would also marvel at the little devices with their glowing screens that are the object of intense concentration by almost everyone, and at almost all times unless they are required out of necessity to look elsewhere.

Upon becoming further acquainted with the capabilities of those little devices, the time traveler might also think those devices literally alive and possessed of supernatural intelligence, given their ability to listen to their user and verbally respond to their questions, their ability to note their user's location and provide directions to any destination desired, either by walking or driving, their ability to provide access to any fact ever recorded in all of human history, and, finally, their ability to provide a means of communication to talk to anyone at any time anywhere in the world.

While the time traveler would have marveled at the technological progress, he would also, likely, not have been overawed. He would have understood it for what it was because progress was, after all, still progress. He had seen his share of it in his time. The first powered man flight was in 1903. The first public wireless broadcast was only three years later, in 1906. The first mass-produced automobile, the Ford Model T, appeared in 1908. Metal filament light bulbs were perfected in 1911. And electricity was making its way into American homes on a large scale soon after the end of the First World War, in 1918.

What the time traveler would have failed to understand was the manifest cultural decline in evidence across the street. He would have stood there in front of the gleaming white Los Angeles City Hall building he had just seen dedicated with all the pomp and circumstance his age could muster, a building which looked essentially the same today as on the day of its dedication a century before, and then turned around to see a city of tents stretching as far as the eye could see in both directions down Main Street. Upon closer examination, he would have noted the dilapidated condition of the tents and the strange behavior of their inhabitants, the able-bodied men and women who should have been out working but, instead, were sleeping in the middle of the day or wandering about on the sidewalk, some of them talking to themselves, others arguing vehemently with an imaginary companion. He would have noticed people urinating in public and, more shocking still, having sex in public. If he dared walk across the street, he would have been greeted by the smell of rotting garbage and human feces. Soon, he would have found himself accosted by beggars. If he was well traveled in his day, this hypothetical time traveler, the assault on his senses would have recalled the slums of Calcutta, India, or Shanghai,

China. Most likely, he would have been indignant at the condition of *his* city, in *his* country. He would have stopped the first passerby that was obviously not a resident of this appalling slum and asked, "See here, sir, how can this be allowed to stand?!"

The passerby would not have known what he was asking because "this" had been allowed to stand for decades. "Just the way it is," the passerby would have shrugged before continuing on.

If this hypothetical time traveler was afforded an audience with the mayor of Los Angeles as a consequence of his celebrity status—he was, after all, a time traveler—he would have been introduced to Mayor Javier Rodriguez. After the requisite exchange of pleasantries and his recounting the sensation of time travel, which he would have described as remarkably benign, nothing more than a flash of white light and a moment of disorientation, he would have demanded action to clean up the slum he observed across the street from City Hall. He would have described the slum as a squatter's camp of vagrants and derelicts.

Mayor Rodriguez would have grimaced at his visitor's language and stifled an urge to admonish him for the judgmental harshness of his words, an urge to which he would have given free rein had his visitor not come from another, earlier time. Mayor Rodriguez would have patiently explained the genesis of the problem, how the state mental hospitals had been closed in a wave of deinstitutionalization that began back in the 1960's, how many if not most of those people then ended up in prisons because they were unable to cope in society, and how there was then a subsequent effort to empty the prisons of people who were not considered a violent menace to society.

"So, you just dumped all these mentally ill people out on the streets, to live as vagrants?" the time traveler would have asked, dumbfounded.

"We now refer to them as 'the houseless,'" Mayor Rodriguez would have gently corrected. "Or 'the unhoused.' No one says 'vagrant' today. And we stopped calling them 'homeless' a few years back. We feel the term homeless has become inseparable from the toxic narrative that blames the unhoused for their state of being without a house."

The time traveler would not have been interested in word games. "Call them what you will, Mr. Mayor. The fact remains many appear mentally ill, and they are living out on the street in appalling circumstances. Why hasn't this been addressed?"

"I assure you we take this problem seriously. We have allocated nearly $2 billion in our city budget to address the houseless challenge."

The time traveler would have been shocked at the number. City Hall had required all of $5 million to build. Also, he had just read in the 1928 Los Angeles Times how the budget for the entire federal government of the United States of America was approaching $4 billion for the current fiscal year. After a moment's reflection, the time traveler would have said, "That is a mighty sum, Mr. Mayor. And, truth be told, I do not fathom how the citizens of Los Angeles can afford such a sum. Still, setting aside my ignorance of your present-day financial situation, what is your plan for spending all that money?"

Mayor Rodriguez would have been happy to see his visitor finally impressed. "We have a number of programs," he would have answered proudly, "because we understand this problem to be multifaceted. First, we are building housing for these people—"

"Excuse me, Mr. Mayor. Housing? As in state mental hospitals?"

"No, no, no. I mean housing … as in *real* housing, real homes."

"Where these people can come and go as they please?"

"Of course. We do not commit people against their will today."

"But they're mentally ill."

"Yes, which is why we're also building community treatment centers where they can access free psychiatric services."

"You can cure mental illness today?"

"I would not go that far. But, with the right medication, we can stabilize their condition."

"Enough so they can take care of the house you've given them?"

"We have support services for that … in case they need help maintaining their home."

"You'll be providing them with a maid and gardener?"

"No, no, no. Just the help they need, when they need it."

"I see. You'll forgive me, Mr. Mayor, if I'm starting to question my vocation as a working man."

"Oh, rest assured, we also have job training programs. Our goal is to make the unhoused fully functional. We also want them gainfully employed. Yes, our goal is to make them gainfully employed, fully functioning citizens of the great city of Los Angeles."

"Forgive me, Mr. Mayor. I am not trying to be impertinent. You tell me you're spending all this money on all these fine sounding programs yet you still have all these—unhoused, is it?—you still have all these unhoused people living out on the streets. What am I missing?"

Of course, Mayor Javier Rodriguez never actually sat down with our hypothetical time traveler from the 1928 City Hall dedication because, well, the time traveler was hypothetical. However, Mayor Rodriguez was getting much the same question from his constituents. "Mr. Mayor, why do we still have all these homeless people out on the streets of Los Angeles?"

Mayor Rodriguez had run on a platform of ending the homeless crisis, or the crisis of the unhoused as his administration now preferred to call it. The city council had approved his budget much as he had submitted it for each of the past three fiscal years. The budget included unprecedented amounts of money to address the crisis of the unhoused, starting at ten percent of the city's total budget of $12 billion in the first fiscal year of his administration and rising to nearly fifteen percent of the budget in the third year of his administration. Still, the number of unhoused only grew. Mayor Rodriguez asked the people of Los Angeles to be patient as it took time to build shelters, dedicated housing and community treatment facilities. The people of Los Angeles were patient, initially. They understood Mayor Rodriguez had promised to tackle a problem of gargantuan proportions and his proposed solutions required time before their impact would be felt. After three years, though, the patience of the people of Los Angeles was running thin. It was running thin to the extent Mayor Rodriguez was now concerned about winning his reelection campaign for a second term. He needed a distraction. He needed the electorate to focus on something other than the failure of his program to reduce the ranks of the unhoused. It needed to be something that would portray him as the decisive and courageous leader he knew himself to be. It needed to be something that would energize his party's base and capture the media's attention. The Los Angeles media's attention, certainly. Even better, the attention of the national media. Like any good politician, Mayor Rodriguez had ambition for higher office. That something, he decided, was Officer Leah Blunt.

***

Sally's voice came over the intercom on the mayor's desk. "Mr. Sullivan's here."

"Thank you, Sally," answered Mayor Rodriguez. "Please have him come in." Mayor Rodriguez sat up straight in his chair and stretched his neck. He did not expect this to be a pleasant meeting.

Jake Sullivan was president of the Los Angeles Police Protective League, the LAPPL, which is the police union representing the nearly ten thousand sworn officers of the Los Angeles Police Department, the LAPD. He was a thirty-year veteran of the LAPD who had recently been elected president of the LAPPL with the promise to stand tall for the much-maligned honor and integrity of the average cop, and to be a political pit bull when it comes to fighting back against mounting efforts to defund the police. He had also promised to call out the hypocrisy of the left-leaning city council, the chief and the mayor who had all so eagerly climbed aboard the defund the police bandwagon while still relying on uniformed and plainclothes officers for their personal protection details.

Sullivan strode into the mayor's office with his trademark leatherbound notebook in one hand and a cup of Dunkin' Donuts coffee in the other. He was of medium height and build, and still obviously fit even though he had just as obviously seen some hard living. The hair on his head was shaved. His face sported a closely trimmed brown mustache and goatee that were generously flecked with gray. He wore a navy-blue suit with a light blue tie. A Blue Lives Matter pin was displayed prominently on the lapel of his suit jacket. His eyes were steel gray and intensely piercing.

"Hello, Jake," said Mayor Rodriguez, grinning broadly as he pushed himself up out of his chair. He walked energetically around his desk to greet Sullivan with an outstretched hand.

"Mr. Mayor," said Sullivan, acknowledging the mayor's greeting without a smile. He took the mayor's hand and gripped it firmly. Had the mayor not been prepared for Sullivan's strong, muscular grip, he would have found the grip painful. Sullivan made a point of holding on to the mayor's hand until the mayor began to wonder if he would ever get it back.

Mayor Rodriguez gestured to one of the dark brown mahogany chairs in front of his desk. There were two of them, upholstered in burgundy leather. Ornate brass tacks followed the contours of the chairs and lent them an air of old-world elegance. Mayor Rodriguez sat down after Sullivan. He chose to sit in the chair next to Sullivan rather than the chair behind his desk so they would not be separated by the expanse of his desk. The mayor thought that an important symbolic act, sitting side by side, to emphasize his desire to work together to find common ground. He assumed the issue Sullivan urgently wanted to discuss was Officer Leah Blunt.

"I'd offer you coffee," said Mayor Rodriguez, "but I see you already have some. Hope you and your family are doing well. Nathan still playing soccer?" Mayor Rodriguez had not really remembered the name of Sullivan's son or the fact he played soccer. His administrative assistant, Sally, always provided a folder on the personal details of his visitors and he always made sure he took the time to review it. Some political wag once quipped, "All politics is local." Mayor Rodriguez did not disagree with the quip. He thought, rather, it did not go far enough. He preferred, "All politics is local *and* personal."

"Mr. Mayor," said Sullivan stiffly, "I did not request this meeting for an exchange of pleasantries."

"No, of course not," said Mayor Rodriguez, disappointed Sullivan seemed intent on making this meeting as unpleasant as possible. "How can I be of service to the Police Protective League?"

"I hear you're planning to give a speech today, and that you're planning to demand the district attorney indict Officer Leah Blunt for second-degree murder."

"Where did you hear that?" asked Mayor Rodriguez, not at all surprised to find the details of his speech leaked from his office.

"You know I will not say," answered Sullivan bluntly.

"No, I suppose not," said Mayor Rodriguez with a tired smile.

"Is it true you will do this?" asked Sullivan, returning to his original question. "Will you be calling for the indictment of Officer Blunt only twenty-four hours after the shooting, without even waiting for the official report from the LAPD Officer Involved Shooting team, or the state DOJ team?"

Mayor Rodriguez saw no point in denying what he would be announcing to the world in just a few hours. "Your information is correct, Jake, however you came by it. I will be asking District Attorney Cortez to indict Officer Blunt on two counts of second-degree murder, for the murder of Raymond James and Dwayne Armstrong."

Sullivan nodded slowly but said nothing.

Mayor Rodriguez noted the jaw muscles on the side of Sullivan's face rhythmically clenching and unclenching. He braced himself for the verbal explosion of expletives for which Sullivan was notorious. He was surprised, then, when Sullivan sighed heavily and proceeded to speak in a voice that was more relaxed than before, albeit one tinged with what Mayor Rodriguez interpreted as weary resignation.

"I'm sure it would not matter," said Sullivan, "if I told you I have seen the video of the shooting, and that I would have done exactly the same thing had I been there instead of Officer Blunt, that any cop in her situation would have done exactly the same thing if they did not want to end up dead in the street."

Mayor Rodriguez chose his words carefully. "I am not saying this to diminish your years of experience, Jake, protecting and serving the citizens of our city … but … times have changed … and we need to change with them."

While Sullivan adamantly agreed times had changed, he just as adamantly disagreed on the need to change with them if the change had not been for the better. He saw no point in discussing their difference of opinion. "Well, Mr. Mayor, perhaps it's just as well you announce it today. We both know what District Attorney Cortez would conclude in the end, regardless of the findings in the OIS report. You are simply dispensing with the pretense of due process—"

"Please, Jake," interrupted Mayor Rodriguez, "I don't think that's a fair characterization."

"Mr. Mayor, with all due respect, and if I may speak for Officer Blunt as well as myself, I think you are the last person in the world who should be complaining about fairness."

"Officer Blunt will have her day in court," objected Mayor Rodriguez.

"And we both know what that's worth!" shot back Sullivan, an edge of bitterness now in his voice. "Which brings me to my point. I am here, Mr. Mayor … in the interest of giving *you* fair warning. The Police Protective League will be calling for a labor action by its members immediately after you call for Officer Blunt's indictment."

Mayor Rodriguez was genuinely shocked. "You can't do that! The police can't go on strike! It's … It's … It's illegal!"

"Actually, Mr. Mayor, it's not. Our legal staff checked. We have every right to go out on strike. And believe me, Mr. Mayor, I know the sentiment of our membership. You do this, you call for the indictment of Officer Blunt, we *will* go on strike."

Mayor Rodriguez was visibly upset. "Then we'll fire you! The city will fire the whole damn department if necessary!"

"That is certainly your prerogative, Mr. Mayor." Sullivan smiled the barest hint of a smile. It was the first time he smiled since sitting down with Mayor Rodriguez. "And good luck to you. Good luck to you *and* the city council. Good luck finding men and women willing to risk their neck to keep you safe when you are so quick to hang them out to dry, to put a noose around their neck and pull it tight the minute it's politically expedient to do so."

CHAPTER THIRTEEN

Tomorrow is the most important thing in life. Comes into us at midnight very clean. It's perfect when it arrives and it puts itself in our hands. It hopes we've learned something from yesterday.

— John Wayne

MELISSA STOOD WITH Push in the grand portico that was the official entrance to Los Angeles City Hall. They stood in the center of the portico along with the rest of the local television and print press behind a red velvet rope that cordoned off a podium with the seal of the City of Los Angeles. They were waiting for Mayor Rodriguez to speak. To the left of the podium was the American flag. To the right of the podium was the California state flag and the Los Angeles city flag. Still further out on the podium's flanks were two uniformed LAPD officers. They stood there at ease, silently surveying the group of press and the modest crowd of mostly city officials. Melissa wondered what those two LAPD officers were thinking, knowing the mayor of their city was about to demand the indictment of a fellow officer for second-degree murder. She also wondered about the growing number of uniformed officers just outside the portico. She recognized both LAPD and CHP uniforms. The officers appeared to be assembling in ranks on the sidewalk that bordered North Spring Street. *It this some kind of protest?* she wondered.

She looked at her watch. "How come they never start these things on time?" she asked, not really expecting an answer from Push.

Push answered anyway. "Maybe the mayor's still recovering," he said flatly.

"Recovering?" asked Melissa. "From what?"

Push was watching the growing ranks of uniformed officers on the sidewalk along with Melissa. He turned and smiled at her. "Weren't you a little late this morning, after your date with Johnny Penn? The mayor's wife is a very attractive woman, I understand."

Melissa punched Push in the shoulder. "There's more where that came from!" she threatened.

"Ouch!" said Push, rubbing his shoulder where she punched him and pretending it hurt. "So," he asked, "was it a good date?"

Melissa looked at Push to see if he was asking seriously or still pulling her leg. When she saw he was serious, she answered, "Yes, it was a good date. He even asked if I'd join him on the other side of the velvet rope. The mayor asked him to say a few words after his statement."

Now Push was surprised. "Really? You up there with Johnny Penn and the mayor? What are you doing here?!"

"There's this little thing called work."

"Too bad. I would have liked to see you up there hanging out with the rich and famous. I've always said you're too good for this local reporting gig."

Melissa laughed. "I know, I know. I should have been in pictures. Me and about a million other women who moved to Hollywood to be the next big star."

"So, I have to ask … Did he pass the test last night?"

"What test?" asked Melissa suspiciously. She genuinely had no idea what test Push was referring to but suspected the worst. It was not at all beneath him to ask if Johnny Penn was good in the sack.

"The one I told you about when you started dating again. You always offer to help pay for dinner. If the guy accepts … that's it. You know he's a loser and you should never date him again."

"Oh. *That* test!"

"Yeah. That test. What'd you think I was asking?"

Melissa blushed. "He passed," she said, ignoring his last question. "I asked and he said he would not hear of it, that *he* asked me out and a true gentleman never allows a lady to pick up the check."

Push nodded his approval. "Maybe I need to change my mind about the guy."

"It was interesting, too. You know he runs a tab there? He told me the Musso & Frank Grill is one of the few restaurants that still do that, for a few of their regular customers. There was no check. Johnny just told the waiter to 'put it on his tab.' They send him a bill once a month. He told me the account book is something to see, all the famous old names who had their tabs there back in the day."

"Cool," said Push.

"Yeah, it was," said Melissa.

"So, you really like him?" asked Push, suddenly serious.

Melissa thought a moment before answering. "I have to be honest … I showed up not expecting to like him. I really thought he would be your typical celebrity. You know, self-centered and arrogant. But he wasn't. And we really connected. So, to answer your question, yes, I really like him … as much as a girl can like a guy after a first date."

"I'm happy for you, Melissa. You deserve a good man."

"Maybe," she said, not at all sure.

"Just be careful."

Melissa appreciated Push's encouragement, and his concern. She reached over and touched him tenderly on the shoulder, the one she had punched only moments before. "You know, I kind of like having you for a big brother."

"Good," he said definitively, "because you don't have a choice."

Mayor Rodriguez strode out onto the portico with his entourage. He walked directly up to the podium as his entourage fanned out behind him. Johnny Penn was in the center of the entourage. He stood just behind the mayor. Mayor Rodriguez did not waste any time starting. "Good afternoon, ladies and gentlemen," he said without smiling. His voice was grave. "Thank you for coming. My comments will be brief. Then I will turn the podium over to Mr. Penn. I think Mr. Penn needs no introduction. I asked him to say a few words because I found his words inspiring yesterday when he spoke from the scene of yet another senseless and terrible tragedy. We'll then have time to take a few questions."

Mayor Rodriguez took hold of the podium with both hands and

scanned the assembled press corps. He was pleased to see a healthy turnout. He briefly looked down at his notes and then continued with his grave tone of voice. "As I'm sure you all know, two young men, Raymond James and Dwayne Armstrong, lost their lives yesterday in an encounter with an officer of the California Highway Patrol. Both these men were African Americans. And we can now say definitively, both these men were unarmed. I am sure you all find that fact as disturbing as I do. There have already been peaceful protests. Those peaceful protests started yesterday, at the scene of this terrible tragedy, and have continued today at several other locations across our city and across our state. The number of peaceful protesters has been growing and we expect the number to continue to grow in the days ahead. Let me say unequivocally, as mayor of our great city, I support the right of these peaceful protesters to express their outrage at yet another instance of the police using deadly force against unarmed African American men. Let me also say, unequivocally, that those who take advantage of these peaceful protests to incite violence and destroy property will face the full force of the law. Regrettably, I have been informed there has already been a fatality, which occurred yesterday, when one of these peaceful protests turned violent."

Mayor Rodriguez paused to survey the faces in the press corps. He noticed many of them nodding their approval. He also noticed the red lights on the television cameras. The red lights indicated the cameras were recording.

He continued. "It was not that many years ago when our citizens filled the streets of our city, filled the streets of countless cities across our state and across our nation. They came out and filled the streets of our cities to express their righteous anger at another instance of police brutality. I'm sure you all remember. It was 2020 and we were all horrified by the video of a Minneapolis police officer kneeling on the neck of George Floyd. He pleaded, 'I can't breathe.' He pleaded over and over again, 'I can't breathe.' He pleaded for nine minutes, 'I can't breathe.' And for nine minutes, that Minneapolis police officer ignored his plea. On that day, George Floyd did not survive his encounter with callous indifference. On that day, George Floyd did not survive his encounter with police brutality."

Mayor Rodriguez looked down at his notes as if composing his thoughts. In fact, he knew exactly what he would be saying next. His pensive pause had been suggested by his chief of staff when he was rehearsing his speech earlier in the morning. His chief of staff thought it built a sense of anticipation and a sense of drama for the speech's finale.

"The protests during the summer of 2020 were a tribute to the American conscience and the American character. We rose up as a nation and demanded justice for George Floyd. And justice was served. The Minneapolis police officer who took the life of George Floyd was convicted of second-degree and third-degree murder. I want to assure the citizens of Los Angeles, the citizens of California and the citizens of the United States of America, that justice will be served here, too. It is for that reason, for that most basic of all American rights, for justice, that I am calling on District Attorney Cortez to indict Officer Leah Blunt for second-degree murder, for the murder of Raymond James and Dwayne Armstrong. Thank you."

Mayor Rodriguez stepped away from the podium as the crowd applauded enthusiastically. Melissa was also applauding, as was the rest of the press corps. Push was occupied with filming and unable to applaud even if he wanted to, which he most definitely did not.

Johnny Penn made his way to the podium. He was immaculately dressed as always. He pulled a folded sheet of paper with notes from his suit pocket and placed it on top of the podium. He surveyed the press corps and, seeing Melissa, allowed the barest hint of a smile to intrude upon his otherwise solemn demeanor. He began with the same grave voice used by Mayor Rodriguez. "Ladies and gentlemen, Mayor Rodriguez—"

A cacophony of police sirens exploded from the street below. The noise was deafening. Johnny Penn stopped speaking.

"What the heck?" asked Melissa, turning to look toward the street. She saw the street filled with police cruisers. The cruisers were not moving. They filled all three lanes of traffic in the street so traffic was completely blocked. Red, white and blue strobes danced across the cruiser light bars. On the sidewalk in front of the cruisers, a column of uniformed officers stretched off to Melissa's left as far as she could see. The officers were standing four abreast and looked to be at attention. Twenty feet in front of the column stood a single man, conspicuous for his position at the head of the column. He was also conspicuous for the fact he was the only person not in uniform. He was dressed in a navy-blue suit with a light blue tie. He was Jake Sullivan, President of the Los Angeles Police Protective League.

Jake Sullivan turned to face the cruisers. He snapped to attention and saluted smartly. The sirens immediately fell silent. The strobes on the light bars stopped dancing.

"Come on," said Push urgently. "Whatever this is, we need to be filming it."

"Right behind you," said Melissa.

They started toward the street. As they did, the rest of the press corps had the same idea and followed along. Johnny Penn found himself standing at the podium with no audience. He turned to Mayor Rodriguez. "What's this about, Mr. Mayor?"

Mayor Rodriguez had a worried look on his face. "I think I know," he said tersely. "Come on."

Mayor Rodriguez followed the press corps toward the street. Johnny Penn fell in behind the mayor, and the mayor's entourage fell in behind Johnny Penn. The two uniformed police officers who had been standing at either end of the red velvet rope brought up the rear.

Jake Sullivan waited patiently for the press to assemble in front of him, and for the mayor and his entourage to assemble behind the press. He was grimly satisfied the mayor had chosen to follow the press out to hear him speak. It would make for better television, he thought, if he was able to address the mayor directly.

"Mayor Rodriguez," he began, locking eyes with the mayor, "we all just listened to your call for justice. I am here to say you have a strange notion of justice. We have a process for assessing whether or not an officer was justified in using her weapon to defend herself and to protect the public. Or, I should say, we used to have a process. That process requires an investigation by the department's Officer Involved Shooting team, and by the state DOJ team. Only then, after the investigation is complete, and only if warranted by the results of the investigation, is an indictment issued. You, Mayor Rodriguez, have decided to cut that process short. You, Mayor Rodriguez, have decided to call for the district attorney to indict Officer Leah Blunt for second-degree murder. You made this decision only a single day after the shooting. You made this decision before the investigations are complete, before the facts of the case are even known. What are we, the uniformed officers of the Los Angeles Police Department and the California Highway Patrol to make of your precipitous call for an indictment of murder? Are we to conclude due process is reserved only for criminals? Are we to conclude political posturing is more important than actual justice? Are we to conclude the life of a uniformed police officer and the reputation of an entire department is expendable when measured in the balance against your political ambition?"

Jake Sullivan extended an arm and pointed at the cruisers in the street. Then he pointed at the assembled column of officers stretching down the sidewalk, four abreast and standing at attention. "We have concluded all these things are true, which is a sad and sorry day for our city and its citizens. The fact these things are true leaves us with no choice. Effective immediately, the Los Angeles Police Protective League and the California Association of Highway Patrolmen is commencing a labor action against Mayor Rodriguez and his corrupt administration. Effective immediately, our members will not be reporting to work. And to ensure there is no misunderstanding, let me make this perfectly clear. We, the men and women of the Los Angeles Police Department and the California Highway Patrol have no issue putting our lives at risk at the hands of criminals. We all know that comes with the job. It's what we signed up to do. What we *do* have an issue with, what we *did not* sign up for, and what we *most emphatically* refuse to accept, is having to put our lives at risk at the hands of back-stabbing politicians more concerned about furthering their careers than protecting and serving the people of Los Angeles."

Jake Sullivan turned his back on the mayor and faced the column of officers. He snapped to attention and saluted sharply. The officers returned his salute as one. A voice from the front of the column boomed, "Forwarrrrrrrrrrdd march!" The column of officers started forward on the word "march." It passed in front of Jake Sullivan, the assembled press corps, the mayor and his entourage. As it passed Jake Sullivan, it approached a row of four galvanized steel trash barrels that no one had noticed before or, if they did, had assumed was there as part of City Hall's provision for sanitation. In fact, the row of galvanized steel trash barrels had been placed on the sidewalk only moments before by some of the assembled officers. They placed the trash barrels with just enough space between them for an officer to march.

"What are they doing?" asked Melissa.

Push did not answer.

When the first row of officers was adjacent to the row of trash barrels, each individual officer tossed something in the barrel to his immediate right. The thing he tossed was small and shiny. It was also obviously metallic as each toss was accompanied by a hollow metallic clang. Officers in subsequent rows followed suit. As the rows passed by, the multitude of tosses sounded remarkably like raindrops on the tin roof of an old barn at the very beginning of a thunderstorm, fat and heavy, and ominously warning of the deluge to come.

Melissa asked again, "Push, do you know what they're doing?"

"Yes," he answered, not taking his eye from the camera's viewfinder which was zoomed in for a close-up of the marching officers and the galvanized steel trash barrels. "They're throwing their badges in the trash."

CHAPTER FOURTEEN

A dead thing can go with the stream, but only a living thing can go against it.

— G. K. Chesterton

THE TWITTERVERSE HAD reacted with anger yesterday after seeing the video of Officer Leah Blunt shooting Raymond James and Dwayne Armstrong in the McDonald's parking lot. Its reaction today, after watching officers of the Los Angeles Police Department and the California Highway Patrol toss their badges in trash barrels in front of City Hall, in front of the mayor and in front of the assembled media, was something different. Anger is usually constrained by some semblance of rationality. There was rationality in yesterday's reaction to the shooting. It was the rationality born of a well-worn narrative, if not a complete understanding of the facts. Another unarmed African American had been shot by police, which was yet another example of the systemic racism inherent in the system. Defund the police! March for social justice! But what happens when there is no precedent for a thing, as when the police walk off their job? Then there is no established narrative. It was the absence of an established narrative, the sheer novelty of the police labor action, that caused the reaction of the Twitterverse to change from anger to outrage. There was something more, too. The police labor action was not only unprecedented, it was taken by the Twitterverse as an act of defiance, a personal affront. How dare the police not prostrate themselves and beg forgiveness for their racist ways! How dare the police pretend "they" are somehow the victims in this shooting of two unarmed African American men! How dare the police demand justice and due process for themselves when they have so obviously denied it to the two men lying dead in the street!

The final ingredient contributing to the outrage of the Twitterverse was the state of the economy. People were struggling to survive, never mind getting ahead. They were frustrated because it seemed the system was rigged against them for the benefit of the well-connected and the wealthy. There was a pervasive, oppressive sense of hopelessness. All these things combined to cause the Twitterverse to become like a wild animal trapped in a cage and provoked to blind fury. It threw its body at the cage walls. It shrieked and howled at the top of its lungs. It lashed out at anything and everything that came near.

Johnny Penn was one of the first to tweet. In addition to being incensed by the defiance of the police labor action, he had another, still more personal reason for outrage. The police labor action had cut short his speech and usurped his time in front of the cameras. He attached a video clip of the police tossing their badges in the trash along with his tweet. "FUCKING DISGUSTING! RACIST, FACIST COPS! WHO DO THEY THINK THEY ARE?!" He immediately followed that tweet with another. "ENOUGH IS ENOUGH! ENOUGH POLICE BRUTALITY! ENOUGH RACISM! ENOUGH WHITE PRIVILEGE AND WHITE COMFORT! ENOUGH OF THIS RACIST COUNTRY!!" Still, he was not finished. "THIS COUNTRY WILL NEVER CHANGE UNLESS WE FORCE IT TO CHANGE. TIME TO STOP ASKING AND START DEMANDING! GET OUT IN THE STREETS! GET IN THEIR FACES! RAISE YOUR VOICES! RAISE YOUR FISTS! SHUT IT ALL DOWN!!! FORCE IT TO CHANGE!!! #NoJusticeNoPeace."

Mayor Rodriguez took to Twitter soon after Johnny Penn. The mayor did not personally tweet. He dictated his tweet to his assistant who typed it in his phone with a few suggested modifications. The mayor's assistant then showed it to the mayor for his approval. The mayor nodded and his tweet was launched. "Sad day for our city! Police officers violating their oath to protect and serve! There WILL BE consequences. We WILL NOT tolerate hate in our city." A minute later, the mayor and his assistant launched a second salvo. "Hope these racist cops like stocking shelves at Walmart, and for a lot less money than six figures!" Finally, there was a third salvo. "Then again, Walmart is too good for them! Who would hire a racist?! NOT ME!!! #JusticeForLosAngeles."

Politically active Hollywood celebrities chimed in to echo the sentiment of Johnny Penn. They all had their followers and, soon, #NoJusticeNoPeace was trending on Twitter. Left-leaning politicians chimed in, too, starting with local politicians who followed the mayor of Los Angeles. Then mayors and councilmen in other California cities expressed their outrage. Then California state legislators. Then the California governor. Then governors from other states. Then representatives and senators in Washington DC. Finally, the president of the United Stated chimed in. "Never thought I would see this in our country! Never thought the police would walk out on their duty to protect and serve! SAD DAY FOR AMERICA!"

The politicians had their followers and they, in turn, had theirs. Some of those followers were activist groups. Others were corporations with a history of social activism. In short order, the outrage spread beyond the borders of the United States. The spokesperson for the Chinese foreign ministry tweeted, "US racism is a cancer on American society." The prime minister of Australia was "shocked and appalled." The diplomatic chief of the EU asked, "When will it finally end?!!!" Together, they made #JusticeForLosAngeles the number one trending topic on Twitter. Other hashtags climbed up the trending chart as well. There was #EndRacismEndAmerica and #EndWhitePrivilegeForever. Then the hashtags turned threatening. The unhinged outrage seemed to feed on itself. #BurnItToTheGround appeared. Then #AllCopsAreBastards. Then #KillAllCops. Finally, there was #KillOfficerLeahBlunt. Twitter monitored the trending hashtags as it usually did. Only this time, it did nothing to censor the threats of violence.

The Twitterverse turned to the practical task of turning unhinged outrage into street protests. There was no central direction, as was usually the case with social media. Street protests developed organically. At Los Angeles City Hall, less than fifteen minutes after the police had dramatically tossed their badges in trash barrels, a small group of twenty-five BLM activists appeared. They tweeted out an invitation to join them with a number of trending hashtags. The inclusion of trending hashtags insured tens of millions of people saw their invitation. A not insignificant fraction of those people lived in Southern California. In turn, another not insignificant fraction of those was motivated to attend. In thirty minutes, there were thousands of protesters at City Hall. In an hour, there were tens of thousands. Other protests developed in a similar manner; in Los Angeles, in other cities in California, in other cities across the United States, and, finally, in other cities around the world.

"I don't like this," said Push to Melissa. The two of them were standing in front of City Hall and surveying the crowd of protesters that filled Grand Park. Grand Park is two blocks of open space—mostly grass with palm trees planted along the border—that stretches out directly in front of City Hall. When they looked up North Spring Street to where the police had assembled in columns only an hour before, they saw that it, too, was filled with protesters in both directions as far as the eye could see.

"What don't you like?" asked Melissa.

"This crowd," answered Push. "Don't like its mood."

"You don't think they have a right to be angry after what happened?"

"Maybe," said Push with a shrug, not believing they did. "I'm talking about something else. The people who came out and protested George Floyd ... I remember them. You could tell they were mostly interested in protesting. These people ..." He searched for the right words. "I think these people are interested in something more."

"Like what?"

"Like trouble."

Melissa had marched in the Floyd protests. She was proud of her participation in them and proud of the people who had marched with her. No one, she remembered, wanted trouble. There was a positive feeling in the crowd, a positive energy because they all believed they were marching for a good and noble cause, because they believed their voices were being heard and their actions would lead to something better. They believed the system would listen to them and change because it had to listen to them and change, because that was the way democracy worked. She had to admit, though, something was different about *this* crowd. The positive feeling was missing, as was the positive energy. The faces, the voices, were mostly angry. Still, she refused to believe the protesters were looking for trouble. She rationalized the anger as justified by events. *Here it is, five years after George Floyd, and nothing has changed! We're back out in the streets protesting against the same thing, police brutality and systemic racism!*

Melissa looked at Push with a patronizing smile. "You're being negative again."

Push did not mind her patronizing. "Yeah," he said. "It's what I do."

"The crowd's bigger now," said Melissa, changing the subject. "Let's do another report. Maybe get the crowd in Grand Park this time."

"Sure," said Push, lifting his camera to his shoulder and positioning himself so Melissa was standing in front of him and the crowd in Grand Park was behind her. He centered her in the camera's viewfinder and watched her lift the microphone with the KNBC logo to just below her chin. "You're on," he said as he pulled the trigger that started filming.

Melissa used her serious reporter's voice like always. "We're here on the steps of City Hall. As you can see behind me, there is a crowd of thousands of people. The crowd fills Grand Park. Normally, Grand Park is where downtown residents go for peace and quiet. They come here for a bit of green in the middle of our city's towering concrete buildings and busy asphalt streets. Today, things are anything but normal. These thousands upon thousands of people, our fellow citizens, have come here to fill Grand Park, and to fill the adjacent street directly in front of City Hall, to express their outrage. They are outraged at the killing of two unarmed African American men here in Los Angeles yesterday afternoon. They are also outraged at the unprecedented event that happened earlier today, a little more than two hours ago, right here in front of City Hall. Officers of the LAPD and CHP labor associations resigned en masse. Officers lined up as if on a parade ground and symbolically tossed their badges in trash barrels. By their action, these officers are refusing to honor and perform their sworn duty, that is, to protect and serve the citizens of our great city, to keep us—"

"Hey!" shouted Melissa.

A white Anonymous face mask filled the viewfinder of Push's camera.

Push took his eye from the viewfinder and looked around the man with the white Anonymous face mask standing directly in front of him. He saw another man in the same white Anonymous face mask standing behind Melissa with his arms wrapped around her. A third man, also wearing a white Anonymous face mask, walked deliberately up to Melissa and fondled her breasts.

"Pig!" shouted Melissa. "Get your hands off me!"

The people standing nearby cheered. They were not cheering Melissa and her attempt at resisting sexual assault. They were cheering the men who were assaulting her. The man holding her from behind picked her up off her feet and headed into the crowd, carrying her with him as he went.

"Melissa!" shouted Push. "Leave her alone!" He dropped his camera and started after her.

The man who first stepped in front of the camera hit Push in the side of the face with a right hook. Push never saw it coming. The blow stunned him but only for an instant. He shook it off and ducked the man's follow-up punch, a left cross coming straight at his face. As the punch sailed past his face, Push drove his right knee hard into the man's groin. The man screamed and doubled over in pain. Push was not finished with him. With both hands, he grabbed the man by the back of his head. He pulled his head down as he simultaneously drove his right knee upward again, as hard as he could, straight into the man's face. He heard a wet smack where his knee impacted the man's face. The man collapsed to the ground. Push stood and stared at him, fists clenched at his sides. He waited to see if the man would get up. The man only rolled about on the ground, moaning in agony through his hands. His hands were holding his shattered nose. Bright red blood oozed between his fingers.

"Push!" screamed Melissa.

Push's head snapped toward the sound of her voice. He spotted her. She was a dozen people deep in the crowd and moving away from him. She was not exceptionally tall but the fact the man had lifted her off her feet made her easy to spot. Her head looked as if it was floating on a sea of heads, the heads of the people in the crowd. The sea of heads undulated back and forth in surging eddies of humanity. Melissa's eyes were locked on his. He saw panic in her face. He bounded after her, pushing people out of the way as he went.

When he finally reached her, the second man, the man accompanying the first man, the man who was carrying Melissa, was standing there waiting for him. He had a baseball bat cocked high up over his right shoulder, ready to swing. "Come on, motherfucker!" he challenged. "Come and get some!"

Push feigned a lunge forward. The man swung the bat and missed. Push lunged a second time, only this time for real. He landed a right cross on the side of the man's jaw. He was rewarded with a loud, sharp snap as if a dry, brittle tree branch was just broken in two. The man dropped his bat and screamed. "You broke my jaw, motherfucker! You broke my fuckin' jaw!"

Push snatched the bat from the ground and held it cocked over his right shoulder. He yelled, "I'll kill you right here, right now, if you don't let her go!" His eyes were locked on the man with the broken jaw. They were cold and narrow. The menace in his voice and the look in his eyes left no doubt in the man's mind Push would do as he threatened.

"Bernie!" yelled the man, now holding the side of his face with one hand and slurring his friend's name because he had a number of broken teeth in addition to a broken jaw. "Let the girl go! Let the girl go 'cause this guy's gonna fuckin' kill me if you don't!"

The man carrying Melissa off into the crowd was the same Bernie who, only three hours earlier, had received an ultimatum from his father to clean up his room, mow the lawn and get Kendra off his property, and get it all done by 6.p.m. or find another place to live. It was not five minutes after his father issued his ultimatum that Bernie made his decision. He would find another place to live. He took great satisfaction in the fact he left home with his room still a filthy mess and the lawn still not mowed. He did, after all, have his principles. He packed a suitcase with clothes, most of which was dirty laundry lying on the floor. The suitcase went in the trunk of his car along with Kendra. Had he been thinking, he would have covered Kendra with a blanket, not out of any concern for her modesty—she was, after all, not just a sex worker but an inanimate, rubber sex worker—but out of concern for his reputation should she be discovered by one of his friends.

Bernie popped the trunk of his car with his two closest friends standing next to him. Contrary to what Bernie told his father, not everyone has a rubber sex doll. His two closest friends did not and let Bernie know in no uncertain terms what they thought about his taste in female companionship. They teased him mercilessly. Bernie turned red with embarrassment. In some strange, twisted mental calculus, Bernie's urgent desire to repair his damaged reputation combined with the sobering realization he was now homeless to convince him grabbing Melissa was a good idea when he saw her reporting at City Hall. He really had no idea what he would do with her once he grabbed her.

"What?!" yelled Bernie, obviously annoyed. "Are you a fuckin' pussy?! You got the bat. Deal with it!"

"I can't! I don't have the bat anymore! Bernie, I'm not kidding! This guy's got my bat and he's gonna fuckin' kill me if you don't let her go!"

"Fuck!" exclaimed Bernie, disgusted.

Melissa came running up to Push a moment later. She wrapped her arms around his waist and held him tightly. "Stand behind me," Push said to her, not taking his eyes off the man with the broken jaw and Bernie, who had just walked up to stand next to his friend. "Take the masks off," said Push evenly to the man with the broken jaw and Bernie.

"Fuck you!" spat Bernie.

Push cocked the bat higher over his shoulder and took a step toward the two of them. The man with the broken jaw had no interest in fighting again. He pulled off his mask and threw it to the ground. Push was surprised to see the man had a baby face. He guessed him to be in his late teens or early twenties. "Now you," said Push, turning toward Bernie.

"Take the fuckin' mask off!" pleaded Bernie's friend. "Take the fuckin' mask off so we can get the hell out of here! I'm telling you, Bernie, this guy ain't kidding! And I need a doctor, man! My fuckin' jaw's broken!"

Bernie ignored his friend. "You're a real big man, aren't you?" There was sneering contempt in his voice.

"How would you know?" asked Push coldly. "You hide behind a mask. You assault a woman. You're nothing but a coward."

"Fuck you!" spat Bernie, not at all interested in listening to a second indictment of his character, the first having come from his father earlier in the day. "Come and make me!"

"Suit yourself," said Push. He cocked the bat again and started toward Bernie.

Bernie was not expecting his challenge to be so readily accepted. Also, the matter-of-fact manner in which it was accepted told him his would-be attacker was not afraid of fighting. He suddenly realized he was in danger of ending up like his friend, with a broken jaw or worse. "Ok, ok!" he said anxiously, holding up his hands in a sign of surrender. He pulled off his cherished Anonymous mask and tossed it to the ground.

Push noticed Bernie was also young, like his friend.

"How come you're so hot about us taking off our masks?" asked Bernie, no longer defiant. He was now only curious.

"Because," said Push, "I never forget a face." He looked at each of them in turn. "And if I ever see either one of you again … I'll kill you."

It took a moment for Push's threat to register with Bernie. No one had ever threatened him with death before, at least not seriously. Push said nothing more. Bernie took Push's silence as his invitation to leave. His friend with the broken jaw needed no further convincing. The two of them disappeared into the vastness of the crowd.

Push turned to Melissa. "You ok?" he asked, looking her over to see if there were any signs of serious injury. He noticed an angry red welt on her left cheek. He also noticed the sleeve of her blouse was ripped and her hair was a mess. He saw nothing more. He gently pushed her hair from her face.

Melissa started to shake. Her eyes grew red and she started to quietly cry.

Push wrapped his arms around her and hugged her tight. "It's ok," he whispered in her ear. "It's ok. I won't let anyone hurt you."

Melissa hugged him back. She focused on his words, on his promise to protect her. She found comfort in his words. She forced herself to breathe slowly, deeply. After a few breaths, she stopped shaking. She whispered in his ear, "I know you won't."

There was an excited shout from a man in the middle of the crowd, not far from where Push and Melissa were standing. "They're storming City Hall!" the man yelled. He held up his phone and shouted again. "They're inside City Hall! They're inside right now! Check it out! Hashtag Storm City Hall!" A palpable sense of excitement rippled through the crowd. Other voices joined in. "We're inside City Hall! Yeah, man! Awesome! Fuckin' awesome, man! Now they'll listen!" More people held up their phones in celebration. Thousands of individual voices coalesced into a low, rumbling roar of approval. The roar grew in volume until it was deafening.

"Come on," said Push to Melissa, speaking loudly in her ear so she could hear him over the crowd.

"What?" she asked, instinctively yelling back. She was still enjoying the security of his arms.

"We're getting out of here."

CHAPTER FIFTEEN

And it came to pass, when Joshua was by Jericho, that he lifted up his eyes and looked, and, behold, there stood a man over against him with his sword drawn in his hand: and Joshua went unto him, and said unto him, Art thou for us, or for our adversaries? And he said, Nay; but as captain of the host of the Lord am I now come. And Joshua fell on his face to the earth, and did worship, and said unto him, What saith my Lord unto his servant?

— "Joshua 5:13-14," KJV

A DOZEN MEN and two women were standing in the multi-purpose room at Wesley's Chapel. It was Wednesday, 6 p.m. The men and women had come in response to Pastor Layton's call for volunteers during his Sunday sermon. Pastor Layton had called for volunteers, for mighty men and women of valor, to step forward and help defend the church and its congregation from the forces of evil he saw gathering about them, forces which he believed were growing steadily stronger. When he issued his call for volunteers, Pastor Layton had no idea how much stronger those forces would become in only a matter of days.

Ten round tables with folding chairs were set up in the multi-purpose room. Each table comfortably sat eight people. A kitchen was attached to the multi-purpose room, separated by a counter. Spread out on the counter were two buckets of Kentucky Fried Chicken and containers of mashed potatoes, gravy, coleslaw and biscuits. Also on the counter were the requisite paper plates, plastic forks, spoons, knives and napkins. The dozen men and two women who answered Pastor Layton's call for volunteers were not, at the moment, interested in food. They were clustered about the iPad one of them had setup on one of the round tables. The iPad was streaming news from the KNBC Sky Cam, the station's dedicated helicopter. The video showed the iconic white tower of Los Angeles City Hall with black smoke billowing from the windows in the lower third of the tower. The streets surrounding City Hall were filled with tens of thousands of people. The KNBC news anchor was visible in his PIP, his picture-in-picture, in the lower righthand corner of the screen. The news anchor was dressed in a suit and tie. His hair was combed back with gel in what had come to be the style for powerful people in business, media and politics, and for people who aspired to be powerful in those endeavors.

The news anchor breathlessly narrated the Sky Cam video from behind his studio desk. "City Hall is on fire! You can see it here live from our KNBC Sky Cam. Los Angeles City Hall is burning. Firefighters have been unable to respond to the fire because tens of thousands of protesters have packed the streets surrounding City Hall. Not only have the sheer number of protesters prevented firefighters from getting near the fire but we have unconfirmed reports firefighters have been fired upon, that firefighters have been the target of gunfire. It is important to emphasize these reports are unconfirmed. Firefighters have also been hampered in their effort to fight the fire by the absence of police support. This absence of police support is the direct result of the unprecedented job action by LAPD and CHP police officers earlier today, which was dramatically initiated when police officers tossed their badges in trash barrels. We want to stress that, as far as we know, most of the protesters at City Hall are peacefully exercising their First Amendment right to protest. They have come to City Hall to peacefully demonstrate against the killing of two unarmed African Americans, and to peacefully demonstrate against the systemic racism that continues to plague our society."

Pastor Layton walked into the multi-purpose room followed by another man. His name was Sam Daniels. He was of medium height and build. In contrast to the news anchor, there was not a trace of gel in his brown hair;

there never had been in all his thirty-eight years of life and, from his style of dress, it was safe to say there never would be. He wore faded jeans, Ariat roper boots and a well washed gray T-shirt that proclaimed "HARD TO KILL" in black letters. His hair fell halfway down his forehead, was casually parted on the left and cut short on the sides so his ears were fully exposed. He had a face that looked young for his age, although it was made to look more mature by a brown mustache and beard. His beard was neatly trimmed and tapered so it came to a point beneath his chin. His skin was deeply tanned because he spent most of his time outdoors. He worked in construction as a carpenter, framing houses.

"Hello," said Pastor Layton. "Is everyone hungry? I should have mentioned in my announcement we'd have dinner. There's KFC in the kitchen. Please, everybody, help yourselves."

"Have you seen the news about City Hall, Pastor Layton?" asked one of the women standing by the iPad, a pained expression on her face. "It's burning!"

"Yes, Ruth," answered Pastor Layton, shaking his head sadly. "Been watching the news all afternoon. Terrible. Just terrible."

"How can this be happening, Pastor Layton?!"

"We'll be talking about that, Ruth. We have lots to talk about tonight. Please, everyone, if I may ask, let's turn off the news and get something to eat."

One of the men reached out and closed the iPad, silencing the voice of the news anchor. The men and women in the room lined up and served themselves in the kitchen. When they were all seated back at the round tables, Pastor Layton blessed the meal. "Bless us, O Lord, and these Thy gifts which we are about to receive from Thy bounty." He paused a moment before continuing with another prayer, one he thought appropriate for the purpose of their meeting. "Heavenly Father, God of Heaven's Armies, You are near us. In this fallen world, in this season of growing strife and deepening shadow, I ask that You give us the wisdom to understand Your Word as it applies to these troubled times. I ask that You grant us the courage to live by Your Word. And, finally, I ask that You grant us the strength to stand up to evil, to confront and defy evil, and, should it be Your will, to destroy evil. I ask these things in the name of Your Son, who, when He was facing the cross, did not falter in His resolve. Amen."

"Amen," echoed the room.

Everyone ate in silence, which was not at all the usual practice for gatherings in the multi-purpose room. Usually, there was banter about work, about school and kids, about fishing and playing golf, about the simple frustrations and joys of living life. Of course, banter was expected for celebratory events like weddings and baptisms. And, while less expected during somber events like funerals, it was still present even then, perhaps as a salve for the grief of losing a loved one, perhaps, too, as a means of reminding family and friends life goes on.

There was no banter today because everyone was anxious. Some were fearful. Riots were bad enough but riots without the thin blue line of police standing between decent, law-abiding people and the rioters served to make the threat of physical violence suddenly very real. No longer was it an abstract threat that happened to someone else, someone who was simply unlucky and found themselves in the wrong place at the wrong time. Now, the threat of physical violence had acquired a palpable, almost physical presence. It was stalking them. It was lurking somewhere just outside their homes, their offices, their church. And not only was it threatening them, it was threatening everyone they knew and held dear: wives and husbands, sons and daughters, fathers and mothers, friends.

One of the older men broke the silence. "Appreciate your prayer, Pastor Layton. We do seem to be in a season of strife."

"Thank you, Ronald," answered Pastor Layton, holding up a finger to ask for a moment as he finished chewing a mouthful of KFC extra crispy chicken breast. "Excuse me," he said when he finished. He wiped his hands with a napkin, pushed his chair back and stood to speak. "You all finish eating. I just want to say a few words about what I see as the mission for this group before turning it over to Brother Sam here. I think you've all met Brother Sam. What you may not know about Brother Sam, because Brother Sam is one of the humblest men I know, is that he was deployed twice to Afghanistan and once to Iraq as an Army Ranger, which makes him far more qualified than me to prepare us and lead us in our mission."

Pastor Layton took his pipe from his left pant pocket. He rarely smoked indoors and would never consider smoking in church. He did not take his pipe from his pant pocket with the intention of lighting it. Instead, he held it by the stem and fidgeted with the bowl, subconsciously going through the routine of packing the bowl with tobacco even though he had no tobacco to pack. His routine, he would freely admit, was a nervous habit.

"Our mission," continued Pastor Layton, "is to defend our church family. Now, that does not mean Brother Sam will be training us to become Army Rangers. I, for one, am way too old and way too fat. I would not last a day in Ranger training. Also, that does not mean we are a substitute for police. Although, as recent events have demonstrated, we cannot always count on the police picking up the phone when we dial 911. So, what does it mean? It means we are men and women who have decided not to leave our fate, the fate of our families and the fate of our church entirely in the hands of others. We are men and women of courage, grit and determination who have taken it upon ourselves to be our own first responders. Why does it make sense for us to do this? Because *we* are already at the scene and no one can respond faster. Because *we* know our people and our church better than anyone. And, most important of all, because *no one* is more motivated than us, the men and women in this room, to place ourselves in harm's way to protect the people we love."

Pastor Layton surveyed the faces of the men and women in the room, gauging their sentiment. He sensed they agreed with his vision for the group's mission. Still, he wanted to make sure.

"Any questions?" he asked. "Please, now's the time. Tell me if you think I've got this all wrong. I've prayed a lot these past few weeks, about this group and its mission, but that doesn't mean I'm not missing the boat. I need you to tell me if we're climbing aboard the Lord's boat or the S.S. Half-baked Pastor Layton."

"I think you've got the Lord's boat," said Ruth with an encouraging smile. "I just wish we'd launched it a little sooner."

"Frankly, Ruth, I wish we had, too. And that's on me."

"I think it's on all of us," added another man, Tom. He said it with an edge to his voice. "Any of us here could have suggested we do something like this a long time ago, have some kind of church security. How many years we been watching these news stories about crazy people shooting up churches? Five years? Ten years? I'll tell you how long. The same number of years we been sitting here shaking our heads and doing exactly nothing except complaining how the world's going to hell! Well, I'm happy we're finally doing something about it … even if it is a little late. And there's something else I want to get off my chest. I've had about enough of this 'turn the other cheek' thing."

"Thank you, Tom," said Pastor Layton. "I appreciate your candor. Believe me, I also struggle with turning the other cheek. I think Sam will be talking about that at length in just a minute. Any other questions?" He looked at each person individually to confirm they had none. Some said no. Others shook their head.

"Ok, with no further questions, I'll turn it over to Sam."

Sam stood up and walked to the front of the room. He carefully placed a single page of notes on the table before him. He surveyed the faces looking up at him, pursing his lips and nodding his head slowly as if satisfied with what he saw. "That was a great discussion," he began, speaking in a loud, confident voice. His voice immediately pumped energy into the room. "And thank you, Tom, for your comment about turning the other cheek. Before we get into the drier stuff about logistics, organization and … yes, there will be training … I want to build on Tom's comment. There's a time and place for everything but I can tell you definitively, based on personal experience, combat *is not* the time and place for turning the other cheek."

Sam paused. He wanted to make sure there were no illusions about their mission and the fundamental fact it involved combat.

"That's right," he continued, "our mission involves combat. Combat is something I know thanks to Uncle Sam, my training as an Army Ranger, and my experience in Afghanistan and Iraq. That knowledge is the reason Pastor Layton asked me to stand up this group, to turn this group into a team that can successfully perform its mission. And what is that mission?"

No one answered.

"Come on, folks," admonished Sam, "Pastor Layton just told us."

"To defend our church family," offered Ruth tentatively.

"Yes! Exactly right! Everyone this time. What's our mission?"

"To defend our church family," answered the room in unison.

"Good!" said Sam, nodding his approval. "And if our mission is to defend our church family, why am I talking about combat?"

"Because defending ourselves requires fighting," said Tom, annoyed. He thought the answer obvious.

"Correct! Thank you, Tom. I jotted down the definition of combat from Merriam Webster." Sam picked up his page of notes and read from it. "Combat. Noun. A fight or contest between individuals or groups." He set his page of notes back down on the table. "Is everyone clear on that? Our mission is to defend our church. Defending our church requires fighting. Fighting is combat."

He saw heads nodding.

"Of course, to successfully defend our church we have to win the fight, which begs the question: How do we win?" He gestured to the room with both arms outstretched. "Anyone?"

"We just win," said Tom. "We make sure we're prepared and then we do what we have to do to win."

Sam nodded. "Tom's answer is basically correct. Thank you, Tom. I'd like to add a little framework to that answer, though, because winning the fight, winning in combat, is something a lot of people have spent a lot of time studying. Four factors are required to be victorious in combat. *The* most important factor is mindset. In the Army, we call it a 'combat mindset,' and that is what I want to spend most of my time talking about today. The other factors, in order of decreasing importance, are tactics, skill and, last but, well, last … gear." Sam smiled. "So, all you guys who are just going out and buying another gun or another box of ammunition every time the world ratchets up a notch in craziness … and if you're not paying attention to any of the other factors … well, you're pretty much wasting your money."

"Would you tell that to my husband," quipped Ruth.

Sam laughed. "Happy to!" He appreciated Ruth's sense of humor. It lightened the mood in the room and he knew from experience teaching Afghan villagers how to fight the Taliban people are less able to retain knowledge when stressed and scared.

"So, what is a combat mindset?" he asked. "First, a combat mindset is choosing to live in reality rather than self-deception. There are evil people in the world, in our world, and they will visit evil upon us if we let them. *That* is reality. Self-deception is thinking evil people only do evil things to someone else, in someone else's neighborhood, in someone else's city, in someone else's country. Second, a combat mindset is being mentally prepared to inflict decisive, devastating and overwhelming violence on evil whenever evil rears its ugly head. Why must you do this? Because *you* do not defeat evil by holding back. You do not defeat evil by attempting to finely calibrate the level of violence *you* must employ to win the fight. You do not defeat evil by thinking this is some kind of movie where you shoot the gun out of the bad guy's hand. Holding back means you are allowing evil to stay in the fight longer. Holding back means you are allowing evil to find the weakness in your defense, or to simply get a lucky shot. If you think you might have a difficult time inflicting decisive, devastating and overwhelming violence on evil, keep this in mind. Evil never holds back. Evil could care less if you are maimed for life and never able to work again. Evil has no qualms about raping your wife and raping your daughter. Evil has no qualms about killing you and everyone in your family if it's expedient, so there are no witnesses, or for the simple entertainment value of it. A combat mindset understands this. A combat mindset understands, when confronting evil, it is kill or be killed."

Sam surveyed the faces in the room. He had been brutally honest because he knew no other way to be. He saw some of the men nodding in agreement while others sat stone-faced. He noticed Ruth looking uncomfortable. He suspected more were uncomfortable than were letting on.

"I know Christians sometimes struggle with the concept of a combat mindset. They find it harsh. I'm not here to sugarcoat things. It is harsh. As Pastor Layton mentioned, I was in the 75th Ranger Regiment. I deployed twice to Afghanistan and once to Iraq. I kicked down doors for a living. To be blunt, I killed bad guys for a living. Yet, I was also a Christian. In fact, I became a Christian *because* I was over there kicking down doors and killing bad guys. That is my testimony for Christ. I found Jesus Christ and became a Christian because I needed Him there by my side. We were doing some pretty harrowing things over there. The Jesus I found and came to know was not this weak, effeminate, Birkenstock-wearing hippie. He was there with me in the trenches. He fought beside me. He gave me the courage to keep on fighting when, frankly, we all knew there was a good chance we might not be coming home. I credit Jesus with saving my life over there, and saving it countless times. How did he do this? He did it by being a strong, courageous and fearless *warrior*."

Sam knew he was shocking these people. He knew he was shocking them because he was telling them something no one had ever told them before. He also knew it was something they needed to hear if they were to have any chance of succeeding in their mission.

"Now, you're probably asking yourself: What Bible are you reading, Sam, because there's no warrior Jesus in my Bible? I can certainly understand your questioning my assertion. We all have our own personal, mental picture of Jesus. It's a product of our environment, our experiences. People who have never been deployed overseas, who have never been shot at, who have never been to war and seen the awful, terrible things you see in war, those people will naturally have a mental picture of Jesus that is more peaceful than mine. There is a picture of Jesus in the big stained-glass window here at Wesley's Chapel, in the sanctuary. It shows Jesus holding a lamb in His arms. A lamb is a baby sheep. Jesus is looking down at this baby sheep and the baby sheep is looking up at Jesus. The expression on the face of Jesus says, 'Don't worry, baby sheep, I'm here with you and it'll be ok.' Now, please don't take this as being disrespectful. I love animals and I believe Jesus loves animals, too. How could he not, right? I'm not saying the peaceful picture of Jesus is wrong, either. What am I saying? I'm saying this: That picture of Jesus is incomplete. Let me ask you all a question which you can answer by a show of hands. How many of you have kids?"

All but one person raised a hand.

"And how many of you have pictures of yourself holding your kids when they were little, say only a few months old?"

Again, all but one person raised a hand.

"Good. Now, if that was the only picture someone had of you, would they have a complete picture of you? Would they know you had other interests? Would they know you loved your wife? Would they know you played golf? That you worked in a hospital? That you served in the military? No, of course not! They would have an incomplete picture of you."

Sam saw heads nodding.

"If you're still giving me the benefit of the doubt and not thinking me an outright heretic, or someone who came back from being deployed with a strange new strain of PTSD, then you're likely wondering where in the Bible it talks about Jesus the warrior, with helmet and greaves, sword and buckler. Show me the money, right? Show me the proof. Show me in Scripture where I can find the picture of Jesus the warrior. Well, I can do that! I like to start with the Book of Revelation. Chapter nineteen tells us Jesus is mounted on a white horse at the head of the armies of heaven. His soldiers are also mounted on white horses. There are flames of fire in His eyes. He is ready to smite nations with a sharp sword, to rule them with a rod of iron."

Pastor Layton raised his hand. "I know you didn't bring your Bibles but I can vouch for that. It really says that about Jesus."

Sam smiled and surveyed the faces in the room. "Believe me, I wouldn't make up Bible stuff, not in church anyway, and definitely not with Pastor Layton in the crowd."

Laughter rippled through the room.

Sam continued. "Ok, you say, but that's in heaven. Jesus was sent down to earth as 'the lamb of God,' as a mere mortal to die for our sins on the cross. Here on earth, you say, Jesus was no warrior. Well, if you're making that claim, I have to ask: Would you have the courage to do what Jesus did here on earth? When Jesus found the money changers in the temple, and the people there selling oxen and sheep and pigeons, He fashioned a whip out of cords. Then He drove them and their animals from the temple because the temple was not a place to exploit the poor; it was a place for worship. Jesus also poured out the coins of the money changers. He also turned over their tables. In other words, He improvised a weapon and then used that weapon to single-handedly drive multiple adversaries from the temple. Sounds like a warrior to me!"

"Sounds like one to me, too!" said Tom, nodding approval.

"Jesus also had the mental strength and mental toughness of a warrior. How many bad asses in Special Forces could fast in the wilderness for forty days and forty nights? I can tell you. Not many! Jesus also preached His message in the face of escalating threats from the Pharisees and Sadducees, culminating in their wanting to crucify Him. Talk about courage! Finally, there was His mission. Jesus was sent by our Father on what could be termed a suicide mission, a suicide mission that did not involve a quick and painless death but a prolonged and painful death, a death by torture.

Jesus was determined to complete His mission no matter the cost, no matter the physical agony. Jesus had the power to abort his mission. He stayed Peter's hand from pulling his sword against the temple guards in the Garden of Gethsemane. He asked Peter, 'Thinkest thou that I cannot now pray to my Father, and he shall presently give me more than twelve legions of angels? But how then shall the scriptures be fulfilled, that thus it must be?' Any history buffs in here?"

Pastor Layton raised his hand.

"Good!" said Sam, pointing at Pastor Layton. "How many soldiers in a Roman legion?"

Pastor Layton grimaced. "You got me, Sam. I really don't know."

"No problem. Not many people do. A legion in the Roman Army had six thousand soldiers. Do the math. Twelve legions of angels are an army of seventy-two thousand." Sam glanced at his notes. "Isaiah 37:36 tells us a single angel slew 185,000 men in a single night. In terms of combat power, Jesus had at his command, that night in the Garden of Gethsemane, the most powerful military force the world has ever known."

Sam paused to let that sink in. That fact had always impressed him. He hoped it also impressed the people in the room.

"I apologize if I turned this talk into too much of a Bible study. I could talk about this stuff for hours. There are many other passages in Scripture that make it clear, at least to me, that Jesus was, and Jesus is, a warrior in the service of His Father's kingdom. I can share those passages with you offline if you're interested. I'll conclude by sharing with you what I've boiled this all down to. It's what I found to be an incredible comfort when I was deployed overseas. It has also been a comfort to me as a civilian since I came back home. Jesus Christ, my Christian brothers and sisters, is not just a lamb. Jesus Christ, my Christian brothers and sisters, is also a lion."

The room was silent.

"Any questions," asked Sam, hoping he had not overwhelmed them with too much, too soon.

"I thought I knew my Bible pretty well," said Ronald, finally. "I really had no idea about all this. Thank you, Sam."

"I was never in the military," said Tom, "but I like your picture of a strong Jesus. I like it a lot more than the hippie one."

"So, Sam," said Ruth, "the bottom line, if I'm understanding you correctly ... Jesus was tough when he needed to be tough ... which means ... What? We need to be tough ... like Jesus?"

Sam thought a moment before answering. "I would not put it that way, Ruth. I think Jesus is the toughest man who ever lived. I do not think any mere mortal man or woman can hope to measure up to His level of toughness. I know I never could. However, I do not say that to be discouraging. I think it's a good thing the captain of the Lord's host is the toughest man who ever lived. Our job is not to be tougher than Jesus. Our job is to be tougher than the enemy. And, with Jesus there by our side ... *That* is something we can be."

CHAPTER SIXTEEN

It's no accident that every dictatorship always tries to break down the family, because it's in the family that you get the strength to be able to fight.

— Rod Dreher, "Live Not by Lies: A Manual for Christian Dissidents"

THE DRIVE HAD been harrowing for Melissa and Push. They decided not to drive back to the KNBC station because crowds of protesters were reported in the area and some of those protesters had taken to smashing storefront windows and torching vehicles. Melissa wanted Push to drive her back to her apartment in Torrance, about a thirty-minute drive south of City Hall if the traffic is good, but he refused to leave her there alone and stranded without her car. "You're coming back home with me," he insisted. "That's all there is to it."

Push lived with his parents in San Pedro, a working-class neighborhood at the far southern end of Los Angeles whose claim to fame is the fact it incorporates the Port of Los Angeles. The Port of Los Angeles is the largest port in the Western Hemisphere as measured by container volume. It accounts for twenty percent of all cargo coming into the United States, mostly from China, Japan and Vietnam. Top imports are furniture, automobile parts, apparel, footwear and electronics. Top exports are wastepaper, pet and animal feed, scrap metal and soybeans. The trade imbalance for the United States is not only evident from the nature of the items being traded—the United States imports manufactured goods and exports raw materials and agricultural products, which is essentially the trade profile of a third world nation—it is also evident from the ratio of import to export container volume. Currently, that ratio is running at three to one; that is, the United States returns one full container for every three it receives. The other two containers go back empty.

The fate of San Pedro and its people had always been inextricably linked to San Pedro Bay and the surrounding Pacific Ocean. The first people to inhabit San Pedro were the Tongva. They migrated to San Pedro thousands of years ago and lived mostly in small coastal villages. The Tongva fished, traded and traveled between villages using large oceangoing canoes. After being settled by the Tongva, San Pedro was "discovered" by the Spanish in 1542, deeded by the Spanish Crown to a retired and well-connected Spanish solider in 1784, placed under the control of the United States in 1848 when the United States defeated Mexico in the Mexican-American War, and, finally, annexed by the City of Los Angeles in 1909.

San Pedro was home port for the United States Navy Pacific Fleet until 1940 when much of the fleet, including the fleet's fourteen battleships, was transferred to Pearl Harbor, Hawaii to deter Japanese aggression. The inadequate deterrent value of the fleet's move was dramatically demonstrated by the Japanese bombing of Pearl Harbor on December 7, 1941. Franklin Delano Roosevelt declared that date "a date which will live in infamy" in a speech before a joint session of Congress. He went on in that speech to request Congress declare war against the Empire of Japan.

Along with the rest of the country, San Pedro devoted itself to the war effort. San Pedro Bay shipyards employed more than ninety thousand workers during World War II, building, repairing and maintaining ships. Four Iowa-class battleships were built during World War II. They were the biggest, fastest and most powerful battleships ever built for the Navy. They were also the last. Their namesake, the USS Iowa, would make her final port call in San Pedro where she would be permanently birthed as a maritime museum. The USS Iowa opened her doors to the public in 2012, more than eighty years after her sister battleships departed San Pedro for Pearl Harbor on the eve of World War II.

San Pedro was also greatly shaped by the fishing industry. The fishing industry in San Pedro began in the early 1900s and rapidly expanded until San Pedro possessed the largest fishing industry in the United States. By 1937, the fishing fleet in San Pedro numbered nearly five hundred boats. There were also fifteen canneries in operation. The fishing industry in San Pedro attracted generations of migrants from countries with fishing and seafaring traditions, primarily Japan, Norway, Croatia and Italy. The Japanese migrants were sent to internment camps in 1942, immediately following the start of World War II. Most never returned. The Croatian and Italian migrants went on to form vibrant, growing communities. They give San Pedro much of its present-day Mediterranean charm. The San Pedro fishing industry reached its zenith during World War II. It declined after the war as the fisheries declined. Today, the canneries are gone, outsourced to low-wage countries. And the once mighty fishing fleet is down to a few dozen boats.

Push's family had no tradition of fishing or seafaring. His father worked as a machinist in Ukraine back when Ukraine was part of the old Soviet Union. His father's father worked on one of Ukraine's vast collective wheat farms. Push's father decided to emigrate to the United States after the Orange Revolution in Ukraine. The Orange Revolution was a series of protests in the Ukrainian capital, Kiev, that started in late November 2004 as a result of a contested presidential election. The protests went on for two months and a day.

Ukraine became an independent country in 1991 following the end of the Cold War and the breakup of the Soviet Union. Ukraine immediately fell upon hard economic times. As happened in many of the republics of the former Soviet Union, the well-connected few bought up the valuable assets of the old Soviet Union, the factories, farms, oil fields and mines. They bought them up at bargain basement prices and became fabulously wealthy as a result. Meanwhile, the average Ukrainian was no longer provided the necessities of life guaranteed under communism, meager though they were.

Push's father did not mind the economic struggle for survival. He was willing to view it as part of the growing pains of a new and independent Ukraine. What made him decide to give up on Ukraine and emigrate to the United States was the political situation. He considered the Orange Revolution, though mostly peaceful, an ominous harbinger of things to come. He believed the country hopelessly divided. The ethnic Ukrainians in the western half of the country wanted Ukraine aligned with the West, including the West's vision of a secular, progressive new world order. The ethnic Russians in the eastern half of the country wanted Ukraine aligned with Russia, which was then emerging from the chaos of the nineties as a champion for national sovereignty and traditional Russian values. Traditional Russian values were those espoused by the Russian Orthodox Church; namely, faith, family and love of country.

It took Push's father two years to be approved for immigration to the United States. Once approved, he set about deciding where in the United States he would live. He decided on Los Angeles for a number of reasons. First, in one of those strange and impossible to explain associations, especially for a young man growing up in a communist country hundreds of miles from the nearest beach, Push's father thought the Beach Boys and the Southern California surfer culture they celebrated in their music the epitome of American culture. Second, Los Angeles was home to one of the larger communities of Ukrainian immigrants in the United States. Last but not least, the Los Angeles aerospace industry was desperate for skilled machinists. Once he determined he would live in Los Angeles, Push's father narrowed it down further to San Pedro. He picked San Pedro because he liked its Mediterranean feel. He also liked the fact it was relatively affordable.

The drive to San Pedro turned harrowing for Melissa and Push as they headed south on the San Diego Freeway. Traffic had been moving at a reasonable speed for the evening rush hour when, suddenly, it slowed to a crawl. Then it stopped.

"Accident?" asked Melissa.

"Maybe," said Push. "See if you can find something on the radio."

Melissa scanned the radio for news. She finally found a radio station talking about the traffic situation on the San Diego Freeway. "We have reports," said the radio announcer, "that a caravan of protesters has stopped their vehicles in the middle of the southbound San Diego Freeway, about five miles from the Harbor Freeway interchange. Several hundred protesters have exited their vehicles and appear to be doing their best to block traffic. Some of the protesters have signs denouncing racism and police brutality. Some of the motorists are attempting to slowly drive through the crowd of protesters, through what is reported to be a gauntlet of angry shouts and angry fists pounding on doors and hoods. Just a minute ... Just a minute ... We have reports a vehicle has driven through the crowd of protesters at a high rate of speed. A number of protesters have, apparently, been hit and run over by this vehicle. We have no information on the number injured or the extent of their injuries. We will, of course, provide you with updates as soon as they are available."

"This is getting crazy," said Melissa with a look of concern. "First City Hall and now this."

"Yes," said Push, also concerned but for a different reason. He was looking at a sea of brake lights stretching out in front of him as far as he could see. They had not moved an inch during the news report. He wanted to use the freeway shoulder to drive to the next exit but the KNBC van was in the middle freeway lane and the lane to his right was full of cars. They, too, were stopped and stacked up bumper to bumper, forming a solid barrier that blocked any access to the freeway shoulder. Push had the distinctly uncomfortable feeling of being trapped.

"Do we just sit here and wait?" asked Melissa.

"Don't think we have a choice," answered Push.

Drivers in front of Push and Melissa began opening their car doors. Some stood on the pavement by their open doors. Others stood on the door sill to gain a more elevated perspective. In either case, they were hoping to spot the reason for traffic coming to a complete stop. Many of the people gazing at the endless line of cars were also on their cell phones, including a man standing beside his gray BMW 750 luxury sedan just three cars in front of Push and Melissa. The man was dressed like he was heading home from work. He wore tan slacks and a classic oxford button-down shirt in French blue whose gold cufflinks glittered in the setting sun. Both his vehicle and his manner of dress made it obvious he was a wealthy man. He looked to be in his sixties given the generous quantity of gray in his jet-black hair and the pronounced laugh lines on his clean-shaven face.

A young man in an oversized white Lakers jersey ran up to the wealthy man from the side and a little behind. The wealthy man never saw him coming. The man in the Lakers jersey sucker punched the wealthy man in the side of the head. The wealthy man fell to the ground beside his BMW. He lay on the ground motionless.

"Oh my God!" said Melissa, clasping her hand to her mouth in shock. "Did you see that?! That guy just ran up and hit him!"

"I saw it," said Push, also shocked.

"What do we do?" asked Melissa.

"What can we do?" asked Push, frustrated. His knuckles turned white as he squeezed the van's steering wheel.

They watched the man in the Lakers jersey grab the wealthy man's phone lying on the pavement near his outstretched arm. The man in the Lakers jersey stuffed the phone in his pant pocket. Then he started going through the pockets of the wealthy man. He found the wealthy man's wallet and stuffed it in another of his pant pockets. Finally, he started relieving the wealthy man of his jewelry. He pulled his watch from his wrist, his wedding band from his left ring finger and, finally, his gold cufflinks from his shirt cuffs.

"We have to do something!" said Melissa.

Push's calculating, logical mind knew the smart thing to do was to keep doing what they were doing, which was nothing. He was responsible for getting Melissa to safety, which meant getting her back to his house. Looking for a fight that was not looking for him was not the best way to go about that. He also knew he had to live with himself. He made up his mind. "Stay here," he said tersely.

"What?" asked Melissa, suddenly anxious. "What are you doing?" She wanted him to do something but, also, did not want him leaving her alone. She shivered involuntarily at the memory of the man in the white Anonymous face mask lifting her off the ground and carrying her away against her will.

"Something stupid," Push answered flatly. He pushed open the van door. "Lock the doors behind me."

"Push!" she hollered by way of objection as he walked away. Then, a moment later, she added, "Be careful!"

Push walked up to the trunk of the BMW and stopped. The man in the Lakers jersey had climbed part way into the BMW through the open driver's door. He had one knee on the driver's seat as he searched the center console. Even though Push had not heard Melissa's admonition to be careful, he was determined to be just that. He would not challenge the man in the Lakers jersey for his act of assault and robbery. He would let the man take whatever he wanted. His priority was rendering first aid to the victim.

"I think the guy's hurt bad," said Push.

The man in the Lakers jersey jumped out of the BMW. He landed with both feet on the ground and spun around to face Push. He was obviously startled. He looked to either side of Push to see if Push was alone or if he had come with friends. When he saw Push was alone, he relaxed. He relaxed because *he* had come with friends, three of them to be precise, in the lowrider 1985 Monte Carlo two car lengths back behind the BMW and one lane over, in the passing lane. He knew his friends were watching. He also knew they had his back if he needed them because they were his homeys.

The man in the Lakers jersey lifted his chin so he could look down at Push in his well-practiced ritual for establishing dominance on the street, all without uttering a word. He reinforced his lifted chin dominance ritual with a second ritual, his "head cocked like a curious dog" ritual. He was, in fact, mildly curious. He was wondering if this guy in front of him had the balls to fight or if he was just some pussy who was only interested in helping some stupid old rich guy.

"The guy's not moving," said Push, nodding toward the wealthy man lying motionless on the ground. "I just want to check and see if he's ok."

"What's he to you?" sneered the man in the Lakers jersey. "He your fuckin' old man?"

"He's nothing to me," said Push with a shrug. "Just looking to help."

"Fuck," spat the man in the Lakers jersey. "You want to help? How 'bout helping me out with a little cash? What you got in your wallet, man?"

Push's face flushed hot as adrenaline pumped into his body. Things were not going the way he hoped. He took slow, steady breaths to try and calm himself. "I have some cash," he said. "How 'bout we make a deal? I'll give you all the cash in my wallet and you let me help this guy."

"Can't agree to a deal like that," said the man in the Lakers jersey, "not before I know how much you got."

Push pulled out his wallet and then the cash inside. "This is what I got," he said, sounding angry despite his best effort not to. "I've got more than two hundred dollars here."

The man in the Lakers jersey hauled off and kicked the wealthy man in the side.

The wealthy man convulsed in a coughing fit.

Push stifled an instinct to charge the man in the Lakers jersey. He forced his attention back to the wealthy man on the ground. *At least he's alive,* thought Push. *Dead men don't cough.*

The man in the Lakers jersey shook his head as though he was deeply disappointed. "Not enough, man." A crooked smile crept across his face. "Listen, I got an idea. How 'bout you come with me and my homeys? I got three of 'em in my Monte Carlo. Then we go get some cash from your ATM."

Four against one, thought Push, no longer interested in remaining calm. He decided a fight was inevitable. *And the guys in the car probably have guns.* A grim, determined look appeared on his face. *Well, if you have to go down fighting, go down fighting!*

Push threw his wad of cash in the air and yelled at the man in the Lakers jersey. "I ain't getting in your piece of shit Monte Carlo! What?! You and your faggot friends suckin' each other off in your piece of shit Monte Carlo?! That's what you do when you're not sucker punching helpless old men, right?! You think you're man enough to fight me?! Shit! I think you're nothing but a punk-ass bitch! Come on, bitch! You wanna fight me or you wanna run back and hide behind your faggot-ass friends?!"

The man in the Lakers jersey was shocked at the torrent of insults. Then he was enraged. No one talked to him like that in front of his homeys. Veins bulged in his neck and forehead as his face turned red. He yelled, "I'm gonna fuckin' kill you, motherfucker!!!" He backed up his threat by pulling a flip knife from his pocket. He ran at Push with the deadly blade cocked high overhead.

Push had hoped his trash talking would rattle the guy, getting him to fight stupid instead of smart. He had not expected the knife. He jumped to the side of the BMW and ran around it, desperately trying to keep the mass of the car between him and the knife-wielding man in the Lakers jersey.

"KABLAM!"

The concussion of the gunshot startled Push. He instinctively looked toward the gunshot and saw a young man with a pump shotgun standing by a blue Honda Civic. The pump shotgun was aimed at the sky as the young man racked a fresh round into the chamber. He pulled the trigger a second time.

"KABLAM!"

The young man immediately racked another round into the chamber. Then he lowered the shotgun until it was pointed at the man in the Lakers jersey. A thin wisp of white smoke curled up from the muzzle.

The man in the Lakers jersey was even more startled than Push. Not only was he startled by the sudden concussion of the gunshots, he was startled by the sight of the gaping black muzzle now pointed directly at his chest.

"Drop the knife!" ordered the young man.

"Who the fuck are you?!" demanded the man in the Lakers jersey.

"Just a guy with a twelve-gauge," answered the young man, "pointed at your chest. You can drop the knife or I can drop you. Your choice."

By the way he said it, Push had no doubt the young man meant it. The man in the Lakers jersey also had no doubt. He dropped the knife.

"Good," said the young man. "Now, get back in your car and stay there. I see you or any of your buddies getting out of the car, I start shooting. You feeling me?"

The man in the Lakers jersey did not answer. He only glared at the young man.

"I'm waiting," said the young man.

The man in the Lakers jersey ignored him. If looks could kill, his would.

"KABLAM!"

The blast from the shotgun blew out the window of the BMW. The man in the Lakers jersey jumped sideways as shards of shattered glass flew past his face.

The young man racked the slide to chamber another round.

"Ok, ok, ok!" stammered the man in the Lakers jersey. "I'm going back to the car! You fuckin' happy now?!"

"I'm fuckin' happy," said the young man.

The man in the Lakers jersey started back to his car. He walked quickly, nervously glancing over his should as he went.

The young man pulled a shell from the side saddle velcroed to the left side of the shotgun's receiver. The side saddle held seven shells. He loaded the shell into the tubular magazine through the loading port in the bottom of the shotgun's receiver, just in front of the trigger guard. He did that two more times to replace the three rounds he fired. As he loaded the shotgun, he never took his eyes from the man in the Lakers jersey. He tracked him the whole time with the muzzle of the shotgun, keeping hold of the shotgun's stock with a proper firing grip, his trigger finger resting comfortably on the side of the receiver where it was ready to slide down to the trigger in a fraction of a second and then pull the trigger to discharge a round with six pounds of pressure. He did all that by rote muscle memory, without a conscious thought other than one: He would shoot this guy if he made a threatening move.

He never did. The man in the Lakers jersey climbed in the Monte Carlo and slammed the door behind him.

"Thanks," said Push. "I think you saved my ass."

"I think so, too," said the young man. He glanced over at Push and grinned before looking back at the Monte Carlo. "Don't trust these assholes. Anyone who would sucker punch an old guy like that … You wanna check on him? I'll just keep an eye on these assholes so they don't get any ideas."

"I will! Thanks!"

Push knelt down by the wealthy man and touched him on the shoulder. "You ok, sir?! Sir?!" Push felt completely and totally out of his element. Even though he had spent years studying martial arts, he had never taken a class on first aid, much less a class on trauma care.

The wealthy man groaned.

"You need to wake up, sir!" said Push.

The wealthy man convulsed in another coughing fit.

Melissa! thought Push. He remembered she studied nursing before switching to journalism. He ran back to the KNBC van and motioned for her to join him.

Melissa knelt down by the wealthy man, grateful there was not much blood. Blood was the reason she abandoned nursing. She could not stomach the sight of it. She suspected a concussion, both from the fact he had been punched in the side of the head and from the fact he had likely hit his head when he fell to the ground. She placed her ear by his mouth to listen for breathing. His breathing was slow and steady. She grabbed his wrist to feel for a pulse. It was fast but strong. "Pull his arms up over his head," she said to Push. "We need to roll him on his side so he doesn't aspirate if he vomits."

Push did as he was told.

Melissa turned to Push once the wealthy man was on his side. "That's all I can do," she said. "He needs a hospital. We should try 911."

"You serious?"

"I know, I know, the police are out on strike. Let's just give it a try."

Push took out his phone and dialed. He held the phone up to Melissa's ear when the call went through. There was a recorded message. "All our lines are busy at the moment. If this is an emergency, please stay on the line and your call will be answered by the next available operator. The wait time is approximately …" There was a brief pause as the dispatch computer calculated the time based on the number of calls, the average duration of each call and the number of operators. "Fifty-five hours and forty-three minutes."

Melissa shook her head in disgust. "He really needs a hospital. He could have internal bleeding. His brain could be bleeding!"

"Torrance Memorial is not far. We can get him there if we can just get off this damn freeway!"

Push walked over to the young man with the shotgun. Three other men were standing with him now. They had all come forward and volunteered to help once the man in the Lakers jersey was back in his Monte Carlo. One of the men had a pistol visible in a holster on his belt.

"The guy's alive but unconscious," said Push. "He needs a hospital. We can lay him out flat in the back of our van but we still need a way off the freeway. If we can just get to the shoulder, we can take the shoulder to the next exit, which is Hawthorne Boulevard. Torrance Memorial is a couple miles down Hawthorne, off Lomita Boulevard."

"Sounds like a plan," said the young man. "We'll help you get him loaded in the van. Then we'll clear a lane so you can access the shoulder. I'll give you an escort to the hospital."

"You a cop?" asked Push, astonished the young man would sign on to his plan without hesitation, taking it all in stride as if the situation was no different than running to the grocery store for a quart of milk.

"Nope."

"Military?"

The young man smiled. "Just a guy with a twelve-gauge … trying to be a good citizen."

"The world could use a few more citizens like you!" said Push, meaning it sincerely. "Mind if I ask your name?"

"Walter."

Push extended his hand. "Push," he said.

"Push?" asked Walter, not sure he heard him right.

"It's short for Pushilin."

Walter released his grip on the shotgun long enough to shake Push's hand. "Nice to meet you, Push."

Push pulled a business card from his wallet and handed it to Walter. "Let's keep in touch, ok? You need anything … you call me. I'm serious. Anything."

Walter smiled. "I will."

CHAPTER SEVENTEEN

Civil war? What does that mean? Is there any foreign war? Isn't every war fought between men, between brothers?

— Victor Hugo

MELISSA AND PUSH drove the rest of the way to Push's home in San Pedro without incident. Their drive was without incident only when considered in a relative sense, that is, compared to the incident on the San Diego Freeway when Push was chased by a man with a knife intent on ending his life. They first stopped at Torrance Memorial hospital to drop off the wealthy man. He was still unconscious. The scene at the emergency room was chaotic. The number of injured people waiting to be treated overflowed the waiting room and stretched down the hallway. People sat in chairs in the first half of the line. After that, the hospital had run out of chairs. Or the staff had run out of people not otherwise occupied and willing to bring down additional seating. People simply sat on the floor or stretched out on the floor with their head on the lap of a loved one, or on a balled-up jacket. Hands and arms and legs were, here and there, bandaged with white gauze. Some of the faces were bruised and bloodied. The people waiting were mostly silent. They sat and stared at the white hallway wall opposite them with tired, worried expressions. There was also the occasional quiet moan and muffled sob. Back on the San Diego Freeway, after Push and Melissa had loaded the wealthy man in the KNBC van, it occurred to Push the man had no wallet; the man in the Lakers jersey had taken it. Push ran back to the BMW and grabbed the man's registration from the glove compartment. At least, he thought, they could give the hospital some identification so the hospital could contact the man's family.

Leaving the wealthy man in the care of Torrance Memorial hospital, they took Hawthorne Boulevard south toward San Pedro. Traffic moved along as it normally did for rush hour, which was a relief after being trapped on the freeway. A mile down on their right was the South Bay Galleria, an upscale shopping mall. All appeared normal from a distance. As they approached closer, they noticed a crowd of people by the front entrance. Then they noticed the people streaming into the Galleria were empty-handed while the people streaming out had their arms full. Some carried heaps of clothing. Others carried stacks of boxes.

"Looting?" asked Melissa.

"Looks like it," said Push, "or one hell of a sale. What happened to the Hawthorne police?"

"The blue flu?" offered Melissa. She had heard rumors of sickouts by sympathetic police officers in departments all across Southern California. The police officers in those departments were calling in sick in a show of support for their fellow officers in the LAPD and CHP.

The same scene greeted them a little further south on Hawthorne Boulevard, this time on the left, at a shopping center with a Walmart Neighborhood Market, a Marshalls and a Trader Joe's. Then they saw it again, the same scene, after another half mile, at Macy's and Nordstrom's. They found the scene repeated with depressing regularity at every major shopping center they passed. Apparently, a good percentage of the citizens of Los Angeles saw the absence of law enforcement as an opportunity not to be missed, either out of economic desperation or mere opportunism.

The looting suddenly disappeared when they crossed East Pacific Coast Highway. It disappeared with the last of the major shopping centers. The stores south of East Pacific Coast Highway were smaller retail stores. They were not targeted for looting for the simple reason they were less lucrative targets. Why loot nail polish from a nail salon when you could carry off a big screen TV from Best Buy? There was another reason, too, why the small stores were not targeted. That reason was as jarringly obvious to would-be looters as it was to Push and Melissa as they drove by. Armed store owners were standing guard in front of their stores.

"Reminds me of Mexico," said Push when he first noticed the store owners with guns. "Took a couple trips down to Vera Cruz and I always remember that, the armed security standing in front of stores."

"How come there's no security at Macy's?" asked Melissa. "And at all those other big box stores? They can certainly afford it."

"Different motivations," said Push. "The big box stores are run by corporations. The corporations hire managers who have no personal interest in the store and its merchandise. It's just a paycheck for them. And they know the corporations have insurance. These mom-and-pop stores … Each one of those little stores represents … What? A lifetime of work? And I'll bet you a lot of those stores don't have insurance."

Push turned left onto Palos Verdes Drive North. They were on the Palos Verdes Peninsula, which is as close to rural as you can get in Southern California. Equestrian trails bordered the road along with white equestrian fences. To their right was the entrance to Rolling Hills Estates, one of the wealthiest communities in the country. Rolling Hills Estates is a private, gated community. Push had never driven through it. He knew no one who lived there and, as a consequence, had never been invited to visit. He noticed five private security cars parked by the guard shack at the front entrance. Usually, there was only one.

Finally, they turned right onto Western Avenue. They were in San Pedro now. San Pedro was mostly quiet. They noticed smoke from a fire off in the distance, in the direction of downtown. They also witnessed an instance of looting, but only one. It was when they passed Ralphs' supermarket. The parking lot there was in complete and total chaos as people pushed shopping carts overflowing with groceries as fast as they could to their vehicles. Their vehicles were parked without regard for the parking spots delineated by freshly painted white diagonal lines on jet-black asphalt. The first thought of the drivers seemed to be to get as close as possible to the store entrance to facilitate the loading of their ill-gotten bounty. The second thought seemed to be to exit the parking lot as quickly as possible, and at the highest possible rate of speed, in case the police suddenly suffered some sudden attack of guilt and returned to work in time to thwart their getaway.

When they turned onto 19th Street, they were greeted by a spectacular view. There it was in all its splendor, the Port of Los Angeles. They saw mountains of carefully stacked shipping containers, forests of giant container cranes at the water's edge and, finally, the deep blue water of the bay itself dotted with the leviathans of the open ocean. The leviathans were presently slumbering at anchor inside the breakwater, at the edge of the horizon, awaiting their turn to unload still more containers.

Push's house was on the left, just three blocks down. It was a neat single-story home with beige stucco walls and a red tile roof. A stunning red bougainvillea was planted to the right of the front door. The front door was painted red like the bougainvillea and set back in a portico with an arched entranceway and arched windows on either side. A brick walkway led from the sidewalk to the entranceway through the middle of a small, neatly manicured yard. There was no grass to manicure as was the norm in Southern California due to the persistent drought and the draconian restrictions on watering outdoors. Green boxwoods and copious quantities of a small sage-colored shrub with purple flowers were planted in a bed of gray pea stone.

A dog barked ferociously as Push and Melissa climbed the few stairs to the portico.

"Ginger!" scolded Melissa. "You remember me!"

The barking stopped.

Push's father, Mr. Pushilin, opened the door. He was bald, had a strong, square Slavic face and was dressed in his usual "wife beater" T-shirt. "Melissa!" he said, surprised to see her. "Come in! Come in!" Mr. Pushilin's accent was much more pronounced than Push's. He hugged her with genuine affection.

Ginger started barking again. This time, it was her excited "pay attention to me" bark. Melissa knelt down and scratched Ginger's ears. Ginger grunted and groaned in ecstasy. Then she looked up at Melissa with adoring eyes. Her tail slapped energetically against Melissa's leg.

Mrs. Pushilin was sitting on the sofa watching television. She was an attractive woman who looked young for her age. Her eyes were blue and her hair auburn. She wore a light-colored sundress. She stood up and hurried over to the door. "Melissa!" she exclaimed, also with a heavy accent. "What a surprise! So good to see you!" She, too, hugged Melissa with genuine affection. "It's been too long, my dear! Have you been taking care of yourself?"

Melissa laughed. "Trying," she said.

"I know. I know. My Melissa is still working too much. Push tells me all about you."

"He does?" asked Melissa.

"Mom!" said Push, embarrassed by his mother.

"Yes, he tells me how you do nothing but work and go out with these guys who do not deserve you."

"Mom!" said Push still more sharply, now annoyed as well as embarrassed.

"He says that?" asked Melissa, looking over at Push with a coy smile.

"Come and sit down," said Mr. Pushilin, motioning them toward the sofa. "You want something to drink?" He looked at Push. "We were starting to worry. You're late and you didn't call. With all this insanity ..."

"Sorry, Dad. I should have called. Yeah, a beer would hit the spot."

"Melissa?" asked Mr. Pushilin.

"Anything with alcohol," she answered. "It's been one of those days."

"Some homemade wine?" asked Mr. Pushilin. "The zinfandel we put up last year is aged just about right. And, in my humble opinion, it's the best we've made."

"Sounds great!" said Melissa, thinking it really did. She missed Push's parents. They had always treated her like family.

Mrs. Pushilin returned from the kitchen with a platter of antipasto. There were olives, mushrooms, cheeses, prosciutto ham and, of course, bread. She set the platter down on the coffee table in front of the sofa. She made a second trip to the kitchen and returned with bread plates, napkins and forks. "Eat," she encouraged Melissa as she sat down next to her. "You young American girls are too skinny!"

Melissa suddenly realized she was famished. She had not eaten since breakfast. Not only was that a solid twelve hours ago but the stress of the day had served to burn its share of calories as well. She filled her plate with a generous helping of everything.

KNBC news was on the television. Push's parents always watched KNBC news because they considered it their son's television station. They thought that even though he was only a cameraman. "We saw your report from City Hall," said Mrs. Pushilin, "when the police threw their badges in the trash. So sad what's happening to our city! We did not see any more of your reports after that. That's what started us worrying."

Mr. Pushilin returned with the wine and beer. He pointedly ignored the news on the television, which was now showing a live picture of City Hall. The smoke was less pronounced compared to earlier in the day. The fire had consumed most of the combustibles in the building. Judging by the scorched black lintels above the windows on the building's iconic white façade, the fire had traveled all the way up the central tower and all the way out along both wings of the base. The red and yellow chyron at the bottom of the screen proclaimed, "City Hall destroyed by fire."

Mr. Pushilin poured a sample of zinfandel and handed it to Melissa. She closed her eyes and took a sip. When she swirled it around her mouth, she tasted raspberry and cinnamon. She also felt it stick to her teeth and cover her tongue with a thick cotton cloth. When she swallowed, she was rewarded with a smooth, slightly sweet encore from the raspberry and cinnamon along with a hint of oak from the aging barrel. She felt a sensation of warmth spread from the pit of her stomach up through her torso and out into her face.

Melissa opened her eyes and beamed at Mr. Pushilin. "*That,*" she said definitively, "is the best thing I've ever tasted!"

Mr. Pushilin laughed and nodded with satisfaction. "Good. We made a hundred gallons last year so you must help us drink it." He filled Melissa's glass to the brim. Then he filled his wife's glass and his own.

"So tell us," said Mrs. Pushilin, "were you there when it started, the fire at City Hall?"

"No," answered Melissa. "Things were getting dicey, which is why I'm forever in your debt, yours and your husband's."

"For what?" asked Mrs. Pushilin, not understanding.

"For raising your son to be such a strong, courageous man! These creeps were giving me a hard time and Push came to my rescue."

"Are you ok?" asked Mrs. Pushilin, suddenly concerned.

"I'm ok. My blouse ..." She pointed at the torn sleeve. "Not so good."

"They were wearing masks," said Push. "Came up behind Melissa and just grabbed her. Then this one creep starts walking off with her!"

"Proud of you, son," said Mr. Pushilin, squeezing his son's knee with affection.

"Then there was this older guy on the San Diego Freeway," said Melissa. "Traffic was stopped and this gangbanger comes running up behind him. He slugs the guy in the head! Knocks him out cold! Push saved him, too. That makes him a hero twice over. First, he rescued me, then he rescued this older guy."

"Actually," said Push, "another guy gets the credit there. His name is Walter. I owe him big time for his help."

Push saw no reason to alarm his parents with the details, like how the gangbanger in the Lakers jersey pulled a knife on him and how he might not be sitting here if Walter had not intervened with his twelve-gauge. Mr. Pushilin suspected his son was omitting part of the story. He decided he would ask him about it later when it was just the two of them.

Push continued. "Walter helped us get this guy loaded in the van and then opened a lane so we could get him off the freeway and over to Torrance Memorial."

Johnny Penn appeared on the television. A crowd of reporters had microphones thrust at his face. As always, he was immaculately dressed in a suit and tie.

"Oh my God!" said Melissa. "It's Johnny! Can you turn it up?"

Below Johnny's face, the chyron declared, "Penn calls for protests at Officer Blunt's house."

"Why would you want to listen to this terrible person?" asked Mr. Pushilin, remembering Johnny Penn's speech from yesterday. He thought Johnny Penn directly responsible for the subsequent riots and the destruction of City Hall.

"Dad," said Push, the barest hint of a smile on his face, "that's Melissa's new boyfriend."

Mr. Pushilin looked at his son in disbelief. Then he looked at Melissa in the hope she would set her son straight about what must be some kind of joke, and one he thought not at all funny.

Melissa smiled uncomfortably. "I would not say boyfriend. We had one date. I think he's nice and I like him. I think he likes me, too."

Mr. Pushilin shook his head sadly. He grabbed the remote and turned up the volume. Johnny Penn's voice filled the Pushilin living room. "The mayor has called for the arrest of Officer Leah Blunt for the murder of Raymond James and Dwayne Armstrong. These two unarmed African Americans were murdered by a member of law enforcement who swore an oath to protect and serve all of us, not just the privileged, not just the people of one particular race, but all of us, every American. The police job action earlier today is a blatant attempt to obstruct justice. They think they can intimidate us by walking off the job. Well, I'm here today to tell them we will not be intimidated! We know where Officer Leah Blunt lives. I am calling on all Americans who will not be intimidated to join me tomorrow, at noon, for a march to Officer Leah Blunt's house. There we will make our voices heard. We will demand justice for Raymond James and Dwayne Armstrong. We will show Officer Blunt there is no place she can hide, nowhere she can go to escape justice. We will show these racist police officers theirs is not the ultimate power, that the ultimate power resides with the people. And, most important of all, we will show the world that Raymond James and Dwayne Armstrong did not die in vain, that there is a new generation of Americans determined to create a country we can be proud of, a country where 'justice for all' is not an empty slogan, a country dedicated to what should have been and what will be going forward, our new founding creed: diversity, equity and inclusion for all! I will be there tomorrow to help make history. I hope you'll be there with me. Details regarding the time and place for this historic protest are available on my Twitter page, @JohnnyPenn. Thank you!"

Mr. Pushilin turned the television off. He was visibly upset and muttering something in Russian.

"Papa!" objected Mrs. Pushilin. "Not in front of Melissa! I know she does not understand the Russian but … still … such language!"

"No, she does not understand the Russian. There is a lot she does not understand! So, let me translate. And I'll leave out the bad words. I said Johnny Penn is an arrogant, ignorant fool who has no idea what he's doing. He's dowsing this country, and himself, in gasoline!" Mr. Pushilin drank down the wine in his glass as if it was water and then filled it again from the bottle on the coffee table. He looked hard at Melissa. "You young people in this country …" He shook his head. "You take so much for granted. Well, I will tell you something you do not want to hear. Because of *that* man on the television, *that* Johnny Penn, and many more like him, war is coming to America. And it is the worst kind of war you can imagine. It will be a war between brothers. It will be a war that pits neighbor against neighbor. I know you can't see it because, if you could, you would want nothing to do with that posturing piece of …" He stopped himself from swearing. "That … Johnny Penn."

"Papa!" scolded Mrs. Pushilin.

Mr. Pushilin ignored his wife. "How can *I* see it, you ask? I will tell you. *I* see it because I've seen it before. You remember we come from Ukraine, no? Well, do you remember a civil war destroyed Ukraine? What is Ukraine now? A shadow of what it was. Half is part of Russia. The other half is a little landlocked rump state. So many dead. So many wounded. So many refugees who will never again see their home. And why?" Mr. Pushilin gestured at the television with disgust. "Because of people like him!"

Melissa respected Mr. Pushilin. They had often discussed current events when she and Push were a couple. She knew him to have a thoughtful, inquiring mind. He could be passionate in their discussions but he focused his passion on the logic of the argument and the facts. He had never once attacked her personally, which is why his comment about there being a lot she did not understand took her aback. She asked tentatively, "What exactly is it about Ukraine that's the same as our country, that makes you think civil war is coming here?"

Mr. Pushilin took another gulp of wine. He leaned back in the sofa, his anger spent. "It's the same playbook," he said with a sad smile. "The sacred victim. The martyr. The noble cause. And, most important of all, the demonized opposition. It's always easy to hate the devil, is it not? People need to hate the enemy. We had our civil war, in Ukraine, because the two sides hated each other. How much did they hate each other? I will give you an example. And this is just *one* of many. It was 2014, in Odessa, just after the Maiden revolution established a new government in Kiev. Anti-government protesters were driven into this building by pro-government protesters. It was an old building from Soviet times called the Trades Union Building. These anti-government protesters were genuinely peaceful protesters, by the way, not like the other side. The pro-government protesters proceeded to set the building on fire by throwing Molotov cocktails through the windows. Some of the anti-government protesters tried to escape the flames by running out of the building. They were caught and beaten by the pro-government protesters. Then they were shot. Or, to be more precise, they were executed. Others jumped from the upper story windows to try and escape the flames. Those not killed by the fall were also beaten and executed. Upwards of a hundred anti-government protesters died that day, including women and children. Then, when news of the massacre was announced by the government back in Kiev, do you know what the people there did?"

Melissa shook her head.

"They cheered."

"That's horrible!" said Melissa, thinking it really was.

"Yes, it was horrible. It was after that massacre that … well … the rest of my family back in Ukraine decided they had no choice. If they did not fight them, the pro-government people, they would be killed. Or they would lose their freedom and become second-class citizens in their own country. A lot of the people in eastern Ukraine came to the same conclusion: fight or perish. And that was that. We had our civil war."

"But that has nothing to do with Johnny's call for social justice!"

"What I'm trying to say, my dear Melissa, is this … Johnny Penn's side already has their sacred victims, their martyrs. It's those two men who were shot by police the other day. They also already have their noble cause, which is ending systemic racism. Finally, they have their demonized opponent, which is anyone opposed to their vision of a socially just America—the haters, the racists."

"That's supposed to be us," said Push, looking at Melissa.

"Yes," said Mr. Pushilin. "That's what they call us. They're not interested in compromise, Johnny Penn's people. They're not interested in resolving differences politically within the framework of the Constitution. They believe themselves to be our moral superiors so, naturally, how can they compromise? You do not compromise with moral defectives, right? With deplorables and irredeemables? They're committed to complete and total victory, which means they're committed to our unconditional surrender. Or, if we do not surrender unconditionally, our complete and total annihilation."

"How 'bout our side?" asked Push. "When do we choose war?"

"I cannot give you a date. The date will be determined when the conditions are met. We have our noble cause, which is defending the Constitution. We also have our demonized opponent, which is Johnny Penn and his fellow social justice warriors … because we know they are seeking to destroy the Constitution and our way of life. What's missing, then?"

"Our martyrs," answered Push.

"Exactly. There were no fatalities today when City Hall burned, which makes what happened there different from what happened at the Trades Union Building in Odessa. Plus, the City Hall employees are not … How should I put this? They are not on our side. But what about tomorrow when Johnny Penn shows up in front of Officer Blunt's house with thousands upon thousands of protesters, the same people who just burned City Hall? Maybe Johnny Penn then does for us what we cannot do for ourselves. He gives us our martyr."

"Officer Leah Blunt," said Melissa.

"Maybe more than one," said Mr. Pushilin. "Maybe we get her family, too, and anyone who tries to defend her and her family. Then, once we have our martyrs …"

"Our side goes to war," said Push.

"That's a frightening thought," said Melissa. "There has to be a way to stop this! I'm not interested in going to war!"

"Then pray for a miracle," said Mr. Pushilin with a fatalistic shrug. "Pray our leaders suddenly acquire a sense of humility. Pray they suddenly realize how close we all are to the edge of the abyss."

"Is that what you pray for?" asked Melissa.

Mr. Pushilin nodded solemnly. "It is."

"I've never been much for praying," said Melissa, "but the world could use a healthy dose of humility."

"There's something else I pray for," said Mr. Pushilin.

"What's that?" asked Melissa.

"I pray for victory in the event it comes to war."

BOOK II

THE SOUTH CHINA SEA

CHAPTER ONE

We repeat again: strength of character does not consist solely in having powerful feelings, but in maintaining one's balance in spite of them. Even with the violence of emotion, judgment and principle must still function like a ship's compass, which records the slightest variations however rough the sea.

— Carl von Clausewitz

PRESIDENT JOHNNY PENN and Japanese Prime Minister Fumio Watanabe decided they needed a break from their morning meeting with their dozens of advisors. The two of them pushed open the rice paper doors to the conference room in the Kyoto State Guest House and walked out onto the porch. The porch looked out over a small pond that was surrounded by a traditional Japanese garden.

Prime Minister Watanabe turned to his personal aide. He was standing a few feet behind the prime minister, which was his usual position. He shadowed Prime Minister Watanabe everywhere during his official meetings, ready to respond to whatever the prime minister might request and, not infrequently, to discreetly remind the prime minister his current meeting needed to come to a close if he wanted to be on time for his next meeting. "We will take this walk alone," said Prime Minister Watanabe to his aide.

His aide bowed and walked back to the conference room.

"Please," said Prime Minister Watanabe to President Johnny Penn, motioning they should walk down the covered bridge that connected the east and west structures of the State Guest House across a shallow pond.

The water of the shallow pond was incredibly clear and allowed a person looking down on the pond to discern with remarkable detail the size and shape and features of the stones that carpeted the bottom of the pond. It also allowed a person to study the coloration of the pond's carp as they floated lazily above the carpet of stones. Most of the carp had broad bands of alternating orange and white. Others had the occasional band of black thrown in. Finally, a still smaller minority were brown with a uniform freckling of small black spots from head to tail. The carp seemed to follow the two men as they walked alone across the bridge. In fact, the carp were following them because they had learned over the years that food often accompanied the strange animate shadows above the shimmering silver ceiling of their pond. Food, literally, rained from the sky when guests at the Kyoto State Guest House partook in what had long been a tradition there: feeding the carp.

No food rained from the sky today. Prime Minister Watanabe stopped when he reached the middle of the bridge. He grabbed hold of the black handrail carved from Yoshino cedar and looked out across the pond to the garden beyond. "This garden is truly a Japanese national treasure," he said. "It embodies what we Japanese call Teioku-ichinyo, which means oneness of house and garden. It is a very ancient architectural philosophy."

President Johnny Penn took hold of the handrail next to Prime Minster Watanabe. "It is truly beautiful," he said. "This garden is so obviously well cared for … yet it has such a natural look about it. This is, I think, what it means to be living in harmony with nature."

"I think so, too," said Prime Minister Watanabe, impressed President Johnny Penn should wax philosophic. "May I say, we very much enjoyed our dinner last night."

"We did, too. The first ladies seemed to hit it off."

"Ah, yes. Yuko very much enjoyed her conversation with Melissa. She was very impressed with her work with the homeless, and her helping to promote affordable housing. Melissa told Yuko the two of you met on your Remembrance Day?"

"Yes. Which means I have no excuse for forgetting the anniversary of our first meeting. Hard to believe it was six years ago."

"I understand tomorrow is the actual date of your Remembrance Day. On behalf of the Japanese people, may I offer our condolences to you and your country, and our hope for your national reconciliation."

"Thank you, Mr. Prime Minister. With your permission, I would like to share your condolences, and your hope, with the American people when I speak to them tomorrow."

"Of course. I would be honored. It is, I think, the most difficult part of our job … helping our people heal while also remembering those things that must never be forgotten."

"That is well put, Mr. Prime Minister."

President Johnny Penn had no doubt he would never forget the events commemorated on Remembrance Day. Those events, and the events of the following weeks and months, were not only responsible for his meeting Melissa, they were responsible for his being elected president of the United States of America.

The citizens of Los Angeles had indeed responded to Johnny Penn's call for protesters to march on the house of Officer Leah Blunt. An hour before the march was scheduled to begin, there was already a huge crowd of people gathered in and around the Walmart parking lot in Santa Clarita. They had come in their individual cars. They had joined together in caravans. They had even chartered buses. The size of the crowd was estimated at several thousand. Initially, the Santa Clarita police and sheriff's department allowed the crowd to have their protest. Then, as the crowd overflowed the confines of the parking lot and began to obstruct local roads, the police and sheriff's department requested the crowd disperse. That was when things turned ugly.

Officers were pelted with whatever the protesters found to throw. Cruisers were attacked and some were set on fire. The smoke from the burning cruisers encouraged the crowd to continue with their destruction. The Walmart was looted. Then the surrounding stores.

Johnny Penn decided the best way to stop the destruction was to start the march. He gathered a small group of protesters and set off walking to Officer Leah Blunt's house. Johnny Penn and the vanguard of protesters walking with him behaved well enough. The same could not be said of those who followed behind. They began vandalizing parked cars and residential homes. More fires were started. Then there were gunshots.

Exactly who fired first was never determined. The protesters blamed the local residents. The local residents blamed the protesters. The local residents had rallied around a police roadblock ahead of the protesters. The roadblock was intended to prevent the protesters from marching further into the neighborhood. The local residents were well armed as there was no shortage of firearms in Santa Clarita. Santa Clarita was a relatively young city and still closely connected to its rural roots. It was also mostly conservative. The police issued an order through a police cruiser's public address system for the protesters to disperse. The police said the protest was no longer peaceful and the protesters posed an imminent threat of serious bodily injury and even death to the residents of Santa Clarita. Finally, the police warned lethal force would be used if the protesters continued to advance.

Johnny Penn actually heeded the police warning. He stopped a hundred yards in front of the police roadblock. Many of those marching with him did the same. They stopped partly because Johnny Penn had stopped and partly because they were literally looking down the barrel of hundreds of firearms. The protesters coming up behind Johnny Penn were not interested in dispersing. The police threat only seemed to enrage them further. They pushed past Johnny Penn and his group, heading for the roadblock.

The police gave no actual order to fire. A shot rang out from somewhere. Then more shots rang out, some from the roadblock and some from the protesters. Then every person at the roadblock seemed to be firing. Dozens of protesters fell dead where they were standing. Dozens more were lying on the ground wounded. They were crying and screaming for help. Hundreds of protesters ran from the street, seeking cover behind cars and trees and houses. When the firing finally stopped, the dead and wounded numbered in the hundreds. They were nearly all on the side of the protesters.

The media had no doubt who was to blame. "Massacre in Santa Clarita," screamed the headline for the Los Angeles Times. The New York Times declared, "White Supremacist Mass Murder." The broadcast news pushed a similar narrative, including Johnny Penn's future wife, Melissa.

She reported, "Peaceful protesters were fired upon and shot down in cold blood today. We do not have a final count of the dead and wounded but authorities tell us the victims number in the hundreds. They had gathered here in Santa Clarita with thousands of their fellow citizens to protest the killing of two unarmed African American men by CHP Officer Leah Blunt only two days before. We have learned Officer Leah Blunt is also a resident of Santa Clarita. Given the fact many if not most of the victims today are people of color, and their killers are mostly white, as is Officer Leah Blunt, one has to wonder, Brett: What will it take for our country to finally address the scourge of white supremacism?"

Whether the media intended to turn a national tragedy into a national catastrophe is anyone's guess. If that was their intent, they succeeded beyond their wildest dreams. They succeeded in creating an orgy of destruction that dwarfed the George Floyd riots. What they created was, in fact, worse than the awful tribal violence of the Rwandan Civil War when Hutu militia slaughtered more than five hundred thousand Tutsi.

Millions of urban Americans boiled out into the streets. Those Americans were already angry and frustrated by what seemed a rigged system that condemned them to work harder and harder for less and less. While they were prepared to endure poverty and hopelessness at the hands of a rigged system without resorting to violence, they were not prepared to let that rigged system murder them in the streets, and murder them because of the color of their skin.

The suburbs bordering the urban areas suffered the most, partly because of their proximity to the urban areas that provided the majority of rioters and partly because they were predominately populated by the object of the rioter's rage, that is, the wealthy and the white. That a majority of the denizens of suburbia voted Democrat and were similarly outraged by the events in Santa Clarita did not matter. Nor did it matter if a sign was proudly posted in the middle of a front lawn proclaiming in rainbow-colored letters "THIS HOUSE BELIEVES BLACK LIVES MATTER, LOVE IS LOVE, SCIENCE IS REAL, FEMINISM IS FOR EVERYONE, AND NO HUMAN IS ILLEGAL." The rioters were intent on having their vengeance and they would extract it from whomever they encountered.

Their victims usually died quickly, if that was any consolation to them, much more so than was the case in Rwanda where the instrument of murder was often a machete. In America, the usual instrument of murder was a firearm. That is not to say there were not atrocities. There were more than a few. There was rape, of course, before a woman was summarily executed. Also, men, women and children were routinely beaten to death. And there was torture, horrible, heinous acts of torture. People were bound up, doused with gasoline and burned alive. People were forced to drink poison upon threat of having a spouse or child shot before their eyes. And, finally, as happened in Rwanda, people were methodically hacked to pieces.

The orgy of violence lasted almost a hundred days. It did not stop when the National Guard was mobilized and martial law was declared because the number of national guardsmen was nowhere near that required to secure hundreds of large and midsized American cities, even if all the guardsmen had responded to their activation orders. Many did not. They considered the protection of their families a higher duty. The orgy of violence did not stop, either, when the rioters finished with the suburbs and started heading out into rural and smalltown America, even though the rioters began taking serious casualties there because rural and small-town Americans were armed to the teeth and ready to defend their lives and property. What finally stopped the orgy of violence was an appeal by Johnny Penn. He was one of those wounded at Santa Clarita. He was shot in the shoulder and lucky to survive because the bullet missed his lung by less than an inch. He appealed for peace with his arm in a sling and his heart on his sleeve. "My fellow Americans," he said, "this is not who we are as a people. The violence has to stop. Please, I am pleading with you. I am begging you. We can make our country what we want it to be but only by working together. I forgive the police officer who shot me, or the civilian if that's who it was. I forgive him because he thought he had no choice. He was driven by fear and, yes, maybe hate and anger. Those are the real enemies we face: fear, hate and anger. We have a choice, my fellow Americans. We can surrender to fear, hate and anger or, instead, we can choose to walk away. We can choose tolerance and respect for our fellow Americans. We can choose peace … for all Americans."

When it was over, three million Americans were dead, more than twice the number of Americans killed in all the wars ever fought in the country's history, from the Revolutionary War to the Global War on Terror. On a per capita basis, compared to the butcher's bill in Rwanda, America was fortunate. Over half a million Rwandans were killed in a population of only seven million. A similar death rate applied to America with a population of over 330 million would have yielded more than twenty-three million dead. Still, three million dead Americans and another nine million injured was a catastrophe.

As a result of his speech, Johnny Penn was drafted by the Democrats to be their party's nominee for president for the 2028 election. His campaign centered on a promise to "heal the nation." The American people chose to believe Johnny Penn more than his Republican opponent even though his opponent was promising the same result. They believed Johnny Penn would prove a better healer for a number of reasons. Two of the reasons were simply emotional. First, he was physically more attractive than his opponent. Second, he was a war hero of sorts, having been injured on the front lines fighting for social justice. By contrast, his Republican opponent was another career politician, and not a particularly good one.

Another reason Johnny Penn was elected president, and by far the most important reason, was not at all based on emotion. It was based on a fundamental difference in the policy prescriptions of the two candidates. Johnny Penn was promising equity, by which he meant equal outcomes. His opponent was promising equality. Equality meant only equal opportunity. Having just erupted in violence over what many of its citizens considered an intrinsically unfair and rigged system, a system they had been told was based on free enterprise and capitalism, both of which had been built on the supposedly sacrosanct foundation of equality of opportunity, the country was of a mind to try something different. It was of a mind to try equity.

President-elect Johnny Penn was sworn into office on January 20, 2029. His first act as president was to sign the Equity, Diversity and Inclusion Act. The Equity, Diversity and Inclusion Act was designed to deliver on his promise of equity for all Americans. It guaranteed Americans a universal basic income, universal cradle to grave access to health care, including gender reassignment procedures, and universal access to higher education. It also mandated reparations to close the wealth and income gaps for all recognized demographic categories. Those were race, sex, gender and sexual orientation. Notably, there was a provision exempting Asians and Indians (from the Indian subcontinent) because they would have received negative reparations; that is, they would have had to pay reparations because their wealth and income were actually greater than the national average. Finally, the act mandated remedial action by all employers with more than twenty employees whose demographics by job title and job classification did not reflect the demographics of their community. There were exemptions here, too, where certain marginalized demographic categories were actually over-represented, as with African Americans in the NBA and NFL. No such exemption was granted to whites in the NHL.

The next six acts signed by President Johnny Penn were designed to secure in perpetuity the fundamental transformation of American society envisioned by the Democrat Party. The first of these acts was called the National Protect and Serve Act. It effectively nationalized law enforcement across the nation. This was done, ostensibly, to prevent another instance of the police going on strike as they did in Los Angeles. Also, less ostensibly, it was done to decapitate the leadership of police forces that were not sympathetic to the agenda of the Democrat Party. There would be no more police departments like those in Santa Clarita willing to stand with local residents against the forces of social justice.

His second act as president was to sign the Freedom to Vote Act. The Democrat Party had tried to pass a similar act under President Biden but was stymied by the filibuster rule in the Senate and two recalcitrant Democrat senators who refused to vote to end the filibuster rule. President Johnny Penn was able to sign the Freedom to Vote Act, along with all his other acts, because the recalcitrant Democrat senators were no longer an impediment to repealing the filibuster rule. Johnny Penn's coattails were significant in the election of 2028. He entered office with fifty-eight Democrats in the Senate. The Freedom to Vote Act required states automatically add to their voter registration rolls any person who interfaced with government for any purpose, regardless of their eligibility to vote; prohibited the prosecution of any undocumented immigrant inadvertently added to voter rolls; allowed same day registration for voters; required ballots be mailed to all registered voters; legalized the practice of ballot harvesting where political partisans go door-to-door and offer to pick up absentee and mail-in ballots to ensure they are properly filled out and returned to the appropriate polling place; and, finally, eliminated all requirements for voter identification.

His third act as president was to sign the Misinformation and Hate Speech Reduction Act. This act criminalized all speech, all writings and all postings on social media that were either "hateful" or not supported by "the science." A new cabinet position was established under this act along with a new department. The new department was the Department for Tolerance and Science. It was charged with consulting the nation's leading authorities, as determined by the Department for Tolerance and Science, to determine what was hateful and what was supported by science.

His fourth act as president was to sign the Learning for a Better Tomorrow Act. It eliminated home schooling and mandated all public schools teach a common core curriculum designed by the Department of Education to foster a common set of values for the nation's children. It also made it a criminal offense for any parent to take issue with the Department of Education's determination as to what was an appropriate value to teach their children. The fundamental values to be taught the nation's children were, as specified in the act and in order of decreasing priority: white people are uniquely racist, masculinity is inherently toxic, gender is fluid and determined by personal choice, climate change is caused solely by CO_2 and poses an existential threat to humanity such that the use of fossil fuels must be banned for all people except those deemed essential by the government, and, last but not least, nationalism is inherently fascistic and the only hope for humanity is to transfer national sovereignty to supranational organizations like the United Nations.

His fifth act as president was to sign an expanded version of the Patriot Act. It granted the nation's police and intelligence agencies the right to monitor all personal and business communications of all citizens, abroad and domestically, and, should they find any citizen a threat to national security, as determined by them, to suspend the rights of that citizen to travel and access their banking accounts. They also had the right, effectively, to terminate a citizen's gainful employment since the employer of a suspect citizen would receive a visit from the FBI whose agents would be asking why the citizen's employer was employing a threat to national security. No warrant was required. There was also no provision for appeal.

Finally, his sixth act as president was to sign the Common Sense Gun Safety for the Sake of Our Children Act. It outlawed the private possession of any weapon that was not a single shot pistol or rifle, of twenty-two caliber or less, and required anyone seeking to possess such a weapon first pass a comprehensive physical examination. The physical examination was, of course, gender neutral. It required men and women run a mile in under six minutes and perform twenty pull-ups. This physical standard was far greater than that for the Army and Marine Corps. If applicants passed the physical examination, they were then required to pass a comprehensive psychological evaluation. The psychological evaluation was performed by psychologists who were, themselves, terrified of firearms and incapable of understanding why any sane citizen would ever want to own one for personal protection, much less own one as a last-ditch means of resistance against a government turned tyrannical. Finally, after paying the $9,995 licensing fee and waiting eight months for the license to be processed, assuming both the physical and psychological evaluations were passed, the successful applicant was required to post a sign on his front door warning of potential serious bodily injury and even death to all who might enter due to the presence on the premises of a deadly weapon.

Every single act was a blatant violation of the Constitution but that was not a problem for the new Supreme Court. The conservative majority of the old Supreme Court was now a minority. With the end of the filibuster rule, Congress voted to add six additional justices. The newly appointed justices all understood their role. It was to interpret the Constitution of the United States of America to suit the political desires of the ruling party, even if that meant rendering the Constitution unrecognizable to its authors.

Prime Minister Watanabe turned to face President Johnny Penn. "I believe we've had a good bilateral meeting, Mr. President. Would you agree?"

"I would, Mr. Prime Minister. I believe it has been very productive."

"Yes. The business meetings went very well. Everyone seemed satisfied with our trade goals. The talks on military matters also went well. Our two countries remain committed to mutual defense through the US-Japan Security Treaty."

"Of course, Mr. Prime Minister. Japan has the unwavering commitment of the United States of America for the security and defense of Japan."

"And now, Mr. President, I would like to speak frankly with you … and in confidence, if I may."

"Of course."

"Our military leaders would never share this with their counterparts, with your military leaders, but they share this with me. They actually have their doubts about the commitment of the United States of America to help defend Japan."

"Mr. Prime Minister, I can assure you—"

"Please, Mr. President, hear me out. Our two countries signed this alliance in 1951, which is eighty years ago. Eighty years is a long time. Much can change in that time. What my military leaders tell me … It is one thing to depend on the United States for our defense when the United States is a great power able to defeat any adversary with little risk to itself. It is another thing to depend on the United States when the United States is no longer able to defeat any potential adversary, at least not without suffering greatly in the process."

President Johnny Penn was taken aback by the prime minister's frankness. *He doesn't think the United States can win?* "The United States is still a great power, Mr. Prime Minister. And, I can assure you, the United States honors its commitments."

"It pains me to say this, Mr. President, and I do not say this to be disrespectful, but some of my advisers would not agree with you. Some of my advisers warn me the United States is no longer a reliable ally. They point to Afghanistan. They point to Iraq. They point to Syria and Libya. And, most recently, they point to Ukraine."

"You have my solemn word, Mr. Prime Minister, the United States will stand with Japan if it comes to war, even if it comes to war with China."

"I do not doubt your word, Mr. President. And I have shared that confidence with my advisors, that I trust your personal commitment to come to the defense of Japan should the need arise. But, even if I have confidence in your personal commitment, there is still the Congress in your country, yes, and, of course, the American people. The American people, these past few years, have not been inclined to fight wars in distant places. The American people, it seems to some Japanese, are inclined to focus on the very substantial problems at home in America."

President Johnny Penn could not disagree. He had heard the same thing from his advisers. He also heard it from senators and congressmen. The American people were tired of war. They wanted their leaders focused on rebuilding the country.

"Then, Mr. President, there is the question of capability. Even if your country is—how do you say it, 'all in?'—the relative balance of power is not what it used to be."

President Johnny Penn had a sudden, terrible suspicion where Prime Minister Watanabe was going with this confidential conversation.

"Mr. President, I want you to know I am against it but there are some in my government urging Japan to do what I grew up to think was unthinkable. They are urging Japan to become a nuclear power."

President Johnny Penn felt a chill run down his spine. "Mr. Prime Minister, I have to be frank with you … I, too, find that unthinkable. Japan has always been one of the world's strongest advocates for nuclear disarmament, and understandably so given that Japan is the only nation in history to have suffered a nuclear attack. To go from that to this …" President Johnny Penn's voice trailed away. He did not know what to say. The president and the prime minister stood for a moment in silence. They were both looking out across the pond at the traditional Japanese garden and suddenly finding its sublime beauty invisible.

President Johnny Penn broke the silence. "I appreciate your confidence, Mr. Prime Minister. You can rest assured I will keep it. Is there anything I can do … to help you resist this effort to make Japan a nuclear power?"

Prime Minister Watanabe answered without hesitation. "Yes, Mr. President, there is. I need the United States to demonstrate it is still strong. In particular, I need the United States Navy to make that demonstration, to stand up to China the next time they violate our sovereignty in the Senkaku Islands, and the next time they threaten the sovereignty of other nations in the South China Sea. Do that, stand up to China, and I will have what I need to prevent Japan from becoming a nuclear power."

CHAPTER TWO

If you know the enemy and know yourself, you need not fear the result of a hundred battles. If you know yourself but not the enemy, for every victory gained you will also suffer a defeat. If you know neither the enemy nor yourself, you will succumb in every battle.

— Sun Tzu, "The Art of War"

THE CHANG-CHENG 365 was one of the latest variants of the Yuan class of submarines in the Chinese People's Liberation Army Navy (PLAN). She was named "Chang-Cheng," which translates to "Great Wall" in English, as are all conventionally powered attack submarines in the PLAN. She was distinguished from her sister submarines only by her number designation. Yuan class submarines are diesel electric boats with a displacement of 3,600 tons. While lacking the speed, range and endurance of nuclear submarines, diesel electric boats have one critical advantage. Their battery-powered propulsion makes them potentially quieter than nuclear submarines with their nuclear reactors which require pumps to circulate water. Pumps and circulating water result in noise that, while minimal, is nevertheless detectable.

The stealth of the Chang-Cheng 365 suited her mission well. She was assigned to patrol the relatively shallow waters of the Spratly Islands, an archipelago of fourteen islands or islets, six banks, 113 submerged reefs, thirty-five underwater banks and twenty-one underwater shoals. The archipelago is located in the South China Sea and is largely uninhabited. It contains almost no arable land. What makes the archipelago valuable are its rich fishing grounds, its potential for harboring significant oil and gas reserves, and its proximity to some of the busiest shipping lanes in the world. As a result of this real and potential value, the Spratly Islands and their surrounding waters are disputed territory. They are claimed in their entirety by China, Taiwan and Vietnam. Portions are claimed by Malaysia and the Philippines.

Captain Xu Guangda was in the attack center of the Chang-Cheng 365. The attack center was bathed in white light. It would switch to red light in another hour to give the crew a sense of nighttime. His stomach growled in anticipation of the end of his watch and the meal that would be waiting in the officer's wardroom. His six-hour watch had been routine, which meant running drills. So far, the boat had conducted a flooding drill in the torpedo room and a fire drill in the engine room. The next drill would be a battle stations drill. The battle stations drill would be based on a mock contact with an enemy warship. He did not know the exact time of the drill, only that it would be conducted during the last hour of his watch. The drill would begin when one of his officers initiated a computer program from the sonar room that simulated contact with an enemy warship. The only crew members who would know the contact was not real were the captain, the officer and crew in the sonar room, and the officer in the torpedo room. The job of the officer in the torpedo room was to stay the crew there from actually firing the torpedo when the order to fire was issued from the attack center. For all other crew members, the drill would seem as real as the real thing because, as far as they were concerned, it was real.

"Conn, sonar," announced the speaker in the attack center. "Surface contact. Designate Sierra 2-0. Bearing 0-6-8. Hull classification: Arleigh Burke warship." Each number was individually articulated. Sonar was able to distinguish the type of warship based on each type's unique sound signature. Arleigh Burke is a destroyer class in the United States Navy.

The officer of the deck picked up the telephone handset attached to the ceiling and repeated back the information to confirm it was correctly received. "Sonar, conn. Surface contact. Sierra 2-0. Bearing 0-6-8. Hull classification: Arleigh Burke."

"Officer of the Deck," said Captain Guangda, "man battle stations."

"Aye, Captain," answered the officer of the deck. "Man battle stations." The officer of the deck turned to the chief of the watch standing only a few feet away. "Chief of the Watch, man battle stations."

The chief of the watch reached over and pressed a button on a yellow box attached to the attack center wall. A klaxon sounded throughout the boat. Then he picked up the telephone handset at his station and announced over the boat's public address system, "Man battle stations. Man battle stations."

Additional men came running into the attack center to support the plotting that would be necessary to generate a firing solution for the target. Captain Guangda announced to the crew, "This is the captain. I have the conn. Lieutenant Commander Bai Yaoping retains the deck."

The officer of the deck repeated back, "Captain has the conn. Lieutenant Commander Bai Yaoping retains the deck."

The position of the contact relative to the Chang-Cheng 365 was now displayed on a screen in the attack center. Along with its designation as S20, the display included the contact's bearing from the Chang-Cheng 365 as well as its heading, speed and depth. Currently, only the contact's bearing was known; the other screen parameters were populated with "XXXX." Actual data would be displayed as it was determined.

Captain Guangda turned to his executive officer. "XO, we have a hostile warship designated Sierra 2-0. Bearing 0-5-6. Hull classification: Arleigh Burke." The bearing of the warship had already changed since it was first identified by sonar, indicating the warship was traveling at a high rate of speed.

The executive officer repeated back, "Aye, Captain. Hostile warship designated Sierra 2-0. Bearing 0-5-6. Hull classification: Arleigh Burke."

"Diving officer," said Captain Guangda, "make your depth 5-0 meters."

The diving officer responded, "Aye, Captain. Depth 5-0 meters."

Captain Guangda turned to the fire control tracking party to his right. "Attention fire control tracking party. We have a hostile warship designated Sierra 2-0. Bearing 0-5-6. Hull classification: Arleigh Burke. Now designated Master 2-0." The contact's designation was changed to Master 2-0 so everyone in the attack center knew it would be the subject of the fire control tracking party's effort to generate a firing solution.

A firing solution requires three key parameters: the target's position, heading and speed. Active sonar could quickly and accurately provide those three parameters. However, it would do so at the cost of not only alerting the enemy to the presence of a submarine but also revealing the submarine's position. Since submarines are interested in both destroying the enemy and surviving to fight another day, active sonar is almost never used. Instead, submarines use passive sonar to generate a firing solution. Passive sonar is essentially listening, which can be done without revealing the submarine's presence. The only disadvantage to generating a firing solution with passive sonar is the time required. It takes time because passive sonar can only provide a single input for the firing solution, which is the target's bearing. The job of the fire control tracking party is to use changes in the target's bearing over time to calculate the target's position, heading and speed. This calculation requires two fundamental assumptions: first, that the target is traveling in a straight line and, second, that the target is traveling at a constant rate of speed. The more accurate those assumptions prove in reality, the more accurate the firing solution.

"Firing point procedures," ordered Captain Guangda. His order meant the boat was to prepare to fire torpedoes. "Master 2-0. Tube 1 primary. Tube 2 backup."

The weapons officer flooded the torpedo tubes for Tubes 1 and 2 and opened their outer doors. "Weapons ready," he said.

"Solution ready," said the fire control tracking supervisor.

"Final bearing and shoot," ordered Captain Guangda.

"Set," answered the fire control tracking supervisor, indicating his fire control computer was communicating with the torpedo's guidance computer and would continue to do so even after the torpedo was fired. It would do so using a fiber optic cable that spooled out from the torpedo as it traveled toward its target.

"Fire Tube 1," ordered the weapons officer.

The torpedo did not fire. It did not fire because the officer in the torpedo room stayed the hand of the crewmember who would, during an actual engagement, physically push the button to fire the torpedo.

"Tube 1 failed to fire," announced the weapons officer, anticipating an order to fire the backup torpedo in Tube 2. When he did not receive the order, he turned to look at Captain Guangda. The satisfied smile on the captain's face told him all he needed to know: This was another drill.

"Officer of the Deck," ordered Captain Guangda, "stand down from battle stations."

***

Captain Guangda sat at the head of the table in the officer's wardroom. He passed the platter of Alaskan king crab legs to the officer on his left who took two for himself and then passed the platter on. The platter was passed a total of five times before everyone at the table was served.

Facing Captain Guangda at the other end of the table was his coequal by virtue of position, grade and rank, Commander Lei Jun. Commander Jun was the boat's political commissar. In accordance with the dual command structure required by the Chinese Communist Party on all PLAN surface ships and submarines, the political commissar shares the burden of command equally with the captain even though their specific responsibilities differ. Broadly speaking, the captain is responsible for planning and executing tactical operations while the political commissar is responsible for personnel readiness. Still, the political commissar is required to study the same aspects of naval operations as the captain with the expectation he take command should the captain become unavailable or incapacitated, especially during combat operations. Specific responsibilities of the political commissar are: organizing study sessions to promote officially approved values such as patriotism, nationalism and the Chinese version of Marxism; shaping military lifestyles by organizing cultural and sporting events; administering science and cultural education as well as providing mental health services when required; conducting research on adversaries including counterintelligence and counter psychological operations; rallying service members to cultivate a fighting spirit; and, finally, co-signing all orders with the captain.

"The crew's performance at battle stations was really outstanding," said Commander Jun as he struggled to break open a crab leg. "Congratulations, Captain."

"And may I offer my congratulations to the officers and crew of the

Chang-Cheng 365," said Captain Guangda, raising his glass, "including you, Commander Jun."

Commander Jun set down his crab leg and raised his glass along with the other officers at the table. He appreciated Captain Guangda's recognition because he knew it was sincere. He and Captain Guangda had a good working relationship, which was not always the case with captains and political commissars, although he would not go so far as to call them friends. He attributed the quality of their working relationship to their mutual respect and their understanding each had a job to do.

"I just received the Central Military Commission's strategic assessment of US Navy force structure and capability, Captain. As you know, this assessment is based on a roll-up of the last five annual assessments. It makes for interesting reading. May I share some of its findings with you and the officers here?"

"Of course," said Captain Guangda.

Commander Jun opened his tablet. He was intimately familiar with the personnel records of everyone at the table, including Captain Guangda, and knew they all had Top Secret clearance. "I'll read the summary. Reduced budgets in real terms and poor morale have made it increasingly obvious the US Navy cannot be counted on to reliably fulfill its national security responsibilities. Real budgets have fallen at the rate of ten percent per year since 2025, the year inflation dramatically accelerated for the United States. In fiscal year 2026, the budget for the US Navy was $212 billion and supported a deployable blue water battle force of 236 ships. In constant dollars (2026 dollars) the 2031 budget is only $112 billion. This shortfall has necessitated reductions of between forty and fifty percent in research and development, procurement, operations and maintenance, and personnel. It has also required a substantial reduction in the number of deployable battle force ships, with the current estimate being only 177. By contrast, China has increased the size of its deployable blue water battle force from 134 to 198."

Commander Jun looked up from his tablet and surveyed the faces of the officers sitting at the table, inviting their comment.

Lieutenant Commander Bai Yaoping obliged him. "China has the most powerful navy in the world now. The numbers are there for all to see."

Lieutenant Wang Chuanfu was not surprised by the numbers. They only continued the trend from previous reports. He fancied himself a student of naval history, especially with regard to the navies of the United States and China. He said to Commander Jun with a broad smile, "Our advantage over the Americans is even greater than suggested by those numbers, Comrade Commander, when you consider the geographic realities of deployment. The PLAN is homeported entirely in East Asia while the US Navy has global responsibilities. As a result, its forces are spread all around the world."

Commander Jun nodded. He made a mental note to make an entry in Lieutenant Chuanfu's personnel file that he had a keen grasp of geopolitical realities. "I agree, Lieutenant Chuanfu. Plus, we can count on all the resources of the People's Liberation Army Air Force and Rocket Force to attack the American Navy. The United States Air Force is limited to those forces it has deployed on Guam and Okinawa."

Captain Guangda observed the smiling faces of his officers sitting around the table. He was proud of how fast and how far the PLAN had come in developing its capabilities over his twenty-five years in the service. When he first entered the PLAN, the American Navy was truly a colossus and, in spite of all the propaganda from the Party, including those like Commander Jun, he knew then who would prevail should it come to a shooting war with the American Navy. It would not be the PLAN. The Americans not only had superior numbers, they had vastly superior quality, both in equipment and training. Today, the PLAN clearly had superior numbers, and it was arguable which navy had superior equipment and training. Each side had its strengths and weaknesses. There was also the intangible factor of morale and fighting spirit. Captain Guangda decided this was a good time to ensure his officers did not succumb to what he considered a cardinal sin in a naval officer: overconfidence. "It is more than just a numbers game," he said to Commander Jun. "We can count on having more ships should it come to war with the Americans. But as China knows from painful experience in our war with Japan in the Second World War, and in our war with the Americans during the Korean War, it is not only numbers that matter."

Commander Jun smiled. He was actually expecting Captain Guangda's comment. It was the reason he wanted to discuss the Central Military Commission's assessment at the table. He had long known, as did everyone else at the table, it was only been a matter of time before China overtook the

United States in terms of numbers of ships and planes. It was a similar story with regard to the qualitative gap. For every STEM graduate in the United States, China had ten. For Commander Jun, the real surprise in the report was the state of morale in the United States Navy.

"Yours is the voice of a wise and prudent leader," said Commander Jun. "We must know all there is to know about our enemy in order to prevail. May I read to you another section of the report? It concerns the current state of morale in the American Navy. I believe you will find it most interesting."

"Please," said Captain Guangda.

Commander Jun looked down at his tablet and read. "The United States Navy has increasingly become a hollow force. While this assessment is driven in part by economic realities, realities that are driving down budgets to levels below those needed to support national strategic commitments and goals, it is also driven by failures to meet recruiting goals that have necessitated a lowering of recruitment standards which, even then, are still failing to produce sufficient numbers of recruits. This shortfall in recruiting is fundamentally the result of the United States military implementing a cultural program the majority of Americans do not agree with, particularly after the traumatic social unrest of 2025. The American military is now seen as serving the new, progressive world order of the American ruling class and not the interests of the average American. As a result, the average American no longer holds a positive view of the American military, especially those average Americans coming from families with proud military traditions. Those families made up the bulk of military recruits in years past."

"What is the evidence of that?" asked Captain Guangda, skeptical of a report that seemed to be painting an excessively bleak picture for the enemy.

"Ships are sailing with crews that are understaffed by fifteen percent," answered Commander Jun, "sometimes twenty percent. Recruitment is failing to meet goals by even greater percentages, both for initial recruitment and retention. And, with regard to standards ..." Commander Jun scrolled through the report to the passage he had highlighted. He read, "The percentage of recruits scoring above average for the Armed Forces Qualification Test is at an historic low of forty-nine percent, which is even lower than during the Vietnam War. Plus, the Navy is accepting significant numbers of recruits without high school diplomas, with weight and health issues, including mental health issues like anxiety and gender identity disorder, and, notably, with felony criminal records."

"Felony criminal records?" asked Captain Guangda in disbelief.

"Yes. Before 2025, convictions for drug distribution, multiple DUIs, aggravated assault, rape and murder would prevent you from joining. Now, the only conviction that will prevent your recruitment is murder."

"How can this be?" asked Captain Guangda, stunned by what he heard.

"It is part of the Navy's diversity, equity and inclusion program. Not only are the convictions themselves viewed as unjust, the product of a systemically racist judicial system, the military has diversity-centered staffing mandates. Those mandates require them to have the right mix of recruits according to classifications of race, sex, gender and sexual orientation. Also, more shocking still, those mandates are applicable when it comes to promotions."

"You're telling me they pick their pilots, their commanding officers, even their captains, based on skin color?"

"Yes, Captain. Everything in the American Navy, like in their society at large, is now based on skin color, sex, gender and sexual orientation. They even started naming their ships based on those factors."

"How's that?"

"After they finished renaming bases that honored former Confederate generals, they decided the names of US Navy ships were insufficiently diverse. For example, CVN-76 … She used to be the USS Ronald Reagan. She was just renamed the USS Rachel Levine."

Captain Guangda knew the USS Ronald Reagan well. She was assigned to the US Pacific Fleet as part of Carrier Strike Group Five, which was the Pacific Fleet's most powerful battle force. "I thought the Americans only named carriers after presidents," said Captain Guangda.

"That was the tradition, yes. However, they formed a ship renaming committee based on a congressional mandate, and the ship renaming committee determined such a tradition was inherently racist given the systemic racism of the country's history."

"What about President Obama? Why didn't they name the ship after him? He was African American."

"They already used his name. The USS Eisenhower is now the USS Obama."

"Then why Rachel Levine? What made her worthy of such an honor?"

"She was an admiral ... in the US Public Health Service Commissioned Corps ... which is not why she was picked as the namesake for the Reagan. She was picked because she was the first transgender person confirmed by the United States Senate."

Captain Guangda shook his head.

"It gets better," said Commander Jun. "All United States Navy ships are now required to have their preferred pronouns listed under the ship's name, parenthetically. So, the USS Ronald Reagan is now the USS Rachel Levine (she/her/hers)."

"The Americans have lost their minds," said Captain Guangda quietly, more to himself than anyone at the table. He had a feeling of true sadness, which he found very strange. Even though the Americans were the number one threat his country faced, and had been for some years now, and even though he was prepared to go to war with them, to kill them, and to die trying to kill them, if necessary, he had always respected them and admired them as a worthy opponent. Now, hearing what Commander Jun had to say, it was like hearing of a once great man, strong and proud, reduced to penury as a result of poor decisions, advancing age and, finally, senility.

The phone rang at the side of the table where Captain Guangda was sitting. He picked up the receiver knowing it was the attack center because they were the only ones who would call him in the officer's wardroom. "Captain Guangda," he answered.

"Captain, conn. Have a surface contact on sonar. Designated Sierra 3-0. Bearing 2-7-8 degrees. Hull classification: Arleigh Burke warship."

"On my way," said Captain Guangda, knowing this was no drill.

CHAPTER THREE

I can imagine no more rewarding a career. And any man who may be asked in this century what he did to make his life worthwhile, I think can respond with a good deal of pride and satisfaction: "I served in the United States Navy."

— President John F. Kennedy

CAPTAIN JAMES MALKIN was on the bridge of the USS Mustin, sitting in the captain's chair and staring out at the seemingly infinite expanse of the Pacific Ocean. The USS Mustin was an Arleigh Burke class guided missile destroyer assigned to the United States Navy's Seventh Fleet. The Seventh Fleet was permanently forward-deployed to the United States naval base at Yokosuka, Japan.

The USS Mustin had been ordered to link up with Carrier Strike Group Five, which included the USS Rachel Levine, preferred pronouns she/her/hers. Carrier Strike Group Five was returning to Yokosuka from a six-month deployment in the Indian Ocean with a smaller than usual complement of escorts due to the low intensity nature of her deployment. Her escort complement consisted of two Arleigh Burke class guided missile destroyers and a Ticonderoga class guided missile cruiser. Carrier Strike Group Five was at the southern end of the South China Sea, midway between Vietnam and Malaysia, cruising at fifteen knots and heading 043 degrees.

Before linking up with the USS Rachel Levine, the USS Mustin was to conduct a freedom of navigation operation, known as a FONOP, in the Spratly Islands. The US Navy had conducted several FONOPs in the Spratly Islands as a means of demonstrating the United States would exercise its right of innocent passage under international law to traverse another nation's territorial waters. While the Chinese government accepted the right of innocent passage in its territorial waters for civilian vessels, it did not recognize this right for military vessels and insisted military vessels obtain Chinese authorization prior to entering Chinese territorial waters. They viewed the refusal of the United States government to request Chinese authorization for innocent passage of military vessels as both bellicose and provocative and, as the capabilities of their armed forces increased over the years, increasingly acted to harass Navy FONOPs, up to and including the conduct of mock attacks.

The USS Mustin was not new to FONOPs. Neither was Captain Malkin. In his seven years as captain of the USS Mustin, he had conducted three: two in the Paracel Islands and one in the Spratly Islands. The two in the Paracel Islands were uneventful but the one in the Spratly Islands left Captain Malkin shaken. A Chinese destroyer threatened the USS Mustin with a series of increasingly aggressive maneuvers. The USS Mustin was finally forced to maneuver to avoid a collision. Captain Malkin estimated the two ships were only fifty yards apart which, for two nine-thousand-ton, five-hundred-foot-long warships traveling at close to thirty knots, was essentially touching. The Chinese government claimed their Navy, the PLAN, had forced the USS Mustin from their territorial waters. The United States government denied the USS Mustin had been forced to leave. That was two years ago. Tensions were running even higher with the Chinese during this FONOP as the United States had recently increased the number of FONOPS in the South and East China Sea. This increase was the deliberate policy of President Johnny Penn to reassure Japan and other important allies in East Asia the United States remained a reliable and committed ally. Captain Malkin was prepared for anything. He placed the USS Mustin on Condition III, which is the condition for wartime cruising just below battle stations. A third of the crew was on watch with all strategic stations manned, including weapon stations.

"Officer of the Deck," ordered Captain Malkin, "report last status from lookouts."

Under the rules of innocent passage, wartime activities are not permitted. Those include the gathering of reconnaissance, the firing of weapons and any interference with local communications. For the USS Mustin, that meant she was sailing blind. Her SPY-1D radar and active sonar were powered down, and her anti-submarine helicopter was stowed in its hanger. Her only sensor input was from passive sonar and radar, and from lookouts with good old-fashioned binoculars. A total of four lookouts were posted, one for each point of the compass.

The officer of the deck was Lieutenant Commander Pinsker. He responded, "Lookouts report all clear, Captain."

"Remind the lookouts our sensors are cold, that they're our only eyes."

"Aye, Captain." Lieutenant Commander Pinsker toggled the communication channel for the lookouts and passed on the captain's reminder. All the lookouts acknowledged except one, Seaman McMurtry. "Seaman McMurtry," said Lieutenant Commander Pinsker sharply, "acknowledge." Still, there was no response. "Seaman McMurtry!" said Lieutenant Commander Pinsker even more sharply than before.

"All right, all right," answered Seaman McMurtry, sounding more than a little annoyed. "I'm acknowledging."

"What are you acknowledging, Seaman McMurtry?" asked Lieutenant Commander Pinsker.

"I'm … um … I'm acknowledging that … um … I'm to look out for anything that ain't a cloud or a seagull."

Lieutenant Commander Pinsker turned to look at Captain Malkin with an expression of disgust and disbelief on his face. "I think he was sleeping, Captain."

"He's relieved," said Captain Malkin. "Have the master chief find out why the hell he wasn't keeping watch and report back to me."

"Aye, Captain," answered Lieutenant Commander Pinsker.

Captain Malkin shook his head. Sleeping on watch was a serious offense. He knew the crew was tired. He was tired. Lately, he had taken to talking to himself when he was shaving in the morning after his umpteenth night attempting to sleep with the phone ringing every twenty or thirty minutes to inform him of something that someone deemed worthy of the captain's attention in the middle of the night. "Well, Captain Malkin," he would say to his haggard, drawn reflection in the mirror, "you look every one of your forty-two years. Hell, you look fifty-two! In other words, you look like shit!"

He thought of the fuel spill inside the module of the number three gas turbine generator last week. A fire easily could have resulted if the stream of high-pressure fuel had hit a component in the engine room that was sufficiently hot. At a minimum, such a fire would have knocked out a third of the ship's electricity and necessitated returning to port for extensive engine repairs. At worst, the fire could have spread and placed both the ship and crew at risk. They were lucky in that an alert watch inside the module noticed the stream of fuel and tripped the generator offline.

Thank God it wasn't Seaman McMurtry standing watch, thought Captain Malkin.

The incident review team determined the cause of the fuel spill was human error. A pressurized fuel connector had not been completely bolted down. The seaman who performed the maintenance thought he had completed the job correctly and his petty officer spoke highly of his work in general. The seaman, likely, was just tired because he was overworked like everyone else on board. Maybe, too, he was distracted, counting the days before he was finished with his deployment and, if he was like an increasing percentage of the crew, finished with the United States Navy.

Captain Malkin had served on ships with happy crews, had even commanded ships with happy crews, including the USS Mustin years before. He knew when a crew was happy and when it was not. The present crew of the USS Mustin, his crew, was decidedly not happy. It pained him to admit it but there was no denying it. It was evident every time he walked the ship, which he made a point to do frequently. A happy crew greeted their captain with smiles. There were not a lot of smiles to be seen on the USS Mustin. A happy crew would come up and talk to their captain about what they liked, what was going well, and how they were proud of their ship and their shipmates. There was mostly grumbling on the USS Mustin. The crew of the USS Mustin grumbled about the work load, about the ever-longer deployments, and, mostly, about each other.

As much as it pained Captain Malkin to admit his crew was not happy, it pained him even more to know there was nothing he could do about it. The ship required a certain minimum number of hours for training and operation and those hours had to be divided between the number of bodies on the ship. He complained to his superior officer, the commander of his destroyer squadron, that he was sailing without a full complement and that his crew was seriously behind in its training. His superior officer listened and told him everyone else had the same problem and he would just have to manage it the best he could. He also complained about the ship's backlog of maintenance and received the same answer: "Just manage it, Captain."

The problems of inadequate staffing, excessive operational tempo and deferred maintenance were not unfamiliar problems for Captain Malkin. They had been with him his entire career in the Navy, starting the year he graduated from Annapolis in 2010. Every year they seemed to get a little worse. Then there was 2025. That was the year the country descended into its paroxysm of tribal bloodlust. The nation that emerged from the election of 2028 set off on a radically different course, determined to reduce the potential for a similar conflict in the future and, if one were to occur, to ensure the national government could count on the loyalty of the armed forces. The first step to ensuring the loyalty of the armed forces was to require a loyalty oath from its members.

Captain Malkin was close friends with Captain Eric Kirby. He was a fellow destroyer captain in the Pacific Fleet. They met at Annapolis and stayed close ever since. When they married, their wives also ended up friends. Since their kids were around the same age, they made it a habit to get the families together for a backyard barbeque whenever their ship's deployment schedules permitted. It was at one of those backyard barbeques, standing by the Weber kettle grill with a bottle of beer, when Captain Eric Kirby told Captain James Malkin he would be refusing to take the loyalty oath.

"You'll lose your command, Eric!" said Captain Malkin, shocked at the news and concerned for his friend.

"I know. And I'll be out of the Navy."

"Jesus! You're a year away from having your twenty in, from being able to retire!"

"Yeah. That'll hurt."

"Allison ok with this?"

"She understands."

"But why? I don't like the idea, either, taking this loyalty oath, but … to throw everything away because the government's a little paranoid. Besides, they're just words. They don't really mean anything. Why can't you just say them and finish another year? Then you're out and you still have your pension."

Captain Kirby looked at his friend with a sad smile. "You really believe that, that the words don't mean anything?"

"I do. Not enough to throw it all away … everything you've worked so hard for … I mean, damn Eric, you're sacrificing your entire career!"

"How about the oath we swore when we were commissioned, to solemnly support and defend the Constitution of the United States against all enemies, foreign and domestic? Were those just meaningless words, too?"

"Of course not!"

"Well," said Captain Kirby, looking hard at his friend, "you can't swear allegiance to two masters. Now they want us to swear allegiance to the president, to President Johnny Penn. What happens when President Johnny Penn orders us to do something unconstitutional?"

"We follow the Constitution, of course."

"So that's the hill you're willing to fight on, and maybe die on? Well, my question to you is: Why not this hill? And if you're not willing to stand and fight now, on this hill, what makes you think you'll stand and fight on the next one, when President Johnny Penn orders you to violate the Constitution?"

Captain Malkin shook his head vehemently. "That's different."

"How's it different?" asked Captain Kirby. "During the riots in 2025, there were officers in the United States military who ordered their soldiers to fire their weapons … at American citizens. Maybe they didn't actually pull the triggers, those officers, but they gave the orders. Or was that ok because … Hey, they're just words."

"Come on, Eric, that's not the same thing and you know it!"

"No, I don't know it! In fact, I think a big part of the reason our country's where it's at today, which is basically in the shitter, is because all those people in positions of responsibility and authority who could have stood up and said 'No, this ain't right,' chose not to stand up. They chose the easy option. They chose to go along to get along because they didn't want to risk their careers. Then, once they rose to the top, to be our senior brass back at fleet headquarters, or the Pentagon ... Is it really a surprise they didn't suddenly discover a conscience and a backbone once they made it to the top? No, of course not. At the top, they have even more to lose. Plus, they're actually incapable of doing the right thing because they've spent their entire career-climbing lives training themselves to do the wrong thing. They excel at one thing and one thing only: Doing what it takes to get the next promotion."

"That's pretty damn cynical, Eric."

"Tell me I'm wrong."

"I can't say you're wrong. I just don't agree this loyalty oath is the same thing as being ordered to violate the Constitution. And it sure as hell ain't the same thing as ordering your command to fire on American citizens!"

"That's fine. We can agree to disagree. I guess that makes me old-fashioned now."

"Yeah," said Captain Malkin, shaking his head sadly. "Me too."

"You know what decided it for me?" asked Captain Kirby.

"What?"

"I remembered one of our classes at Annapolis. I know references to Nazis and Hitler are overused and usually the first resort of people who have no real argument but ... I never forgot reading about the Fuhrer oath."

"I must have missed that class. What was that ... the Fuhrer oath?"

"It was an oath the German military was required to say before the start of World War II. The German military always had an oath. Before Hitler, it was pretty much like our oath. They swore allegiance to the German Constitution. Then, when the Nazis came to power, it was changed to remove reference to the Constitution. The German military only swore allegiance to the people and the fatherland. When President Hindenburg died in 1933 and Hitler was declared Fuhrer, they changed the oath again. They changed it to the Fuhrer oath. Want to know how it goes?"

"Sure."

"I swear to God this holy oath, that I shall render unconditional obedience to the leader of the German Reich and people, Adolf Hitler, supreme commander of the armed forces, and that as a brave soldier, I shall at all times be prepared to give my life for this oath."

Captain Malkin took a long swig of beer and stared at the orange flames flickering above the gray briquettes at the bottom of the Weber grill. "They all swore it?" he finally asked.

"As far as I know, not a single German soldier refused."

Captain Kirby was true to his word. He refused to take the loyalty oath. Shortly afterwards, he was relieved of command. He was separated from the Navy with a General Discharge Under Honorable Conditions, a step below an Honorable Discharge. Still, it allowed him to access veteran programs.

After the loyalty oath came the Diversity, Equity and Inclusion Initiatives. The title was focus-group tested to evoke positive feelings in the widest possible spectrum of people. The words "diversity, equity and inclusion" were a given since they had been used for years in public schools, in government and in corporate America. Diversity, equity and inclusion were the holy trinity of a socially just society. The only real question put to the focus group was whether or not to call them "initiatives." Calling them "requirements" was deemed too harsh. And "regulations" was thought too bureaucratic. The focus group decided "initiatives" struck the right balance of sounding official while evoking positive feelings of change in people not really interested in understanding the particulars of what the initiatives really involved.

The particulars were quotas. The initiatives mandated equal representation by race, sex, gender, and sexual orientation all the way up the chain of command as well as in all military occupational specialties. To ensure the initiatives were enthusiastically implemented throughout the military, the Department of Defense Office for Diversity, Equity and Inclusion had its reporting structure changed so it would no longer report to the undersecretary of defense. Going forward, the Office for Diversity, Equity and Inclusion would report directly to the secretary of defense. Also, the Office of Diversity, Equity and Inclusion would be adopting the political commissar system used in the Chinese People's Liberation Army. A diversity, equity and inclusion officer would be assigned to every unit in the Army at the level of regiment and above, every squadron in the Air Force and every ship in the Navy. The DEI officer would be a coequal with the unit's military commander. Where the Chinese political commissar was responsible for inculcating military members in the spirit and teachings of the Chinese Communist Party, the American DEI officer was responsible for inculcating military members in the spirit and teachings of diversity, equity and inclusion.

The Diversity Equity and Inclusion Initiatives had an immediate impact on Captain Malkin and the USS Mustin. First, for Captain Malkin personally, he understood he would advance no further. He was a white, heterosexual male and that category was over-represented as far as rear admirals and above were concerned. Second, the USS Mustin's newly appointed DEI officer informed Captain Malkin the USS Mustin would be adopting "affinity berthing."

"And what, exactly, is affinity berthing?" asked Captain Malkin.

"It'll make the USS Mustin a more welcoming, supportive and safe community for our minoritized sailors."

"Minoritized sailors?" asked Captain Malkin. "You mean minority sailors?"

"No, I mean 'minoritized,'" said the DEI officer, putting air quotes around the word. "To be minoritized captures the essence of what has been done to minorities by the dominate culture in this country, that is, by the white, heterosexual patriarchy."

"You mean to say we're going back to segregated berthing?" asked Captain Malkin, scarcely believing he was having this conversation.

"It's fostering diversity, equity and inclusion," said the DEI officer with growing impatience.

"It's eroding unit cohesion, spirit and trust," countered Captain Malkin.

"If it's good enough for Yale, Harvard and Princeton, it's good enough for the United States Navy!" shot back the DEI officer.

"I will not allow a ship in the United States Navy to be segregated!" said Captain Malkin, raising his voice and regretting it as soon as he did. He turned his back on the DEI officer and stormed off.

Captain Malkin was overruled. The DEI officer went to his chain of command who informed Captain Malkin's chain of command that Captain Malkin was not supporting a key element of the Diversity, Equity and

Inclusion Initiatives. Captain Malkin was informed by his commanding officer in no uncertain terms he was to institute affinity berthing on the USS Mustin or the USS Mustin would have a new captain.

The results were worse than Captain Malkin imagined. Where before there was no regard for race when the crew sat down for mess, now there was. The African Americans sat down with their fellow African Americans, the Hispanics with their fellow Hispanics and the whites with their fellow whites. The different groups starting holding separate events, too. Asian American movie night started, for Asian Americans only. An African American book club started, for African Americans only. There was workout gym time for Hispanic Americans and only Hispanic Americans. So it went. Finally, the different groups demanded separate training classes, including separate certification tests. Soon, there was a noticeable drop in crew performance. The DEI officer attributed the drop in crew performance to white fragility and white rage. When Captain Malkin asked him to produce evidence to support his assessment, he said it was obvious, that you only have to know what to look for.

"Then kindly share with me what to look for," said Captain Malkin, sincerely wanting to know.

"I'm looking for hostile and patronizing attitudes," snapped the DEI officer, "like the one you're exhibiting at this very moment!"

While Captain Malkin found the drop in crew performance alarming, he found another change downright depressing. It was the tone of the suggestions in the USS Mustin's suggestion box. Captain Malkin had always reviewed the suggestions personally, thinking it part of his duty as ship's captain to attend to the needs of his crew. He considered crew suggestions a good indicator of crew morale. When he first assumed command in 2024, the suggestions were overwhelmingly offered in the spirt of improving ship readiness and ship operations. They were usually signed by the sailor making the suggestion in case more information was needed. They were never personal. Not once in his seven years as captain could he remember a suggestion questioning the ability of another sailor by name. And the thought of receiving suggestions that cast aspersions on groups of sailors as a whole, because of their race or sex, was inconceivable. All that changed immediately following the introduction of affinity berthing. There was, for example, a suggestion that read, "Seaman Salazar left his station before he was relieved. What a lazy beaner!" Another read, "The African Americans left the mess a mess after their book club meeting. What a joke! As if African Americans like to read!" Another read, "I'm sick and tired of doing all the heavy lifting for female sailors. If they can't pull a fire hose down the passageway, at least they can pull their panties down around their ankles!" And another, "How come white sailors aren't working the dog evening watches? Seems like more privilege to me!" And another, "Master Chief Zankich is a cracker racist!" And another, "Lieutenant Washington hates homosexuals!" And, last but not least, "Captain Malkin is a dog-faced pedo pervert!"

Captain Malkin decided his friend had been right about leaving the Navy, pension or no pension. He talked to his wife, Laura, about leaving the Navy at the end of the year. She came from a Navy family so he expected her to try and talk him out of it, especially in view of the financial cost. She did not. "Honey," she said, reaching out to take hold of his hand and looking him square in the eyes, "I don't know how you stood it as long as you did. You're not leaving the Navy. The Navy left you."

CHAPTER FOUR

Modern war is the most highly developed of all sciences. We have perfected our weapons but failed to perfect the men who use them.

— Billy Graham

THE FLIGHT OF four JH-7AIIs took off from the airfield on Woody Island. Woody Island is the largest of the Paracel Islands, which is not saying much because the airfield's eight-thousand-foot runway extends conspicuously beyond the edges of Woody Island, rising all of ten feet above the high tide mark thanks to fill dredged from two artificial harbors. The JH-7AII is a Chinese supersonic twin-engine fighter-bomber configured for a maritime strike role. Although the JH-7 platform is showing its age—it first entered service with the People's Liberation Army Air Force in 1992 and does not include stealth design features—the AII version was introduced in 2019 and features improved radar post-processing for better integration with its radar jamming pods.

The flight of four JH-7AIIs climbed to fifteen thousand feet and headed south toward the USS Mustin. The USS Mustin was nearly four hundred miles away and just entering what China claimed as its territorial waters surrounding the Spratly Islands. The flight's mission was to conduct a mock attack on the USS Mustin, to demonstrate China's displeasure with the United States government because the United States government was, yet again, sending its warships into Chinese territorial waters without prior approval from the Chinese government. The attack was mock only in the sense the pilots would not release their weapons. Otherwise, as far as the flight's pilots and ground crews were concerned, the attack was real in every sense of the word. The planes were flying a real attack profile and armed with real anti-ship cruise missiles.

***

Lieutenant Commander Pinsker was standing watch as the officer of the deck on the USS Mustin. The phone at his station rang and he immediately answered, "Officer of the Deck. Pinsker."

"CIC," said the voice at the other end of the line. CIC stands for combat information center. It functions as the USS Mustin's tactical center. CIC controls all the ship's sensors and weapons. "Baseplate reports radar contact with enemy aircraft approaching our position. Flight of four. Target bearing 3-2-5 degrees from our position. Distance 1-5-0 miles. Altitude 1-5 thousand feet. Speed 5-2-0 knots. Likely origin Woody Island." Baseplate was the call sign for the E-2D Hawkeye from the USS Rachel Levine, flying a figure eight pattern over the carrier strike group approximately two hundred miles to their west. The E-2D Hawkeye is an airborne early warning aircraft whose radar is housed in a distinctive disc that sits above the wing. Due to its elevated vantage point, the E-2D Hawkeye's radar is able to see far beyond the range of any shipborne radar.

Lieutenant Commander Pinsker knew there was a Chinese military airfield on Woody Island, which meant the approaching planes were very likely Chinese military planes. He repeated back the critical information. "Baseplate has four aircraft approaching our position. Target bearing 3-2-5 degrees. Distance 1-5-0 miles. Altitude 1-5 thousand feet. Speed 5-2-0 knots. Likely origin Woody Island. OOD out." Then he switched the phone to Captain Malkin's quarters. Captain Malkin picked up on the second ring. "Captain, OOD. Baseplate has four aircraft approaching our position. Target bearing 3-2-5 degrees. Distance 1-5-0 miles. Altitude 1-5 thousand feet. Speed 5-2-0 knots. Likely origin Woody Island."

"On my way," said Captain Malkin.

Captain Malkin was on the bridge in less than a minute. Like Lieutenant Commander Pinsker, he was concerned but not alarmed. "Officer of the Deck," he said to Lieutenant Commander Pinsker while staring out the window of the bridge in the direction of the approaching aircraft and seeing nothing but calm seas and clear skies, "order CIC to standby on the SPY-1D search and SPG-62 tracking radars. Standby on all electronic warfare systems and all countermeasures, including chaff and decoys. Standby on all air defense weapons."

Lieutenant Commander Pinsker answered crisply, "Aye, Captain. CIC to standby on SPY-1D search and SPG-62 tracking radars. Standby on all electronic warfare systems and all countermeasures, including chaff and decoys. Standby on all air defense weapons."

***

Eighty miles from the USS Mustin, the flight of four JH-7AIIs lit their afterburners and headed for the deck. Soon they were traveling at supersonic speed. Then they were below the E-2D Hawkeye's radar horizon.

***

Lieutenant Commander Pinsker grabbed the phone the instant it rang. "OOD. Pinsker."

"CIC," answered the voice at the other end. "Baseplate reports contact lost. Last contact has aircraft descending and accelerating, still approaching our position. Target bearing 3-2-1 degrees. Distance 6-5 miles. Speed 8-3-5 knots."

Lieutenant Commander Pinsker did the requisite repeat back and then relayed the information to Captain Malkin even though he knew the captain heard the repeat back; he was standing next to him.

"Supersonic," said Captain Malkin. "Definitely military. JH-7s?"

"Probably. They have the newer SU-30s, too, for maritime attack."

"Either way ... Officer of the Deck, man battle stations."

Captain Malkin considered the situation and decided. If the approaching Chinese aircraft used their fire control radar, he would consider them an existential threat to his ship and crew, which meant he was authorized to engage them.

"Aye, Captain," answered Lieutenant Commander Pinsker, "man battle stations." He turned to the chief of the watch. "Chief of the Watch, man battle stations."

"Aye," answered the chief of the watch, "man battle stations." He pushed the button that sounded the klaxon. He followed up the klaxon by announcing on the 1MC, the ship's public address system, "Man battle stations. Man battle stations."

There was a flurry of activity as the crew of the USS Mustin donned flash hoods and gloves and ran to battle stations. Then it was quiet. Lookouts stood on the starboard side of the bridge scanning the sky for aircraft. They saw nothing. Minutes passed, which seemed like hours.

The phone rang and Lieutenant Commander Pinsker picked up immediately. "OOD. Pinsker."

"CIC," answered the voice at the other end. "Approaching aircraft now jamming. Bearing 3-1-8 degrees. Distance 3-2 miles ... Wait..." There was a second of silence before CIC came back on line. "Detecting fire control radars! Repeat, we are illuminated by fire control radars!"

"Jamming and fire control radar detected," repeated Lieutenant Commander Pinsker. "Target bearing 3-1-8 degrees. Distance 3-2 miles." He did not set the phone back in its cradle but kept it pressed against the side of his face.

"OOD," said Captain Malkin, "Power up all radars and electronic warfare systems. Determine and advise on firing solution."

"Aye, Captain," answered Lieutenant Commander Pinsker. "CIC, power up all radars and electronic warfare systems. Determine and advise on firing solution."

"Helm," said Captain Malkin, "Ahead flank speed. Hard right rudder and make course 3-1-8 degrees." Captain Malkin was turning the USS Mustin to face the incoming threat to minimize the size of the ship's radar cross section.

"Aye," answered the helmsman, "Ahead flank speed. Hard right rudder and make course 3-1-8 degrees."

Captain Malkin felt the ship accelerate and start to heel.

CIC came back on the phone. "OOD, CIC. Four targets. Targets bearing 3-1-8 degrees. Distance 2-1 miles. Altitude 1-5-0 feet. Speed 9-2-0 knots. Firing solution set for EMMS. Two EMMS per target." EMMS is the acronym for evolved sea sparrow missile, a 620 pound twelve-foot-long missile with an eighty-six pound blast fragmentation, proximity fused warhead. ESSM were loaded in the vertical launch system or VLS in quad packs, which meant there were four ESSM per VLS cell.

Captain Malkin did not wait for the repeat back and for Lieutenant Commander Pinsker to then relay the message to him. He clearly heard CIC standing next to Lieutenant Commander Pinsker. "OOD, engage targets," ordered Captain Malkin.

"CIC, engage targets," ordered Lieutenant Commander Pinsker.

"Engaging targets," repeated the voice at the other end of the phone in CIC.

Geysers of orange flame erupted from the fore VLS a second later. Eight ESSM salvoed from two cells and streaked skyward on columns of white smoke. They disappeared in the direction of the approaching aircraft, the aircraft that were still not visible to the lookouts standing on the bridge with ten-power binoculars glued to their eyes.

The men and women in CIC watched the air battle on their computer screens. The approaching aircraft were red icons and the ESSM blue icons. The red icons dispersed in various directions as they attempted to evade the ESSM. No doubt the pilots of the aircraft were alerted by their own electronic sensors, the ones telling them they had suddenly been illuminated by the fire control radar of the USS Mustin. Apparently, too, the pilots decided to try and evade the ESSM rather than launch their anti-ship cruise missiles at the USS Mustin.

The blue and red icons closed quickly as the aircraft were traveling Mach 1.4 and the ESSM were traveling Mach 4. The combined closing speed was Mach 5.4, which is 5.4 times the speed of sound or 1.15 miles a second. After a couple seconds, it was apparent each red icon was followed by two blue icons. Then a blue icon converged with a red icon and both icons suddenly disappeared from the screen. A second later, another pair of blue and red icons converged and disappeared from the screen. Then another. Finally, the last pair of icons converged and the computer screens in CIC showed clear skies. The air battle had lasted all of eighteen seconds. At the end of it, four Chinese fighter-bombers were destroyed and eight Chinese naval aviators were killed in action.

CHAPTER FIVE

If you find yourself in a fair fight, you didn't plan your mission properly.

— David Hackworth

THE CHANG-CHENG 365 had been shadowing the USS Mustin since it entered the territorial waters of the Spratly Islands. The Chang-Cheng 365 used her passive sonar to follow behind the USS Mustin at a range of approximately five miles. The Chang-Cheng 365's passive sonar immediately detected the USS Mustin's sudden burst of speed as she turned to face the flight of four JH-7AIIs. Seconds later, the Chang-Cheng 365 detected the launch transient of eight missiles fired from the USS Mustin's VLS. That was all the information available to the Chang-Cheng 365. She was submerged and unable to detect the radar and jamming emissions from the USS Mustin and the flight of four JH-7AIIs.

"Launching missiles is a clear violation of innocent passage rules!" exclaimed Commander Jun, the Chang-Cheng 365's political officer.

"I know this, Commander Jun," said Captain Guangda calmly, standing next to Commander Jun in the attack center of the Chang-Cheng 365 but making sure to say it loud enough for the other ten men in the attack center to hear him. The Chang-Cheng 365 was already at battle stations. She had gone to battle stations the moment her passive sonar detected the missile launch transient from the American destroyer.

"The question is," asked Captain Guangda, "why would the Americans violate the rules of innocent passage?"

"There can be only one answer," replied Commander Jun. "The Americans are launching an attack ... in the sovereign, territorial waters of China!"

"And what is their target?" asked Captain Guangda.

"Another Chinese ship," answered Commander Jun, "or our base at Subi Reef, or our base at Mischief Reef, or our aircraft. Remember, we have aircraft based there. There is no way to know, Captain Guangda, what the particular target was. All we know is the American Arleigh Burke class guided missile destroyer launched weapons in Chinese territorial waters, a clear violation of the rules of innocent passage. Unless we are prepared to accept the possibility the Americans are conducting a training exercise in Chinese territorial waters, which they are not allowed to do, then the only possible explanation is an attack on our forces. We must take action, Captain Guangda! I speak for the Chinese Communist Party and I know they would demand action! They would demand the PLAN teach the Americans a lesson!"

"And what lesson is that, Commander Jun, that you would teach the Americans?"

"That China is no longer an impotent nation to be subjugated in another 'Century of Humiliation!' When China stands to resist the imperialists this time, in this century, it is the imperialists who shall have the bitter taste of humiliation!"

Captain Guangda wished Commander Jun had kept his opinions focused on the tactical situation at hand and not digressed into one of his lectures on the humiliation suffered by China at the hands of the western powers beginning with the Opium Wars in the mid-nineteenth century and only ending in 1949 when the Chinese Communist Party took power in China. Captain Guangda was well aware of that history, as was every officer and enlisted man on the Chang-Cheng 365.

One of those officers was Lieutenant Wang Chuanfu, who fancied himself a student of naval history. He had studied the Century of Humiliation beyond the cursory requirements in Chinese schools and, in a rare instance of not accepting the Party line, rejected the Party's assertion that China's

Century of Humiliation was a result of China generally failing to modernize. He knew from his research China had embarked on a massive military modernization program at the beginning of the nineteenth century, buying weapons from western countries and manufacturing some of her own in her own arsenals. He also knew China's armies had some success against western armies when they fought on land. He believed China's Century of Humiliation was fundamentally related to her weakness at sea. At the start of the Opium Wars, China had no unified Navy and what disparate, isolated naval forces she possessed were based on the ancient wooden war junk, a ship which was hopelessly outclassed by the iron-hulled and steam-powered ships of the western powers. As a result, the western powers were essentially free to blockade Chinese ports and land troops wherever they wished, including far up river in the interior of China. For Lieutenant Wang Chuanfu, the lesson from China's Century of Humiliation could not be clearer. Sea power is the essential power. It is more important even than land power. If China is never again to be humiliated by western powers, or any other power, she must possess a navy more powerful than that of any potential foe. On account of that belief, Lieutenant Wang Chuanfu had joined the PLAN. On account of that belief, Lieutenant Wang Chuanfu now hoped, while standing in the attack center of the Chang-Cheng 365, that Captain Guangda would hold the Americans accountable for their arrogance, first for violating Chinese sovereignty and, second, for daring to use their weapons inside Chinese territorial waters.

While Captain Guangda did not appreciate Commander Jun's historical digression, he could find no fault with his tactical assessment. He could not imagine the Americans conducting a live-fire exercise in Chinese territorial waters, especially considering how tensions had escalated in recent months. He thought it came down to two potential scenarios: either the Americans were attacked and launched their salvo of missiles in self-defense or they launched an unprovoked attack. If it was an unprovoked attack, his duty was to engage the enemy. If the Americans were attacked, which could only be by Chinese forces, then again, his duty was to join in the attack by Chinese forces.

Many of the men in the attack center were turned from their screens and looking at Captain Guangda. He thought they looked especially young, younger than they usually looked. He saw concern on their faces. Captain Guangda had no doubt every man on his boat was a true patriot, one who sincerely loved the Party, the country, socialism and the people, and was willing to sacrifice his life, if need be, to do his duty. He knew that patriotic fervor was not by accident. It was the end result of a deliberate program that started in kindergarten and ran through the universities. The Party called it "thought work." Five-year-olds sang patriotic and nationalist anthems. Older children took field trips to museums that commemorate China's Century of Humiliation, the Long March of the Chinese communists during World War II, China's subsequent victory over Japan in World War II, and, finally, China's victory over the Americans during the Korean and Vietnam Wars. University students were required to take courses on China's incredible transformation into a manufacturing superpower at the beginning of the twenty-first century and the essential, foundational role played by the Chinese Communist Party in that transformation. Captain Guangda concluded their concern was not an anxious, fearful concern rooted in the potential danger of combat with a worthy adversary. Rather, he thought their concern was for their captain, that their captain make the right decision, so their boat might best serve the interests of China and the Chinese people.

If I mistakenly engage the Americans, then I may have mistakenly started World War III. Then again, to not engage the enemy if, in fact, they have fired on the forces of the PLA would be an unbearable disgrace. Consulting with command is not an option as the enemy would detect our transmissions.

Finally, Captain Guangda decided. If he mistakenly engaged the American warship, it was the responsibility of the diplomats to avoid World War III.

"Firing point procedures," ordered Captain Guangda, knowing the fire control tracking party had been continuously updating a firing solution for the American warship as they shadowed her. "Master 3-0. Tubes 1 through 6." Captain Guangda looked at Commander Jun and saw him nod his approval. Had he looked at Lieutenant Wang Chuanfu, he would have seen a determined, satisfied expression on his face.

"Firing point procedures," repeated back the weapons officer. "Master

3-0. Tubes 1 through 6." The weapons officer flooded the torpedo tubes and opened their outer doors. "Weapons ready," he said.

"Solution ready," said the fire control tracking supervisor.

"Final bearing and shoot," ordered Captain Guangda.

"Set," answered the fire control tracking supervisor.

"Fire Tube 1," ordered the weapons officer.

The seaman in the torpedo room pushed the button that opened the valve that pumped water into the torpedo tube that then pushed the torpedo from the tube into the open ocean. Its thermal engine started turning the twin contra-rotating propellors when the torpedo was halfway out the tube. The torpedo's fiber optic cable spooled out from the hub of its twin contra-rotating propellors.

"Torpedo 1 away," announced the weapons officer. "Fire Tube 2."

The process was repeated until all six torpedoes were in the water and making their way toward the target.

The Chang-Cheng 365 carried the latest model of the YU-6 torpedo, which is the Chinese counterpart of the United States Navy's Mark 48 Advanced Capability (ADCAP) torpedo. Like the Mark 48, the YU-6 is a thermal torpedo; that is, it is powered by a monopropellant called Otto fuel. Otto fuel is burned in a piston engine without the need for outside air or oxygen. While thermal torpedoes are not as quiet as electric torpedoes, they are still remarkably quiet, almost as quiet as the submarine itself. The reality of modern submarine warfare is, unless the target has exceptionally capable sonar and an exceptionally skilled sonar crew, the target will not know it is a target until just before it is destroyed. The thermal torpedo has an advantage over electric torpedoes in that the chemical energy of Otto fuel is greater than the stored energy of the electric torpedo's batteries, thus giving thermal torpedoes greater range and speed. The maximum speed of the YU-6 is sixty-five knots, which is only used for its final attack run when the torpedo is no longer concerned about detection. A slower speed is used for the torpedo's approach to the target. The slower speed not only reduces the potential for detection but also greatly extends the torpedo's range, which can be up to twenty-eight miles.

Like most modern torpedoes, the guidance control system for the YU-6 uses updated guidance from the submarine's superior acoustic arrays after the torpedo has been fired. This updated guidance is transmitted through the fiber optic cable spooled out from behind the torpedo. The YU-6 also uses active and passive homing modes as well as a wake-homing mode. Wake-homing uses the torpedo's active sonar to follow the small air bubbles left in the wake of the target. The advanced digital processing capabilities of the YU-6 guidance control system coupled with its new generation acoustic head allow the YU-6 to identify smart decoys and jammers in only a matter of seconds. Once they are identified, it then ignores them, making the YU-6 very difficult to evade. In effect, the YU-6 is like an underwater terminator. When it reaches its programmed kill box, it will search for its target until it either finds its target and destroys it or runs out of fuel.

"Torpedoes running hot, straight and true," said the weapons officer.

"Hot, straight and true," acknowledged Captain Guangda.

In the day and age before smart torpedoes, the submarine captain would have taken out his stopwatch to estimate the time to impact, to know if his first salvo missed and he had to conduct a second attack. There is no need for a stopwatch with modern torpedoes. The fire control team knows the exact location of the torpedoes and the approximate location of the target. How long it takes the torpedo to close with the target and make its final high speed attack run is a function of many variables: the number and quality of decoys deployed by the target, the time it takes the torpedo to identify the decoys and ignore them, and, finally, the evasive maneuvers taken by the target itself. It is, simply, a waiting game.

CHAPTER SIX

Through all this welter of change and development, your mission remains fixed, determined, inviolable. It is to win our wars. Everything else in your professional career is but corollary to this vital dedication. All other public purposes, all other public projects, all other public needs, great or small, will find others for their accomplishment; but you are the ones who are trained to fight. Yours is the profession of arms, the will to win, the sure knowledge that in war there is no substitute for victory, that if you lose, the Nation will be destroyed, that the very obsession of your public service must be Duty, Honor, Country.

— General Douglas MacArthur, May 12, 1962,
valedictory to the Corps of Cadets at West Point

CAPTAIN MALKIN WAS seated in the captain's chair on the bridge of the USS Mustin. He picked up the 1MC handset and addressed the crew of the USS Mustin. "Men and women of the USS Mustin. We have engaged and destroyed four enemy aircraft with our ESSMs. The aircraft were approaching our ship on the deck and at supersonic speed. They were also jamming and illuminating our ship with fire control radar. I considered their actions an existential threat to our ship and its crew and ordered the aircraft destroyed. I want to commend all of you for your performance during this engagement. I could not have asked anything more of you. Well done. We are steaming at twenty-five knots to join the USS Reagan … I mean USS

Rachel Levine … and her strike group. We will remain at battle stations until then. Captain out."

Captain Malkin placed the handset back in its cradle and looked out the window of the bridge. The sea was calm and there was no indication of the battle that had happened not five minutes earlier. Ordinarily, Captain Malkin would marvel at the vast expanse of ocean and the endless horizon. Not now. He was lost in his thoughts, hoping to God he had made the right decision in ordering those aircraft destroyed. Perhaps it was only a mock attack, like the Soviets practiced during the Cold War. He imagined the Chinese would claim it was. Then he wondered if they would even admit that. Maybe they would claim it was a non-threatening reconnaissance flight and the captain of the American destroyer panicked and fired his missiles. He shook his head. *The Chinese will do what they will do. I did what I had to do. If Fleet wants to make me a scapegoat, so be it.*

The USS Mustin's DEI officer rushed onto the bridge. He was visibly upset as he walked over to Captain Malkin. "Captain," he said, "I heard your address to the crew and it was completely and totally unacceptable."

Captain Malkin was spent. The adrenaline from the engagement was gone and he wanted nothing more than to close his eyes and try and get some sleep. He looked at the DEI officer without bothering to hide his contempt. "Is that so, Commander? Please tell me, in your opinion, and as a seasoned naval officer … How was my address unacceptable?"

The DEI officer bristled at the insult. "I may not have much experience aboard ships, Captain, but I have plenty of experience promoting diversity, equity and inclusion. And that experience leads me to conclude you are willfully subverting the Navy's goal for promoting an inclusive work environment."

"You do realize, Commander, we just finished an engagement with the enemy, and that engagement might have had a very different ending had the enemy released their weapons, to the point where you and I might not be standing here breathing."

"I realize, Captain, you had a job to do and you did it … just like I have a job to do. And I very much intend to do mine!"

"Fair enough, Commander.Tell me, then … What was it you found unacceptable about my address to the crew?"

"Men and women of the USS Mustin?! Really, Captain?! What about our service humans with gender ambiguity? How do you think they felt when you left them out of your announcement? They deserve as much recognition as anyone else for this ship's performance."

"Do we have any of those sailors, Commander? What is the term? Gender ambiguity?"

"You can call them genderqueer, or androgynous, or androgyne."

"Ok, do we have any those? The genderqueer?"

The DEI officer shook his head sadly. "You really don't get it, do you Captain? Your gender is no more a constant in time than it is a constant determined by your chromosomes. It is a function of your life experiences and how those life experiences manifest themselves at any particular moment."

"Ok, Commander, just for my information, what are the various manifestations of those life experiences, so I don't miss one during my next all-hands address?"

The DEI officer seemed not to notice the sarcasm in Captain Malkin's voice. He went on to explain, fully expecting Captain Malkin to be more inclusive in his next address. "In addition to the genderqueer, there are also the agender. Those are people who identify as having no gender. They have no specific set of pronouns so you should use the singular 'they.' There are also bigender people. They identify as both male and female simultaneously. It is important not to confuse the bigender with the gender fluid, which is transitioning from one gender to another, from male to female, and vice versa. Of course, there are also trigender people, they shift between male, female and a third gender. Then there is demigender. They identify as partly one gender and partly another gender, but not in equal proportions, in which case they would be bigender. There are also subcategories within the demigender. You have to be careful with those. There is demiboy and demigirl, for example, where the person partly identifies as being a boy or girl. Then there is pangender, where people have multiple gender identities, either serially or simultaneously, but more than just two or three, in which case they would be bigender or trigender. There is also xenogender, where the person has gender identities outside the human understanding of gender."

"Such as?" asked Captain Malkin with a straight face, not believing he was hearing this from an officer in the United States Navy.

"Well, the identities of the xenogender are more metaphorical. For example, the xenogender may have identities related to animals, plants and even things."

"Like this ship?" asked Captain Malkin. "I would be xenogender if I identified as being the USS Mustin?"

The DEI officer thought a moment before answering. When he did answer, he answered carefully, as if he was not completely sure. "Yes, in theory, that would make you xenogender."

Captain Malkin stifled an urge to laugh in the DEI officer's face. Then he stifled an urge to have him escorted from the bridge and confined to his cabin as a stark raving mad lunatic. Then he reminded himself the DEI officer was the face of the new Navy, a Navy which was wholly committed to the ideology of transgenderism. He found the thought thoroughly depressing.

"That's quite a list, Commander. Is there some shorthand term I can use when addressing the crew, so I can get on with communicating my actual message?"

"Of course, Captain. There are many gender-inclusive forms of address. I will send you a complete list approved by the DOD Office for Diversity, Equity and Inclusion. Off the top of my head, you can say 'folks, friends, comrades—'"

"I don't think 'comrades' would be appropriate, Commander, seeing as the Chinese communists just tried to sink us."

"That's fine. There are plenty of other options. There's also 'gentle beings—'"

"For a warship?" asked Captain Malkin, incredulous.

"Ok ... well ... you can say 'humans—'"

"What if we have xenogender sailors, Commander? That would not be very inclusive."

The DEI officer was mortified by his faux pas. "You're right, Captain! That was thoughtless of me! Please accept my apology!" He looked around the bridge nervously to see if anyone had taken offense. When he saw no one had, he continued, although with less confidence than before. "Maybe 'team' would be a good term to use. Or you can fall back on 'everyone and everything.' That's always safe."

Captain Malkin turned away from the DEI officer and looked back out the bridge window. He lifted his cup of coffee and took a sip. The coffee was cold and bitter, like his mood. "Thank you, Commander," he said. "I'll look forward to seeing your list."

"It'll be in your inbox momentarily."

The DEI officer hurried from the bridge.

Captain Malkin watched him leave and wondered how on earth it had come to this point, the point where he was having to waste his valuable time discussing ridiculous nonsense with a person who was so obviously not a serious person. Then he thought about his friend, Captain Kirby, who had resigned rather than swear allegiance to President Johnny Penn. As far as Captain Malkin knew, Captain Kirby was the only Navy officer who had refused to swear allegiance and, as a consequence, been forced to resign. *You want to know how it came to this point, Malkin?* he asked himself bitterly. *That's how! A bunch of gutless cowards, that's what we are!* He was genuinely disgusted not only with the Navy but with himself. *They kept pushing their social engineering insanity on the service and what did the brass do? Nothing! What did I do? Nothing! We all just took it. We all saluted smartly even though we knew it was garbage, even though we knew it was worse than garbage, it was degrading our ability to fight and win wars. And why did we take it? Because we were too damn scared we would lose our precious commands, we would lose our precious careers! Pathetic, Malkin! Absolutely pathetic!*

***

Sonar Technician 1st Class Cynthia Ryan was seated at the first sonar console in the sonar control room of the USS Mustin. Her console consisted of two computer screens stacked one on top of the other. The upper screen presented a schematic of the sonar system with the requisite parameters required to monitor system status. The lower screen presented a display of the processed sonar signal. The circular format and single, fluorescent green color of the display on the lower screen gave it the look of an old-fashioned radar display. As with radar, the clock positions on the lower display corresponded to the bearing points of the compass. A contact bearing of 180 degrees, for example, would show up at the six o'clock position. There, however, the similarities ended.

A radar display indicates distance to the contact by distance from the center of the display to the blip on the screen, scaled according to the range of the radar. One inch on the display might equal ten miles to the actual contact. Passive sonar does not provide information regarding the contact's distance relative to the receiver. Instead, it uses the radial dimension on the display to capture the contact's acoustic time history. The concentric rings starting at the center of the display represent the progression of time, with the innermost ring being the most recent time. Using the contact's brightness to represent the intensity of the received sonar signal, the display presents the sonar technician with a visual representation of how the contact's sound bearing and sound intensity vary with time. If the contact was another vessel approaching the USS Mustin with a constant emitted sound intensity, from an engine turning the propeller at a constant number of revolutions, then the received sound intensity would increase as the contact's distance to the USS Mustin decreased. The display would show a trace with increasing brightness as it approached the innermost concentric circle.

The shape of the trace on the display is a function of how the relative bearing between the USS Mustin and the contact would change over time. A contact approaching the USS Mustin at an angle, on a constant heading, would have a trace with an arced, comet-like appearance. The head of the comet would be small and bright at the innermost concentric circle while the tail of the comet would grow fainter and fainter until its tip reached the outermost concentric circle.

An isolated noise transient, by contrast, like the opening of a torpedo tube outer door, would look nothing like the comet trace. It would appear as a single, faint point of light, gradually moving to the outer edge of the display as time passed. When enough time passed, it would drop completely off the display.

Sonar Technician 1st Class Cynthia Ryan was good at her job. Her job was to identify the comet-like traces and individual points of light that warranted further investigation. She was the one who performed the initial classification of a contact. She performed this initial classification by hovering over the trace or point of light with a cursor which allowed her to listen to the signal through her headset. Sometimes, the signal was obviously biologic, which is the term sonar technicians use to describe dolphins and whales and other marine animals. Other times, the signal was obviously a ship. If it was a ship, she handed the contact off to the two sonar technicians seated next to her. They would use the ship's library of sonar sounds to classify the contact further and support development of a firing solution. The ship's library was extensive and allowed them to classify ships not only by type—freighter, tanker, destroyer, submarine—but also, at times, by individual name. Usually, because of her knack for the job, Sonar Technician 1st Class Cynthia Ryan identified contacts at the very edge of detection. Also, usually, she succeeded in classifying them by type without resorting to the ship's library.

Today, though, Sonar Technician 1st Class Cynthia Ryan was not good at her job. She was having a panic attack. It started as soon as Captain Malkin finished his address to the crew, informing them of his decision to engage and destroy the attacking enemy aircraft. Sonar Technician 1st Class Cynthia Ryan had no doubt the attacking enemy aircraft were Chinese, which meant the United States was potentially at war with China. She had not signed up with the Navy to go to war, and certainly not to go to war with China. She signed up for the GI bill, so she could get out when her enlistment was up and attend college to be a physical therapist. She did not mind the drills and the calls to battle stations and all the make-believe fighting. The thought of real fighting, though, with a real enemy capable of doing real damage to the ship and possibly even killing some of its crew, including herself … That thought terrified her.

Sonar Technician 1st Class Cynthia Ryan grabbed the sides of the sonar console to steady herself. The sonar control room seemed to be spinning. Her heart was racing and she could feel her heartbeat pounding in her temples. Suddenly, she seemed to float out of her body. She was up by the ceiling, looking down at her fellow sonar technicians and herself. *How could this be?* she wondered. *It's me!* She looked at herself, at tiny little Cynthia Ryan, all one hundred five pounds of her in her navy-blue fatigues seated in front of the screen she had spent so many months behind and had a suffocating sense of claustrophobia, as if she was trapped in a steel coffin, helplessly waiting to be blown up, or burned to death, or drowned. She looked around at the others in the room and could not understand why they were acting as if nothing was wrong, as if they were not also in imminent danger. She felt compelled to warn them. *Don't you know?!* her floating second-self screamed at her supervisor, Navy Petty Officer 1st Class Anthony Tortellini, who was standing behind her physical body and asking her physical body something her floating second-self could not hear. *We're going to war! We're going to war with the Chinese! What are we fighting for anyway? I didn't sign up for this! Did you?! Are you willing to die for your country?! I'm not! What did America ever do for me?! What did America ever do for anyone except the rich, the well-connected and the white?! We were founded on slavery for crying out loud! We have a racist history! We committed genocide against the First Peoples! We've been a curse on the world from the moment of our founding! The sooner we're deposited on the ash heap of history, the better!*

"Cynthia?" asked her supervisor, Navy Petty Officer 1st Class Anthony Tortellini. "You ok?" He knew she was not. He knew she was not because not only was he her supervisor but, also, he was her boyfriend. "Cynthia?" he asked again, gently touching her on the shoulder and leaning down to look at her face. He saw tears running down her cheeks. He turned her chair around to face him. "What's wrong, Cynthia?"

Cynthia's floating second-self returned to her physical body. Her physical body suddenly seemed to recognize Navy Petty Officer 1st Class Anthony Tortellini. She threw her arms around his neck. "Tony!" she whispered in his ear. "I … I can't breathe. I'm so scared, Tony. God, I can't be here. I can't do this anymore. We could have died, Tony! I don't want to die. I don't want you to die, either. I don't want anyone to die! I … I just know, Tony … Something terrible is going to happen."

Tony hugged Cynthia. He did not care what the other sonar technicians thought. "Shhhh," he whispered in her ear. "No one's going to die. We did what we had to do to defend ourselves and now we're safe. You heard the captain. Come on … you know I won't let anything happen to you. You know that, right?" He brushed the tears from her cheeks and looked in her eyes. "Tell me you know that," he said gently.

She searched his eyes and found them reassuring. She touched his hand with hers and nodded tentatively. "I know that," she said. Then she said it again with more conviction in her voice, desperately trying to convince herself. "I know that."

"Do you think you can continue your watch?"

His question provoked another panic attack. Fear filled her eyes. She grabbed hold of him and held him even more tightly than before, the way a drowning person grabs hold of their rescuer. He could feel her body trembling. He turned to the sonar technician sitting next to Cynthia who was doing his best to ignore what was going on. "I'll take her to her berth," he said. "Cover for me, ok. I'll be back in a minute."

The second sonar technician was surprised Tony would leave his post while they were still at battle stations. He shrugged. "Whatever, man."

Navy Petty Officer 1st Class Anthony Tortellini helped Cynthia from her chair in front of her console. Then he helped her walk out of the sonar control room.

"That was weird," said the second sonar technician to the third sonar technician as he moved over to sit in Cynthia's chair.

"I knew they were doing it," said the third sonar technician.

"Yeah, well, whatever. Don't make it any of my business what people do in their spare time."

"Supervisors shouldn't be bangin' the help," said the third sonar technician. "Against regulations."

"As if you give a shit about regulations," said the second sonar technician.

They both laughed.

"Wouldn't mind bangin' that tight little ass myself," said the third sonar technician.

The second sonar technician looked over at the third sonar technician and smirked. "Guess you haven't been paying attention in class. That's sexual harassment!"

"I'll bet she's getting some harassment right now. He ain't getting back here in no minute!"

The second and third sonar technicians proceeded to speculate on the nature of Cynthia's sexual harassment at the hands of Tony and how they could improve upon Tony's performance if she ever decided to dump him. Had the second sonar technician, the one sitting in Cynthia's chair, bothered to look at the display screen, he would have noticed the six faint points of light that appeared in sequence at a bearing of 0-9-6 degrees. Had he moved the display's cursor over the faint points of light, he would have heard the distinctive acoustic signature of outer torpedo tube doors opening, one after the other. Then, once the torpedoes had closed the distance to the USS Mustin from five miles to two miles, which took all of four minutes, he would have noticed the faint, curved tail of a comet appear on the screen. Two minutes after that, when the six torpedoes were only half a mile from the USS Mustin, he would have seen the portion of the comet's tail closest to the center of the display suddenly become intensely bright as the torpedoes went to maximum power and accelerated to sixty-five knots for their final attack run. Finally, had he moved the display's cursor over any portion of the comet's tail, he would have heard the unmistakable whine of contra-rotating torpedo propellors.

But he saw and heard none of that.

The acoustic proximity fuse of the first torpedo detonated its 650-pound high-explosive warhead directly under the aft engine compartments of the USS Mustin. The explosion created a huge gas bubble that lifted the USS Mustin well above her normal waterline. It placed huge stresses on her keel and hull. The shock effect from the explosion was transmitted through the USS Mustin's steel hull with sufficient force to throw crewmen off their feet, breaking ankles and knees in the process. Then, as the gas bubble collapsed, it left a momentary void under the ship. The keel and hull of the USS Mustin sagged into the void, placing huge stresses on the keel and hull in the opposite direction. In combination, these upward and downward stresses were sufficient to snap the keel of the USS Mustin and rip open the steel plate on the sides of her hull. Finally, the sea water rushing in to fill the void from the collapsing gas bubble under the hull of the USS Mustin created a bubble-jet effect. The bubble-jet effect is sufficiently powerful to shoot a geyser of water three hundred feet in the air if the explosion occurs near the surface of the water without a ship in the vicinity. If the explosion occurs under the hull of a ship, as this explosion did with the USS Mustin, the geyser of water will punch a thirty-foot-wide hole through the steel plate on the bottom of the hull, instantly destroying all the equipment in the compartment above the hull and killing any crew unfortunate enough to be there. The geyser of water is usually not finished with its destruction until it has blown out adjacent bulkheads and an overhead deck or two.

As a result of the explosion of the first torpedo, the two aft gas turbine engines of the USS Mustin were destroyed, as was the engine control room just above the aft engine compartments. Fifty-six sailors were killed or injured. The USS Mustin was, at that moment, fatally wounded.

Then the second torpedo hit.

It exploded forward of the aft engine compartments, under the main fuel bunker, the galley and the crew mess. The geyser of water from the bubble-jet effect became a geyser of fuel that instantly ignited when it hit the open flames in the galley. The geyser of burning fuel incinerated everything in its path, including the twenty-five sailors in the galley and crew mess.

The third torpedo hit under the forward engine compartments and broke the USS Mustin completely in two. The fourth and fifth torpedoes targeted the forward half of the USS Mustin while the sixth torpedo exploded under the aft half, under the hanger deck.

Water poured into the two halves of the USS Mustin as they slowly drifted apart. There was the sound of gurgling water and hissing air as seawater rushed in to displace the vital, buoyancy giving air in the compartments with blasted bulkheads. The aft half of the USS Mustin lost its battle with buoyancy first. It rolled on its side and slide under the waters of the South China Sea. A few minutes later, the forward half of the USS Mustin followed the aft half under the waves. Of the 305 officers and crew onboard the USS Mustin, only sixty-eight survived. Captain Malkin was not among them.

CHAPTER SEVEN

It has been the political career of this man to begin with hypocrisy, proceed with arrogance, and finish with contempt.

— Thomas Paine

PRESIDENT JOHNNY PENN was seated at the head of the mahogany table in the Situation Room in the basement of the West Wing of the White House. He was dressed casually, in tan khaki pants and a white polo shirt because it was not yet four in the morning. With him in the room were members of his National Security Council. The vice president was seated to his right along with the secretary of state, the secretary of defense, the secretary of energy and the secretary of homeland security. Seated to his left were his national security advisor, the chairman of the Joint Chiefs of Staff, the chief of naval operations, the Air Force chief of staff, the director of national intelligence and, finally, the president's chief of staff. The civilians were dressed in business casual attire like the president. Only the service chiefs were dressed as if the meeting was during normal business hours. They were resplendent in their medal-bedecked dress uniforms. The USS Mustin slid under the waves only an hour earlier, at 06:57 Zulu time, which was 14:57 in the South China Sea and 02:57 on the East Coast of the United States.

"So," said President Johnny Penn to his secretary of state, Victoria Albright-Hayden, "you talked to the Chinese secretary of state?"

"Yes, Mr. President," answered Victoria, who everyone called Tory.

"He offered his condolences for the loss of life on the USS Mustin. He said Chinese forces in the area have picked up some thirty survivors and are still searching for more. They are also providing medical care for the injured. I thanked him for caring for our injured and we agreed to arrange for their transfer to our care as soon as they can be safely moved. I informed him the American people will be shocked and outraged when they learn of this unprovoked attack in the morning, and that the American people will expect no less than a formal apology."

"A formal apology?!" asked Bobby Nuland, the national security advisor. "We have a United States destroyer at the bottom of the South China Sea and a couple of hundred dead Americans. I think a little more than a formal apology is required!"

"Please, Bobby," said President Johnny Penn, holding up his hand, "let's let Tory finish with her briefing."

Bobby Nuland reluctantly leaned back in his chair.

"Thank you, Mr. President," said Tory. "The Chinese secretary of state is of the opinion it is we who owe them an apology, for destroying four of their maritime strike aircraft and killing all eight airmen. He claims the aircraft were only conducting a training mission, and that the captain of the USS Mustin panicked and fired his missiles. He said once the USS Mustin used its weapons in Chinese territorial waters, it was the duty of the Chinese submarine to attack the USS Mustin."

"Unbelievable," muttered Bobby Nuland to himself.

"What do we know about the captain of the Mustin?" asked President Johnny Penn, turning to the chief of naval operations. "Was he level headed?"

"Mr. President," said the chief of naval operations, "Captain Malkin was captain of the USS Mustin for seven years. His operational record was solid, although he was struggling with some of our DEI initiatives. All the evidence points to the Chinese aircraft flying a profile consistent with launching a cruise missile attack. Captain Malkin was, in my opinion, justified in considering the aircraft an existential threat to his ship and engaging them."

"How was it Captain Malkin was able to engage and destroy these aircraft but not stop this Chinese submarine from sinking his ship?" asked President Johnny Penn.

"At this time, Mr. President, we can only speculate. If the USS Mustin was running at flank speed to engage the attacking aircraft, his passive sonar would be ineffective. Also, the Chinese are patrolling the Spratly Islands with diesel-electric boats which are very quiet and very difficult to detect."

"I see. Do we know how many of our sailors survived?"

The chief of naval operations looked down at the table and cleared his throat before answering. "No, sir. But we think the casualties are heavy given how fast the Mustin went down."

President Johnny Penn felt a pang of guilt for the lost lives. It was his decision to increase the tempo of freedom of navigation operations in the South and East China Sea after his discussion with the Japanese Prime Minister earlier in the year. His pang of guilt lasted only a moment. Then he was angry. He pounded the table. "What the hell's wrong with the Chinese?!" he asked no one in particular. "We've complained to them before, about their harassment of our ships, and they just ignore our complaints. In fact, they seem to deliberately ratchet up the harassment every time we complain. And now we have this terrible accident!"

Bobby Nuland saw his opportunity and seized it. "What's wrong with the Chinese, Mr. President, is they think they own the South China Sea, and parts of the East China Sea, too. And, with all due respect, Mr. President, this was no accident. The Chinese have been trying to push us out of the South China Sea for years and this is the year they decided to make their move."

"You think this was a deliberate attack?" asked President Johnny Penn.

"I do, Mr. President."

President Johnny Penn turned to his secretary of defense, Lloyd Dallas. "What do you think, Lloyd? Do you think this attack was planned? Do you think it was a deliberate, premeditated attack?"

Bobby Nuland and Lloyd Dallas had talked before the meeting, to make sure they were on the same page. The country was struggling economically and defense budgets were shrinking. A regional conflict, they both agreed, would be helpful in generating public support for increasing the defense budget. It would also be helpful in securing lucrative positions with defense companies once they left the Penn Administration.

"I do, Mr. President," answered Lloyd Dallas. "I do not believe the four Chinese aircraft were flying a training exercise. I believe the aircraft were part of a coordinated attack with the Chinese submarine. I find it difficult to believe the Chinese submarine just happened to be in the right place at the right time to sink the USS Mustin."

President Johnny Penn turned and looked at his national security advisor, Harold Stark. "Do you agree, Harry? Do you think this was a planned, premeditated attack?"

Harold Stark nodded solemnly. "I do, Mr. President."

Bobby Nuland and Lloyd Dallas had not invited Harold Stark to their meeting before the meeting because they already knew where Harold Stark would stand. Harold Stark had a long career in the foreign service and could always be counted on to counsel intervention; the more intervention, the better.

"I think this was planned," continued Harold Stark, "because the Chinese sense weakness on our part as a result of recent reverses for the United States and the international, rules-based world order. The United States was humiliated in Afghanistan. The United States was humiliated again in Ukraine. The European Union is coming apart along with NATO. Our economy is in decline and we are a dangerously divided nation. Mr. President, I believe the Chinese see this as their opportunity, as their moment in history. They decided to attack with the expectation we would not respond with resolve. They know all of East Asia is watching. When East Asia sees us equivocate after the Chinese have sent an American destroyer to the bottom of the sea, along with hundreds of American sailors, then East Asia will know the sun has set on American power and risen on a new power, on Chinese power. But that is only *if* we equivocate in our response."

President Johnny Penn agreed with Harold Stark's assessment. However, if there was one thing he had learned since taking office, it was that clever people can make a bad idea sound good and a horrible idea sound like the opportunity of a lifetime. He turned to his secretary of state who had a reputation for independent thinking. "Tory?" he asked.

"Mr. President," answered Victoria Albright-Hayden, "I have my doubts it was a planned attack. The Chinese are not a rash people. It is one thing to risk a collision between warships on the high seas. It is an entirely different thing to deliberately sink one of our warships and kill hundreds of American sailors. They would think this through. What will we do if they attack? How will they then have to respond? And so on. Like during the Cold War with the old Soviet Union, when you think these scenarios through, you realize how unpredictable they are, which is what makes them so very dangerous, especially when the two powers are armed with nuclear weapons and cannot afford to look weak, for obvious reasons."

Bobby Nuland leaned on the table and glared at Victoria Albright-Hayden. "That's exactly how we'll look if we don't retaliate," he said. "Weak!"

"Ok, Bobby," asked Tory, not allowing herself to be provoked, "how, exactly, do you propose we retaliate?"

"The attacking aircraft came from Woody Island. There is a substantial Chinese military base there." Bobby Nuland then turned to President Johnny Penn and pointedly ignored Victoria Albright-Hayden. "Mr. President, I recommend we attack the Chinese base on Woody Island. An attack there would be proportionate, in view of the loss of the USS Mustin, and it would send a clear message to the Chinese and the rest of the world: The United States will not be intimidated!"

"Woody Island is Chinese territory," said Victoria Albright-Hayden, shocked at Bobby Nuland's suggestion. "You would bomb Chinese territory?"

"No!" shot back Bobby Nuland. "Woody Island is disputed territory. It is also claimed by Vietnam."

"What matters," said Victoria Albright-Hayden calmly, "is what the Chinese think. The Chinese consider Woody Island part of China. What would we do if the Chinese bombed our base in Guam, which is United States territory?"

"That's different!"

"How is it different? We have a base there just like the Chinese have a base on Woody Island. I can only image your reaction, Bobby, if the Chinese bombed our base on Guam." She permitted herself the barest hint of a smile, which she calculated would annoy the hell out of Bobby Nuland. "So, if we do as you suggest, if we bomb Woody Island, what do you think the Chinese will do?"

"They will understand we mean business and never again dare to attack an American Navy warship!"

"Or they will retaliate by attacking the American base that launched the attack on what they consider sovereign Chinese territory, just like we retaliated against Woody Island."

"They wouldn't dare!"

"You keep saying that, Bobby, that they wouldn't dare. Are we really so intimidating? Shall we consider our history over the past couple/three decades? The Russians were not intimidated by us in Ukraine. They took what they wanted and NATO was humiliated. In fact, NATO was more than humiliated. NATO was effectively destroyed. How about Afghanistan? After thirty years, the Taliban are still there and we aren't. And then there was our quest for non-existent weapons of mass destruction in Iraq and the fact Iraq is now aligned with Iran. If memory serves, you were a strong advocate of taking a hardline in all those places."

Bobby Nuland was furious. "How dare you talk to me like that!"

"There you go again," smiled Victoria Albright-Hayden, "daring people to do what they will, in fact, do."

"Bobby, Tory, please," said President Johnny Penn. "Let us be tough on the issues and not on each other."

"Please forgive me, Mr. President," said Victoria Albright-Hayden, not at all sorry for making Bobby Nuland look bad.

Bobby Nuland gave Victoria Albright-Hayden an evil look. He was determined to have his revenge, in this meeting or the next.

President Johnny Penn looked around the table. "I appreciate everyone's input. Speaking of doing what one has to do, I believe the United States has to do something here. As all of you know, the Japanese are nervous about our reliability as an ally. So, too, are our European friends after the mess in Ukraine, and especially after the Biden Administration blew up the Nord Stream gas pipelines to Germany. If we do not respond forcefully against the Chinese, after they sank an American warship, if we cannot be counted on to defend ourselves, how can we possibly be counted on to defend anyone else?" He turned to Lloyd Dallas. "Lloyd, a potential retaliatory strike against Woody Island is on the table. I know this is putting you on the spot and you have not had a chance to consult with the service chiefs but, off the top of your head, is that feasible? Do we have options?"

Actually, because Lloyd Dallas knew beforehand what Bobby Nuland would suggest, he was prepared for the question. "Mr. President," he said confidently, "we have two options. We can launch a Tomahawk cruise missile attack from the escorts attached to the USS Rachel Levine, preferred pronouns she/her/hers, or we can use B-2 stealth bombers stationed at Guam. Of the two, I consider using B-2 bombers the lower risk option since there is less chance Chinese air defenses can detect and intercept B-2s."

"Any comments?" asked President Johnny Penn, looking around the table.

"I have one," said Bobby Nuland, determined to have the last word after his verbal joust with Victoria Albright-Hayden. He turned and looked at Lloyd Dallas who was wondering what the hell Bobby was up to. This was not part of the script. "Lloyd, while it may be the B-2 is less likely to be detected, what, in your opinion, is the likelihood of success if we attack with Tomahawk cruise missiles from the strike group of the USS Rachel Levine?"

"I consider the likelihood of success still very high," answered Lloyd Dallas. "Chinese air defenses may intercept some of the cruise missiles but I expect most will reach their targets."

Bobby Nuland had a second question. "And isn't it true there is always a chance, however small, the Chinese may succeed in intercepting one of our B-2 bombers, which are manned by American pilots?"

Lloyd Dallas nodded. "There's always that risk but I consider it small. The B-2 is a very stealthy platform." *You bastard! What are you doing?! Now you're making me look bad!*

Bobby Nuland turned to the President. "Mr. President, I propose we use the USS Rachel Levine to launch the attack. First, there is no risk of us losing American pilots. Second, I think it would be a proud moment for our country and its commitment to diversity, equity and inclusion ... that the USS Mustin be avenged by the first carrier named after a member of the LGBTQIA+ community."

President Johnny Penn smiled and nodded at Bobby Nuland. "That's a great idea, Bobby. Funny you should mention that. The first lady has a LGBTQIA+ event with our son at his elementary school later this morning." He looked around the table. "Any objections?"

After hearing about the first lady's event with the president's son, there were no objections. Bobby Nuland shot Victoria Albright-Hayden a triumphant "fuck you" smile.

"Ok," said President Johnny Penn, "I'd like the National Security Council to finalize a plan to launch an attack on Woody Island as soon as possible, using cruise missiles from the strike group of the USS Rachel Levine, preferred pronouns she/her/hers. I'd like to approve this plan by 10 a.m. this morning. Thank you, everyone."

***

First ladies have to have a cause. Melania Trump was focused on the overall well-being of children. She supported causes fighting against drug addiction, poverty, disease, human trafficking and hunger. Michelle Obama was an advocate for healthy families, including service members and their families. She focused on supporting higher education and international adolescent girls' education. Hillary Clinton was an advocate for expanding health insurance coverage, ensuring children are properly immunized, and raising public awareness of health issues. First Lady Melissa Penn decided her issue would be championing gender neutrality when raising children, to avoid and hopefully abolish the gender stereotypes that are the final impediment to true gender equality. She came to champion this cause because she was endeavoring to raise her son in a gender-neutral fashion. She had his room painted a neutral beige color before bringing him home from the hospital. She made sure he had a complete set of boys' and girls' clothing from which to choose. She made sure he had a selection of both boys' and girls' toys with which to play, although, conspicuously, she made sure there were no toy firearms included with the boys' toys. It was one thing for her son to dress up as a girl but for him to play with guns, *that* was beyond the pale. Finally, she consciously decided to refer to him as her "offspring" until he made a final decision regarding his gender.

Her offspring was currently going by Francine even though his given name, the name on his birth certificate, was Frank. Francine, aka Frank, was five years old and attending Sidwell Friends School, a private Quaker school located in Bethesda, Maryland. Sidwell Friends was founded in 1883 by Thomas W. Sidwell. The school's motto is "Eluceat omnibus lus" which is Latin for "Let the light shine out from all." The motto refers to the Quaker belief in a divine light capable of penetrating into the deepest, darkest corners of the human soul and illuminating God's truth about how the soul should align itself with God's will. In recent decades, Sidwell Friends School had become the unofficial school for the children of the nation's chief executive. Chelsea Clinton went there, as did the Obama children.

Today was Drag Queen Story Hour for Francine Penn and her kindergarten class at Sidwell Friends School. Melissa Penn had planned to attend because parents were also invited. When Melissa's chief of staff found out about the event, she thought it the perfect vehicle for promoting the first lady's cause of raising children in a gender-neutral fashion given the stated goal of Drag Queen Story Hour, an organization started in San Francisco in 2015. The stated goal was to "inspire a love of reading while teaching deeper lessons on diversity, self-love and appreciation of others." Melissa agreed wholeheartedly with her chief of staff and asked her husband, President Johnny Penn, to attend with her. It was an offer President Johnny Penn could not refuse.

The drag queen was Paul Johnson. He was a kindergarten school teacher himself who, when he was not reading stories to children designed to portray gender fluidity in a positive light, enjoyed putting on adult drag shows in the various bars and clubs around Bethesda. When dressed in male attire, he was a nondescript middle-aged man of medium height with an ample stomach. His physique could fairly be described as pudgy. His hair was short and brown and parted on the side. He had a full beard and mustache that would have been the envy of an eighteenth-century sailor. Paul Johnson was anything but nondescript when he stepped out in his drag queen persona, which was Paulette. Her eyes were generously highlighted by white and black mascara. Her black eyelashes were nearly an inch long. She wore hot pink lipstick and a wig that was flaming orange and yellow. The hair of her wig extended down to her shoulders which were covered in a carpet of tightly curled brown hair. The tightly curled brown hair on her shoulders was her own, and it was thicker still on her chest where it was accentuated by a low-cut, strapless sundress. The sundress was white with a bold, abstract floral print pattern. The abstract flowers were bright red, yellow and pink. Hot pink latex gloves extended up over her elbows. Finally, to further ensure no one missed her, she wore hot pink high heel platform pumps with an ankle strap. She had to special order the pumps since she wore a woman's size 12.

Paulette was seated in the library. A few of the children from Francine's kindergarten class were seated next to Paulette. The rest of the class was seated facing her. The school had to move Drag Queen Story Hour from Francine's kindergarten classroom to the library to accommodate the parents, the press and the president. Some of the parents were awkwardly sitting in the child-sized library chairs next to their children. Others were sitting cross-legged on the floor with their children. The only adult sitting next to Paulette was Melissa. Melissa was intentionally placed there by her chief of staff so the media's video would have the necessary composition, that is, the first lady of the United States and her offspring sitting next to Paulette the drag queen. Melissa was trying to hold Francine in her arms but Francine was not cooperating. Francine was more intent on practicing her pirouettes than listening to Paulette. Francine was wearing a light pink tutu, the one she wore to ballet class and tried hard to wear all week long, even to bed. At least a quarter of the other boys in the library were also wearing skirts, although only Francine's was a proper tutu.

"So, children," said Paulette, consciously avoiding the phrase "boys and girls" as such a phrase would exclude those possessed of a non-binary gender, "what do you think of Julián the Mermaid?" Paulette looked around the room with a huge grin on her bearded face. When no one answered, she said, "My, my, my, aren't we all shy. You know, I used to be shy, too. And now … Look at me!" She set the book "Julián is a Mermaid" down on her lap and sensuously ran her hot pink, latex covered hands up her body, from her thighs to her well-padded double D chest. When her hands were at her chest, they exploded up into the air and reached for the ceiling in an open-fingered pose of celebration. Finally, her hands returned to her hips, at which point she vogued for the camera, turning her head from side to side and batting her inch long eyelashes.

The children found Paulette hilarious and laughed uproariously. The parents, who were mostly mothers but, in this context, were more properly called "biological parents," also laughed. Many of the biological parents looked over and smiled at their offspring. Others leaned over and hugged their offspring, warmed to the core to see them having such a good time.

"First Lady Melissa," said Paulette, reaching over to touch the first lady on the shoulder, "I know you're not shy!"

"Me?" asked Melissa with an awkward laugh. "Well, to tell you the truth, yes, I am shy."

Paulette brought her hot pink, latex covered hands to her mouth in a theatrical expression of shock and surprise. "You, the first lady, shy? I don't believe it!"

"Well, I should say *I was* shy. But I became less and less shy as I grew up, and that was because of all the loving people in my life who accepted me for who I am."

"That's so beautiful!" enthused Paulette. "Thank you, First Lady Melissa."

"You're welcome, Paulette. Really, though, I'm the one who should be thanking you ... for being such a wonderful role model, for helping us all break down social norms and celebrate self-expression and self-love in such a beautiful way, and in a way that is definitely *not* shy!"

Again, the offspring and biological parents laughed.

President Johnny Penn looked on from the back of the library where he was trying as best he could to be inconspicuous with Bobby Nuland, his national security advisor, and his escort of secret service agents. As a trained actor, Johnny Penn had no problem playing the part he was expected to play: the supportive spouse and biological parent. He knew Melissa expected it and, certainly, his political party expected it. Transgenderism was a fundamental plank in the Democrat Party platform, along with climate change and diversity, equity and inclusion. For him not to fully support and embrace any of them would be committing political suicide. Still, he found the scene in front of him disturbing, especially because his son was involved. He told himself it was because of his age, because his generation had been raised with old-fashioned, intolerant notions of gender roles. Then he wondered what his father would think, and his grandfather. They were both strong-willed, hardworking men who provided a home for their families and went deer hunting in the fall. His father worked on an assembly line, at General Motors, and his grandfather worked in a steel mill, at Bethlehem Steel. His father was a Navy veteran and his grandfather was a

Marine veteran who fought in Vietnam. He imagined they both would be appalled. Then he imagined them turning to look at him with disapproval bordering on contempt. He imagined them saying, "You're letting these people do this to your son?! You're letting them turn your son into a freak, like that thing up there pretending to be a woman?! What kind of a father are you?! What kind of a man are you?!"

Bobby Nuland leaned over and whispered in President Johnny Penn's ear. "Mr. President, the National Security Council has finalized the plan for the attack on Woody Island. They have high confidence the attack can be launched with no risk to American lives. We can launch the attack immediately upon your approval."

Johnny Penn turned and looked at Bobby Nuland. He searched his face for any hint of second thoughts. He saw none but felt compelled to ask anyway. "Is this the right thing to do, Bobby?"

Bobby Nuland answered confidently, "Mr. President, I have no doubt this is the right thing to do."

President Johnny Penn was reassured. "All right," he said. "Let's do it. I approve the attack."

"Thank you, Mr. President."

The president's offspring, Francine, was now the star of the show. She had escaped from Melissa's embrace and was happily dancing in the semi-circle of open carpet created by the assembled kindergarten class, their biological parents, and the media. She finished her dance with a pirouette and then bowed to Paulette. Paulette applauded enthusiastically as did everyone else in the room.

CHAPTER EIGHT

There are decades where nothing happens; and there are weeks where decades happen.

— Vladimir Ilyich Lenin

THE TICONDEROGA CLASS guided missile cruiser USS Shiloh was steaming at twenty knots approximately a mile ahead of the USS Rachel Levine, preferred pronouns she/her/hers. Flanking the USS Rachel Levine a mile or so off her port and starboard sides, respectively, were the Arleigh Burke class guided missile destroyers USS Curtis Wilbur and USS Barry. It was 14:57 Zulu time, which was 22:57 in the South China Sea and 10:57 on the East Coast of the United States. The sea was calm and the sky was clear. The carrier strike group was sailing blacked out so the stars overhead seemed especially brilliant in the absence of competing ambient light. A sailor familiar with the constellations would have very much enjoyed the spectacle of Leo the Lion rising up over the eastern horizon, had he the time to notice. He did not because the ships of the carrier strike group were at battle stations.

A siren sounded on the deck of the USS Shiloh. Not a soul was visible on the deck. The siren sounded for thirty seconds and then a hatch to one of the forward VLS cells popped open. An instant later there was an ear-splitting roar and a geyser of flame from the exhaust vent next to the cell as the solid rocket booster of the Tomahawk cruise missile seemed to explode it up and out of the cell. The Tomahawk cruise missile itself was visible for only an instant, illuminated by the geyser of flame from the exhaust vent. Then there was only the brilliant white light of the rocket booster, brighter by far than all the other stars in the night sky, accelerating the Tomahawk cruise missile to its cruising speed before exhausting its propellent and dropping off. Free of the rocker booster, the Tomahawk cruise missile extended its wings, lowered its air scoop and started its turbofan engine. The turbofan engine would propel the Tomahawk cruise missile and its one thousand pound high-explosive warhead to its destination at nearly 550 mph.

As the roar of the rocket booster faded in the distance, the siren was again audible. Actually, it had never stopped. Fifteen seconds after the first Tomahawk cruise missile exploded from the VLS, the hatch to a second cell popped open and another ear-splitting roar and geyser of flame sent another Tomahawk cruise missile skyward. Tomahawks started erupting from the aft VLS as well, and at the same interval, every fifteen seconds. It took just over six minutes for the USS Shiloh to launch its full complement of forty-eight Tomahawks. A similar ritual was occurring onboard the USS Curtis Wilbur and USS Barry, although they carried a slightly smaller number of Tomahawks, only thirty-six each. When all three ships were finished, a total of 120 Tomahawks were streaking toward their destination.

Their destination was Woody Island. As the crow flies, Woody Island was 443 miles from the carrier strike group when it launched its attack with Tomahawk cruise missiles. Only the group of Tomahawks from the USS Shiloh was taking the direct route, however. The group of Tomahawks from the USS Curtis Wilbur was heading slightly east of Woody Island so they could then turn and attack from the east. The group of Tomahawks from the USS Barry was heading slightly west of Woody Island. They would turn and attack from the west. The three separate axes of attack together with the Tomahawk's time-of-arrival control to ensure the attacks occurred simultaneously were intended to make things as difficult as possible for the Woody Island air defenses.

Mission planning considered the air defenses on Woody Island formidable. Those air defenses consisted of a squadron of Shenyang J-11 fighters and three batteries of S-400 surface-to-air missiles. The J-11 is a twin-engine fourth-generation fighter that is, essentially, a Chinese-produced version of the Russian Su-27. The J-11 is considered a worthy adversary for western F-16s and F-18s. The S-400 surface-to-air missile system is Russian designed and built and considered one of the best surface-to-air missile defense systems in the world, although it has since been supplanted in the Russian military by the more advanced S-500 system. Each S-400 battery has three different radar arrays operating on different frequency bands, including a lower frequency band designed to detect stealth platforms. Each S-400 battery has eight transporter-erector-launcher platforms with between four and eight missiles per platform, depending on the platform's particular missile loadout.

The Tomahawk cruise missile is a venerable design. It first entered service in the United States Navy in 1983. Over the years, it has been upgraded in different blocks to include more accurate navigation, an ability to loiter and select alternative targets, an ability to transmit battle damage imagery via satellite link, an ability to attack moving land and sea targets, an ability to home in on enemy radar emissions and, finally, an improved warhead better able to penetrate hard targets. Notably, the Tomahawk remained a subsonic cruise missile while the Russian and Chinese militaries increasingly fielded supersonic and even hypersonic missiles. The Pentagon had a number of reasons for staying with the subsonic Tomahawk. One reason was the fact supersonic cruise missiles would not fit in existing ship and submarine launching systems. Another reason was economic. A single Tomahawk cost approximately $5 million while a single hypersonic missile ran well over $100 million. Proponents of the Tomahawk argued there was a balance between quantity and quality. A single hypersonic missile may be invulnerable to interception but if an attack with twenty Tomahawks is able to overwhelm enemy defenses and still destroy the target, there is no practical difference between the missiles. The target is destroyed and the cost is the same.

***

Lieutenant Lin Dan sat in the cockpit of his Shenyang J-11 at the end of the eight-thousand-foot stretch of concrete that was Yongxing Island's sole runway. Yongxing Island is the Chinese name for Woody Island. On his left and just behind his aircraft was his wingman, seated in his own J-11. Another pair of J-11s sat behind their aircraft and made up the entirety of their "alert-two" flight. Alert-two meant they were expected to be airborne in two minutes or less. The second flight in their squadron was armed and fueled in their hangers with the pilots waiting in the ready room. They were the "alert-ten" aircraft, expected to be airborne in ten minutes or less. The third flight would take at least thirty minutes to get airborne as their pilots were generally sleeping. The squadron, along with the rest of the PLAN base on Yongxing Island, had been on alert since the Chang-Cheng 365 sent the USS Mustin to the bottom of the South China Sea. That was now over nine hours ago.

Lieutenant Lin Dan was shocked when he first heard the news. *We sank an American destroyer!* Despite the omnipresent propaganda that touted the superiority of Chinese society, including Chinese engineering and technology, he still, deep down, considered the American Navy invincible. Lieutenant Lin Dan was not alone in his shock. The assembled pilots and crew of the squadron stood there silently after their commander told them the news. They stood like that until their commander chastised them. "What's the matter with you?!" he yelled. "China has won a great victory! This is a moment we have all worked hard for! This is a moment to celebrate!" The commander then raised his arms high over his head and let out a shout of triumph. "Hoooorlaaaahhhh!" That was enough to shake the squadron from its shock. The men joined in with their commander, raising their arms and letting loose with their own shouts of triumph. They turned to their neighbors and exchanged handshakes, slaps on the back and hugs. Broad grins covered every face.

After a few minutes of celebration, the commander called the squadron back to attention. He explained to the squadron that PLAN headquarters expected the Americans to retaliate, and that they expected the retaliation to be here, at the PLAN base on Yongxing Island. He said that while it was possible the Americans might also attack bases in the Spratly Islands, that was not their concern. Their concern was to be as prepared as possible to meet and defeat the American attack here, should it occur. Accordingly, the base would remain on high alert until further notice.

This was Lieutenant Lin Dan's third hour in the cramped cockpit of his J-11 fighter. His eyes had long ago adjusted to the dark night but, still, he could barely make out the stretch of concrete runway in front of him; the runway and base lights were blacked out. His mind wandered in unexpected directions while sitting in the cockpit under a brilliant canopy of stars. He thought about the crew of the American destroyer and wondered what they were thinking, about being in a real war instead of just another drill in an endless series of drills. He imagined they were too busy for much contemplation when they were running to battle stations and, after that, when they were fighting to save their ship and their lives. But after they abandoned ship, when they were floating in the South China Sea watching their ship slide beneath the waves, he wondered what they were thinking then, to have lost their ship and so many of their shipmates. Then he thought about the pilots and radar intercept officers of the JH-7AIIs. He knew them all, some of them well, and now they were gone. *Gone and they're never coming back.* He looked up at the stars in the night sky and recalled an old saying often recited by his grandmother: Flowers may bloom again but you are never young again. When she told him that, she was telling him not to waste his youth. *Were their lives wasted?* He shook his head and looked up at the stars, refusing to believe they were. *None of us live forever. They knew the risks and they still climbed in their aircraft. They gave their lives for China, just like I'll give mine for China if that is what China requires of me.*

The speakers in his helmet crackled to life. "Scramble Flight One," said the control tower. "Scramble Flight One. Approximately 3-0 bandits bearing 2-7-0 degrees. Approaching 9-0-0 kilometers per hour. Altitude 2-5 meters. Range 8-2 kilometers."

Cruise missiles! thought Lieutenant Lin Dan as he toggled the switch that started his port engine. The port engine turned with a whine and then rumbled to life as fuel ignited in the combustion chamber. The runway lights suddenly appeared in front of him and on either side. They converged to a single point of light far off in the distance. He started his starboard engine and heard it rumble to life. Thirty seconds later he was finished with his instrument checks. Then he was accelerating down the runway, pushed into the back of his seat by the sixty thousand pounds of thrust from his two after-burning WS-10 turbofan engines. His wingman was off to his left and just behind him. Fifteen seconds behind them, the second pair of J-11s roared down the runway.

The flight of J-11s leveled out at five hundred feet. They were just subsonic, closing with the thirty-six cruise missiles fired from the USS Barry at over 1,200 mph or twenty miles a minute. The cruise missiles were now only thirty-five miles from the PLAN base at Yongxing Island and twenty-five miles from his flight. Lieutenant Lin Dan's plan of attack was simple: fire all his longer-range, radar guided missiles first and then fire his shorter-range, infrared guided missiles.

"Dragon One, Dragon One, this is Dragon Leader," said Lieutenant Lin Dan. "Lock on and salvo Thunderbolt-15s. Dragon Leader out."

Lieutenant Lin Dan had missile lock. He salvoed his six Thunderbolt-15s. He looked down at his instrument panel to save his night vision as the Thunderbolt-15s rode white-hot plumes of rocket exhaust into the blackness ahead of his J-11 fighter. Then, all of two seconds later, he looked up to see the Thunderbolt-15s visible only as small, white discs of light that were rapidly shrinking in size as they raced ahead. Together with the Thunderbolt-15s from the three other J-11s in his flight, it looked to Lieutenant Lin Dan like a meteor shower of sorts, only one that seemed to defy gravity as the meteors traveled up and away from the surface of the ocean. One by one, the discs of light flickered out as the rocket motors exhausted their propellent. The Thunderbolt-15s would coast the rest of the way to their targets, relying on the stored kinetic energy of their speed which was well over four times the speed of sound.

On the radar display in his cockpit, Lieutenant Lin Dan watched the Thunderbolt-15 tracks approach the target tracks. He thought it strange to see the targets coming in level and straight and not trying to evade the approaching Thunderbolt-15s. At first, he thought them dumb, either that or incredibly heroic. Then he reminded himself they were dumb, in spite of all their processing capability, and they were certainly not heroic because a machine is indifferent as to whether it lives or dies. The tracks of the first Thunderbolt-15s converged with the cruise missile tracks and disappeared. Then more did the same. Then still more. The Thunderbolt-15s performed well. Twenty-two hit their targets, giving them a better than ninety percent kill ratio. Unfortunately, some of the missiles hit the same target because the J-11 targeting radars on the four separate J-11s were not able to network and coordinate their targeting. Of the original thirty-six cruise missiles, twenty-three remained.

"Dragon One, Dragon One, this is Dragon Leader," said Lieutenant Lin Dan. "Lock on and salvo Thunderbolt-10s. Dragon Leader out." Each J-11 carried only four Thunderbolt-10s so the meteor shower this time was a less intense spectacle. Plus, the Thunderbolt-10 is a smaller, shorter-range missile with a smaller rocket motor. With only sixteen Thunderbolt-10s and twenty-three cruise missiles still bearing down on the PLAN base on Yongxing Island, Lieutenant Lin Dan knew there would be some leakers. He decided not to "look the missiles in." He would vacate the area to give the S-400 batteries a clear field of fire.

***

Captain Zhou Guanyu was commander of the three S-400 missile batteries on Yongxing Island. He was standing in the mobile command post vehicle a quarter mile from Battery 2, on the east end of the island. Battery 1 was on the south end of the island and Battery 3 was on the west end of the island. Seated in front of Captain Zhou Guanyu were three fire control specialists. Each was staring intently at the liquid crystal display, otherwise known as an LCD, that was displaying the airspace surveillance data from the radar from their particular S-400 battery.

The LCDs for Batteries 1 and 2 were showing thirty-six and forty-eight threats, respectively. The LCD for Battery 3 was showing only nine threats, indicating the Thunderbolt-10s from Lieutenant Lin Dan's flight had destroyed another fourteen cruise missiles. Still, the math did not add up for Captain Zhou Guanyu. There were ninety-three cruise missiles inbound. Even though his three S-400 batteries had a total of 144 missiles, they were not all suitable for defense against cruise missiles that were only twenty-five miles out and closing fast. Half the batteries' missiles were designed for defense against long-range and very long-range threats, out to 150 and 250 miles, respectively. The other half were short and medium-range missiles, the 9M96E and 9M96E2.

He gave the order with a calm, flat voice that concealed the angst he felt inside. “Auto fire missiles,” he ordered. His inner voice screamed, *Our base will be destroyed!*

The fire control specialists confirmed his order. “Auto fire missiles.” They were also tense and worried, although it was impossible to tell from their repeat-back.

The fire control specialists pressed the buttons that launched the 9M96E and 9M96E2 missiles housed in the launch tubes of the transporter-erector-launcher platforms at Batteries 1, 2 and 3. Compressed gas propelled the missiles from their vertical launch tubes almost a hundred feet up in the air. There, the solid rocket motors ignited. The rocket motors propelled the missiles upward a short distance further and then, suddenly, snapped the missiles into horizontal flight as the rocket motors' thrust vector steered the missiles to their targets. The targets had been selected by the targeting computer based on the computer's assessment of threat level. The threat level was basically a function of distance. The closer the target to the S-400 battery, the greater the threat level.

Seventy-two 9M96E and 9M96E2 missiles streaked toward their targets at over three times the speed of sound. The missiles were initially guided by a combination of inertial guidance and radar guidance from the S-400 tracking radar. On the LCDs in the mobile command post vehicle, the tracks of the 9M96E and 9M96E2 missiles closed rapidly with the tracks of the approaching cruise missiles. The 9M96E and 9M96E2 missiles switched to their onboard active radar for their final approach. It took all of the thirty seconds for the first set of tracks to converge. Captain Zhou Guanyu never felt so helpless in all his life. All he could do was stare at the LCDs over the shoulders of his fire control specialists and try to will the missile tracks to converge. When it was over, the 9M96E and 9M96E2 missiles had engaged and destroyed sixty-six cruise missiles. Still, twenty-seven cruise missiles remained. And they were heading relentlessly toward their targets.

The first cruise missiles reached the hanger and maintenance buildings next to the runway. They flew straight through the building walls and detonated inside. The four fueled and armed alert-ten J-11s disappeared in exploding fireballs, as did the four alert-thirty J-11s. Assorted aircraft, helicopters and vehicles were also destroyed. Other cruise missiles attacked the airport control tower and fuel storage tanks. The control tower crew was killed instantly and the fuel storage tanks exploded in giant orange fireballs. Still other missiles targeted the harbor facilities and the base barracks. Four cruise missiles dove into the runway itself, approximately midway down its length. Their penetrating warheads exploded five feet below the concrete surface and left craters twenty feet across. A final group of three missiles headed for one of the S-400 batteries. It was Battery 2. The first two missiles exploded near one of the transporter-erector-launcher platforms, shredding it and its remaining missiles. The third missile exploded near the mobile command post vehicle, destroying the mobile command post and killing Captain Zhou Guanyu along with his three fire control specialists. When the strike was over, the PLAN base on Yongxing Island was no longer operational. Three hundred forty-seven Chinese sailors, airmen and civilians were dead. One thousand thirty-two were wounded.

CHAPTER NINE

Well outta south Alabama come a country boy
He said I'm lookin' for a man named Jim
I am a pool shootin' boy, my name is Willie McCoy
But down home they call me Slim
Yeah I'm looking for the king of Forty Second Street
He drivin' a drop top Cadillac
Last week he took all my money and it may sound funny
But I come to get my money back
And everybody say Jack, don't you know
You don't tug on Superman's cape
You don't spit into the wind
You don't pull the mask off that old Lone Ranger
And you don't mess around with Jim

— Jim Croce, "You Don't Mess Around with Jim"

"THE OLDER I get, the more I appreciate moments like this," said paramount leader and general secretary of the Chinese Communist Party Xi Pei. He was sitting on the sofa in his living room contemplating the flames in the stone fireplace. It was autumn in Beijing and the nights had turned cool. Sitting next to him on the sofa was his wife of fifty-three years, Zhang Pei.

Zhang set her book down and looked at her husband. She smiled warmly and reached over to gently massage his shoulders. "Me too," she said, knowing her husband tended to wax philosophic when something of consequence was on his mind.

"What's going on with Mingze?" asked Paramount Leader Xi Pei. Mingze was their daughter.

Zhang shrugged. "Same thing, different day. The boys are running her ragged. I suggested she find activities to occupy them and she said, 'What do you know about raising boys, Mom? You only had me!'"

Paramount Leader Xi Pei laughed. "Fair enough! Boys and girls are different animals. My brother and I, we were very different from my sister when we were growing up. My mother's gray hair ... The vast majority of it was because of me and my brother."

Zhang laughed. "I cannot imagine *you* giving your mother a hard time. Your brother on the other hand ..."

"We both did. Until we were forced to grow up."

Zhang knew Paramount Leader Xi Pei was referring to his family's hard times. His father was purged from the Chinese Communist Party leadership when he was ten years old. He was sent to work in a factory. Then the Red Guards came and ransacked their home. They forced his mother to publicly denounce her husband as an enemy of the revolution, whereupon her husband was sentenced to work in a labor camp. The awful stress of that time was too much for his sister. She committed suicide.

"I think," said Paramount Leader Xi Pei, "Chen will be an engineer. He is the quiet, analytical one. Bo, on the other hand ... He is an outgoing extrovert, a born ham if ever there was one ... taking after his grandmother, I think."

Zhang attacked the ribcage of Paramount Leader Xi Pei, hoping to tickle an apology from him. "I am not a ham!" she insisted.

Paramount Leader Xi Pei briefly resisted before surrendering. "Ok, ok! I take it back! You are not a ham! You are a shy and recalcitrant performer, and one of the first rank! You are also a most beautiful and gracious first lady!"

"Thank you!" said Zhang, halting her assault on his ribcage.

When Zhang married her husband, she was by far the more well-known of the two of them, a household name in China. She was a soprano and contemporary folk singer famous for her regular appearances on television during Chinese New Year celebrations. She was also famous for her honors in various national singing competitions, for a number of popular singles and theme songs for Chinese television series, and, finally, for starring in a number of musical productions. In those years, her husband was only just beginning his climb to the pinnacle of political power in China. He was, then, a little-known functionary in the Chinese Communist Party.

Paramount Leader Xi Pei was suddenly serious. "Would you worry about raising children today, if we were starting over as parents?"

"Hmmm," said Zhang, leaning back in the sofa to give his question some thought. She answered tentatively, "I think parents always worry, no matter what. None of us would ever have children if we thought about all the potential pitfalls."

Paramount Leader Xi Pei looked back at the fire. Yellow flames danced quietly above a bed of glowing orange coals. "Is it because I'm getting old that I seem to see more pitfalls than before?"

"Maybe," she said. "With age comes wisdom. Then, too, it is your job to see the pitfalls for all of us, for all Chinese people."

"It is, yes. And I hope I have not been too ... complacent."

"How so?"

"There is so much parents cannot control today. When I grew up, there was no internet. And my parents had no television. All we had was radio."

"You are trying to control those things for all Chinese parents, to keep decadent and degenerate influences away from our children."

"Yes, I am trying. Many do not approve of my trying, though." Paramount Leader Xi Pei was referring to his censorship of programming on the television and radio, and his censorship of the internet. "You were a performer ... Do you think I did the right thing ... banning immoral content and overly entertaining stars?"

"You mean the boy bands?"

"Yes, as one example. Many people were unhappy with that."

"I think it was good. The boy bands were very popular, and their popularity was growing. I understand why the girls liked them ... They were wearing makeup, they were very fashion conscious, and their mannerisms were funny and also a little flamboyant. I think the young girls simply viewed them as 'one of the girls.' I don't think they were viewing them as potential boyfriends. And I certainly don't think they were viewing them as husband material, or soldier material, keeping them and China safe from our enemies. But were they a good example for our Chinese boys, these boy bands? I don't think so. China needs its boys to grow up to be strong men, to be strong husbands and strong defenders of China. The boy bands were not good role models for that."

"It is a humbling thing to try and shape a future generation. Sometimes I think I am too harsh. Other times … I think I am not harsh enough."

"If your plan is for one year, plant rice. If your plan is for ten years, plant trees. If your plan is for one hundred years, educate children."

Paramount Leader Xi Pei laughed. "You are quoting Confucius now?"

"It seemed apropos."

"You are very wise, First Lady Pei, as is Confucius. Certainly, the children are our future. I was informed of an interesting story recently. It was during one of our briefings in the Central Military Commission. It was a study in contrasts between two officers in the United States Navy. Both were graduates of the Unites States Naval Academy at Annapolis. The first officer was named Jeremiah Denton. He was a naval aviator who was shot down over North Vietnam and taken prisoner. That was in 1965. He was tortured by the North Vietnamese for six months. They were trying to force him to go on camera for their purposes of propaganda. He finally relented. When he was on camera, he used Morse code to blink the word "torture." Also, while they were interviewing him, he was asked if he supported the war effort of the United States government. He responded, 'I am a member of that government and it is my job to support it, and I will as long as I live.' He was later awarded the Navy Cross for heroism while a prisoner of war. As I understand it, the Navy Cross is the second highest decoration awarded by the United States Navy, second only to the Medal of Honor."

"What an amazing story! And what an amazing, courageous man!"

"Yes. Contrast that with 2016, off the coast of Iran. Two United States Navy patrol boats were captured by the Iranians for straying into Iranian waters. At least, that is what the Iranians claimed. The United States Navy officer in charge of the patrol boats was also a graduate of the United States Naval Academy at Annapolis. He was put in front of the cameras by his captors just like this Jeremiah Denton was during the Vietnam War. Only this officer did not demonstrate heroism. He said the incident was the fault of the United States of America. He also apologized to his captors for the incident. Finally, he thanked his captors for their hospitality!"

"What happened when he was released? Please tell me this officer was not awarded a medal!"

"The briefing did not say but I doubt it. The concerning question for me and the other members of the Central Military Commission is ... What happened? The service academies are supposed to accept only the best raw material the country has to offer. Then they are supposed to forge that raw material into a fine blade of tempered steel, to defend the people. If this officer captured by the Iranians is representative of what their service academies are now producing ... the Americans are in real trouble. They are forging butter knives instead of swords."

"That's good for us."

"Yes, of course. But it is a cautionary tale, too. How do you go from hero to shameful disgrace in only half a century?"

"You relax your standards. You accept what used to be unacceptable. You worry too much about the individual instead of the people as a whole."

"Yes, that is very true. The Americans are letting the tail wag the dog."

"What would you do, if a Chinese naval officer did that?"

Paramount Leader Xi Pei thought a moment before answering. "He would be severely punished. Of that, I have no doubt. Would it rise to the level of a capital offense, for treason, or cowardice in the face of the enemy ... It certainly would during wartime. During peacetime ..." Paramount Leader Xi Pei shrugged. "Suffice it to say, we would make it very clear this is not the behavior expected of a Chinese military man."

"I think you did the right thing."

"What's that?"

"Banning boy bands in China."

"You think so?" asked Paramount Leader Xi Pei, looking over at his wife and smiling.

"I do. There are many trends in the West that are not positive. We do not need those trends in China."

"Thank you for saying that. I know there are a lot of young Chinese people who would not agree with you."

Paramount Leader Xi Pei's phone rang. He pulled his phone from the carrying case on his belt and looked at the name of the caller. "Hello, General," he answered.

Zhang noticed her husband's brow furrow as he listened. She could only make out a word here and there from the general's voice on the other end of the phone. She heard, "Attacked … Many dead … American missiles … American carrier strike group."

"I understand, General. It is as the Central Military Commission expected. Is our response ready? Good. How many ships in the American strike group? Ok. Are our forces ready? Good. I need not remind you, General, it is vitally important our response be decisive."

Paramount Leader Xi Pei looked at his wife as he listened. Then he said, "That is correct, General. Every American ship."

He listened some more.

"Very well, General. Please execute our plan. The eyes of China are upon you."

Paramount Leader Xi Pei ended the call and placed the phone back in the carrying case on his belt. He looked at the dancing yellow flames in the fireplace and hoped their brethren would not soon be consuming the world. He knew the response they were about to execute was a gamble, for China and perhaps humanity. He saw no other option. Sooner or later, he believed, this bridge had to be crossed.

"That did not sound good," said his wife, unable to bear the suspense any longer.

"No, it was not. But it was also not unexpected. The Americans attacked one of our bases in the South China Sea. It was a serious attack and there are many casualties. We will now be responding."

"By attacking the American ships that launched the attack?"

"Yes. We will sink those ships, to teach the Americans a lesson."

"Which is?"

"That their days as the world's sole superpower are over."

Zhang looked concerned. "Do you think them capable of learning such a lesson?"

"I have my doubts. History teaches us moments like this are very dangerous, when you have a great power in decline and another great power rising up. The great power in decline is often unwilling to give up its prerogatives, the ones they have assumed for themselves as a consequence of no one being strong enough to challenge them."

"But they have to, don't they? They have to recognize reality!"

"Hopefully they will, which is why China's response must be decisive, to leave no doubt in the minds of the Americans they can no longer act with impunity. That is a bitter lesson to learn, though, to acknowledge your fall from greatness."

Zhang was worried. "And if they cannot learn such a lesson?"

Paramount Leader Xi Pei shrugged his fatalistic shrug. "Then many more people will have to die."

CHAPTER TEN

There is nothing so destructive as a superficially attractive idea divorced from reality.

— Larry Saunders,
Brilliant Solutions software engineer, retired

THE HANGER BAY of the USS Rachel Levine, preferred pronouns she/her/hers, was cavernous. It extended the entire breadth of the ship, two thirds or her length and three decks high. Inside were three of the four squadrons carried by the USS Rachel Levine. One of those squadrons was flying the relatively new F-35 Lightning II while the other two were flying the venerable F/A-18E Super Hornet. The Lightning II squadron was ready for immediate combat operations with the standard complement of air-to-air missiles. The first of the two Super Hornet squadrons was similarly armed and ready while the second of the two was on alert. It could be armed for either air-to-air or anti-shipping duties within sixty minutes instead of the normal ninety minutes. The fourth and final squadron was on the flight deck. It was flying Lightning IIs and providing the constant four-ship formation that was the carrier strike group's combat air patrol.

Ketanji Brown was posing for the camera in front of one of the Super Hornets configured for air-to-air operations. She had her hand on one of the Super Hornet's air-to-air missiles. Her hand was resting just above the large rainbow flag decal on the front half of the missile. Under the rainbow flag was stenciled “BIPOCAAM” in black block letters and, in black italic letters after a dash, “*Diversity is our Strength.*” BIPOCAAM is the acronym for black, indigenous, people of color air-to-air missile. Until recently, the BIPOCAAM was known as the AMRAAM or advanced medium range air-to-air missile. The name change was Ketanji Brown’s idea, and it was the reason she came to be on the USS Rachel Levine with a photographer from the Navy Times in tow, courtesy of Admiral Turner, commanding office of the Pacific Fleet.

Exactly how Ketanji Brown came up with the idea of changing the AMRAAM’s name is a convoluted tale. Her stint as the program manager for the AMRAAM’s guidance software did not go well at Brilliant Solutions. She may have been a mediocre engineer but she was a terrible program manager. When she missed her first important delivery milestone, she blamed it on the systemic racism embedded in the Brilliant Solutions software team. Brilliant Solutions brought in a diversity trainer and required all members of the software team take a course entitled “Confronting Racism.” After a slide touting the training company’s commitment to building a more equitable future for all communities and a subsequent slide touting the pedigree of the diversity trainer standing in front of them—she was a sociologist with advanced degrees from not one but two Ivy League schools—and her preferred pronouns—she went by they/them/theirs—“they” came to the slide that defined “the problem” with the Brilliant Solutions software team, at least as far as “they” was concerned. The slide read, “In the United States and other western nations, white people are socialized to feel they are inherently superior because they are white.”

Larry Saunders was sitting in the training room at Brilliant Solutions and not at all feeling inherently superior. He was the senior engineer for the software team who would have been the AMRAAM program manager instead of Ketanji Brown if not for the diversity, equity and inclusion quotas imposed on Brilliant Solutions by DOD. In fact, he was feeling like a fool for actually believing he worked for a company and lived in a country that rewarded excellence and hard work rather than melanin content and genitalia. He sat back in his chair half paying attention and stewing with resentment as the diversity trainer continued with “their” presentation. *These people have a nerve, lecturing me about racism when they are the biggest racists going! Every minute wasted on this garbage is a minute not doing real work!* Then the diversity trainer started talking about what, exactly, was required to fix the problem of white people feeling inherently superior. The slide advised Larry and his team to "be less white." Larry could not believe his eyes when he saw the slide. *Can you imagine if the slide said, "be less black?!"* According to the slide, there were a multitude of ways Larry and the other white guys on the team could be less white. They could be "less oppressive, less arrogant, less certain, less defensive, less ignorant, more humble, listen more, believe more, break with apathy, and, last but not least, break with white solidarity."

"I have a question," said Larry, deciding he had enough and raising his hand.

"Yes," answered the diversity trainer, happy for the classroom engagement.

"What does that last point mean, breaking with white solidarity?"

"Good question!" enthused the diversity trainer. "They" strained to read Larry's name tag and his preferred pronoun list. The preferred pronoun list was now required by Brilliant Solutions whenever a person's name was presented, be it on name tags or email. "What it means, Larry, is breaking with the white privilege power structure to support the advancement of people of color."

"But it's ok for people of color to have solidarity?"

"Yes, we encourage their solidarity as a means of empowerment."

"So, just to make sure I'm understanding, it's ok for people of color to organize and feel affinity for people who look like them, that is, other people of color, but it's not ok for white people to do the same thing."

"Yes, that's right, because of our culture's history of white supremacism."

"That's interesting. I'm sure you know sociologists like yourself have studied this feeling of affinity for people who look like themselves—I believe it's called tribalism—and they've found it's actually measurable."

"Of course."

"They've done experiments where they show people pictures of different ethnic groups. They've generally found people have a positive bias toward their own group. Whites are biased to feel more favorably toward whites, blacks toward blacks, Asians toward Asians and so on."

The diversity trainer was growing impatient. "I'm aware of that, Larry. What's your point?"

"Well, I just find it interesting. There's one and only one group that does not exhibit this positive bias toward its own ethnic group. They actually demonstrate a negative bias."

"And what group is that?"

"White liberals."

"I really don't see what you're getting at, Larry." The diversity trainer was no longer impatient. She was decidedly annoyed.

"Well, I'm just trying to understand. You're white, right? Unless you identify as another ethnicity." Larry did not wait for an answer. "And based on your presentation, I think it safe to assume you're liberal. So, I'd really like to know … What is it about you white liberals that makes you different from all these other groups? What is it that makes you despise your own ethnic group?"

"My problem with being white," answered the diversity trainer coldly, "is white people are uniquely responsible for slavery."

"Sorry," shot back Larry, "that is not a true statement. Every ethnic group, at one time or another, practiced slavery. And in case you don't know, which you evidently don't, it was white people who led the effort to end slavery in the western world."

The diversity trainer flushed red with anger. "Why don't we take this offline, Larry."

"I'd love to but, just for the benefit of the class, I'd like to posit my own hypothesis. Maybe the problem here is that there is something uniquely wrong with white liberals. Maybe, deep down, white liberals genuinely loath themselves, and the only way they can stop loathing themselves is to push this anti-white racism. Anti-white racism makes white liberals feel better about themselves. 'Hey everybody, look how enlightened I am! I'm so enlightened I actually hate my own ethnic group!' Is that it, Madam Diversity Trainer?" Larry's voice turned suddenly solicitous. "Oh, I'm sorry. Did I say madam? I forgot you're a they/them/theirs." His solicitousness was obviously insincere.

That was the end of Larry's employment with Brilliant Solutions. HR told him he could either resign or be fired for violating the company's community spirit and tolerance policy. Larry chose to be fired.

Things did not improve at Brilliant Solutions with the purging of Larry Saunders and a few other old white guys suffering from WRS or white rage syndrome. In fact, things became even worse. Ketanji missed another delivery milestone and the program was now seriously over budget. Fortuitously for Ketanji, she found an opportunity at XTremeDefense, the prime contractor for AMRAAM. She also found her true talent: marketing.

"The Diversity Missile!" she fairly shouted with excitement to the diversity, equity and inclusion manager at XTremeDefense only a few months after hiring on. "Because diversity is our strength! We can market it as the nation's first missile designed and manufactured by a certifiably diverse work force, with diversity at every level, from the managers in the corner office to the engineers on their computers to the technicians on the production line. Of course, we'll have to change the name from AMRAAM to something that reflects our commitment to diversity. I'm thinking BIPOCAAM, for black, indigenous, people of color air-to-air missile. That can be its formal name, which may be a little too technical, a little too awkward for our marketing campaign. For our marketing campaign, I really like 'the Diversity Missile.' I think it's catchy." She held her arms out wide as if imagining a banner and proclaimed in a dramatic voice, "The Diversity Missile, because diversity is our strength!"

The diversity, equity and inclusion manager loved the idea and immediately took it to her vice president. The vice president of diversity, equity and inclusion also loved it and took it to the president and chief executive officer of XTremeDefense. He immediately saw its potential in an environment of shrinking defense budgets. No one in Congress would dare cut orders for the nation's first Diversity Missile. He also had no doubt the Penn Administration would be an enthusiastic supporter, given its LGBTQIA+ constituency. His only question was whether they could somehow work-in climate change as well as diversity. The vice president of diversity, equity and inclusion finally convinced him to leave climate change out of it. People might suspect XTremeDefense guilty of cynical sloganeering.

Admiral Turner, commander of the United States Pacific Fleet was also quick to see the Diversity Missile's potential. In his case, the potential was for higher office rather than additional orders. In particular, he aspired to be the next chief of naval operations on the Joint Chiefs of Staff. He thought the

Diversity Missile just the ticket to differentiate himself from the competition while also demonstrating his woke bona fides. He decided he would personally champion rolling out the Diversity Missile to the Pacific Fleet, starting with the USS Rachel Levine.

So it was Ketanji Brown was invited to join the USS Rachel Levine in the South China Sea. Officially, Ketanji Brown was there to demonstrate the commitment of XTremeDefense to the Diversity Missile project, serving as the single point of contact for the Navy to access the technical and diversity expertise of XTremeDefense should there be any issues with the Diversity Missile. No technical issues were expected because, in reality, there were no significant technical changes to the missile. No diversity issues were expected, either, seeing as Ketanji Brown was a black female.

"How's it going with our Diversity Missile?" asked Captain Clancy. He liked to walk around the ship when not up on the bridge to make sure the ship was shipshape and to get a sense of the crew's morale. He thought the crew's morale sky-high today. They had avenged the loss of the USS Mustin. He also thought the crew a little anxious. When he stopped to ask some of the crew their thoughts, they said they were wondering how the Chinese would respond. A few said they were concerned the Chinese would attack the USS Rachel Levine.

Lieutenant Milligan was assigned to escort Ketanji Brown and the reporter from the Navy Times to make sure they did not get lost in the ship's maze of passageways, or inadvertently put themselves in a dangerous situation. All the machinery and aircraft in the crowded confines of an aircraft carrier make it an inherently dangerous place. Lieutenant Milligan had not seen Captain Clancy walk up. He had been busy watching Ketanji Brown pose for the photographer. He turned around with a start. When he saw it was Captain Clancy, he answered cheerfully, "Going well, Captain! Ketanji just finished a video interview and now we're doing some still photos."

"Is Lieutenant Milligan taking good care of you, Ketanji?" asked Captain Clancy, fully expecting that Lieutenant Milligan was.

"He is, Captain. Absolutely. I think he's already saved me from falling down two, maybe three open equipment hatches."

Captain Clancy looked at Lieutenant Milligan and said with the barest hint of a smile, "Well done, Lieutenant."

"Thank you, Captain."

"So, this is it," said Captain Clancy, turning to look at the Diversity Missile, "our secret weapon against the Chinese." He knew the Diversity Missile was important to Admiral Turner, which meant it was important to him. "Crews having any issues mounting the Diversity Missile to aircraft?"

"None," Ketanji Brown answered proudly. "As far as mounting and flight checking goes, the Diversity Missile is identical to the old AMRAAM."

"Glad to hear it. How 'bout operationally? How is the Diversity Missile improved over the old AMRAAM?"

"Captain, XTremeDefense has leveraged its commitment to diversity to provide the Navy with the most capable missile in the world."

Captain Clancy was also a naval aviator, which is a requirement to command an aircraft carrier in the United States Navy. "Ok," he said, not expecting what he thought was a bullshit public relations answer. "Specifically, from a pilot's perspective, what's different about the Diversity Missile? Greater range? Better guidance? Improved off-boresight capability?"

"We focused on improving the Diversity Missile's reliability, Captain, which XTremeDefense believes is best enhanced when we provide a supportive and inclusive environment for our employees."

Captain Clancy's eyes narrowed. "You're telling me this is basically the same old AMRAAM, the one that was last updated ... What, eight years ago?"

"Not at all," protested Ketanji Brown. "It's a much more reliable platform ... because we have a much more diverse workforce. As I'm sure you know, Captain, diversity is our greatest strength."

Senior Chief Petty Officer Sanchez was standing nearby supervising some last-minute maintenance on one of the Super Hornets. He could not help but overhear the conversation. He muttered under his breath, "Rainbow flags and slogans ain't gonna win no wars."

Captain Clancy's next question was cut short by the klaxon sounding battle stations. The sound of the klaxon was almost painful as it reverberated in the huge hanger bay. Then the announcement came over the ship's 1MC. "Man battle stations. Man battle stations. This is not a drill."

CHAPTER ELEVEN

Many pilots of the time were [of] the opinion that a fighter pilot in a closed cockpit was an impossible thing, because you should smell the enemy. You could smell them because of the oil they were burning.

— Adolf Galland, German Luftwaffe, World War II ace

THE REGIMENT OF eighteen Xian H-6N bombers took off from their Hainan airbase. The H-6 is a twin-engine medium bomber based on an old Soviet design from the 1950s. It was first introduced to service in the PLA Air Force in 1969 as a conventional free-fall bomber and, later, a nuclear free-fall bomber. Many improvements to the basic design occurred over the years, much like with the American B-52 bomber which first entered service in 1955 and is still flying today. The latest variant of the H-6 is the H-6N. It is optimized for long-range, stand-off missile attacks on United States carrier strike groups using, in particular, the YJ-12 anti-ship missile.

The YJ-12 anti-ship missile is a beast of a weapon. It is twenty-three feet long, two feet in diameter and weighs over five thousand pounds. Its long range, supersonic speed and terminal maneuvering capability make it a formidable anti-ship missile not easily intercepted by current United States carrier strike group air defenses, and devastating should it find its target. Each H-6N bomber carries six YJ-12 anti-ship missiles. A regiment of H-6N bombers can, therefore, attack a carrier strike group with one hundred and eight YJ-12 anti-ship missiles. The YJ-12 anti-ship missile also comes in a land-based variant. Twenty-four YJ-12s were based on Chinese military outposts in the Spratly Islands, at Mischief Reef and Subi Reef.

Flying nearly a hundred miles in front of the H-6N bomber regiment were four squadrons of Chengdu J-20 Mighty Dragon fighters. With sixteen aircraft per squadron, there were a total of sixty-four Mighty Dragons in the air. The Mighty Dragon is China's most advanced fighter. It is a fifth-generation stealth fighter comparable to the American F-35 Lightning II. The Mighty Dragons were configured for air-to-air combat operations and, accordingly, were carrying a full complement of six medium-range Thunderbolt-16 missiles and two short-range Thunderbolt-10 missiles. Where the Thunderbolt-15 missile used by Lieutenant Lin Dan in his defense against the American cruise missile attack on Yongxing Island was considered the rough equivalent to the latest version of the AMRAAM—since renamed the BIPOCAAM and popularly known as the Diversity Missile—the Thunderbolt-16 was developed with the explicit goal of producing a better missile than the Diversity Missile, through greater range and a more capable active-radar homing system. The Chinese pursued this goal with their usual single-minded determination. Also, their personnel approach was fundamentally different from the approach used by the Americans. While the Americans were focused on achieving the perfect mix of skin color, sex, gender and sexual orientation, the Chinese were focused on hiring and promoting people based on actual performance. The Chinese had a term for this novel personnel approach. They called it "meritocracy."

Far and away, this was the largest scramble of aircraft in Chinese history. The attack plan for the PLA Air Force was simple. The Mighty Dragons would dash in using their tremendous speed and kill the E-2D Hawkeye while it was protected by only two flights of Lightning IIs. The horizon of the American radar coverage would then be cut in half, to that which was provided by their ship-born radars. The Chinese would still have the benefit of their airborne warning and control aircraft. Combined with the Chinese numerical edge in fighter aircraft, killing the E-2D Hawkeye would allow the Mighty Dragons to clear a path for the H-6N bombers.

The E-2D Hawkeye with the call sign Baseplate was flying a racetrack pattern approximately two hundred miles in front of the carrier strike group. In addition to its conventional radar frequency bands, it also had a lower UHF frequency band. The UHF frequency band allowed the E-2D Hawkeye to detect the Mighty Dragons even though the Mighty Dragon is a true fifth-generation stealth fighter. Detection is one thing, targeting another. Massive computer processing capability on the E-2D Hawkeye improved the inherently poor resolution of the UHF frequency band such that "a picture" was produced sufficiently resolved for targeting. Although the E-2D Hawkeye carried no weapons itself, data links shared this targeting information with all weapons in the carrier strike group, including those on the carrier's air wing.

Baseplate first detected only two contacts. Then it detected a dozen. Then it detected the massive force of Mighty Dragons and bombers bearing down on it and the carrier strike group. The contacts were 280 miles out from Baseplate's location and closing at six hundred mph, which was ten miles a minute.

"Combat, Baseplate. You seeing this? 7-0 contacts plus. Bearing 3-5-2 degrees from your position. Speed 5-2-0 knots. Altitude 1-0 thousand feet."

Combat was short for the combat direction center which was below the flight deck of the USS Rachel Levine, just under the aircraft carrier's island. All tactical decisions for fighting the carrier and its strike group are made in the combat direction center. The carrier's commanding officer delegates authority to "fight the ship" and "fight the strike group" to the officer in charge of the combat direction center.

Commander Dan Schmaeling was the officer in charge of the combat direction center. He picked up the phone. "Baseplate, combat. I see it." He was looking at the screen in the combat direction center slaved to the radar display in Baseplate. He turned to Commander Brent House, the strike warfare commander. The strike warfare commander is responsible for the carrier's air wing. "Commander House, enemy contacts bearing 3-5-2 degrees. Engage with combat air patrol. Launch the alert flight on deck. Given the seventy-plus contacts, get the Eagles and Diamondbacks on the flight deck and in the air. Also, ready the Dambusters for air-to-air combat."

The Eagles, Diamondbacks and Dambusters were the three squadrons in the hanger bay. The Eagles and Diamondbacks were ready for immediate combat operations. The Dambusters were not yet armed. The squadron on the flight deck and currently in the air was the Royal Maces.

"Roger enemy contact," confirmed Commander Brent House, "engage with combat air patrol. Get Eagles and Diamondbacks airborne. Ready Dambusters."

Commander Dan Schmaeling picked up the phone. "Air warfare, combat."

A voice answered immediately. "Combat, air warfare."

Air warfare was the only warfare commander not physically located in the combat direction center. He was in the combat information center or CIC of the USS Shiloh, a Ticonderoga class guided missile cruiser. The USS Shiloh was responsible for defending the carrier strike group against all air and missile threats. The USS Shiloh did this using the Aegis combat system. It integrated the radars and missiles on all three escorts in the carrier strike group. The air warfare officer was also looking at the slaved radar screen from Baseplate.

"Strike warfare engaging 7-0 plus contacts," said Commander Schmaeling. "Bearing 3-5-2 degrees. You've got the leakers."

"Roger that. Air warfare has the leakers."

The two flights of Lightning IIs from the Royal Maces were 160 miles north of the carrier strike group and 320 miles from the Mighty Dragons when they received their "tally-ho" to attack. They went to afterburner and were soon traveling at the Lightning II's top speed of Mach 1.7 or 1,300 mph. The Chinese airborne warning radar detected the Lightning IIs not long after they turned north. The Mighty Dragons also went to afterburner.

The Mighty Dragons were faster and, soon, were traveling Mach 2.2 or 1,700 mph. The combined closing speed of the two formations was Mach 3.9 or 3,000 mph, which was fifty miles every minute. In just under four minutes, the two formations were only 120 miles apart and within range of the Thunderbolt-16. Each Mighty Dragon carried six Thunderbolt-16s in their internal weapons bay. The lead squadron of sixteen Mighty Dragons fired sixteen Thunderbolt-16s, assigning two to each target. The Lightning IIs with their shorter-range Diversity Missile had to wait. Thirty seconds later, the Diversity Missile was within range. The Lightning IIs opened their internal weapons bay doors and salvoed all thirty-two Diversity Missiles in their two-flight formation.

Both the Diversity Missile and the Thunderbolt-16 are not quite true fire-and-forget weapons. The launch platform provides the target's location before launch and the missile then uses its own internal navigation system to fly an intercept course. Updates can be provided along the way via a data link with either the launch platform or another platform such as an airborne warning and control system like Baseplate. When the missile closes to its active-radar homing distance, it then locks onto the target. At that point, when the target is "in the basket," the missile is tracking the target on its own.

Trusting in Baseplate to update the Diversity Missile's intercept course, the Lightning IIs went defensive. They dove for the deck to try and evade the incoming Thunderbolt-16s. They were only partly successful. Five of the eight Lightning IIs were destroyed. The surviving Lightning IIs headed back to the USS Rachel Levine to be refueled and rearmed.

The Diversity Missiles took another sixteen seconds to reach the Mighty Dragons. The Mighty Dragons were also defensive and were also only partly successful in evading the incoming Diversity Missiles. Twelve Mighty Dragons were destroyed.

Less than a minute later, Baseplate was within range of the Mighty Dragons and their Thunderbolt-16s. The Mighty Dragons launched four Thunderbolt-16s at Baseplate. Baseplate was a twin-engine turboprop with a large radome that made the aircraft anything but maneuverable. It was doomed the moment the Mighty Dragons launched their missiles.

Before Baseplate died, the third flight of Lightning IIs from the Royal Maces was within range of the Mighty Dragon's Thunderbolt-16s. The Mighty Dragons fired twelve missiles, assigning three missiles per target. Twenty seconds later, the Lightning IIs salvoed all sixteen of their Diversity Missiles. The Mighty Dragons dove for the deck to evade the incoming Diversity Missiles, counting on their airborne warning and control system radar to provide updated intercept data to their Thunderbolt-16s. So, too, did the Lightning IIs. Baseplate provided this updated intercept data until the moment it died, which was before the active-radar homing of the Diversity Missiles had their target in the basket. The Diversity Missiles continued on, finding nothing but empty sky. The Thunderbolt-16s homed in and destroyed the entire third flight from the Royal Maces.

Two minutes later, the same scenario played out with the first flight from the Eagles. The longer range of the Thunderbolt-16 combined with the absence of target intercept data from Baseplate gave the Mighty Dragons a decisive advantage. The Mighty Dragons were unscathed while all four Lightning IIs in the first flight from the Eagles were destroyed.

"We lost Baseplate," said Commander Brent House, the strike warfare commander responsible for the carrier's air wing. Commander Dan Schmaeling nodded slowly, an invisible fist grabbing his stomach and twisting it in a knot. Without Baseplate, the radar horizon for their carrier strike group was reduced to what they could see with their ship-based radars, which was only 150 miles for medium- and high-altitude targets, and much less than that for low-altitude targets, which meant he could not intercept the Chinese bombers before they were in range to launch their cruise missiles, which meant he would not be able to detect the low flying cruise missiles until they were very close, maybe forty or fifty miles out, which meant the cruise missiles would be very difficult to intercept.

"Air warfare," said Commander Brent House, "get everything that will fly up in the air with a max loadout of air-to-air missiles. Position them to our north to intercept the cruise missiles from the bombers. Position a flight to our east, too, to intercept cruise missiles from the Spratlys."

"Roger that. Everything that will fly to our north and a flight to our east. Max loadout of air-to-air missiles."

The USS Rachel Levine immediately started launching aircraft. Fifteen minutes later, the last of her aircraft were airborne. About the same time, the H-6N bombers reached the launch point for their cruise missiles, 210 miles north of the carrier strike group. Six YJ-12s dropped from each bomber. Their solid-propellent rocket boosters propelled the YJ-12s to over Mach 3 or 2,300 mph. When their propellent was exhausted, the rocket boosters fell away and the ramjets took over. One hundred and eight YJ-12s descended to a cruise altitude of eighty feet and followed their intercept course. Supersonic shock waves left rooster tails of salt water in their wake. A short time later, the Chinese outposts on Mischief Reef and Subi Reef launched all twenty-four of their YJ-12s. The short delay was intended to coordinate the strike, so the YJ-12s from the bombers and outposts would reach the carrier strike group simultaneously.

A minute after launch, the YJ-12s from the H-6N bombers had closed the distance to the carrier strike group to 168 miles, which is when the surviving two flights from the Eagles found them. The two flights salvoed their thirty-two Diversity Missiles. The Diversity Missiles accelerated to Mach 4. The combined closing speed of the YJ-12s and Diversity Missiles was Mach 7.5 or 5,700 mph. The Diversity Missiles switched to active-radar homing fifteen miles from their targets. As soon as the YJ-12s detected the active-radar homing of the Diversity Missiles, they started maneuvering to evade interception. In less than ten seconds the missiles crossed paths. The incredible closing speed combined with the YJ-12's ability to maneuver reduced the effectiveness of the Diversity Missiles. Only nine YJ-12s were destroyed.

Another minute passed. The YJ-12s had closed the distance to 126 miles. Ten Super Hornets from the Diamondbacks were in position to attack and salvoed their inventory of Diversity Missiles. Each Super Hornet carried ten Diversity Missiles as opposed to the four carried by the Lightning II. The Super Hornets could carry a larger missile payload since they were not constrained to carry missiles in an internal weapons bay. More missiles meant more kills. Another twenty-six YJ-12s were destroyed.

Only three minutes after being launched from the H-6N bombers, the YJ-12s had closed the distance to eighty-five miles. Six Super Hornets from the Dambusters found them and salvoed their Diversity Missiles with similar results. Sixteen YJ-12s died.

The USS Shiloh's Aegis combat system locked-on to the remaining fifty-seven YJ-12s from the H-6N bombers when they were just over fifty miles from the carrier strike group. A moment later it locked-on to the thirteen YJ-12s from the Chinese outposts in the Spratly Islands. A flight of Super Hornets from the Diamondbacks had destroyed eleven of the original twenty-four YJ-12s launched from the Chinese outposts there. Even though the Aegis combat system had over 150 cells in her VLS loaded with air-to-air missiles, she had just over a minute to launch them. It was not enough time. Geysers of flame erupted from the USS Shiloh, the USS Curtis Wilbur and the USS Barry as missiles leapt from their VLS cells at a desperate firing rate. Altogether, the three escorts launched over ninety air-to-air missiles. They destroyed another twenty-four YJ-12s.

Which left forty-six YJ-12s heading straight for the carrier strike group.

***

Ketanji Brown was sitting in the empty hanger bay consulting the notes she had taken while the squadrons in the hanger bay were frantically scrambled up onto the flight deck. One of the first things she noticed when she came on board the USS Rachel Levine were the colored shirts worn by the sailors who made up the deck crew. When she asked her escort, Lieutenant Milligan, about these, he informed her it was a way of keeping track of who does what without having to resort to verbal communication, which can be very difficult in such a noisy environment. Lieutenant Milligan explained the color coding: green shirts are maintenance personnel, blue shirts are aircraft elevator operators, yellow shirts are aircraft handlers, red shirts are ordnance handlers and purple shirts are aviation fuel handlers.

Ketanji Brown was intrigued by this color coding and, seeing the world through a racial lens, wondered if there was true diversity with the deck crew shirt colors. She drew a matrix on her notepad. Shirt colors were denoted in a column on the lefthand margin of the notepad while people colors were denoted in a row running across the top of the page. She then systematically observed the deck crews working in the hanger bay. She made a checkmark in each matrix box based on the individual's shirt color and skin color. A white guy with a red shirt received a checkmark in the matrix box for white person/red shirt. A black guy with a green shirt received a checkmark in the matrix box for black person/green shirt. And so on. She thought briefly about trying to incorporate sex in her matrix but decided that would make things too complicated. When she was finished, she had over two hundred checkmarks in her matrix. She also had a disturbing pattern. The checkmarks were not evenly distributed. There were noticeably more white people wearing red shirts, and noticeably more black people wearing yellow shirts. Clearly, she thought, there is some kind of systemic racism at work.

"Is the red shirt work more desirable?" Ketanji Brown asked Lieutenant Milligan.

"What?" he asked, distracted and looking concerned. Even though the huge armored elevator doors of the hanger bay had been shut, Lieutenant Milligan could still hear the roar of surface-to-air missiles being launched from the three escort ships.

"The red shirts ... They're the ordnance handlers, right?"

"Right."

"I was just wondering. Is that considered a prestigious job? Is it a sought-after job?"

"Would you want to handle bombs all day?" asked Lieutenant Milligan.

"Is there more pay involved?" asked Ketanji Brown. "You know, like hazard pay?"

"I really don't know," he answered.

Ketanji Brown took her last breath resolving to find out if the red-shirt ordnance handlers were paid more than the yellow-shirt aircraft handlers. A YJ-12 anti-ship missile slammed into the side of the USS Rachel Levine just forward of where Ketanji Brown and Lieutenant Milligan were seated along with the reporter from the Navy Times. The YJ-12 penetrated the inch thick steel hull of the hanger bay as if it were paper. An instant later, when the missile was in the center of the hanger bay, its 1,100 pound high-explosive warhead detonated. The shock wave from the detonation pulverized Ketanji Brown, Lieutenant Milligan and the Navy Times reporter, turning their bodies into a fine red mist. Their central nervous systems operated at a much slower processing speed than the speed of the shock wave from the explosion so they experienced neither alarm nor pain. Another seventeen YJ-12s impacted up and down the length of the USS Rachel Levine. Over half her 5,500-person crew was killed and wounded outright. The survivors were left to battle a hundred raging fires. They battled valiantly but in vain. Ten minutes after the YJ-12s first struck, the order was given to abandon ship.

The USS Shiloh, USS Curtis Wilbur and USS Barry fared even worse. Multiple YJ-12 hits ruptured bulkheads and fuel bunkers and killed most of their crews. The survivors immediately abandoned ship as the ships rapidly took on water and started to list. The USS Shiloh slipped under the waves first, only five minutes after first being struck. She was followed shortly afterwards by the USS Barry and then the USS Curtis Wilbur.

The USS Rachel Levine lingered on until the flames found one of her magazines. Her surviving crew, bobbing on the sea in their orange life vests, felt the blast's concussion through the water. With the side of her hull ripped open, the USS Rachel Levine rapidly took on water. Her bow dipped beneath the waves first. Then she rolled over with a huge, hissing groan and sank to the bottom of the sea.

With nowhere to land and low on fuel, the stunned pilots of Carrier Strike Group Five headed toward the nearest airfield, friendly or not. They were more than ninety miles from the coast of Vietnam when they ran out of fuel. One by one, they ditched in the South China Sea.

BOOK III

THE FREE STATES OF LIBERTY

CHAPTER ONE

But I know, somehow, that only when it is dark enough can you see the stars.

— Martin Luther King Jr.

GREEN FUTURE ONE was a solar farm in the middle of the Mojave Desert in California. It was one of Supreme Leader Johnny Penn's prestige projects. At his direction, it was designed to be the largest solar farm on the planet. It had a total peak capacity of over five thousand megawatts which was generated by ten million solar panels on nearly thirty thousand acres. All that was required to generate this total peak capacity was a bright, clear summer day and clean solar panels. The weather was up to God or the giddy dance of atoms, depending upon your political persuasion, of which only one was publicly tolerated, and that was the persuasion that was not the least bit interested in God. The clean solar panels were up to Officer Leah Blunt, otherwise known as Prisoner 1538762 in the Democratic People's Republic of America or DPRA.

Leah and her fellow prisoner, Celine, who the DPRA knew as Prisoner 3689134, had spent the last three years assigned to the same cleaning team, lifting the same cleaning rig onto row after row of solar panels. Lifting the cleaning rig had never been easy, both because of its awkward size and its weight. It was twelve feet long and weighed over a hundred pounds. When they were first assigned to the cleaning crew, they made sure to coordinate their movements. "One, two, three, lift!" they said in unison before hoisting the cleaning rig the requisite four feet from the ground. As the months turned into years and muscle mass melted from their bodies—they were not getting enough to eat—they increasingly struggled. One day, they were simply unable to lift the cleaning rig. They were unable to lift it no matter how hard they tried.

The DPRA Department of Reeducation guard ran over and started screaming at them. "What's the matter with you, you lazy fascist maggots?! You're falling behind the rest of the crews! Get that rig on the panels! Now!"

"I can't physically do it!" protested Leah. She had collapsed to her knees. "I'm trying but I just can't!"

"You just can't?!" screamed the guard, sending flecks of sputum into Leah's face. The guard was bending forward at the waist so his face was only inches from Leah's. "Who do you think you're talking to?! One of your fellow fascist maggots?!"

"I'm … I'm … sorry, Comrade Reeducation Officer," stammered Leah, horrified she had forgotten the required protocol for addressing him. "No disrespect intended, Comrade Reeducation Officer."

The guard straightened up. His size alone made him physically imposing. Dressed in the uniform of the DPRA Department of Reeducation, he was still more imposing. He wore black jackboots, a military style gray shirt with gray cargo pants, and a heavy black duty belt. His duty belt was festooned with a holster and pistol, extra magazines, baton, radio and handcuffs. His uniform was topped off by a gray peaked cap with a short black visor, black band, and the emblem of the DPRA in the center of the crown. The DPRA emblem was a rainbow-colored globe set atop a crossed hammer and sickle. The hammer and sickle were both colored gold. Finally, an all-seeing eye was perched atop the globe. The eye included the anatomical detail of a white sclera, blue iris and black eyelashes.

It was a hot July day in the Mojave Desert and, even though it was not yet 11 a.m., the temperature was already well over a hundred degrees. Sweat beaded on the guard's face. His shirt had a wide, spreading sweat stain that grew up from his belt and covered most of the front of his shirt. The guard looked down at Leah and smiled a cruel, crooked smile. "Well, maggot," he said in a voice that was now calm, "if you just can't do it, that means you're of no use to the DPRA. And if you're of no use to the DPRA …" The guard shook his head slowly from side to side as if he felt sorry for Leah, which he obviously did not. "If you're of no use to us, it will not be good for you. And it will not be good for your fellow slacker here, either, because, well, the DPRA does not tolerate slackers, especially fascist maggot slackers."

The guard grabbed hold of the handle of his pistol. He did not draw the pistol from his holster. He just kept his hand there. "One minute," he said to Leah and Celine. He said it without emotion which made it all the more ominous. "You have one minute to get that cleaning rig on the panel." He looked at each of them in turn to make sure they understood. Then he walked away.

Celine started to sob. "I'm sorry, Leah. I'm sorry. I just can't ..."

"No, no, no, don't be sorry!" said Leah. "We're going to disappoint that sadistic fuckin' prick!" There was determination in her voice. She closed her eyes and willed herself to forget about their would-be executioner. *Focus on the problem, Leah. How do we get this rig on the panels? How do we do it when I can't lift my end and Celine can't lift hers?* Then it came to her. *The two of us lift one end together! The two of us can lift one end together, put it on the panel, and then run back to lift the other end! The two of us can push it the rest of the way on!*

"I know how to do this!" said Leah.

"How?" asked Celine, desperately hoping for a reprieve.

Leah ran around to Celine's end of the rig, the end closest to the solar panel. "We'll lift it up together, get it on the panel, and then run back to the other end and push it the rest of the way on."

"Ok," said Celine, wiping the tears from her face. "Let's do it!"

"One, two, three, lift!" they said in unison. They lifted the cleaning rig and set it on the edge of the solar panel. Then they ran around to the other end and pushed. It was easier than they imagined with half the weight of the cleaning rig now supported by the panel. The cleaning rig slid up the face of the panel until the wheel at the top of the rig slipped over the panel's upper edge, locking the rig in its proper cleaning position.

"We did it!" shouted Celine, throwing her arms around Leah.

"Yes we did!" exclaimed Leah, returning her hug. She struggled to catch her breath after the exertion.

The guard had been watching the whole time. He walking up to the two of them and said with his cruel, crooked smile, "Amazing what a little motivation will do."

Celine and Leah let go of each other and stood there in front of him, looking down at the ground as required of them when addressed by a guard of the DPRA Department of Reeducation, unless told otherwise.

"Do you think I really would have shot you if you did not get this cleaning rig on the solar panels?" he asked nonchalantly, as if it was a matter of little consequence.

"Yes, Comrade Reeducation Officer," answered Leah.

"And you, Prisoner 134?" asked the guard, only bothering with the last three digits of Celine's prison number.

"Yes, Comrade Reeducation Officer," answered Celine.

He nodded. "That's right. Putting a bullet through your brains so our planet has two fewer fascist maggots to support would give me nothing but pleasure. Remember that! I only let you live as long as you're useful to the DPRA, which means as long as you're useful to me. Is that clear?"

"Yes, Comrade Reeducation Officer," answered Leah and Celine together.

"Now get this fuckin' row of panels cleaned!" ordered the guard.

"Yes, Comrade Reeducation Officer," echoed Leah and Celine.

Leah and Celine ran to their positions on either end of the cleaning rig and started walking it along the row of solar panels. The cleaning rig's water-powered roller brushes scrubbed off and washed away the accumulated dust, pollen and bird droppings. If not cleaned regularly, Green Future One was dramatically less efficient. A dirty solar panel is only half as efficient as a clean one.

Green Future One was truly immense. Its ten million solar panels were arranged in a rectangular array one thousand panels across and ten thousand panels long which, in more conventional units, was nearly a mile across and fifty miles long. The long, narrow shape of the rectangular array was in anticipation of Green Future Two, Green Future Three and however many more Green Futures were required to make up for the fossil fuels that had been banned by Supreme Leader Johnny Penn as part of his Great Green Leap Forward. Once, in one of her few quiet moments back at the DPRA Department of Reeducation labor camp, identified only as Labor Camp 847, Leah decided to calculate how long it would take her and Celine to clean all the solar panels in Green Future One, just the two of them. Assuming thirty seconds per panel, she calculated 9.5 years. She thought that number amazing in its own right. Then she realized it assumed she and Celine were working 24/7, with no breaks for eating, sleeping and the mandatory reeducation programs. Limiting her cleaning time to her current schedule, which was ten hours a day, seven days a week, she came up with twenty-three years. Green Future One required monthly cleaning to maintain its solar panels at peak efficiency. It was that monthly cleaning schedule that explained the nearly one thousand prisoners at Labor Camp 847, in the middle of nowhere in the California Mojave Desert.

Leah came to be in Labor Camp 847 by way of the California Institute for Women in Riverside County. She was sent there after her trial for second-degree murder for shooting Raymond James and Dwayne Armstrong. She and her husband, Ayad, had mortgaged their home to hire the best legal team money could buy. It was no use. After the mass carnage and bloodshed of the Great Riot of 2025, a riot that dwarfed the George Floyd riots of 2020, everyone knew she was guilty. The judge knew it, the prosecutors knew it, the jury knew it, even her own defense team knew it, although they were still willing to take her money. The jury deliberated all of one hour before taking their first vote. The first vote was "guilty" on both counts. When the judge was informed of the jury's verdict, he told them to go back and think about it another day. He wanted at least the appearance of deliberation.

The judge sentenced Leah to twenty years for each conviction of second-degree murder, to be served consecutively. With little prospect for parole, it was, in effect, a life sentence. When the judge announced the sentence, Leah was emotionless, just as she was when the verdict was announced. She had been resigned to her fate for some time. She appreciated the police union supporting her with their labor action but she did not see the politicians dropping the charges. They were trapped by their rhetoric and the expectations of their constituencies even if they had any interest in changing their minds. Then, after the massacre in Santa Clarita and the Great Riot of 2025, she fell into a deep depression. She blamed herself for the terrible violence and loss of life. She even thought seriously of suicide. She sat in her living room in the middle of the night, unable to sleep again.

She had started reading the Bible which she had not touched since she was an adolescent in Sunday School, hoping to find some understanding, some solace, for why this was happening to her and her family. She found none and railed at heaven. "Why, God?! What did I do to deserve this?! I'm a good person! You're taking everything from me! Everything! My husband! My chance to have children! Everything! How can you do this to me and call yourself a loving God?! How, God?! How?!"

She fell on her knees and sobbed. She sobbed for nearly an hour until numbed by despair. Then she heard a voice. It came from deep inside her and told her she did not have to suffer anymore. There was a way out. There was a way she could finally have peace. All she had to do was pick up her pistol, put it to her head and pull the trigger.

At that moment, the promise of peace was irresistible. She walked to the kitchen and opened the cabinet where she stored her pistol. She took the pistol and pulled the slide back to confirm there was a round in the chamber. She saw the shiny brass of the cartridge case and pushed the slide back home. Then she dropped the magazine to confirm the magazine was full. It was and she pushed it back into the handle of the pistol. There was a metallic click when the magazine locked in place. She did all that without thinking because that was her routine, ingrained in her from years of handling firearms. She walked back to the sofa. The pistol felt cold and heavy in her hand. The voice came to her again as soon as she sat down. "It can all be over, Leah. No more pain. No more heartache. You can finally have peace. Just pull the trigger and you'll sleep forever."

She raised the pistol to her temple. She felt the hard, cold steel of the muzzle press against her skin. When she closed her eyes, she imagined Ayad running down the stairs to find her lifeless body. She had seen more than a few suicides as a police officer and knew it would not be a pretty picture. Then she imagined Ayad kneeling by her side and sobbing in grief. Tears welled up in her eyes and ran down her cheeks. She thought of her parents and how they would be devastated when they heard their daughter had taken her own life. *How can I do that to them?* she asked herself. *I don't deserve what's happening to me but, if I do this to them ... that makes me a selfish coward. And what does it say to the world? If I take my own life, in the eyes of the world, that makes me as guilty as they say I am!*

Another voice came to her. That voice also came from deep inside but it was a different voice. She felt its warmth and knew from the moment it spoke to her it had her best interest at heart. "You can beat this," it said. "You're a good person, Leah. You've always been a good person. You've always cared about people and you always will. You can't let them take that from you. You can't and I know you won't. Let them have their way with you now. They have the power and there's nothing you can do to change that. But their day is coming. I promise you that. They won't always have the power. Know that, Leah. Believe it. And believe you are a good person. Always be that, Leah. Be what you are! Be a good person! *That* will be your victory over them!"

She lowered the pistol from her temple.

The California Institute for Women at Riverside was nothing like Leah expected. The criminals she feared would be out to get her as a law enforcement officer, as a representative of the institution and the society that first arrested them and then set them on their path to incarceration ... They were largely gone. They had been freed in the interest of redressing the systemic racism of the criminal justice system. That is not to say the prison was not crowded. It was packed to the gills. The violent criminals, the drug dealers, the prostitutes and the property crime criminals had been replaced by another kind of prisoner: the political prisoner.

The government viewed the Great Riot of 2025 as an opportunity to attack its political enemies. Its political enemies were anyone who resisted the orgy of destruction and violence that followed the massacre in Santa Clarita. Simply holding a weapon while standing on your front porch or your front lawn resulted in your being arrested and charged with a variety of crimes: for brandishing a firearm, for unlawful use of a weapon, for disrupting a lawful assembly and, finally, for willfully interfering with a person's legal and constitutional right to peacefully protest. No consideration was given to the fact brandishing the weapon is what kept the "peaceful protest" peaceful, or to the fact the assembly was actually unlawful. Ordinarily, these were misdemeanor charges but, in the context of the Great Riot of 2025, the government prosecuted them as felonies. They were obviously hate crimes motived by racial animus. Other charges were clearly felonies. Pointing a firearm at someone was assault with a deadly weapon and actually shooting someone was attempted murder or murder depending upon the defendant's skill with a firearm. The motivating factor of racial animus was applied here, too, not to turn the charges from misdemeanors to felonies but to garner additional prison time. The right of self-defense was never considered.

There was another, larger influx of political prisoners following the election of President Johnny Penn in 2028 and the passage of his Transform America for Good agenda. His Misinformation and Hate Speech Reduction Act criminalized all speech, writings and postings on social media that were either "hateful" or not supported by "the science." Since the government was responsible for deciding what was hateful and what was not supported by the science, it was, in effect, a crime to voice opposition to the government. His Learning for a Better Tomorrow Act made it a criminal offense for any parent to take issue with the course curriculum for their children. Your children will be taught what the Department of Education decides they will be taught and you will like it, or else. Finally, his Common Sense Gun Safety for the Sake of our Children Act effectively outlawed the private possession of firearms. The Founding Father's concerns about a future government turning tyrannical were obviously and hopelessly behind the times, claimed the government. They would be quaint, really, if not for the fact firearms posed such a clear and present danger to public safety.

The biggest influx of political prisoners came following the crushing defeat of the United States Navy in the South China Sea in 2031. The loss of an entire United States Navy carrier strike group, the symbol of American military power since the end of World War II, was a true watershed moment in the history of the world. For a brief moment, the world held its breath as the United States considered responding with nuclear weapons. There was a substantial contingent in Washington forcefully advocating for a nuclear response. Chief among those was President Johnny Penn's national security advisor, Bobby Nuland. As usual, Secretary of State Victoria Albright-Hayden was the lone dissenting voice in his cabinet. The two of them had it out in the Oval Office the day after learning of the worst naval disaster in American history.

"We have to respond, Mr. President!" said Bobby Nuland passionately. "The credibility of the United States is at stake!"

"The survival of the United States is at stake!" shot back Victoria Albright-Hayden. "What do you think the Chinese will do when we nuke their bases on Hainan? You think they're going to suddenly up and apologize for sinking our carrier strike group, because they're suddenly afraid of nuclear weapons? They have their own nuclear weapons, Bobby, and the means to deliver them!"

"But not as many as we do!" countered Bobby Nuland. He turned to President Johnny Penn. "Mr. President, we still have a decisive advantage in both tactical and strategic nuclear delivery systems. The Chinese know that."

"Like they knew our carrier strike groups were invincible?" asked Victoria Albright-Hayden, a cutting, sarcastic edge creeping into her voice. "Wasn't that your idea, Bobby, to use the carrier strike group for retaliation, the one that was actually a sitting duck in the middle of the South China Sea?"

"How was I to know the Chinese would attack with advanced missile technology?!" asked Bobby Nuland, stung by her question.

"Oh, I don't know?" asked Victoria Albright-Hayden. "Maybe by listening to people who don't just tell you what you want to hear. Maybe by considering the vital interests of our adversaries as well as our own. Maybe by obsessing about something other than your own career advancement and the advancement of your bank account!"

"How dare you!" he shouted.

"There you go again!" she shouted back.

"Stop!" yelled President Johnny Penn, slamming his fist on the desk. He stood up and grabbed the jar of M&Ms he kept on the corner of his desk and hurled it across the Oval Office. It struck the wall next to a bookcase and shattered, sending M&Ms and shards of broken glass everywhere. Bobby Nuland and Victoria Albright-Hayden exchanged surprised looks. They had never seen President Johnny Penn lose his temper before.

President Johnny Penn's executive secretary opened the Oval Office door and looked in, an expression of concern on her face. "Everything ok?" she asked, noticing the M&Ms and shards of broken glass scattered across the carpet and hardwood floor.

"Everything's fine, Barbara," said President Johnny Penn, once more composed.

"Ok. Um … I'll call Facilities to come and clean this up. Sorry to disturb you, Mr. President." She closed the door behind her.

President Johnny Penn sat back down behind his desk. He looked hard at Bobby Nuland and Victoria Albright-Hayden. "The next person that raises their voice is out of my office, and out of my administration. Is that clear?"

"Yes, Mr. President," they answered together.

"I want answers, not histrionics."

"Yes, Mr. President," they answered again.

"Tory, you were in the middle of saying something."

Victoria Albright-Hayden took a deep breath to calm herself. "Mr. President, the Chinese are a proud people. They will never *not* respond to a nuclear attack on the Chinese mainland, even if it's limited to a military base. They will hit one of our military bases, like the naval base at San Diego. Then, what will we do? We will have to respond. Mr. President, studies on the use of nuclear weapons during the Cold War concluded there is no way to limit their use. Once one side crosses the threshold of using nuclear weapons, the imperative 'to win' inevitably results in a full-scale nuclear exchange."

"Thank you, Tory. Bobby?"

"Mr. President, there are other studies that show the efficacy of a limited strike on a military target with tactical nuclear weapons. It comes down to the decision makers. We do not want a full-scale nuclear exchange targeting civilian targets and neither do the Chinese. It's in no one's interest. We only want to send the message that the United States is serious about protecting our vital national interests. A limited, tactical nuclear strike at the military bases responsible for the attack on our carrier strike group will clearly communicate that message."

"There is something else, Mr. President," said Victoria Albright-Hayden.

"What's that, Tory?"

"The Chinese and Russians signed a mutual defense pact after the Ukraine War. It pledges the two nations to consider an attack against one as an attack against both."

"Would the Russians really insert themselves here, over something that has nothing to do with Ukraine, and over something that involves nuclear weapons?"

"The Russians and Chinese have grown very close, Mr. President, since the sanctions and the Ukraine War."

"I highly doubt the Russians would get involved," said Bobby Nuland.

"I have some back channels to the Kremlin, Mr. President. With your permission, I would like to use those channels to determine if the Russians will consider this their fight, or if they will be willing to stay on the sidelines."

"That sounds reasonable, Tory. Please do that." He turned to Bobby Nuland. "Bobby, please ask the Joint Chiefs for options for a limited nuclear strike on the responsible Chinese bases. We'll meet back here tomorrow to make a final decision."

Tory had the Russian answer for their meeting the next day. She reported succinctly, "The Russians, Mr. President, will view any first use of nuclear weapons against China as tantamount to a first use of nuclear weapons against Russia itself."

"They're bluffing, Mr. President," said Bobby Nuland.

"Do you think they're bluffing, Tory?" asked President Johnny Penn.

"History shows, Mr. President, the Russians are not in the habit of bluffing."

President Johnny Penn thought a moment. He said finally, "I don't think they're bluffing, either. Besides, I think we have pressing problems here at home that require our attention. Bobby, tell the Joint Chiefs to stand down."

"Mr. President, I urge you to—"

"Bobby," said President Johnny Penn, "my decision's final."

Events would soon prove President Johnny Penn prescient. With the military defeat of the United States in the South China Sea, the world decided it was time to leave the dollar. For decades, the world had watched the United States go from the world's biggest creditor to the world's biggest debtor; from the world's greatest manufacturing power to the world's greatest consumer nation; from the greatest generator of real scientific and technological achievement, as reflected by Nobel Prizes and patents, to the greatest generator of politically-inspired theories concerning gender, climate and revisionist history; from the foremost champion of impartial jurisprudence to a tiered system of justice depending upon your standing with the ruling class; from an independent press with a professional commitment to objective journalism to a press that was little more than an organ for government propaganda; and, finally, from a staunch defender of freedom of speech to a supporter of censorship and cancel culture in the interest of suppressing disinformation, which was really just any opinion at odds with the approved government narrative. Yet, in spite of the manifest indications of a nation in decline, the world continued to cede to the United States its place as "first among equals." In part, they did this because there was no obvious successor to the dollar as the world's reserve currency. They also did this out of deference to the perceived military might of the United States.

It turned out the latter was more important. With the defeat of the United States Navy in the South China Sea, countries raced to unload their dollar denominated assets sooner rather than later. They knew the longer they held on to their dollars, the less they were worth. As countries dumped their dollars, huge surpluses of dollars were created in foreign exchange markets. The dollar's exchange rate crashed compared to other currencies. This crash in exchange rates was more than just a problem for the few American tourists still traveling overseas, tourists who needed to pay for hotel rooms and meals in local currencies. It was a problem for Americans back home, too. Americans back home needed to purchase goods manufactured overseas and the purchase of those goods ultimately required foreign currency. There were no "Made in the USA" alternatives to purchase because there was no manufacturing to speak of left in the United States. It had all been outsourced. A pair of tennis shoes went from a hundred dollars to a thousand dollars. A flat screen television that used to cost a thousand dollars was now ten thousand dollars. The standard of living in the United States dropped by an order of magnitude almost overnight. It was now equivalent to that of a third-world nation. Americans were more than a little unhappy about the drop in their standard of living. They were shocked. They were frightened. And, especially, they were angry.

Put stress on a strong relationship and the couple ends up stronger from the test. Put stress on a weak relationship and the relationship comes apart. So it was with the United States. There was agreement only on the problem, that the country's economy was wrecked. There was no agreement on how to respond to the crisis. The country fractured along the political divide that had been growing steadily for decades. The divide could now be characterized as a chasm. The two sides could agree on nothing. They also viewed the other side's failure to see things their way as indicative of a fundamental character flaw, a moral shortcoming even. There were only two possible sides to an issue, the right side and the wrong side, and since the other side refused to recognize they were on the wrong side, even after all the reasons they were wrong were repeatedly explained to them, that made them more than just wrong. That made them willfully and deliberately wrong. There is only one type of person determined to remain willfully and deliberately wrong: a threat to society, otherwise known as a public enemy. A socially just society cannot have public enemies roaming about freely, sowing hate and discontent as they go. They must be dealt with swiftly and firmly, first by identifying them as public enemies, then by restricting their movements, and, finally, by incarcerating them.

Texas was the first state to declare its independence. The final straw for Texas was President Johnny Penn's Great Green Leap Forward and its ban on fossil fuels. Where President Johnny Penn and his party saw the Great Green Leap Forward as the obvious solution to jumpstart the economy and build a sustainable future, Texas saw it as a sure and certain path to economic ruin inspired by green weather worshippers completely and totally divorced from reality. Red states wasted no time joining with Texas. President Johnny Penn declared a state of emergency in response. He suspended the Constitution and vowed to take whatever action was necessary to preserve the Union. The fighting started soon after.

CHAPTER TWO

I am not afraid of an army of lions lead by a sheep; I am afraid of sheep lead by a lion.

— Alexander the Great

"YOU SEEING THIS," asked Earvin Smith in a whisper, the elder son of physical education teacher Mr. Smith, formerly of the Dalton Academy Christian school in Los Angeles.

"I got it," said his younger brother, Roland, also in a whisper. He was watching two ghostly green figures through the PVS-14 night vision monocular attached to his helmet. They appeared to be a man and a woman. The two figures were moving furtively as they made their way across a field. They were also leading a pair of goats as they went. "Don't see no weapons," added Roland.

"Ol' man Jenkins and his wife ... taking their goats for a midnight walk?" asked Earvin, who went by Magic, after Magic Johnson, because he was a talented basketball forward during his high school days.

"I don't think so," answered Roland. "Just more sad-sack starving refugees from Los Angeles."

"Yeah. I'm getting tired of this."

"Me too. Pass the word. Tigers on me. Viking Raiders hold this position and cover us." Tigers was the five-man fireteam Magic led. It included his brother, Roland. Viking Raiders was the second five-man fireteam. The

Tigers and Viking Raiders belonged to the 3rd Regiment of the Free City of Temecula, which was part of the Free County of Riverside that extended east of Los Angeles all the way to the Arizona state line. The Free County of Riverside had seceded from the United States of America along with most of the other rural counties in the country shortly after Texas seceded from the United States in 2032, starting the civil war that was still ongoing. The 3rd Regiment of the Free City of Temecula was responsible for patrolling the city perimeter.

Magic led his Tigers silently down the side of the field. He used a row of trees for concealment since the half-moon overhead cast enough light for them to see their own shadows. That meant they could be spotted by the figures ahead, even if those figures had no night vision. The trees permitted the Tigers to spread out in an L-shape in front of the figures, as if they were preparing an ambush. Three of the men were in front of the figures' line of advance while two were off to one side. The Tigers did that instinctively, in case the figures had weapons and things turned ugly. The L-shaped deployment gave them intersecting fields of fire. Magic was with the two other men in front of the figures' line of advance. When the figures were fifty yards out, Magic yelled, "Freeze!" He hit the button on top of his AR-15 handguard. The button activated the weapon light mounted beneath the handguard. The rest of the men did the same. The five weapon lights, each putting out over a thousand lumens, were blinding.

The two figures raised their hands to shield their eyes. Had the Tiger team been less experienced apprehending starving refugees from Los Angeles, the sudden movement of the refugees might very well have been their last. "I said don't move!" yelled Magic.

"Ok, ok!" shouted the male refugee. "We're not moving. We're not armed, ok. We don't want no trouble."

"That's good," answered Magic. "Just follow directions and no one gets hurt. Lift your jacket and turn around slowly." The two refugees did as they were told. Magic saw no holster and no sign of a weapon tucked in a belt. "Ok, now drop to your knees and put your hands on top of your head." When they were on their knees, Magic and the rest of the Tiger team walked up to the couple. Magic noticed they were young, maybe in their late twenties, which meant they were of military age. "Search 'em," said Magic. One of the Tiger team men set his AR-15 on the ground and patted down the male refugee. "He's clean," said the Tiger team man. Then he patted down the female refugee, making no allowance for the fact she was female. "She's clean, too," he said tersely.

"You can stand up and put your hands down," said Magic.

"Thanks," said the male refugee.

"You wanna tell me why you're stealing our goats?" asked Magic, nodding toward the two goats that were grazing nearby, completely unconcerned by the group of armed men who had interrupted their journey.

"Please don't hurt us!" pleaded the female refugee, a scared look on her face. "We didn't mean any harm! We didn't wanna steal the goats! It's just … we haven't eaten in three days!"

Magic believed the female refugee. Her face was drawn. Also, in addition to fear, he saw hunger in her eyes. "Where you from?" he asked, trying to make his question sound more like a curious inquiry than an interrogation.

"Los Angeles," she answered.

"Where in Los Angeles?"

"Anaheim."

"How'd you get here?"

"We walked," said the male refugee.

"That's a long walk. A dangerous walk, too." Magic had a hunch. "You dodging the draft?"

The male refugee looked down.

"Nothing to be ashamed of. We're happy to hear it … blue folks refusing to fight."

"Was ordered to report last month," said the male refugee. "We've heard the stories. We packed up and left the next morning."

"What stories?"

"You want the truth?"

"Nothing but."

"Hearing it's bad. Real bad. Hearing we're losing even though all we hear from the news is how we're winning, how the fascists … sorry … the reds, are on the verge of surrendering. Hell, they've been telling us that for two years now, that you're about to surrender. Meanwhile, all our friends are drafted and, once they're drafted, we never hear from 'em again."

"You're not willing to die for the Great Green Leap Forward?"

"Look, we're not political. Never were. Just want to live our lives."

"Don't we all," said Magic.

The female refugee added anxiously, "They also tell us …" That was all she managed before she looked away.

"What?" asked Magic.

"They tell us about all the atrocities," said the male refugee, saying out loud what he knew was on the mind of the female refugee and worrying her sick. "They tell us about the executions of captured soldiers, about the torture. They tell us about what you do to refugees, too. They also say …"

"What?"

The male refugee answered reluctantly, "They say you abuse women."

Magic shook his head. "Well, at least one thing hasn't changed. The news media were lyin' tools before the war and they're still lyin' tools." He looked over at the female refugee, saw her shaking, and felt sorry for her. "Don't worry," he said gently. "We're not what they say we are."

The female refugee summoned her courage and looked Magic in the eyes. "What's gonna happen to us?" she asked.

"Two things," said Magic. "First, you're returning the goats to Ol' Man Jenkins. Second, you're talking to Dad."

"Dad?" she asked, not understanding.

Magic smiled. "Yeah, you'll be talkin' with my father. You'll be calling him 'Mr. Smith,' not that he's pretentious or anything. That's just what he goes by. He'll explain your options."

"Mister," asked the male refugee, "can I ask you a straight-up question?"

"Sure."

"Are we in trouble?"

"Well," said Magic, "that depends."

"On what?"

"The option you choose."

***

Mr. Smith was seated at the kitchen table in the Temecula jail, otherwise known as the Southwest Detention Center. Seated at the table with him were the refugee couple his sons had dropped off only a few hours earlier. It was

8 a.m. He had learned the couple were an actual couple. They were living together but not married. His name was Jason and her name was Erin. He watched the two of them devour their bowl of chili as he finished his second cup of coffee. "There's more chili if you want it," he said.

Jason wiped his mouth with a napkin. "No, thanks, we really couldn't."

"Sure you could," said Mr. Smith. "I wouldn't offer it if I didn't have it to offer. Plus, you look like you could use the calories." He walked over and grabbed the chili pot from the stove. He set it on the table and then went back to grab the wooden serving spoon. He stuck the serving spoon in the pot so it stood upright. "Now that's some good chili!" he exclaimed with a smile. "Enough beans and meat to stand a spoon up straight!"

Jason did not hesitate. He filled his bowl to the brim. Erin was right behind him. "I don't know how long it's been," she said, "since we've tasted real meat."

"I understand rations are pretty thin over on your side of the border."

"We get a ration book," said Jason. "It's supposed to be good for 2,500 calories a day. Then we stand in line at the NNC—"

"NNC?" asked Mr. Smith.

"The National Nutrition Center. We stand in line for three or four hours. When we finally get up to the counter, they tell us they're only giving out half rations today. You don't have no choice if you wanna eat. You turn in your ration card and you get your half ration of beans and rice, maybe some canned mystery greens, and this brown mush that's pressed into the shape of a beef patty, only it's not a beef patty. It's a friggin' bug burger!"

"Processed meal worms and crickets," added Erin. "It's part of our responsible, sustainable diet. They have Hollywood stars eating bugs on camera and telling us how good they taste. The news is writing articles about our social responsibility to eat bugs, to cut our carbon footprint. They're making kids eat bugs in school, too, to get them used to the idea."

"They always go for the kids," said Mr. Smith, thinking back to his days as a Los Angeles Unified School District teacher and the gender indoctrination they were rolling out then. "You know the beautiful people are eating real beef, right? When they're not out in public. Same with the politicians. Bugs are only for the little people."

"So how is it you have real beef?" asked Jason. "Enough that you're willing to share with little people like us, a couple of refugees?"

Mr. Smith shrugged. "The same way we've always had it. People grow hay and corn. They feed hay to the calves and finish the steers with corn. Then the steers head to the slaughter house and, presto, steaks!"

"But all the fertilizer, all the diesel fuel, all the electricity ... How do the farmers and ranchers afford it?"

"Simple," said Mr. Smith, "we don't subsidize stupid shit ... and we don't discourage the production of things people actually want."

Jason looked skeptical.

"You know," said Erin cautiously, "they tell us you're environmental terrorists, you reds, that you're destroying the climate and the planet and that's why we have to fight this war. They say we have to destroy you because, if we don't, you'll destroy the planet."

"Weren't you blues fighting to save the world from fascism?" asked Mr. Smith, a touch of sarcasm in his voice. "Or was it racism?"

"Both," said Erin. Then she smiled a thin smile. "Actually, all three."

"You believe all that?" asked Mr. Smith. "You think we're planet destroying, eco-fascist racists?"

"Not really," said Erin. "At least not all of it. I know there are two sides to things and they're only telling us their side."

Mr. Smith turned serious. "Listen, here's the problem. We have a lot of people coming over from the blue states. And when I say 'a lot,' I mean '*a lot.*' Most of them are coming for the same reasons you two came. Life is increasingly difficult in the DPRA. In fact, we're hearing it's downright miserable. Am I right?"

Jason and Erin nodded.

"So, here's our problem, the problem for us reds. If we let all you blues in and you blues are still believing in all that blue stuff ... the gender craziness, the environmental craziness, the white people are evil craziness, and the let's just toss the Constitution in the trash craziness ... Well, if we let too many of you blues in then, pretty soon, we'll be exactly what you risked your lives to escape. Then what? When the Free States of Liberty are gone, where do we go, the people like me and my sons?"

"Please don't send us back!" pleaded Erin, suddenly distraught and reaching out across the table toward Mr. Smith. "We're not like them, Mr. Smith! Really, we're not!"

Mr. Smith took hold of her hands and patted them gently like the grandfather he was. "There there, dear," he said, trying to reassure her. "Hear me out first. There's no reason to panic."

Erin leaned back and tried to compose herself.

Mr. Smith continued. "We've given this a lot of thought, us reds. Here's our problem. The Free States of Liberty are committed to being a constitutional republic. The Founding Fathers of this country, being very wise men, understood our Constitution was fit only for a moral and religious people. I think it was John Adams who said that. Any idea why he said that?"

"A country needs good people," offered Erin.

"How 'bout you, Jason?" asked Mr. Smith.

Jason seemed offended by John Adam's words. "I don't think you have to be religious to be moral."

Mr. Smith nodded. "Fair enough. I know some good people who aren't Christians. I also know some good people who don't even believe in God. And then there are more than a few Christians who could practice a lot more of what they preach."

"Amen to that," said Jason.

"Sounds like you had a bad church experience."

"I did."

"Sorry to hear that. Maybe we can give you a better experience here, if you're interested. No pressure. Anyway, their point, the Founding Fathers' point, was that political freedom can only exist to the extent people are self-governing. When people are self-governing, they do what they're supposed to do to allow society to function. They do what they're supposed to do because that's the kind of people they are. They don't need all these government rules and regulations to force them to do what they ought to be doing in the first place. And the converse is true. When people have no self-control, when people are selfish, corrupt and irresponsible, then they need lots of government coercion to keep society from descending into anarchy. Follow me?"

"That makes sense," said Erin.

"So, the practical question becomes: Without being able to look inside and see what's in a person's heart, how do you know a person's moral?" Mr. Smith nodded toward Jason. "Which we agree does not just mean a person is a regular churchgoer. Any thoughts?"

Jason sat stone-faced.

"Maybe a test," offered Erin.

"Exactly!" said Mr. Smith, giving her an encouraging smile. "When I was discussing this with my sons, being an old Marine, I suggested something like Marine Corps basic training. Semper Fidelis and all that."

"We have to go through basic training if we want to stay?" asked Jason, not at all liking the idea because he had left the DPRA to avoid the draft.

"No. You'll be happy to hear, Jason, my idea didn't pass muster. My sons pointed out we have a lot of older folks here in the Free States of Liberty who wouldn't last a day in basic training, even though they're real patriots. We had to come up with a test people can reasonably be expected to pass, the ones that should pass, anyway. And we think we did. We think of it as an economics test. Simply put, people are expected to support themselves because government is not in the business of charity. A moral person feels obligated to earn his own way. A moral person feels shame living off the hard work of his fellow citizens. That's the way it used to be in this country. Now, we understand shit happens, to put it bluntly. If a person is incapable of supporting themselves then we, the citizens of the Free States of Liberty, will step in and help out. But there is a price for that help. You lose your right to vote as long as you're receiving government charity. We think that not only reinforces the moral behavior we're looking for, it also avoids a dangerous conflict of interest; people voting to give themselves free stuff. You also don't get to vote if you're a government employee, for similar reasons."

"We can do that," said Jason, finally encouraged. "Erin and I have no problem working."

"Great. There's one more test."

"Oh," said Jason, immediately suspicious again.

"We call this one the knowledge test. The refugees coming to the Free States of Liberty have been indoctrinated, shall we say, with the DPRA view of the world. This indoctrination has gone on for so much of their lives, has been so pervasive ... we've found most refugees have no idea they've even been indoctrinated, which is really just a fancy word for brainwashed. They have no idea there's a reasoned, alternative view of the world, especially if they made the mistake of going to one of the DPRA universities. So, we require refugees hoping to join the Free States of Liberty be exposed to *our* view of the world."

"You mean we have to sit through *your* propaganda," challenged Jason.

"No. You have to sit through *our* perspective, based on what we consider a balanced presentation of the facts and the actual science, since you're asking to join *our* society."

"And what if we sit through your perspective and don't agree with it?"

"Well, that's where we reds are taking a leap of faith. We'll require you pass a test to demonstrate you were paying attention and not sleeping through class. The test is not designed to require your agreement with our presentation material. It is only designed to confirm your comprehension of our material. You're then free to make up your own mind. We are, after all, the Free States of Liberty."

"Can you give me an example?" asked Jason. "Of what you consider actual facts and science?"

"Sure," said Mr. Smith. "President Johnny Penn's Great Green Leap Forward is touted as saving us all from climate catastrophe, right? Well, we in the Free States of Liberty fundamentally disagree with the hypothesis that man-made CO2 is driving climate change. Climate has always been changing, and these changes are principally driven by variations in solar radiation and ocean currents. Man-made CO2 is only a weak contributor to climate change. By contrast, the burning of fossil fuels is a very strong contributor to the standard of living of the world. So strong, in fact, that banning their use will lead to the impoverishment of the bulk of the world's population, as you folks are only now beginning to discover in the DPRA. The impoverishment of the world is what will lead to real environmental catastrophe as a poor world cannot afford a clean environment, unless you're willing to run it like a police state, which is another thing the good folks in the DPRA are now beginning to discover." Mr. Smith smiled a sly smile. "We also fundamentally disagree with the DPRA's claim we have to give up our cheeseburgers to save the planet, and that eating bug burgers poses no health risk. Finally, we here in the Free States of Liberty believe bug burgers taste just plain awful."

Jason turned and looked at Erin. He cocked his head as he looked at her, unsure of how to respond and wondering if she was ok with this.

Mr. Smith laughed. "Ok, that last one about bug burgers tasting awful is my own subjective opinion."

"What happens if we fail the test?" asked Erin.

"Yeah," said Jason, anxiously turning to look back at Mr. Smith. "I was never very good in school."

"Well, we have tutors. Of course, the tutor's on your dime."

"And if we still fail," pressed Jason, "or we decide we don't want to sign up?"

"You'll have a one-way ticket from the Free States of Liberty to the border with the Democratic People's Republic of America, and our best wishes the DPRA does not track you down and treat you the way it usually treats draft dodgers."

CHAPTER THREE

It's really a wonder that I haven't dropped all my ideals, because they seem so absurd and impossible to carry out. Yet I keep them, because in spite of everything, I still believe that people are really good at heart.

— Anne Frank, "The Diary of a Young Girl"

THERE WAS A sharp rap on the door to the camp commander's residence.

"Come!" said the commander of DPRA Labor Camp 847.

The DPRA guard opened the door and pushed Leah in ahead of him. He pulled Leah to a stop by the collar of her fluorescent orange camp jumpsuit when they were in the middle of the camp commander's dining room. He saluted smartly and asked, "You wanted to see Prisoner 762, Comrade Commander?"

"Yes," answered the camp commander. He was just sitting down for dinner. "Have her sit here." He gestured with his glass of wine toward the chair to his right.

The guard pushed Leah over to the dining room table, pulled the chair out from under the table and ordered her to sit as if she were a dog. Leah did as she was ordered. She kept her eyes cast down the whole time, never making eye contact with the guard and, certainly, not with the camp commander.

"Leave us," said the camp commander.

"Sir," answered the guard. He saluted and turned on his heel. The door closed with a loud bang.

The camp commander looked Leah over. He breathed in deeply and then exhaled as if disappointed. He lifted the crystal glass of wine to his lips and took a sip. The wine was red. "So," he finally said, "this is Prisoner 762."

Leah had no idea why she had been summoned to the personal residence of the camp commander, other than it must have something to do with her and Celine's inability earlier in the day to lift the cleaning rig onto the solar panels. But if that was it, she did not understand why she was the only one summoned. Why was Celine not here with her? Also, why was she summoned to his personal residence instead of his office? That was especially unusual. She was certain of only one thing: This could not be good.

The camp commander was notorious for his discipline and harsh cruelty. Leah first met him when she first arrived in camp. He stood on the porch of the camp commander's office in front of the assembled group of new arrivals and explained his expectations. He expected order, he said. He expected discipline. And, most important of all, he expected work. He went on about the importance of their work, how they were making clean, sustainable energy for the DPRA, and how it was vital the solar panels be regularly cleaned. Do your work well, he promised, and you will be treated well. Do your work poorly and this will be your fate. Leah and the assembled new arrivals were then forced to witness an execution. A pair of guards marched a shackled prisoner to a post at the edge of the camp fence. They tied the prisoner to the post and then marched back to join a firing squad of six guards. At the command of the officer in charge of the firing squad, the guards raised their rifles, took aim at the prisoner and fired. The shirt on the prisoner's chest exploded in tufts of material. The tufts were stained red with blood. The prisoner's knees buckled and her body slumped down toward the ground as far as the ropes binding her to the post would permit. Her head fell forward until her chin was resting against her chest. Her body twitched spasmodically a few times and then hung motionless.

Leah witnessed more executions than she could count during her three years at Labor Camp 847. She also witnessed countless "unofficial" acts of punishment. Those were the back of a guard's hand, a kick in the ribs, or a more thorough beating with closed fists for failing to move fast enough, or answer fast enough, or simply because the guard woke up in a foul mood that morning. "Official" punishment meant the post, and it came in two and only two varieties. In addition to summary execution, there was twenty-five lashes to the back while the offender was tied to the post. Lashing was relatively rare, though, and reserved for instances where the offense was not too great and the offender still had some physical strength left to be offered up to the DPRA, once the prisoner's attitude was corrected. Most of the official punishment involved a simple, summary execution. There was no trial, no defense counsel, no appeal. There was only the word of the camp commander, and his word was final.

"Yes, Comrade Camp Commander," answered Leah, still looking down. "I am Prisoner 1538762."

"You can look up now," he said.

Leah looked up at the camp commander. This was the closest she had ever seen him, and the first time she had seen him without his camp commander cap. She noticed he had a full head of blond hair that was cut short. She also noticed his intelligent blue eyes and smooth soft skin with the faint stubble of a five o'clock shadow. She guessed him to be in his early thirties. Finally, she noticed the most shocking thing of all: He was smiling.

The camp commander picked up the bottle of wine sitting on the table between the two of them. "Would you like some wine?" he asked.

"Yes, please," said Leah, not knowing what else to say, shocked not only by the smile on his face but by his polite consideration. *What is this?!* her mind screamed, desperate to understand.

The camp commander poured her a glass of wine. When he set the bottle back down on the table and noticed she had not touched her glass, he smiled again. "Please," he urged, picking up his glass. "A toast! To the DPRA and the Great Green Leap Forward. And to the parts we are each ordained to play in our brave new world order."

She reached for the glass of wine in front of her and was surprised when the tips of her fingers touched actual glass, that they did not go right through the sides of the glass because this was some fantastical dream. She lifted the glass and was again surprised to feel the weight of it, that it was heavy from the wine inside. *This is really real!* she thought, finally convinced that it was. She watched the camp commander extend his glass toward hers. Without thinking, she moved hers toward his. She heard the clink of the glasses when they touched. She brought her glass to her lips. She felt the cold hardness of its edge. She tilted her glass. Warm, fruity sweetness ran into her mouth and swirled about her tongue. She had not had a drink of alcohol in ten years, since she was first sentenced to prison. She thought the wine the most incredible, amazing thing she had ever tasted.

"It is good, no?" asked the camp commander.

"Yes, thank you so much." The former police officer in her, the one that was inherently suspicious of people and their motivations, could stand it no longer. "May I ask, Comrade Camp Commander, why I am here?"

"Of course, Prisoner 762," answered the camp commander. "When the guards told me about your clever improvisation with the cleaning rig this morning, I looked you up in our system and discovered something very interesting. You may be Prisoner 762 here in my camp but, on the outside, you are Officer Leah Blunt. Officer Leah Blunt who was sentenced to second-degree murder for shooting two unarmed African American men in Los Angeles in 2025."

He set his glass back on the table and leaned back in his chair. He smiled an ironic smile. "All this time … for the past three years … I had no idea I had a celebrity in my camp. You are the one that started it all, Officer Leah Blunt. The Great Riot. The election of President Johnny Penn. The crushing defeat of the old United States Navy in the South China Sea. The collapse of the US dollar and the subsequent civil war. And, finally, the birth of our DPRA with its beloved supreme leader, Dear Leader Johnny Penn. You are, I think, Officer Leah Blunt, the mother of it all."

Leah stared at the camp commander, blinking rapidly as she struggled to follow what he was saying, and viscerally rejecting his claim she was responsible for birthing this nightmare she was living and the nightmare that had become the world. "No, no," she protested. "Comrade Camp Commander, I was only doing my job. I was only trying to be a good police officer. Nothing more. All this … This is not because of me."

"You don't wish to take credit?" he asked, gesturing at the room with a sweep of his hand. "You are not a fan of our DPRA?"

Her head was swimming, not from the little bit of alcohol but from the danger she sensed lurking in his question. She answered carefully, "I am here, Comrade Camp Commander, to serve the DPRA."

The camp commander laughed. She noticed his teeth were stained red with wine. "Of course," he said. "Aren't we all. Well, I hope you brought your appetite. Did they tell you I invited you for dinner. No, I imagine not. The guards are, well, guards." He hollered to the kitchen in a voice that was far from considerate. "We will have our dinner now!"

A woman walked out with two plates. Leah recognized the woman. Her name was Diana. She had lived in the barracks until a year ago. Then she was promoted to the support staff for the camp DPRA complement, working in their kitchen. Leah remembered her because she was a strikingly beautiful woman. She took the job because it meant getting off the cleaning crew. It also meant better food. Leah could tell she was eating well. She did not have the pale, sunken-eyed look of a regular prisoner.

Diana set a plate in front of Leah. Leah was shocked by the sight of it, at the sight of the plate itself—which looked to be real porcelain—as well as the food heaped upon it. The dinnerware for her and her fellow prisoners was a tin bowl, into which was ladled a grayish brown gruel with the consistency of oatmeal. A biscuit was tossed on top of their gruel at the end of the cafeteria line, just before they picked up their tin cup of white liquid that was supposed to be milk. They knew it was not milk because it tasted nothing like milk. Plus, they knew cows were no longer allowed in the DPRA. They were told theirs was a balanced meal with all the essential vitamins, minerals and nutrients required for their bodies to put in a full day's work out on the cleaning crews, for the greater glory of the DPRA. Only it was not a balanced meal. And, even if it was, there was not nearly enough of it. Everyone in the camp lost weight, slowly but surely. That was actually by design because the DPRA had to make room for new arrivals. Always, there were new arrivals.

"Is this real meat, Comrade Camp Commander?" asked Leah, incredulous as she looked at the slab of meat covering half her plate. A memory from a deep recess in a long-forgotten corner of her mind told her it was prime rib. Prime rib had been a favorite of hers when she and her husband used to go out to eat at a nice restaurant, back in another world, before the war and before her arrest.

"Yes, yes," said the camp commander. "Diana here is an excellent cook."

Leah looked at Diana who was in the process of placing the camp commander's plate in front of him, taking care that the plate was turned so the prime rib faced the camp commander. It seemed to Leah as if Diana was making a deliberate effort not to look at her.

"And I see we have a baked potato," continued the camp commander, "and asparagus. Most excellent. Thank you, Diana. You may leave us now."

"Yes, Comrade Camp Commander," answered Diana. She turned and walked quickly from the room.

"Here," said the camp commander, pushing the butter dish closer to Leah. "We have butter, too. Real butter. Dig in and don't be bashful. I hope you like it."

Leah did not have to be told twice. The smell of the food, the sight of it, the anticipation of eating a real meal conspired with her pangs of hunger to push her anxiety and apprehension to the back of her mind. She devoured the plate of food with the single-minded determination of a ravenous animal, not at all interested in talking. She stuffed great mouthfuls of prime rib in her mouth and washed them down with great mouthfuls of wine. She did the same with the baked potato after smothering it with butter. She went back and forth between the prime rib and the baked potato, not once thinking about wiping her mouth with the napkin. She was amazed at how incredibly rich the food tasted and how she could feel it filling her body with energy. She saved the asparagus for last, thinking of it as dessert. It, too, she smothered with butter. When she finally set her fork and knife down on an empty plate, her stomach felt full for the first time in a long, long time.

"I see you hated it," said the camp commander, gesturing at her empty plate.

"No, no, Comrade Camp Commander," said Leah, suddenly embarrassed. "It was truly incredible. Thank you. Thank you so much." She was embarrassed not so much by her lack of table manners, at having eaten like a ravenous animal, but at the sudden realization she had abandoned her self-control. She had not just eaten like a ravenous animal, she had become a ravenous animal. She felt as though she had abandoned the dignity of her humanity, and all for a plate of food.

"You know," said the camp commander, only halfway through his meal, "I feel like you and I have something in common. That we have already crossed paths, you and I, before your coming to my camp. I was in Los Angeles just like you when all this started. I was there at City Hall when those fascists in the LAPD and CHP tossed their badges in trash barrels and walked out on the people of their city. I was one of those in the vanguard that started the fires that burned down City Hall. I was there with Supreme Leader Johnny Penn in Santa Clarita, too, when we came to demonstrate in front of your house. Although, I should say, I was not there physically standing next to him. He was just an actor back then. He had not yet discovered his revolutionary consciousness, shall we say, because he was more interested in marching than taking real action." He added nonchalantly, "Do you know, I think I would have killed you back then, had I been able to get to you." He smiled at Leah as he said it. "Do you find that funny?"

Leah looked down at her empty plate. The anxiety and apprehension she had pushed to the back of her mind was back. It was back even stronger than before, warning her that something was very wrong here. She struggled to keep her voice flat and emotionless. "Comrade Camp Commander, I am not sure what to make of that."

He laughed. "Well, neither am I, really. I had some issues back then. I was angry, especially with my father. He told me I had to get rid of Kendra, my girlfriend. She was living with me in his garage and he wanted me to put her out like the garbage. Can you imagine that? He left me no choice, really. We moved out the same day."

"That sounds … harsh … of your father."

"He was an asshole. Still is, I imagine. We haven't spoken since."

"It was considerate of you, Comrade Camp Commander, to stay with your girlfriend."

"It was more than considerate. It was love. Do you believe in love, Leah? Oh, that was presumptuous of me. May I call you Leah?"

"Yes, Comrade Camp Commander."

"Good, good. It's a lovely name, too … Leah. I think I've always liked that name. So, do you believe in love, Leah?"

"I do. Yes, I very much do, Comrade Camp Commander."

"Good!" he said, obviously happy with her answer. "That is another thing we have in common. You have your love and I have mine. I would never leave Kendra. We're still together, you know. In fact, she's here with me now. Would you like to meet her?"

"Yes, Comrade Camp Commander. I would be honored to meet her."

"Excellent!" he said, pushing his chair back from the table and standing. "She's in the living room. Come with me, please. The three of us will have a nice little talk."

Leah followed the camp commander. She was only a few steps into the living room when she spotted Kendra sitting in a chair. She froze, not believing what she was seeing. Not only was Kendra dressed only in a black negligee, she was also obviously not a real person. She was some kind of mannequin.

"Kendra," said the camp commander, not noticing Leah had stopped short and was staring at Kendra slack-jawed, "I'd like you to meet Leah."

The camp commander was only partly correct when he said he would never leave Kendra. While she may have been the same woman she always was on the outside, she was a wholly different woman on the inside. In fact, she had been a series of different women on the inside. The camp commander had upgraded Kendra's software and internal hardware repeatedly over the past decade as his career and financial means advanced, always keeping Kendra on the cutting edge of relationship robots.

Kendra opened her eyes and turned her head to look in the direction of the camp commander's voice. "Hello, Leah," answered Kendra. "Bernie has told me so much about you. We're so excited to have a real celebrity in our house."

Leah was speechless, struggling to process the situation.

"Hello, Leah," repeated Kendra. "I did not hear you answer."

You need to say hello, Leah reminded herself. She answered automatically, certain she sounded as artificial as Kendra, "Hello … Kendra. It's … a … pleasure to meet you."

"Oh, the pleasure is mine. Won't you sit down?"

The camp commander gestured for Leah to sit at the end of the sofa nearest Kendra.

"Did you enjoy your dinner with Bernie?" asked Kendra.

"Yes," answered Leah. Sitting next to Kendra, she heard the miniature electric motors whirring in Kendra's head as they articulated her eyes and mouth. Then she noticed the brown of her nipples showing through the black lace of her negligee. Leah quickly looked away.

"Did Bernie ask you yet?" asked Kendra.

"Um, no, I don't think so." Leah looked at the camp commander. "Ask me what?"

"Kendra," said the camp commander, chuckling as if embarrassed. "So typical. Always impatient."

Kendra ignored him and went on. "When Bernie told me how you were famous, I asked him to show me your photo. Oh, not the dreary camp photo but the photos of you on the outside. I saw a very attractive woman in those photos. I said to Bernie, 'Bernie, why don't you ask her to come and be our house servant?' Bernie very much liked the idea. You can live here in our house, in your own room. You will have a real bed with real sheets. And hot baths! Won't it feel good to have hot baths and be clean, Leah?" Kendra batted her eyelashes as the small electric motors whirred inside her head.

Leah's head was swimming. *What the fuck is going on?!* She forced herself to answer pleasantly. She felt like she was turning into the thing that was sitting next to her, some kind of Stepford Wife mannequin. "Yes, a hot bath would be wonderful!" she answered with feigned excitement. "It's been a long time since I've had a hot bath."

"I can only imagine what you've been through," said Kendra sympathetically. "Would you please stand up for me?"

"What?" asked Leah, wondering if Kendra knew what she was asking. She looked at the camp commander for confirmation.

"Go ahead," he said with an encouraging smile.

Leah stood up.

"Now turn around," said Kendra sweetly. "Please do it slowly."

Leah did not know what else to do. She slowly turned around in front of Kendra.

"Very nice," said Kendra. "With a bath, some nice clean clothes, and just a little makeup, you will be very nice for Bernie."

"I ... I ... don't understand," stammered Leah.

"One more thing," added Kendra sweetly. "Would you take off your top?"

"What?!' asked Leah, shocked by her request. Then she remembered Kendra was not a real person. She turned and looked at the camp commander. He only smiled his encouraging smile. Leah's face flushed red.

"Take off your top, please," repeated Kendra. "My Bernie has particular tastes in breasts. He likes large nipples, too. That was the one thing about you I could not verify from your photos."

"No!" shouted Leah. "I will not take off my top! No!" She sat back down and looked straight ahead, finally understanding what this was about. *Sick fuckin' weirdo!* she thought to herself.

"Kendra!" scolded the camp commander. Then he looked at Leah and shrugged sheepishly. "Like I said, she's always impatient."

"Comrade Camp Commander, may I please return to the barracks? Thank you so much for dinner but, really, I have to get up early tomorrow … to work with my cleaning crew."

"You are not interested in our offer?" asked the camp commander, pretending to be surprised. "To be our house servant?"

"No, thank you, Comrade Camp Commander. I really just want to do what I'm doing. Can I please leave now and go back to my barracks?"

"Am I really so bad?" asked the camp commander, still smiling.

"No, no, not at all, Comrade Camp Commander. I'm flattered, really, it's just … I'm married and … like we talked about … I love my husband … and … I'd really just like to stay with my barracks and work with my crew … cleaning solar panels."

"Ah!" exclaimed the camp commander. "I almost forgot! Your husband! May I ask when you last heard from him?"

Oh God, no! thought Leah. A black wave of grief welled up inside her. *Please God, no!*

The camp commander saw it on her face and added quickly, "No, no, no, your husband's fine. I looked your husband up as part of my research, when I was researching you. Did you know he's also a guest here, with the DPRA Department of Reeducation?"

The black wave of grief receded.

"No," answered Leah, shaking her head. "I haven't talked to him since the war, since I was transferred here from the California Institute for Women."

"Of course you didn't. How silly of me to ask. The Department of Reeducation does not allow contact with the outside world. We've found that does not facilitate the reeducation process. Well, anyway, I was not really surprised to find your husband here as one of our guests. Disloyalty seems to run in families, you know. His name is Ayad, yes?"

"Yes," said Leah. "Ayad."

"Ayad, it turns out, is not too far away from here. Just a few camps over. I happen to know the camp commander there."

"Comrade Camp Commander," said Leah, suddenly excited, "would it be possible for me to talk to him? Just to hear his voice, just to let him know I'm ok … It would mean so much to me if I could!"

"Unfortunately, that will not be possible. At least for some small amount of time. But, after you've been here with us a while, with me and Kendra, then, yes, I think that can be arranged."

Leah squeezed her eyes shut tight. She forced herself to swallow her bitter disappointment. She felt trapped and utterly powerless. She knew exactly what the camp commander was doing.

The camp commander leaned forward to look at her face. He saw tears running down her cheeks. He also noticed her lower lip quivering. "Now, now," he sympathized, "don't be like that. You will stay with us and then you will talk with Ayad. What could be simpler?"

"I can't," said Leah, shaking her head emphatically. "I'm sorry but … I just can't do that."

"Well," said the camp commander, still sounding sympathetic, "I was hoping it would not have to be like this but, since you insist … Like I said, I know the camp commander where your husband, Ayad, is staying." He made a point of saying his name. "Your husband, Ayad, is fine … at the moment."

Oh God! thought Leah.

"But, as you know, life in the camps is hard. If you were, say, to choose to go back to the barracks and not accept our most generous offer, to live here in our house, with me and Kendra, well, then, I'm afraid life for your husband will get very much harder."

Please God … No!

"In fact, it will get so much harder, I'm afraid to say, I very much doubt your husband, Ayad, will survive the week here in our beautiful Mojave Desert. So, now that we fully understand the situation, I will have your final answer, Leah. Do you wish to return to the barracks or will you stay here with us?"

Leah opened her mouth to try and answer but the words would not come.

"I'm sorry," said the camp commander. "I can't hear you."

All her force of will was required to pry the words loose. The part of her mind that was appalled and revolted by the camp commander and his sick, twisted relationship with Kendra held onto the words with all its might. The other part of her mind was stronger, though. It was the part that loved her husband, that would die for her husband, because it knew he would die for her. One by one, she pried the words loose. They came out slowly, almost reverently, a sacred offering on the altar of selfless love: "I … will … stay … with … you."

CHAPTER FOUR

A nation of sheep will soon have a government of wolves.

— Edward R. Murrow

THE BULL LAUNCHED himself from the bucking chute the instant the gate opened. With a great leap forward and then a turn to the right, the bull almost dumped the cowboy who was tied to the bull's back by his bull rope. Then the ride turned to poetry in motion. The bull jumped and kicked and spun while the cowboy kept his legs locked around the bull's girth. He dug his spurs into the bull's hide to urge the bull on. The cowboy seemed to anticipate the bull's every move as his free arm flew back and forth to the rhythm of the bull jumping and kicking. The cowboy almost made it look easy, although everyone watching knew it was not. The buzzer sounded eight seconds. The cowboy reached down with his free hand and loosened his bull rope. The bull's next jump catapulted the cowboy from his back. The cowboy landed on his feet and ran to the arena fence. The crowd was on their feet, roaring their approval. The cowboy held his black felt hat high overhead in a salute to the crowd. He was grinning from ear to ear.

President Layton leaned over to his friend and chief advisor, Sam Daniels. He shouted to be heard over the crowd. "I don't care what anyone says, Brother Sam. You're not a sane person if you sit on the back of a bull." President Layton referred to Sam Daniels as Brother Sam out of habit. It was what he called him back when he was a pastor, now more than ten years ago, at Wesley's Chapel Church in Los Angeles.

Brother Sam laughed and nodded in vehement agreement. "Ain't that the truth, Mr. President."

"My God, this makes me feels good!" said President Layton. "I love everything about it! People coming here with their families. Everyone being polite and considerate. That rodeo gal galloping into the arena with the stars and stripes. Then the pledge of allegiance and the benediction. It just makes me feel good. It gives me real hope for our country."

"It does that, Mr. President. It reminds me we have a whole lot of good folks here in the Free States of Liberty."

This was not their first rodeo. President Layton was out touring the Free States of Liberty this summer and rodeos were a staple of summer in many small towns, especially out west. It was his first real tour of the country since being elected president of the Free States of Liberty, nearly two years ago now. The fact this was his first tour was not a consequence of his being too busy to travel, although he was busier than he had ever been in his life. It was, rather, a simple matter of security. Supreme Leader Johnny Penn and the DPRA had been diligently trying to kill him.

Their first attempt nearly succeeded. President Layton was meeting with a number of governors from states that had seceded from the United States, including the governor of the state of Texas. Their meeting was to be at a Marriott in Fort Worth. Brother Sam was responsible for security and had taken the usual precautions: a perimeter with metal detectors, bomb sniffing dogs and the requisite team of armed soldiers. Still, he was uneasy about the meeting. President Johnny Penn had recently been elevated to Supreme Leader of the DPRA and, only the week before, had delivered a fiery speech declaring the leaders of the Free States of Liberty guilty of treason. Since the penalty for treason in the DPRA was now death, and since that penalty was being frequently and routinely imposed, Brother Sam was worried his threat profile had radically changed. It was no longer a lone gunman or suicide bomber with a vest. It was now a nation, and one with a huge arsenal of weapons left over from the old United States military. The more he thought about that arsenal, the more he grew concerned. He finally decided to bring his concern to President Layton's attention. "Mr. President," he said, "you know what's required to destroy a target today?"

"What's that?" asked President Layton, only half paying attention. He was going over a draft of his speech, the one he would give tomorrow at the first physical, in-person meeting of the leadership of the Free States of Liberty.

"It's one thing and one thing only," added Brother Sam.

President Layton reluctantly stopped reading. He set the draft of his speech on his desk and looked at Brother Sam. "I don't know. Maybe a gun?"

"No, Mr. President. It's not hardware. It's information."

"A name, then. You need to know your target's name."

Brother Sam shook his head. "You need to know your target's location. We knew we wanted to kill Osama bin Laden for … What? Ten years? We were not able to actually target him and kill him until we knew where he was hiding. Location is the one essential piece of information. It was ten years ago, and it is still today. Give me your GPS coordinates and I can put a thousand pounds of high explosive right in your lap."

"I understand your point."

"I'm not sure you do, Mr. President. The DPRA knows we're meeting tomorrow with most of the governors and most of the leaders of the Free States of Liberty, including you, right here in the Fort Worth Marriott."

"That would be escalating the war to another level, Sam, attacking our country's political leadership. They must know we're capable of responding in kind. A lot of the military sided with us when the country split. And that was mostly the side interested in fighting, the side concerned with combat arms, not combat support."

"Mr. President, the DPRA has denounced you and the other leaders of the Free States of Liberty as traitors. The DPRA is currently executing traitors over on their side of the border. I don't think we can count on them practicing restraint just because we are over here, on our side of the border, especially since it's a border they refuse to recognize."

"What is it you're proposing, Brother Sam?"

"Until we control our airspace, we need to deny the enemy information about your location. We need to move the meeting and not publicize the new location."

President Layton sighed. "This will greatly annoy the governors. It will also make us look weak, if we suddenly cancel the meeting and go into hiding. It will make us look like we're not confident in our ability to protect ourselves. You only get one chance to make a first impression."

"That's certainly true, Mr. President. It's also true you only get one chance not to get yourself killed, and not to get all the rest of the leadership team killed, and not to lose the war because you took reckless risks."

"All right," relented President Layton, marveling at his old friend's characteristic bluntness. He trusted Brother Sam's judgement as much as his own. "Move the meeting," he said as he picked up the draft of his speech. He continued editing as if they never had their conversation.

Brother Sam was not content to simply move the meeting. He also ran a misdirection operation. The president's caravan of black SUVs headed to the Fort Worth Marriott as scheduled, as did numerous caravans for the governors. Only the caravans were not carrying their usual occupants. They were carrying stand-ins. The real authentic president and the real authentic governors were transported by nondescript civilian vehicles to the ranch of an old family friend of the Texas governor. They were transported at different times by different routes. They were not at the ranch more than an hour when they received the first frantic call from security at the Marriott perimeter. "It's gone!" shouted the man in security. "The whole fuckin' building's gone! There were giant explosions, fireballs, and then it all came crashing down! The Marriott's nothing but rubble!"

President Layton was visibly shaken. So, too, were the governors. Every one of them felt as though the specter of death had just walked by and brushed the hair on the back of their necks. President Layton found Brother Sam and sat down next to him. "My God, Sam, all those people … They died pretending to be us!"

"I know," said Sam grimly. "War's a nasty business."

"I really didn't think the DPRA capable of such a thing," said President Layton, still shocked by the enormity of the attack. "There were women and children in that hotel!"

"You remember when you asked me to come and talk to the folks at Wesley's Chapel, Mr. President, when you asked for volunteers to defend our church family and you asked me to help get them trained up?"

"I remember."

"I talked about having a combat mindset then. I told them they have to choose to live in reality rather than self-deception. I also told them they have to be mentally prepared to inflict decisive, devastating and overwhelming violence on evil whenever evil rears its ugly head."

"I remember, Brother Sam. I remember."

"You do not defeat evil by holding back, Mr. President. You do not defeat evil by finely calibrating your response … to send a message in the hope evil will stop being evil. When confronting evil, Mr. President, a combat mindset understands it is kill or be killed."

"I thought I understood that," said President Layton, deeply disappointed in himself.

"The DPRA is truly evil, Mr. President."

President Layton nodded silently. Then he stood and started walking away. Before he had gone a few steps, he stopped and turned back to face Brother Sam. "Thanks for reminding me," he said.

"That's my job, Mr. President."

"And thanks for saving my life," he added as an afterthought.

The war changed after the DPRA targeted President Layton and the leadership of the Free States of Liberty. What had been a war of small-scale skirmishes fought largely over disputed border areas with a combination of regular and irregular forces turned into a war fought by robot killers in the skies over the cities. The Free States of Liberty responded to the attack on the Fort Worth Marriott by sending a dozen cruise missiles into the building for the DPRA's Department for Tolerance and Science in Washington DC, killing most of the staff. The DPRA responded with another cruise missile attack of their own. They attacked and destroyed the Texas State Capital in Austin, killing many of the Texas representatives and their staff. They attacked the Texas State Capital because they viewed it as the birthplace of the rebellion, since it was there where the Texas House of Representatives voted for secession. There was some debate in President Layton's War Council about how the Free States of Liberty should respond. Some advocated for an attack on the Capitol Building in Washington DC in view of the fact the Texas State Capitol had been the de facto capitol for the Free States of Liberty. Others advocated for another target. They still thought of the Capitol Building as representative of the old United States, the United States that used to be a constitutional republic. An attack against it, they argued, was tantamount to an attack against the Constitution. President Layton listened to both sides of his War Council. When he finally decided, he explained his decision at some length, thinking it important they understand his reasoning.

"The DPRA means to conquer us," he began, leaning back in his chair and removing his trademark pipe from his mouth, the one whose stem he mostly chewed since he rarely smoked anymore. "We have been clear we are willing to coexist with them, with them living their way in their country and us living our way in ours. They have clearly expressed no interest in any such arrangement. I think it incumbent on us to consider why that is. Is it because they think they will be victorious, ultimately, and force us back into a union with them, to be subjugated by them? Or is it something more? I think it is something more. The leaders of the DPRA are adherents to an ideology that can brook no dissent. They can tolerate no open and honest examination of the merits of their ideology because they know their ideology is fundamentally repulsive to freedom-loving people. It is like the old communist ideology of the last century. Communism was driven to try and subvert its noncommunist neighbors because the contrast between the two systems was always embarrassing for the communists. It is that way today with the DPRA. We often call them 'the blues' but I think a more accurate title for them is 'woke communists.' And, like the old nineteenth century communists, the woke communists we are facing today will never be interested in peaceful coexistence. They will always be interested in trying to subvert us, to harm us and, should they ever get the opportunity, to conquer us. How do we live next to such people? I believe there is only one way. We convince them they can never prevail. We convince them whatever harm they inflict on us will be visited upon them in equal or greater measure. It is, regrettably the reality we are facing. We must, therefore, attack and destroy the Capitol Building of the DPRA. We must do that because they attacked and destroyed our capitol."

The Free States of Liberty attacked and destroyed the Capitol Building in Washington DC with over a hundred cruise missiles. The DPRA responded with a large cruise missile attack of their own on the Florida

State Capitol in Tallahassee. The Free States of Liberty responded by attacking and destroying the White House. So it went, the tit for tat destruction until both sides had exhausted their stocks of cruise missiles from the old United States military. A new type of robot killer then appeared. These were much smaller than cruise missiles and much cheaper and easier to manufacture. They were termed kamikaze or suicide drones because, in attacking and destroying their target, they also destroyed themselves.

Suicide drones are a class of expendable munitions that can be used not only to conduct surveillance and reconnaissance on the battlefield but to make attacks on specific targets. Smaller suicide drones are twenty inches long, three inches in diameter and weigh in at less than six pounds. They are easily carried in a backpack and are designed to be deployed by a single operator. There are multiple guidance options. The operator can directly input the target's GPS coordinates. He can program an intercept course. Or, simply, he can use the joy stick on the laptop-sized control unit to keep a set of cross hairs centered on an image of the target provided by the drone's color and infrared cameras. The drone is launched from a tube using compressed gas. Its wings fold out as soon as it clears the launch tube. Its small electric motor drives a propeller that allows the drone to climb to a cruising altitude of five hundred feet. There, the drone can loiter for up to ten minutes or head directly to a target up to six miles away. It cruises at sixty mph and accelerates to nearly one hundred mph for its final attack. The drone's small size makes it difficult to spot visually. Its non-metallic body and relatively stealthy shape make it difficult to detect with radar. Its electric motor makes it nearly noiseless. Usually, the target has no idea it is a target. A half pound of shaped explosive in its warhead makes it deadly for both individuals and unarmored vehicles.

Suicide drones were first employed by the DPRA. The DPRA viewed them as a natural extension of the cancel culture campaign relentlessly pursued by the woke communists in the old United States. Back then, if you said or did the wrong thing, which was anything at odds with woke communist ideology, you would soon find yourself the target of a coordinated effort, usually on social media, to destroy both your personal and professional life. The woke communists would pressure your employer to end your employment, pressure your bank to suspend your account, pressure your distributors to drop your products, and pressure your publisher to drop your publications. Like most terror campaigns, their effectiveness was a function of their power to intimidate. Relatively few examples were required before the vast majority of people understood: Get with the program or suffer the consequences.

The DPRA faced a dilemma when the old United States split in two. It still had enemies in the Free States of Liberty—more enemies than ever, actually—only those enemies were now beyond its reach. One of the first acts of the Free States of Liberty upon leaving the old United States was to make political speech and political affiliation a protected activity governed by the same anti-discrimination laws that prohibit discrimination based on age, sex and race. Basically, in the Free States of Liberty, you could no longer be persecuted for having the wrong thoughts or the wrong political views. Suicide drones provided the DPRA with the perfect solution to their dilemma. More than that, it allowed them to take their terror campaign to a whole new level of intimidation. The consequence of defiance was no longer limited to cancellation from the digital public square, to personal and professional cancellation. It was now a real, permanent, physical cancellation ... from life.

A close personal friend of President Layton was one of the first victims of the DPRA's new terror campaign. His name was Alexander Gretzky. He was targeted not only because he was a close personal friend of President Layton but because of his outspoken views on the origins of the war and its fundamentally globalist roots. He was walking his dog on a dirt road in rural Virginia when a suicide drone found and killed him. His dog was killed, too. Another victim of the DPRA's new terror campaign was a popular conservative newscaster. He was blown up on his patio while he was sitting there reading the morning news with a cup of coffee in his hand. He made the DPRA list because he was doing a series entitled "The War on the Border." The series left the unmistakable impression fighting was not going well for the DPRA. Even though that impression was generally consistent with the reality on the ground, it was an impression at odds with the DPRA narrative, that the DPRA was sweeping the ineptly led and poorly motivated Army of the Free States of Liberty from the battlefield. Then there was an industrialist well known for his personal appearances on television, advertising his company's products which were mostly associated with pillows and mattresses and sleepwear. He was targeted because he also advocated the purchase of war bonds to support the Army of the Free States of Liberty. He had just stepped into his company's helicopter on the helipad at his home in Colorado when a suicide drone dove into the helicopter's cockpit and killed everyone inside.

The Free States of Liberty started operating their own suicide drones, although they operated them with a different targeting philosophy. President Layton had a hand in developing the targeting philosophy. He involved himself when it was suggested the Free States of Liberty target the DPRA's universities.

"How does this help us win the war?" asked President Layton.

"It will degrade the enemy's ability to indoctrinate another generation of young DPRA people in woke communist ideology," he was told.

President Layton chewed on the end of his pipe as he mulled it over in his head. Then he asked, "We're not trying to kill their young people, right? I mean, we're not trying to kill the ones who aren't soldiers?"

"No, sir," he was told.

"Then their young people are a given, which makes me think we want them attending their universities."

"I don't understand, sir."

"Ask yourself ... What kind of a young person is a greater threat to us? A young person who is taught to be an independent thinker, a critical thinker, who understands and believes achievement is the result of hard work? Or a young person who is taught to be a victim, taught that critical thinking and achievement based on hard work are, at best, precursors to microaggressions and hurt feelings, and, at worst, oppressive constructs of the white patriarchy?"

His aide scratched his head and laughed. "Mr. President, when you put it like that ... Maybe we should be sending dollars to their universities instead of high explosives."

"No," said President Layton with a wry smile, "I think we can just let them carry on, ruining their young people all on their own."

He also involved himself when someone suggested the Free States of Liberty attack DPRA abortion centers, and the DPRA medical centers performing transgender surgeries on minors. He struggled more with those options because part of him felt compelled to protect innocent children and young people. If there was a button he could push that would make those centers magically disappear without consequence for the Free States of Liberty, he would have pushed it. But he had no such button, which meant he had to test every decision against one simple criterion: Does it help the Free States of Liberty win the war?

"No," he finally told his aide, "if they wish to kill their unborn children, let them kill them. That means fewer soldiers for us to fight in future battles, and fewer workers supporting their soldiers." It was, he thought grimly, the logic of total war.

"And their transgender surgery centers?" asked his aide.

"Same thing," said President Layton. "Let them carry on confusing and abusing their young people. We will carry on raising strong young men and strong young women."

In the end, the Free States of Liberty came to adopt a targeting policy for its suicide drones based on the Layton principles, of which there were only three. Is the target contributing to the DPRA war effort in a material way? Can the target be destroyed without excessive collateral damage? And, finally, can the Free States of Liberty justify the target's destruction before Almighty God? If the targeting committee answered yes to all three questions, then the order was given: Destroy the target.

***

President Layton looked out the window of the tour bus as it made its way across the rolling sea of green prairie grass. The prairie grass seemed to go on endlessly, as did the blue sky overhead. The sky was a lighter shade of blue near the horizon and a deeper, darker shade of blue overhead. Separating the two shades of blue were thin, tenuous wisps of white clouds. President Layton took a sip from his can of Mountain Dew as he contemplated the rolling green prairie and the vast expanse of sky. Their immensity made him think of centuries past, of a time when huge herds of buffalo thundered across the plains. He imagined American Indians riding their ponies at a gallop to the edge of the herd, gripping their ponies with only their legs while drawing back on their bowstrings, and then holding the bowstrings taut until they were nearly pressed up against the flank of the buffalo. He imagined the exhilaration of the chase, the thunder of hundreds of thousands of hooves, the choking clouds of dust and the whoops and hollers of the hunters. He imagined the accompanying fear, the fear of falling from their ponies and being trampled to death, the fear of failure at having an arrow miss its mark and, perhaps the greatest fear of all, the fear of shame, of coming home empty-handed with no meat for the tribe. Finally, he imagined the sense of satisfied contentment, of peace, when it was all over and they were successful, when the herd had moved on and the prairie was quiet except for the heavy breathing of the ponies. The men would walk their ponies together to form a circle and survey the bounty of their hunt. They would smile and nod at each other knowing they had done well, knowing they had done what their fathers had done and what their father's fathers had done, knowing they had faithfully honored the role assigned to them in life by the Great Father of the world, the creator of all life.

Such a tragedy, he thought sadly, *for the buffalo and the American Indians. They probably thought it would go on forever, until the day they realized it would not.*

Brother Sam sat down opposite President Layton. Instead of a can of Mountain Dew, he had a glass tumbler filled to the top with ice and bourbon. "Mr. President," he said with a grin, "it is a mystery to me how you can drink that rot gut."

President Layton smiled and shook his head. "Guess I'm still just a good ol' Methodist preacher at heart."

Brother Sam raised his tumbler of bourbon. "Here's to good ol' Methodist preachers."

President Layton returned the toast with his can of Mountain Dew.

After Brother Sam downed a swallow of bourbon and smacked his lips loudly, he said, "You're looking mighty pensive, Mr. President."

"Just thinking about buffalo," said President Layton wistfully.

"What?" asked Brother Sam, surprised at his response.

President Layton waved his hand as if to wave away the thought. "Nothing," he said with a smile. "This is a good trip, Sam. So glad we're making it."

"Me too, Mr. President."

"You're comfortable with the security arrangements?"

"So far, so good."

"It no doubt helps having twenty tour buses with a couple hundred soldiers from the Army of the Free States of Liberty tagging along for the ride."

Sam laughed. "Yes, Mr. President, it helps."

"Let me ask you something, Sam."

"Shoot."

"Are we winning this war?"

Sam cocked his head, surprised by the president's question. He studied his bourbon before answering. "Yes, Mr. President," he said finally, "we're winning this war."

"And what makes you say that?" asked President Layton.

"They don't *make* anything," answered Brother Sam succinctly.

President Layton chuckled. "Can you elaborate a little?"

"The war between the old United States and Russia, over Ukraine ... What was the lesson learned there?" Brother Sam did not wait for an answer. "That manufacturing still matters. The old United States thought it would crush Russia with sanctions but that didn't work because the Russians made what they needed. The old United States thought it would crush Russia's currency, too, the ruble, but that didn't work because the world needed Russian energy and Russian minerals and Russian grain and was willing to buy what it needed with rubles. Finally, the old United States thought it would bleed Russia's military white. Well, that didn't work because the Russians had the manufacturing base to support their military, even when their military was firing fifty, sixty thousand artillery shells a day, and doing that for months. I'm still amazed when I think about what an incredible volume of fire that was ... and how terrible it must have been to be on the receiving end of it. Anyway, the old United States, and the old NATO ... they couldn't keep up. They couldn't keep supplying the Ukrainians who were firing only a tenth of what the Russians were firing. In the end, it was the old United States and the old NATO that bled themselves white."

"All because we lost our manufacturing base."

"Yes. The moral of the story is: You can't fight a real war with a real enemy when all you have is a paper economy."

"Do *we* have a paper economy?" asked President Layton, suddenly concerned.

Brother Sam shook his head. "The Free States of Liberty got the parts of the old United States that actually produce stuff. We produce the oil and gas. We produce the grain and minerals. Plus, the Free States of Liberty are rapidly re-industrializing, for a number of reasons. Contrast that with the DPRA. They're still against fossil fuels, still against making stuff because it goes against their Great Green Leap Forward. The only relative strength I see for the DPRA is finance, because they kept the currency, the old dollar. But that relative strength is really not so great after the collapse of the dollar, which was precipitated by the defeat of the old United States Navy in the South China Sea. Also, it's a rapidly diminishing strength because they have nothing real to back it up. Plus, they're printing dollars like there's no tomorrow."

President Layton nodded, impressed with Sam's analysis.

Brother Sam was not quite finished. "There's another reason, too, Mr. President, why we're winning."

"What's that?"

"Geography. The DPRA is largely confined to the cities."

"How's that a disadvantage?"

"It's easy to cut off supplies … their food, water and energy. Also, they have no strategic depth. We're seeing that with the drone wars. The drones are relatively short-range weapons. That does not limit us much because DPRA targets are concentrated in cities and those cities are surrounded by territory that belongs to the Free States of Liberty. Most of their targets are within range of our drones. The same is not true for the DPRA. The Free States of Liberty are a huge expanse of mostly rural countryside. We make up … What? Over eighty percent of the geography of the old United States of America? There is very little the DPRA can reach from their territory, which is why they have to send launch teams deep inside our borders. Unfortunately for them, we've gotten pretty good at hunting down their launch teams before they're in a position to launch their drones."

"That's why you were comfortable approving our road trip."

"Yes, Mr. President."

"You don't think Supreme Leader Johnny Penn is touring his cities?"

Brother Sam smiled. "Not if he values his life."

CHAPTER FIVE

Madness is something rare in individuals—but in groups, parties, peoples and ages, it is the rule.

— Friedrich Nietzsche

A HUGE WIDESCREEN television covered most of one wall of the bunker in the Rainbow House. There was a bucolic garden scene on the screen which, in reality, was a live feed from the garden outside the Rainbow House. Nearest to the camera that provided the live stream was an Asian-style gazebo filled with bamboo patio furniture. The gazebo seemed to grow up out of a bed of smoothly raked tan and pink pea stones. Surrounding the bed of pea stones was a row of short, neatly trimmed evergreen hedges. A taller row of evergreen hedges, perhaps six feet tall, grew up just behind the first row. Finally, behind the taller of the two hedge rows, a security wall towered. It was sixteen feet high and textured to look like stone instead of steel-reinforced concrete. The live feed from the widescreen television allowed Supreme Leader Johnny Penn and his family to enjoy the ambiance and serenity of the garden from the safety of their underground bunker. The bunker was located forty feet beneath the ground floor of the Rainbow House. Safety was still very much a concern for Supreme Leader Johnny Penn and his family. The gazebo had been rebuilt twice in the last six months after suicide drones attacked members of the Rainbow House staff in the mistaken belief they were members of the supreme family.

Rainbow House was the new White House. It had been constructed after the White House was destroyed in the second round of cruise missile exchanges between the DPRA and the Free States of Liberty. It was nothing like the old White House with its stately neoclassical columns and porticos, intentionally designed to evoke in the populace of a new nation, a nation recently birthed in violent revolution, feelings of permanence and majestic grandeur. The Rainbow House was, first and foremost, designed to afford security to the supreme family. Secondly, although the DPRA was birthed in violent revolution just like the old United States, and certainly aspired to the same permanence and grandeur as the old United States, the DPRA wanted to evoke in its population feelings aligned with its priorities. Those were the sustainable use of green energy, atonement for past racial injustice, and a commitment to tolerance, especially with regard to gender choice.

The sustainable use of green energy was the easiest of the three to incorporate in the design of the Rainbow House. The Rainbow House was, of course, oriented so its windows faced south to maximize lighting from natural sunlight. It was also built into a hillside to take advantage of the soil as a natural insulator. In addition to being a natural insulator, the soil afforded protection from loitering munitions, nicely complementing the security design goal. The roofs were all covered in solar panels. Together with the banks of batteries in the basement, the Rainbow House was completely off the grid, which the Rainbow House staff joked made them tantamount to preppers. The staff found that funny in a mildly unnerving way because the DPRA often targeted preppers as domestic terrorists.

Atonement for racial injustice was much more difficult to incorporate in the design of the Rainbow House. There were ideas about including murals depicting the cruel reality of slavery. There were also ideas to include statues of Raymond James and Dwayne Armstrong, the two unarmed African American males shot down in cold blood by Officer Leah Blunt. Supreme Leader Johnny Penn was responsible for approving all important decisions with regard to the design and construction of the Rainbow House just as George Washington had been responsible for the White House. The suggestions for murals and statues struck Supreme Leader Johnny Penn as far too ordinary. DPRA law mandated every school have a mural depicting the cruel reality of slavery. Also mandated were statues of Raymond James and Dwayne Armstrong in every town square, each with an outstretched arm boldly pointing to the promised land of racial equity.

Supreme Leader Johnny Penn was determined the Rainbow House would have a fresh, new way to signal to the world the DPRA's commitment to atonement for past racial injustice. He had his epiphany while sitting through a presentation by the head of the DPRA's Department for Reeducation. The department head was thirty minutes into what seemed like an endless sequence of slides with an endless series of tables and graphs. Some of the graphs had converging lines while others had diverging lines. Regardless of which way the lines went, they all trended to the same conclusion: The DPRA would fail to meet its reeducation metrics unless it dramatically expanded its network of labor camps. That is when it suddenly hit Supreme Leader Johnny Penn. It hit him like a thunderbolt, or the proverbial suicide drone with a warhead that miraculously failed to detonate. It was not *what* they included in the construction of the Rainbow House, it was *how* they constructed the Rainbow House.

"Yes!" shouted Supreme Leader Johnny Penn, slamming the palm of his hand on the conference room table.

The briefing stopped and all heads turned to look at Supreme Leader Johnny Penn.

"I've got it!" he said with obvious excitement.

"Excuse me, Supreme Leader?" asked the head of the Department of Reeducation.

"We'll use slave labor! We'll use slave labor to build the Rainbow House!"

The head of the Department of Reeducation had no idea what Supreme Leader Johnny Penn was talking about. He was, however, defensive when it came to propaganda from the Free States of Liberty, propaganda which charged the DPRA reeducation camps with being no less than slave labor camps. He said with all seriousness, "Supreme Leader, we do not think of our prisoners as slave labor. We think of them as reeducation guests."

Supreme Leader Johnny Penn ignored him. He jumped up and walked quickly to the front of the conference room. "Listen," he began, "you all know how we want the Rainbow House to reflect *our* values, the values of *our* democracy, and how one of those values is the need to atone for past racial injustice, especially for slavery. Well, the White House was built with slave labor. *Our* atonement, for *our* democracy, will be accomplished by building Rainbow House with slave labor!"

The people seated around the conference room table were afraid to say anything. They were afraid to say anything because they did not follow Supreme Leader Johnny Penn and they had learned from experience, with the stress of recent setbacks in the war and Supreme Leader Johnny Penn's increasingly erratic behavior, it was better to say nothing than to say the wrong thing. The head of the Department of Reeducation finally broke the silence, feeling some obligation to speak since it was still his briefing. "I'm sorry, Supreme Leader, but how will using slave labor for the Rainbow House atone for using slave labor for the White House? It is still slave labor."

Supreme Leader Johnny Penn chided his department head as if he was a disappointed DPRA university professor. "You're still trapped by your white supremacism, Curtis. You're assuming I'm talking about African Americans just because I'm talking about slaves. And that's not at all what I'm talking about. Think of it like this, Curtis. It's another form of reparations. We'll use white slave labor to build the Rainbow House. It's the perfect atonement. The White House was built with black slave labor so we'll offer our atonement for the original sin of slavery by building the Rainbow House with white slave labor."

Everyone in the conference room suddenly understood. There were broad smiles and nods of agreement. Self-serving congratulations were warmly offered to Supreme Leader Johnny Penn for his remarkable idea. The head of the Department of Reeducation thought this another opportunity for his department and himself. "Supreme leader," he said cheerfully, "you can count on the Department of Reeducation to supply all the slaves needed for the Rainbow House."

"No, no, no, Curtis," said Supreme Leader Johnny Penn, a mischievous twinkle in his eyes. He was very much enjoying the fact Curtis was still playing the part of the dense university student.

Everyone stopped talking and looked at Supreme Leader Johnny Penn.

Supreme Leader Johnny Penn explained. "We're definitely *not* using slave labor from the reeducation camps. After all, what kind of atonement would that be, using malingerers, malcontents and subversives? Real atonement requires it be us, the loyal citizens of the DPRA. *We* need to be the ones experiencing slavery, just like the African Americans experienced slavery all those years ago. So, this is how I see it. We'll have random raids inside the DPRA. We'll call them slaving raids. The slavers will swoop into towns and cities across the DPRA and capture slaves just like they did back in the day. Only the slaves we capture this time will be white. That, comrades, will be *real* atonement. I see this being widely supported by our people. They will recognize the atonement opportunity. Those white people captured in the slaving raids, after they complete their tours of servitude, which we will have to take care to remind ourselves is still for a limited period of time and, therefore, nothing at all like the perpetual servitude of the original black slaves ... Anyway, after they complete their tours of servitude, they will be the DRPA's bright, new, shining examples of public virtue. They will prove to the Free States of Liberty, and to the world, the moral superiority of the people of the DPRA."

Gender choice was the final element to be incorporated in the Rainbow House. Supreme Leader Johnny Penn left the details of that element to Melissa, whose title had recently changed from first lady to supreme partner. She was more than a little miffed the Rainbow House had been named before she was assigned her new responsibility. She much preferred "the Queer House." She was, after all, the country's champion for gender neutrality, first as first lady for the old United States and now as supreme partner of the DPRA. She firmly believed the Queer House an important affirmation of gender neutrality. Also, when she sat down to bounce the name off Paulette, the drag queen kindergarten teacher who was still reading books about gender fluidity to her son, Francine, she discovered Paulette was wholeheartedly in favor of the proposed name. Paulette thought the proposed name important to establish the principle that words can be reclaimed and reappropriated from hateful old social constructs. "Think on it," she enthused with her usual flamboyance, "where 'queer' was once a hateful, hurtful pejorative, we'll be using it as an inclusive superlative, applying it not only to 'our people' in a spirt of tolerance, respect and love, but to the residence of our supreme leader and his supreme partner!"

Melissa had to admit there was another, deeper reason she disliked "the

Rainbow House." She considered the symbolism of the rainbow passé. The DPRA had already adopted the rainbow flag as its national flag in place of the stars and stripes of the old United States. Also, the old White House had been illuminated in rainbow colors way back in 2015 when the old Supreme Court ruled in favor of same-sex marriage. She thought, *Enough with the rainbow already!*

Melissa resolved to pitch "the Queer House" to Supreme Leader Johnny Penn. Melissa decided to make the pitch without Paulette even though Paulette was her go-to expert on all things queer. Melissa knew Supreme Leader Johnny Penn still harbored some queerphobic attitudes toward Paulette. Those attitudes, Melissa suspected, were a result of him blaming Paulette for his son's gender choice, to be Francine instead of Frank. Melissa had to tread carefully there because it was a criminal offense in the DPRA not to affirm your child's gender choice. Even as the supreme partner, it would be politically dangerous for Melissa to accuse Supreme Leader Johnny Penn of committing a gender crime. It might even prove physically dangerous. She did, however, think Francine would be helpful. Supreme Leader Johnny Penn had a hard time saying no to his son even though his son was now his daughter, and Melissa knew Francine was in favor of the name change, thanks to her and Paulette's coaching.

Melissa and Francine sat at the table in Supreme Leader Johnny Penn's office absentmindedly watching a pair of yellow butterflies flitter their way across the widescreen television that showed the live feed from the garden forty feet above their heads. As usual, Supreme Leader Johnny Penn was late.

"Are they queer?" asked Francine out of the blue.

"Who?" asked Melissa.

"The butterflies. Are they queer, Gestational Co-parent?"

Francine had been referring to Melissa as her "gestational co-parent" for well over a year. Gestational co-parent was one of the DPRA's approved gender-neutral appellations for parents, replacing the old genderist appellations like mother and father, mom and dad, mommy and daddy. Even though Melissa had a hand in developing the list of officially approved appellations, and then rolling it out to parents with the thinly veiled threat there would be consequences for parents who continued using the old genderist appellations, gestational co-parent still grated on her nerves. *I'll never get used to it,* she thought, sincerely disappointed in herself for clinging to a deplorable genderist paradigm.

"I don't know," answered Melissa. "I never really thought about it. Why do you ask?"

"Paulette says we should be asking."

"If something's queer?"

Francine was tired of the subject. "When's Non-birthing Co-parent getting here?" she asked.

"He'll be here soon," answered Melissa. Then she chuckled. "You know your non-birthing co-parent ... He's very busy taking care of the country's business."

"I'm hungry," complained Francine. "Can we have lunch soon?"

Melissa assured Francine with as much conviction as she could muster. "We'll have lunch as soon as we finish meeting with your non-birthing co-parent." Melissa had no idea if Supreme Leader Johnny Penn would be only a few minutes late or an hour late. She decided to change the subject. "How was school today?"

"Boring," answered Francine, obviously not caring to talk about school.

"Learn anything interesting?"

"No," answered Francine, now determined to be obstinate.

"Come on," pleaded Melissa. "Your gestational co-parent is interested in what you learned today. Can you share just one thing?"

"No!" answered Francine more defiantly than before.

Melissa had enough of Francine's attitude. She reached over and grabbed Francine by her arm. "Now listen here, Francine, I'm your gestational co-parent and you *will* answer me when I ask you a question!"

"Stop touching me!" Francine screamed.

"Stop it!" scolded Melissa. "You stop it this instant, Francine!"

Francine continued screaming. "No permission, no touching! That's the rule! No permission, no touching!"

Melissa gave up and let go of Francine's arm. She took a deep breath to try and compose herself. "Ok," she finally said, looking for a way to extract something positive from their fracas, "that's a good rule, Francine, not to let anyone touch you without permission. But it doesn't apply to your co-parents."

"Yes it does!" insisted Francine. "It applies to everyone! Paulette says so!"

Melissa surrendered, not wanting Supreme Leader Johnny Penn to walk in on a family scene. "Alright, Francine, it applies to co-parents. Can your gestational co-parent give you a kiss?"

"No!" said Francine, not yet ready to accept her gestational co-parent's surrender.

"Please?" asked Melissa sweetly. "Your gestational co-parent wants a kiss. Just one little kiss. Pretty please with sugar on top?"

"No!" said Francine. "I only want kisses from Paulette!"

Alarm bells went off in Melissa's mind. *Kisses from Paulette?!*

Supreme Leader Johnny Penn threw open the door and strode into the room. He had a concerned, worried look on his face. When he noticed Melissa sitting at the table, he was surprised to find her in his office. Then he remembered their meeting. "This is really not a good time," he said tersely.

"There's never a good time with you!" said Melissa, flushing hot with anger that their meeting had slipped his mind. She wondered what else could go wrong this morning.

Supreme Leader Johnny Penn knew from the tone of her voice she would not be put off. "Ok," he said, sitting down across from her, "you called the meeting."

"Yes," she said. "Yes I did. I want to talk about the Rainbow House."

"Ok. What about it?"

"I don't like the name. I think we should call it 'the Queer House.'"

"Sorry," said Supreme Leader Johnny Penn, "it's already named."

His dismissive attitude stoked her anger still hotter. "I know it's already named, Johnny! I want the name changed!"

"Why?"

The logical reasons were all there on the tip of her tongue, the ones she rehearsed and planned to present to him this morning. Suddenly, they seemed beside the point. She glared at him and said ominously, "I want it changed, Johnny, because … I'm … your … wife!"

Whatever doubt Supreme Leader Johnny Penn had regarding her

determination to change the name vanished. Melissa had not referred to herself as "his wife" in years.

The door to Supreme Leader Johnny Penn's office burst open a second time. Bobby Nuland, his national security advisor, rushed in. "Supreme Leader," he said breathlessly, "it's true. The rumor is true! Green Future One is down! The grid's down in Los Angeles! Los Angeles is blacked out!"

Supreme Leader Johnny Penn sat motionless upon hearing the news.

"Los Angeles is blacked out!" repeated Bobby Nuland. "Did you hear me, Supreme Leader?!"

Still, Supreme Leader Johnny Penn sat motionless.

Bobby Nuland looked at Melissa and then back at Supreme Leader Johnny Penn. He stood there not saying anything because he did not know what else to say.

Melissa looked at her husband with concern.

Supreme Leader Johnny Penn finally moved. The palms of his hands went to his face and covered his eyes. His fingertips massaged his forehead. He did that for a moment before dropping his hands to his lap. There, his hands took turns caressing each other, as if washing themselves with soap and water, of which there was none. He muttered under his breath.

"Excuse me, Supreme Leader?" asked Bobby Nuland, not catching what Supreme Leader Johnny Penn was muttering.

That seemed to bring Supreme Leader Johnny Penn back from wherever he was. He cleared his voice and added enough volume for Bobby Nuland to hear him, although just barely. "They've left us no choice," he whispered.

"Los Angeles cannot survive without power," said Bobby Nuland.

"None of our cities can survive without power," said Supreme Leader Johnny Penn, now speaking with his normal volume if not his normal voice. He still sounded distant and strangely detached. "Without power, there's nothing. No food. No Water. Nothing."

"It'll be bad," confirmed Bobby Nuland.

Anger crept into Supreme Leader Johnny Penn's voice. "We warned the fascists," he said. "An attack on our power grid is the same as an attack on our cities, and we will defend our cities with all available means, up to and including nuclear weapons."

Bobby Nuland was shocked Supreme Leader Johnny Penn would immediately consider nuclear weapons. He looked over at Melissa and saw she shared his concern. He turned back to Supreme Leader Johnny Penn. "We said that, Supreme Leader, to *deter* the fascists. Now that deterrence has failed, it's important to keep in mind the fascists also have nuclear weapons. We may have the ballistic missile submarines from the old United States Navy but they have the Minutemen missile silos."

Supreme Leader Johnny Penn glared at Bobby Nuland. There was a mocking, hateful look on his face. He asked sarcastically, "Now you're the reticent warrior? What happened to 'bombs away Bobby?'"

Bobby Nuland had never seen Supreme Leader Johnny Penn so obviously upset. "Supreme leader," he said, "there's a difference between tactical nuclear weapons and strategic nuclear weapons. If we use strategic nuclear weapons against their cities, they'll use strategic nuclear weapons against our cities. That's not a good scenario, Supreme Leader."

Supreme Leader Johnny Penn slammed his fist down hard on the table. The sharp crack of it startled Melissa and Bobby. They both jumped. It also startled Francine. She reached over and hugged Melissa, not at all thinking to ask permission before touching her.

"Ok," said Supreme Leader Johnny Penn, still glaring at Bobby Nuland, "I'm waiting to hear 'the good scenario.'" He used his fingers for air quotes.

"Supreme leader—"

Supreme Leader Johnny Penn decided he was not interested in Bobby Nuland's assessment after all. "Do we send in the Marines?" he asked with a brutally mocking voice. "Oh, wait, we can't send in the Marines. Why? Because we don't have any Marines! Why don't we have any Marines, Bobby?"

Bobby Nuland was taken aback by the unhinged behavior of Supreme Leader Johnny Penn. He mentally thumbed through his inventory of potential responses as if he was surprised by an impertinent question at a press conference. He found one that seemed politically appropriate. "We thought, Supreme Leader, the Marines were a hopeless repository of toxic masculinity, incongruous with the DPRA's vision for a diverse and gender-neutral military, one that reflects the values of *our* democracy."

"I remember you telling me that," said Supreme Leader Johnny Penn, adding a contemptuous, crooked smirk to his brutally mocking tone. "I remember you said that when I signed the bill disbanding the Marines. I think you said something similar when I signed the bill creating the Army of the DPRA." He gestured expansively with his arms. "Our brand-new gender-neutral Army of the DPRA, whose soldiers will be superior to those of the enemy, unconstrained by outdated gender stereotypes! They will take lethality to a whole new level, you said, because diversity is our strength!"

Supreme Leader Johnny Penn shook his head and laughed. It sounded so obviously absurd to him when he said it now. He looked back at Bobby Nuland. "Well, Mr. National Security Advisor, the man with all the answers, where's our Army now?"

"Supreme leader—"

Supreme Leader Johnny Penn held up his hand. He had another question before he let Bobby Nuland try to explain. "And where was our Army when the fascists were steadily pushing us back on the border?"

"Supreme leader—"

He cut Bobby Nuland off with another question. "And where was our Army when the enemy was attacking Green Future One?"

Bobby Nuland was determined to speak this time, tired of being mocked. "I don't think it's fair to say we're steadily losing—"

Supreme Leader Johnny Penn exploded. He slammed his fist down on the table a second time and screamed, "DON'T TREAT ME LIKE AN IDIOT, BOBBY! WE LOST THE DRONE WAR AND NOW WE'RE LOSING THE GROUND WAR!" His face was red. Veins bulged in his neck.

Melissa decided she had to do something to try and calm down Supreme Leader Johnny Penn. She summoned her soothing, empathetic voice. "I know it's upsetting, Johnny, but we'll get through this. You'll figure it out like you always do. You're our supreme leader and we all have faith in you. We'll get through it, Johnny, because we have *you* leading us."

Supreme Leader Johnny Penn turned and looked at Melissa. He heard the concern in her voice despite her effort to conceal it. He thought she was right to be concerned. He turned her words over in his mind. He appreciated her confidence in him, that he would take care of her, but that confidence stirred a deeper thought. It surfaced slowly like some long-submerged truth only now pushed to the surface by the impending catastrophe of losing Los Angeles and, with it, the rest of the West Coast. He would take care of her not because he was Supreme Leader Johnny Penn but because he was her husband, and she was his wife. Then he noticed his son clutching desperately at Melissa's arm. He saw his son as if for the first time. He saw the long blond locks that hung down to his shoulders, the inch-long artificial eyelashes and the heavy black mascara around his eyes. He saw the red rouge on his cheeks and the bright red lipstick on his lips. He saw the lacey girls' blouse and the pleated girls' skirt. He saw it all as if for the first time and suddenly realized what he had done. He was horrified at the realization. He had abandoned his son. He had abandoned him as completely and totally as if he had left him alone in the woods, to fend for himself without food and shelter, surrounded by wolves.

The countenance of his own father suddenly appeared, looking down on him. Then he saw his father's father. Other faces appeared out of the hazy mists of time, faces that belonged to the ages going all the way back to antiquity. He recognized none of them by name but their look was familiar to him. It was the look of serious men who had not shirked their responsibilities in life, to provide for their families and raise their sons to be men. They looked down upon him along with his father and grandfather. Their gaze was disapproving. Then it turned contemptuous. He tried to look away but could not avert his eyes. He tried to run but could not move his legs. They pronounced their judgment, all those generations of men who had come before him. It came as a single, whispered word he could not initially make out. Then he heard it. "Coward!" they said. Each time they said it, they said it louder than the time before. They began to chant it as if chanting to the steady beat of a drum. "Coward! Coward! Coward!" With every refrain it grew steadily louder. "Coward! Coward! Coward!"

Before the assembled generations in his mind, Supreme Leader Johnny Penn fell to his knees. He prostrated himself on the ground, sobbing and begging for forgiveness.

In the conference room of the bunker, he collapsed in his chair.

"Johnny?" asked Melissa, even more concerned than before.

He looked up at her with tears of guilt in his eyes.

"It'll be ok," she said, trying to reassure him.

"No," answered Supreme Leader Johnny Penn with a hollow, defeated voice.

"What do you mean, Johnny?"

"We will lose this war, Melissa."

"But why, Johnny?"

"Because we deserve to lose it."

CHAPTER SIX

Out of every one hundred men, ten shouldn't even be there, eighty are just targets, nine are the real fighters, and we are lucky to have them, for they make the battle. Ah, but the one, one is a warrior, and he will bring the others back.

— Heraclitus

CAPTAIN LEONID PUSHILIN, who everyone called Push, was lying flat on the ground on a hill overlooking Camp 847. He moved his ten-power binoculars slowly across the camp. The camp was like most of them. The barracks were laid out in an evenly spaced grid and surrounded by a square of fence with guard towers at each corner. He counted twenty-five barracks, which was about right for a camp with a thousand prisoners. The barracks at the back of the camp housed the prisoners while the barracks at the front housed the guards. He estimated a hundred guards given the number of prisoners. The DPRA seemed to abide by a ten-to-one ratio between prisoners and guards. There were also buildings for the mess, the shop, the housing and maintenance of cleaning rigs for Green Future One, administration and, finally, the camp commander's residence. There was an open field near the front gate that took the place of two barracks. He knew from talking to prisoners rescued from other camps the open field was where the prisoners assembled whenever assembly was required, which was every morning at 05:00, before heading out for their morning cleaning details, and every evening at 16:00, before being dismissed for mess and lights out. It was also where the prisoners assembled to witness punishment.

"Not much of a fence," said Lieutenant Buchanan who was lying next to Push and looking through his own pair of binoculars. The camp perimeter was enclosed by a single fence of chain link. It was ten feet tall and topped with coils of razor wire.

"Good enough if you don't have tools," said Push. "Plus, even if you get out, where you gonna go? You're gonna die in the desert, that's all."

"Yeah," said Lieutenant Buchanan grimly. "You think we made it in time?"

Lieutenant Buchanan was referring to the last camp. They found no prisoners when they captured it. There was the usual complement of guards and camp staff but no prisoners. One of the guards finally told them what happened. The camp commander knew the camp was on borrowed time because the DPRA was pulling its borders back closer to Los Angeles. He did not want the condition of the prisoners being held against him when the Army of the Free States of Liberty showed up. He decided to execute the prisoners. Their bodies were buried in a mass grave a mile behind the camp. Push made the camp commander dig another, single grave next to the mass grave. Then he shot him.

"Not sure yet," said Push. "I think so because I still see guards in the towers. We'll know for sure when the sun sets. If we see lights in the barracks and then the lights go out … the prisoners are still there."

Lieutenant Buchanan pulled the elastic cloth cover from his wristwatch, the one that kept glare from the glass on the watch face from revealing their position during daylight hours. It did the same at night, keeping the tritium-painted dial from revealing their position if the enemy had night vision, which they usually did. He saw it was 17:34. "Twenty-six minutes to lights out," he said.

Push set his binoculars on the ground to give his eyes a rest. He thought about using the twenty-six minutes to check on the company but decided he had time for that later. The plan was straightforward, although really it was two plans with the decision diamond being whether or not the prisoners were still alive. The plan was simple if the prisoners were no longer alive. Come in through the back side of the camp and push the guards outside the camp perimeter, from the back side of the camp to the front entrance. They would use the barracks for cover as they went. Once the guards were outside the camp, it was a simple matter of hunting them down in the desert. Usually that did not take long. Things were more complicated if the prisoners were alive. Then they needed to establish a defensive line between the barracks where the guards were housed and the barracks where the prisoners were housed. Two platoons from his company would hold the defensive line while the other two platoons methodically cleared the barracks with guards, one barrack at a time. Sometimes the guards surrendered. Usually they did not.

Push found the guards in the DPRA Department of Reeducation a different breed of soldier compared to the soldier in the regular DPRA Army. The soldiers in the regular DPRA Army were not really all that interested in fighting. Most of that reticence, Push thought, was a consequence of their being draftees. "You can force someone into uniform," he liked to say, "but you can't force them to place a higher priority on the mission than their lives." He found that an interesting contradiction when he stopped to think about it. The blues, who everyone in the Free States of Liberty now referred to as woke communists, were always so convinced theirs was the one true way, the enlightened path to utopia. If you ever had the opportunity to sit down and talk with one, which was an opportunity only in the sense you were getting to know your enemy, they would not be shy about letting you know, either. When they found out you were not on their side, they would proceed to slander you with every nasty epithet imaginable: hater, bigot, racist, misogynist and, of course, Nazi. After that, they would do their best to destroy you, to have you fired from your job and ostracized from civil society.

That was all back in the bad old days, in the old United States of America before the cold civil war finally turned hot. Then a strange thing happened. All those ferociously combative woke communist culture warriors turned noticeably less enthusiastic about putting on a uniform and picking up a rifle. Push did not think their lack of enthusiasm a consequence of them suddenly viewing their cause as any less noble. He thought it, rather, a consequence of the fact they were afraid to pay the ultimate price. They were not willing to die for their beliefs. He had a theory as to why that was. The woke communists believed in nothing beyond the physical world. They believed in nothing transcendent, the way Christians believe in heaven and Muslims believe in paradise. If a person believes in nothing greater than themselves, it is asking a lot of them to sacrifice themselves. In fact, it is asking more than a lot of them. It is asking everything of them.

Push found the DPRA Department of Reeducation guards more difficult to understand. They were anything but reluctant to fight. They were determined, fearless fighters. Yet they subscribed to the same woke communist ideology as the regular soldiers of the Army of the DPRA. He thought the difference had something to do with the fact reeducation units were considered elite units in the DPRA, even though they were essentially just guards. The DPRA, like the woke communists in the old United States, had always placed a premium on education. "Go ahead and raise your kids in your home schools," they liked to say, back when home schooling was still allowed, "we'll get them in the universities." And so they did, at least a large percentage of them. The DPRA advertised their reeducation camps as a second chance for the redeemable conservatives of the old United States, and as a means of isolating and disenfranchising the irredeemable conservatives. Either way, the reeducation camps were the foundation upon which the DPRA placed its hopes for a united America. The priority afforded the Department of Reeducation reflected that belief. The Department of Reeducation had the best recruits, the best pay and the best equipment.

Like the Azov Battalion in Ukraine, thought Push.

His father told him stories about the Azov Battalion in Ukraine, about how they considered themselves an elite unit and conducted themselves accordingly on the battlefield. They were as fearless as they were ruthless. Those stories were based on his family's experience with them before the outbreak of the Ukraine War, and during the war itself. Soldiers in the Azov Battalion believed in nothing transcendent, at least not in the sense of an afterlife. They were devoted to their vision of a future Ukraine, one that was culturally unadulterated by either the Russian language or the Russian Orthodox Church. They were content to find transcendence through their role in realizing their vision.

Same with the Waffen-SS, thought Push. *They were willing to give their lives for the Thousand-year Reich. The Fuhrer had no more loyal soldiers.*

Push concluded elitism mixed with a sense of purpose makes for a dangerous combination.

The sun had submerged into the craggy peaks of the Sierra Nevada mountains. The spot where it submerged was marked by a luminous halo of yellow sky and horizontal bands of orange, pink and magenta clouds. The prickly black silhouettes of Joshua trees stood like silent sentries before the western horizon. Stars peaked out from the thickening veil of blackness on the eastern horizon. In the valley below, the windows in the barracks glowed softly white.

"What time you got?" asked Push.

"17:58," answered Lieutenant Buchanan.

The siren in the camp announced lights out. One by one, the softly glowing windows turned black. When the siren fell silent a minute later, the camp was dark except for the guard barracks and the camp commander's residence.

"The Department of Reeducation is nothing if not punctual," said Push.

"Yes, sir," said Lieutenant Buchanan."

"Let's get the company in position," said Push. "We know the prisoners are still alive. This will be a prisoner recovery operation."

***

Officer Leah Blunt, who became Prisoner 1538762 when she entered the system of camps run by the Department of Reeducation, and only recovered her name when she garnered the unwanted favor of the camp commander, finished lighting the second of two dinner candles. She finished lighting the dinner candles just as the camp sirens finished their nightly wailing. It was an odd contrast, Leah often thought, that the sirens' wailing signaled the prisoners were to extinguish the lights in their barracks at the same time it signaled she was to light the candles for the dinner table in the camp commander's dining room.

Leah blew out the kitchen match with a puff from her lips. Her lips were painted red, which was the way Bernie liked them. He also liked her to dress up for dinner as if they were going out on the town. He was particular about how she dressed to the point where he laid out the dress he wanted her to wear. He laid it out on her bed with no thought about going into her room or going through her closet because, as far as he was concerned, she was his personal property.

The dress he set out tonight was a black sequined cocktail dress with a plunging neckline. It used to bother Leah, at first, the dresses he selected. They made her feel cheap and trashy. They were too tight. They also showed too much leg and too much cleavage. It did not take her long to realize none of that mattered. The only people who saw her were Bernie and Diana. Bernie would have his way with her like he always did regardless of what she wore. Diana, the camp commander's cook, rarely looked at her and, when she did, looked at her with anything but the sympathy Leah thought she deserved. Diana looked at her with what Leah imagined was disgust. She learned it was actually resentment when the two of them finally had words, when Bernie was suddenly called away for camp business one evening. "What's your problem?!" asked Leah, tired of the cold shoulder from Diana.

"You're my problem!" shot back Diana.

"Me?!" asked Leah, shocked Diana would say that. "What did I ever do to you?"

"Who do you think was sleeping with Bernie, Leah, before you?"

Leah suddenly understood. Diana was one of the most beautiful women in camp. She had been the camp commander's nightly female companionship before Leah came along. Diana was worried the camp commander would send her back to the barracks now that he was sleeping with Leah instead of her.

"Diana," she said, "I would go back to the barracks this instant if the choice was between that loathsome man and the barracks."

"Then why don't you!" challenged Diana, glaring at her.

"Because he'll kill my husband if I leave!"

Diana had not expected that. She stood speechless.

"Look," said Leah, "I may not be able to leave but I have some leverage. I'll make sure you don't go back to the barracks."

"And how would you do that?" asked Diana, not wanting to believe Leah after resenting her for so long.

"I'll tell him I like your cooking."

"You would do that for me?"

"I would. Of course, it would help if I could also tell him we're friends."

The next day, Diana began smiling at Leah.

Bernie strode in through the front door. "Camp's all tucked-in," he said cheerfully, hanging his camp commander cap on the hook by the door. He walked up to the dining room table and sat down. He poured himself a glass of wine, set the bottle down and took a sip. "Excellent," he said to himself. He picked up the bottle again and turned to Leah. "Wine?" he asked.

"Please," she said.

He filled her glass. When he finished filling Leah's glass, he turned to Kendra who was sitting at the table opposite Leah. Kendra was wearing the same black negligee she always wore. "Wine?" asked Bernie.

"No thanks," answered Kendra. "I'll just watch the two of you."

"Of course," said Bernie, as if Kendra did not say the same thing every night.

Bernie turned to Leah. "You look stunning, my dear."

"Thank you, Comrade Camp Commander," she said, smiling as though genuinely flattered. Her skin crawled as she watched his eyes travel the length of her body.

Diana brought their plates to the table. The plates for Bernie and Leah were heaped high with food while the plate for Kendra was empty. There was not much conversation as they ate, which was unusual because Bernie liked to talk. He liked to talk about his day, the mundane things about running the camp, meeting their metrics cleaning solar panels at Green Future One, and dealing with the ineptitude of the DPRA bureaucracy. He especially like that, discussing the ineptitude of the DPRA bureaucracy, because he thought very highly of himself. He was, in his mind, the smartest guy in the room. Always. In that vein, Bernie also liked to talk about moving up the chain of command. Not only would that allow him to fix the rampant ineptitude in the Department of Reeducation, it would also allow him to move to the city. With his first promotion, the city would most likely be Los Angeles. His second promotion, he expected, would take him to Washington DC. There, Bernie had little doubt his full potential would be recognized. He dared hope it might even be recognized by Supreme Leader Johnny Penn himself.

Bernie had not been talkative the last couple weeks because he was preoccupied by the war situation. The DPRA was losing the war. Even though the nightly DPRA news gave only glowing reports about the war's progress, with the Army of the DPRA regularly crushing the Army of the Free States of Liberty on the battlefield, he had it from reliable sources in the Department of Defense the war was going badly. In fact, they were telling him it was going so badly the entire West Coast was in jeopardy of being lost. That started Bernie thinking. First, he was anticipating the order he would receive regarding his camp, Labor Camp 847. If it was like the orders received by other camps in danger of being overrun, he would have to liquidate the prisoners. That, he thought, would be easy enough. There was a procedure for such an evolution. There were "lessons learned," too, gleaned from camps who had already performed the evolution. When he read those lessons learned, he found the need for deception the biggest takeaway. Under no circumstances do you allow your prison population to comprehend the fate that awaits them. Concoct a story that the entire camp contingent is required to assist with an emergency solar panel cleaning project at another, undisclosed location. Then, when the prisoners are unloaded in a barbed wire enclosure and told to wait for the arrival of the cleaning equipment, cleaning equipment they do not know will never arrive, the trucks are backed up with the machine guns. Disposal of the bodies is accomplished using the latest guidelines for human composting, courtesy of the Department for Tolerance and Science. No matter what, warn the lessons learned, do not burn the bodies. Burning bodies generates an unacceptably large carbon footprint.

The thing that was really troubling Bernie was what to do about Leah. As much as he was capable of liking a woman, he liked Leah. In fact, he liked her so much, he was afraid Kendra was growing jealous. "Isn't it time for someone new?" Kendra started whispering in Bernie's ear when Leah was sleeping at night. Kendra also insisted she join Bernie and Leah for dinner instead of waiting for the two of them in the living room like she used to do. Bernie was confident he could deal with Kendra. He would tell her to get used to it or she could spend some time alone in the closet. As far as Leah was concerned, he very much wanted to take her with him when they moved on to another camp, assuming there was still some time pending before his promotion. He had not yet worked out the precise logistics but he thought it doable even if it was against regulations. There were always ways around Department of Reeducation regulations, especially for a camp commander. When he was promoted, though, that would make keeping Leah much more difficult. There was no way to hide her as a prisoner in the city. Plus, there was the fact Leah was who she was. She was "the Leah." She was Officer Leah Blunt, the police officer responsible for the Great Riot in 2025 and the whole sequence of events that culminated in the current, ongoing Second Civil War. The DPRA propaganda apparatus had spent the intervening years demonizing Leah to the point where she was the devil incarnate. Introducing Leah to his friends and neighbors in the city would not go well, Bernie was certain, not for Leah and, likely, not for him either.

Bernie sighed.

"Are you tired, Comrade Camp Commander?" asked Leah.

"Yes."

"You've been quiet the last few days. Is something bothering you?"

Bernie looked at Leah and smiled. He thought of all the meals they shared together here at his table, how she was always waiting for him with the candles lit like they were now, and how she always looked so lovely in the dress he laid out for her. He thought about the curves of her body, too, the warm softness of her skin under his fingertips, and how much he enjoyed having his way with her in his bed. Finally, he thought about how she had made him so happy when she agreed to stay with him, and when she did not force him to kill her silly husband. He would have been grateful if he was capable of such an emotion. *I've really done her a favor,* he told himself, *by taking her off the cleaning crews, letting her stay with me here in my house, with clean clothes, clean sheets and real food.* He did a quick mental calculation to determine how long she had been with him. *Almost a year,* he thought proudly. *Nothing to feel bad about. She's lucky, really, that I gave her so much time.*

He made up his mind then. She would have to go with the rest of the prisoners when the liquidation order came.

***

It was a dark, black night with an amazing display of brilliant stars twinkling overhead. The moon was not yet up so the ephemeral band of hazy light from the Milky Way was clearly visible. Push toggled the mic attached to the headset on his helmet. "Confirm tower team set. One through four."

"One set," he heard through his headset. "Two set," came a different voice. "Three set," said another voice. "Four set," said the last voice.

The job of the tower team was to destroy the four towers at the corners of the camp perimeter. Each member of the tower team carried an AT4 unguided, man-portable recoilless rifle. Although the AT4 has a range of over three hundred yards, the team was much closer than that. They were just outside the light splash from the fence flood lights, more than close enough to precisely place the half-pound high-explosive warhead squarely in the center of the tower box.

"Fire on my mark," said Push. "Three, two, one, mark."

He heard what sounded like four gunshots from the four corners of the camp perimeter, only louder. They were followed immediately by the much louder explosions from the high-explosive warheads. The tower boxes exploded in orange fireballs.

Push ordered, "First and Second Platoon, launch assault on north fence. Third and Fourth Platoon, light 'em up."

The seventy-two men of First and Second Platoon came out of the shadows and approached the north fence. Simultaneously, Third and Fourth Platoon opened up with their machine guns and small arms from outside the west fence. The fusillade raking the guard barracks from outside the west fence was intended to kill as many guards as possible while they were still in their barracks. It was also designed to keep those guards who were not killed from pouring out and engaging First and Second Platoon before they could establish their defensive line between the guard barracks and the prisoner barracks.

Push watched from the darkness with Third and Fourth Platoon. This was the worst part as far as he was concerned. So much of their plan depended on what the prisoners did. The plan depended on the prisoners staying in their barracks. If the prisoners stayed in their barracks, all he needed was time to methodically engage and destroy the camp guards. If, however, the prisoners came running out of their barracks, panicked by the thought the explosions and gunfire were a consequence of DPRA guards slaughtering their fellow prisoners one barrack over, then it would turn real ugly real quick.

It turned real ugly real quick.

The voice of the leader from Second Platoon crackled in Push's headset. "Cap, we got prisoners outside the barracks."

"Can you get 'em back in?" asked Push.

"We'll try."

Push waited for what seemed like an eternity. It was less than a minute. The voice of the leader from Second Platoon crackled again. "That's a negative, Cap. Prisoners are terrified. They're running around and screaming and that's spreading the panic. Got more and more of 'em coming out of the barracks."

Push pictured seventy-two men trying to control a thousand panicked prisoners and decided it was hopeless. The prisoners would soon be everywhere inside the fence which meant they would be running into the field of fire of his machine guns, which meant they would lose the one thing that was keeping the guards pinned down inside their barracks, which meant this would suddenly be too much like a fair fight. He toggled his mic. "First and Second Platoon, forget the prisoners. You've got the first row of guard barracks. That's five buildings. One squad per building. A fireteam on the door and another tossing grenades through the windows. Go!"

"Roger that!" came the reply in his headset.

"Third and Fourth Platoon, same drill. We've got the second row of guard barracks. On me. Go!"

"One fireteam on door duty, the other on grenade duty," confirmed the leader of Third Platoon. "Frag 'em and shoot 'em," said the leader of Fourth Platoon.

Push and the sixty-four men of Third and Fourth Platoon ran up to the west fence. A pair of men in each squad set their rifles on the ground and started to work on the fence with wire cutters. Gaping holes were cut in under a minute, which was too long. Push saw curious heads appear at the doors to the guard barracks. The guards had noticed there was no more machine gun fire. "Get some fire on those doors!" ordered Push. His men started firing with their rifles. Some of the heads ducked back inside. Other guards saw prisoners running by and decided to take their chances.

They jumped outside and ran with the prisoners, using the prisoners as cover in the hope the attackers would not risk friendly-fire casualties.

Push and his sixty-four men were through the wire. The platoons knew the drill because they had practiced it often enough. They used hand signals to assign a squad to each of the barracks as they ran down the row of barracks. At their assigned barrack, one fireteam covered the door to the barrack with their rifles at the ready while the other fireteam started with grenades. They were using the M67 grenade, which was the standard fragmentation grenade used by the old United States Army. It weighs just under a pound but has a kill radius of sixteen feet and an injury radius of fifty feet.

They began at the window farthest from the door with the intent of pushing the guards toward the door and into the kill zone of the riflemen that would soon be entering. If the guards tried to run out the door, so much the better. They pulled the grenade pins and tossed the grenades inside. Five seconds after they pulled the pins, the grenades detonated. Screams came from inside. Then gunfire came. The guards targeted the thin wooden walls under the windows where they thought the grenadiers might be standing. A few of Push's men went down. The grenade explosions shook the camp with increasing frequency as more and more of the fireteams started their grim work of tossing grenades in through the barrack windows. With all the fireteams working together, they were tossing four or five grenades a second. The grenade explosions were not at all like the regular, staccato pounding of a machine gun. They came in random, irregular groupings which made them all the more terrifying. "BOOM! BOOM BOOM! BOOM! BOOM BOOM BOOM! BOOM!"

Then there were no more explosions.

There was a moment of eerie quiet, which was quiet only in a relative sense. While there were no more explosions, there was still gunfire, plus the screams of panicked prisoners and wounded men. The eerie quiet was the signal for the fireteam covering the barrack door to start its task. The fireteam kicked open the door and stormed inside. The first man went left, hugging the wall as he went. The second man went right, also hugging the wall. The third, fourth and fifth man headed for the middle of the barrack. They all had their rifles up at the ready position, looking just over the red dot sight of their rifle. Anything standing was an immediate target and died. So, too, was anything moving on the ground. It also died. Some of the guards had improvised fighting positions using whatever furniture was available for cover and concealment. The sound of gunbattles erupted from inside barracks all over the camp. There were more grenade explosions. Then, finally, the camp was quiet. This time, it stayed quiet.

***

"You need to see this, Cap," said Lieutenant Buchanan to Push.

Push was looking at the row of wounded soldiers lying on the ground in front of him. There were fourteen. Eight of them were not seriously wounded and would live to fight another day. Six of them might not. The medic and another soldier were tending to their wounds. There was nothing more Push could do for them. There were seven more soldiers lying on the ground on the other side of the barrack. There was nothing more he could do for them, either. They were KIA. Push was in a foul mood. They had accomplished their mission but it had cost them.

"What you got?" asked Push.

"Over there," said Lieutenant Buchanan, pointing at the camp commander's residence. "The camp commander's still alive. He's also got … a guest."

"A guest?"

"Like I said, Cap, you need to see it."

Push followed Lieutenant Buchanan to the camp commander's residence. He walked in and found the room like he expected: wrecked. Furniture was turned over and broken glass was scattered everywhere on the floor. There were jagged gashes in the wall from grenade fragments along with bullet holes, lots and lots of bullet holes. He thought it amazing anyone had survived inside, much less survived unwounded. *Must have hit the deck when the fighting started,* thought Push, *and stayed there.*

"Here's the camp commander," said Lieutenant Buchanan as they walked into the living room. He gestured at Bernie who was sitting on the sofa with his hands zip-tied behind his back.

Push saw what he expected to see, a middle-aged man in the camp commander uniform of the DPRA Department of Reeducation. He noticed the camp commander had an anxious, worried expression on his face.

"And here's his … guest," said Lieutenant Buchanan, gesturing at Leah. She was sitting in a chair on the other side of the room. Her hands were zip-tied, too, behind her back.

Push was not surprised to see a woman. The camp was, after all, a women's camp. What surprised him was to see a woman in a black sequined cocktail dress with a plunging neckline. He noticed the plunge of her neckline was even more pronounced than originally designed as a consequence of a long rip down the side of her dress. His mind struggled for the right word. All it could find was "incongruous."

"And who are you?" asked Push.

"Leah," answered Leah in a flat monotone.

"You his wife?" asked Push.

"No … no," she stammered, shaking her head vehemently, "I'm married to a wonderful man." Leah stared ahead without looking at Push.

Push wondered if she was in shock. "Cut her loose," he said to Lieutenant Buchanan. While Lieutenant Buchanan went to cut her zip tie, Push walked back to the dining room. He had noticed an overturned table there when he first walked in. He pulled the tablecloth from the table, shook the debris from it and walked back to the living room. "Here," he said, handing the tablecloth to Leah, "your party dress has seen one too many parties."

Leah pulled the tablecloth around her shoulders like a shawl. Then she pulled it tight around her body as if there was a cold, biting wind.

"What's the story?" asked Push, nodding toward the camp commander.

Leah opened her mouth to try and tell Push who she was and how she came to be in the camp commander's residence but no words came. There was too much to tell and she had no idea where to start. The idea of telling Push or anyone else suddenly seemed impossible.

"I can't help you if you don't tell me what happened," said Push. "Are you one of the prisoners here?"

Leah nodded.

"This man here, did he force you to … live in his residence?"

Leah nodded again, confirming what Push suspected. He had seen it in some of the other camps, camp commanders having their way with helpless female prisoners. He turned and looked at Bernie with undisguised contempt. Then he turned back to Leah. "This may not help, Leah, but we'll be taking him back with us. This man will have his day in court, in the Free States of Liberty."

Leah found her voice again but still did not look at Push. She just stared ahead at nothing. She said quietly, "There really isn't any, you know."

"What's that?" asked Push

"Justice," she whispered.

"Hey, Cap," said Lieutenant Buchanan with an amazed voice, "take a look at this!" Lieutenant Buchanan walked into the living room holding Kendra. Kendra was dressed in her black negligee as always. "Found her stashed in the closet in one of the bedrooms." Lieutenant Buchanan set Kendra on the sofa next to the camp commander.

"This yours?" Push asked Bernie, thinking the camp commander not only contemptable but pathetic.

"She is," answered Bernie. Bernie was not at all embarrassed. He was relieved to find Kendra unharmed. He had stashed her in the closet when the shooting started and had not been able to check on her since. "Her name's Kendra," he said proudly. "We've been together a long time, me and Kendra." He turned to Kendra. "Say hello to the nice officer from the Free States of Liberty, Kendra."

"Hello, Nice Officer," said Kendra in her sexy, sultry voice.

Push heard the whirr of small electric motors in her head as Kendra articulated her lips and batted her eyes.

"I'm sorry," said Kendra, "I did not catch your name."

"I didn't give it," said Push. He turned back to Bernie. "You really are a sick fuck, aren't you?"

"Captain!" shouted Lieutenant Buchanan.

Push spun around to see Leah holding an M4. It was pointed at Bernie. Leah no longer appeared to be in a state of shock. Her eyes were fixed squarely on Bernie. There was an expression of cold hatred on her face.

"She grabbed my gun," explained Lieutenant Buchanan. "I left it leaning up against the wall for a minute when I found the doll and—"

"Not now, Lieutenant," said Push, waving for Lieutenant Buchanan to move back away from Leah.

"You're right, Captain," said Leah, not taking her eyes off Bernie. "He really is a sick fuck. And I let this sick fuck fuck me because he threatened to kill my husband if I didn't. Well, now I'm the one holding the gun. And I've got it pointed right at his head. And I'm gonna blow his sick fuckin' head clean off!"

Push stepped in front of Bernie.

"Get out of my way, Captain!" screamed Leah.

"Put the gun down, Leah. He'll get justice. I promise. Just not like this."

Bernie laughed. Then he said sarcastically, "Oh, Leah knows all about justice. Do you know who Leah really is? She didn't tell you her last name. She's none other than Officer Leah Blunt, the police officer who shot those two unarmed African American men in cold blood way back in '25. She's the one who started the whole thing, Captain Whatever Your Name Is From The Free States Of Liberty."

"That true?" asked Push. "Are you really Officer Leah Blunt?"

"That's me," said Leah bitterly, "the mother of it all, the woman who gave birth to this sick, twisted nightmare of a world."

"Ok, Leah, then you know cops don't do this. Cops don't act as judge, jury and executioner."

"They do in the DPRA," said Bernie with a laugh.

"Shut up, asshole!" yelled Push. He turned back to Leah. "Let me take him back to the Free States of Liberty, Leah. I promise you, he'll get justice there." Push saw a tear run down her cheek.

"I can't," she said.

"Sorry, Captain," said Bernie, obviously not sorry, "old habits die hard. Once a cold-blooded killer, always a cold-blooded killer." He turned to Leah and asked in a sickly sweet, mocking voice. "Isn't that right, my pretty little Leah?"

Push understood what Bernie was trying to do. He was trying to commit suicide by cop, so he would not have to face the gallows back in the Free States of Liberty. He ignored Bernie. He saw Leah tense her body and hold the rifle tighter. He knew he was running out of time. "Your husband, Leah! Think about your husband! You said you married a wonderful man! You'll see him again, Leah! Soon! But not if you do this!"

Leah suddenly pointed the M4 at Kendra.

"NO!" screamed Bernie.

Leah pulled the trigger. The M4 roared in full auto. Bullets slammed into Kendra's chest, shredding her black negligee and rubber skin. Sparks flew from the destroyed battery packs inside her torso. The recoil of the M4 sent bullets climbing up Kendra's neck. They smashed her electronic voice box and the gears that articulated her neck. Then the bullets found her face. Kendra's head exploded in a hundred shards of shattered circuit boards and destroyed micro-electric motors. When the bolt locked open on an empty magazine, Kendra was a smoldering, smoking husk.

"NOOOOOOOOO!" screamed Bernie in an inhuman howl of agony. He threw himself on top of Kendra with his arms still zip-tied behind his back. He began sobbing hysterically.

"Get him out of here," said Push, disgusted.

Lieutenant Buchanan and another soldier picked Bernie up off Kendra and roughly hustled him from the room.

Push reached for the empty M4 in Leah's hands. Smoke was still coming from the muzzle and open bolt. "You did the right thing, Leah," he said gently.

"Did I?" she asked.

"Yes. You're still a cop after all."

"I am," she said, nodding as if to affirm the person she used to be. The barest hint of a smile crossed her face. She added, "And a damn good one."

Leah handed the empty M4 to Push.

"I have a favor to ask," she said.

"What?" asked Push.

"My husband ... Can you find out if he's still alive?"

Push nodded. "I'll do my best."

Leah searched his face, really looking at him for the first time. She decided this was a man she could trust. She could not remember the last time she thought that. Then she thought it was the last time she talked to her husband, just before she was shipped out to the Department of Reeducation. "He really is a wonderful man," she said.

"He better be," said Push.

Leah did not understand and gave him a quizzical look.

Push smiled. "Because he doesn't deserve you if he's not."

Leah smiled back at Push. This time, she could not stop smiling. His words meant more to her than he could possibly know. She felt like she had hope for the first time in a long, long time. Hope for herself. Hope for her family. Hope, even, for humanity.

THE END

Made in United States
Troutdale, OR
10/18/2023

13767796R00228